I0674293

the
'idiot spy'
(the series)
book six of ten

the sanctuary

c. benjamin lattimore

© C. Benjamin Lattimore

the sanctuary
Published: July 2021
Printed in the United States of America
ISBN: 978-1-7334945-5-7

ALL RIGHTS RESERVED. Except as permitted under the U.S.
Copyright Act of 1976, no part of this publication may be reproduced,
distributed, or transmitted in any form or by any means, or stored in a
database or retrieval system, without the prior written permission of the
C. Benjamin Lattimore or his legally designated representative.

DISCLAIMER: This is a work of fiction. Names, characters, businesses,
places, events, and incidents are either the products of the author's
imagination or used in a fictitious manner. Any resemblance to actual
persons, living or dead, or actual events is purely coincidental.

a lattidreamer™ publication
© C. Benjamin Lattimore, 2021

To Marisa, my wife, and number 1 reviewer!
Thanks for your commitment to my passion.
I appreciate all that you do to help me with my projects!

ACKNOWLEDGEMENTS

To my children, Christopher, Monica, and Courtney, as well as my grandchildren, Isaiah, and Desmond for just being exceptional. A special hello to Travis, my godson. A unique and heartfelt expression of love to my sister Mary E. and my brother Darryl A. Yet again, venerate regards to Maurice Cheeks and Reggie Wilkes.

Special acknowledgements to Marisa, Dawn Marie, Nikki, and Jill.

Lots of love ethereally to my mom, Mary Alice, my dad, Walthro M, my little sister, Barbara Ann, and my big brother, Walter Eugene. Also, to my friends, Gordon Gant, Joseph Bongiavanni III, Monique Gorham, Rahsaan Stevens, and my newest guardian angel, Mrs. Marjorie C. Cheeks.

CHAPTER ONE

Ben Beckmire and his crew traveled from St. Thomas in the U S Virgin Islands to Valencia, Spain, to search for a child purportedly fathered by Zanthius Beckmire De Lombardo. It was alleged that the child was being housed in a monastery. The possibility of it being a hoax with a much more sinister plot attached to it, was extremely conceivable. It was a festive flight, in that 50% of the women on the flight were happy and pregnant.

Two hours out of St. Thomas, Juan walked up to where the Sarge and Courtney were sitting and asked, "Mr. Beckmire, is it possible for me to have a word with you in private?"

The Sarge looked at him and asked, "Do we have a problem?"

Juan said, "I don't think so, but I would like to speak with you privately."

The Sarge rose from his seat and appeared to be giant next to Juan who said to himself, "This man is going to kill me".

In the back of the plane, Juan fumbled so extensively with his words that the Sarge said, "Dude, you're confusing me. What exactly are you trying to say to me?"

"I just want to tell you that your daughter is pregnant—by me."

The Sarge said in a loud voice, "You've been sleeping with my baby? You had unprotected sex with my daughter?"

Overhearing the conversation between the Sarge and Juan, Jilkes slapped John Lee on the shoulder and said, "The Sarge is getting ready to go ballistic. You know how he feels about that child. If that guy doesn't say the right words, we're all doomed. He's going to open that door and throw him off the plane."

John Lee jumped up and said to Somara, "This here situation ain't good. When he done been enraged, it takes all of us to hold him down. He be stronger than Superman. I don't like this."

Somara and Yeshida walked to the back of the plane, and Yeshida announced, "Mr. Sarge, Sir, your intense response to your personal problem has involved my child. I need you to stop yelling because it upsets my child."

The Sarge looked at her, then at Somara and said, "I need you ladies to go back to your seats and buckle up. I'm about to whup this dude's ass."

Jilkes said, "Sarge, no one is going to get their ass whupped on this flight. I need you to calm down. Your daughter is a grown ass woman. Now, if he took advantage of her forcefully, then, John Lee and I will dispense of his ass when we land. However, if Rashida rode that train willingly, then we have another kind of story to discover. In any event, I need you to take some deep breaths. Please back the hell away from Juan."

John Lee exclaimed, "Sarge, please! We be too high in the sky for some bullshit. Please, sit down. Let me and Jilkes have a word or two with Juan."

Juan interjected, "I came to you to tell you I want to marry her when we land."

The Sarge smiled and said, "Why the hell didn't you say that? My wife and I were beginning to wonder what on earth was going on. Now you tell me my daughter is pregnant and not married. My way of thinking, still requires me to try to beat your ass."

Courtney walked to the back and said, "Ben Beckmire, if you don't leave your future son-in-law alone, I'm going to put you in that box that has no fringe benefits."

"Honey, I'm just messing with him. You know I'm a peace-loving kind of guy." The Sarge reached out guardedly, hugged Juan, and said, "Man, I was only messing with you."

"Sarge, Sir, it sure didn't feel like it to me."

The Sarge walked back towards his seat and saw Rashida looking out of the window crying. He sat down in the seat next to her, whispered in her ear, "You have choices. You don't have to marry someone you don't love. That child will have so much love and a husband might get in the way."

"Sarge, I love that dude so much. He's means the world to me and LaGina."

"Then why are you crying baby?"

"I feel that I failed you and mom."

"Nonsense! You're a grown woman. Your decisions are yours. We only hope you make good ones. Listen, damn near every woman on this plane is pregnant. I'm happy for you because he had enough respect for you that he wanted to discuss the issue with me. I knew something was up when you went 'MIA'. Your mom and I talked about you this morning prior to boarding this plane. Honey, if you don't know that we're two old smart people, then we need to put you back in school. Oh, here is your future husband. I guess he wants me to get out of his seat on my damn plane. The nerve of that guy."

The Sarge stood up, bowed to Juan and said, "We depend on you in so many ways. Now you have gone to the next level to secure my daughter. Welcome to my family. My daughter has her own mind, get used to it, but also insist that she hears your side of reality. You two make a wonderful couple. I'm so happy she's pregnant, by you, Juan. This is good news. I have to go tell my wife the details."

"Sir, Ms. Courtney knows all of the details. She thought it was best that I told you when we were 30,000 feet in the air so you wouldn't open the door and attempt to throw me out of the plane," Juan stated.

"Juan, if I open a door, trust me, someone is going the hell out of it, and it ain't going to be me. Just information for you to sort through in the future. We'll have a drink when we land to celebrate the marvelous event. Thanks, my brother."

The Captain piped in the latest news from around the world. Everyone knew that a new Commander in Chief was about to take office and wanted to watch aspects of his inauguration. People saw that infamous few seconds when it appeared that the new First Lady was totally happy about her husband's inauguration. During her euphoria, the president elect turned to her, uttered something and her entire facial/body expression turned from joy to disdain.

The group also watched as the incoming occupant of the White House met with the outgoing occupants. The new president got out of the limo and walked up a few steps to greet the outgoing president. The incoming First Lady was left to fend for herself. It was a clear message to the world that he respects nothing, or no one. Rumor had it that he still begrudged his wife for those explicit magazine photos seen around the universe.

# # #

Juan ventured towards the front of the plane with LaGina holding on to him, picked up the microphone and asked, "May I have your attention for just a minute?" After the group settled down, he said, "Hi everyone, this is Juan, I just want to announce that Rashida and I are madly in love. She's pregnant, we would appreciate your support and assistance. LaGina is happy about what we're planning. I would like to marry Rashida in Valencia or Barcelona, both of which I consider my home. It would be our delight once we have confirmed and obtained certain certificates that you all will join us in our blessing and our bliss. Thanks for your attention."

The Sarge stood up first, followed by Jilkes who began to clap. He headed back towards where Rashida, Juan and LaGina were sitting. He asked Juan, "So, do I have your permission to kiss the bride to be?"

"Absolutely, and as a matter of fact, everyone can extend their well wishes to us and have some champagne."

In the interim and without notice, Mike picked up the microphone and said, "Hello, sorry to disturb the moment, but I just wanted you guys to know that the captain and I are dating. We don't have any baby news, but we're certainly looking at a long-term relationship."

Everyone clapped and congratulated him. It had been many moons since Rashida had a relationship with a man due to her terrible encounter with Malik, her nemesis, as well as Monica's. (That story resides in "The Edge", another journey featuring the Sarge, Courtney, Larry, Rashida, as well as Mallory and Monica.)

As the trip reached the halfway point, most of the passengers were sound asleep including John Lee who kept everyone up with his loud snoring. His snoring drowned out the cries of the baby. Somara nudged him but that didn't work. Jilkes got out of his seat, shook him until he jumped up and instinctively pushed Jilkes backwards. Jilkes calmly said, "Slow down my brother. You're keeping the entire plane up. I didn't mean to shake you so hard, but you were really in another time zone."

John Lee sat down and began to cry. Jilkes took a knee and asked, "What's wrong Big Country? I know it's not the interaction between the two us that just transpired. What's going on?"

Somara asked, "Honey, John Lee, did I offend thee in some manner?"

John Lee grabbed her little hand and kissed it. He whispered, "No, my Baby Girl, you didn't do anything. I guess I was dreaming about all the souls Jilkes and I done dispatched. We done hurt a lot of people in our day. I guess it's catching up with me. I'll be alright. I'm going to fix me a nightcap and try to go back to sleep. Sorry about my reaction, but I was still in that there unconscious state."

Jilkes said, "I'll have a nightcap as well. Come on back to the galley and let's figure this thing out." When they arrived in the galley, Jilkes asked, "WTF? What's going on with you?"

"I had a bad nightmare. I sure am glad you woke me up. It was about someone like that Scottie woman I gutted. I mean she had Somara, my baby, had gutted them, and hung their inners over the banister in my house. Much like Scottie did to my other woman. It was so real! It was like I was tied down, had to watch her as she disemboweled Somara first, and then the baby."

"Damn, Man. Okay, keep this between us. No need in anyone else hearing about your nightmares."

"Wait, what was so scary was it seemed so real. It happened in the old house."

"In your new house?"

"No, in my old house.

"Well, thank goodness for that. That place has been demolished—you know. Both of our new houses are almost completed. They're enclosed with a roof, windows, and doors. As a matter of fact, we should spend some time with the women finding toilets, knobs, and shit like that. I think we should have Monica and Courtney help us as well. After all, they did the work at the resort. That's some pretty fancy shit, but practical."

"I also cried because I done pushed you in a mean manner. I should have known you were near. I was just in the middle of that there nasty dream. Sorry I demonstrated my friendship in a negative way."

"So, are you calling that a long-ass-winded apology?"

"I guess you can say that without me apologizing. You can call it whatever you want, but I ain't apologizing to your black ass for anything. Salute!"

The two men took swigs of their drinks. The Sarge and Mallory entered the galley, and the Sarge asked, "What are you people up to?"

"We just be having a drink, thinking about some of the bad shit we done did to people," John Lee stated.

Mallory said, "Well, kiss my ass. The Sarge and I were having the same damn discussion."

"Mallory, this ain't no time for bullshit. He literally tried to push me out of the plane," Jilkes announced.

The Sarge said, "What are you talking about?"

"I be dreaming, snoring, he grabbed me, and shook me. I didn't know what was going on, so I jumped defensively at him. I didn't mean to bruise his delicate ass, but he got his nose all bent out of shape and, therefore, we be back here trying to make his highness feel better about me kicking his ass once again."

"John Lee, you didn't win that fight. As a matter of fact, I thought Jilkes was going to kill you on your final charge. I nodded to Mallory to end the fiasco."

"Now, Sarge, don't you be going down that road called 'alternative facts'. Everybody knows I whipped his ass. Anyways, you and Mallory weren't even there."

"John Lee, let me ask you a question. What year did that happen? How many times have you two been apart? Do you know two people who are building new homes next to each other? And how about this question, do you know two dudes who married Asian women and both ladies are now pregnant?"

"Yeah, yeah! It really don't matter that no one but me realizes I kicked his ass, but if you people from the north want to still imagine you won something, then by all means, keep chasing my pigs. They know what happened."

Jilkes said, "Enough of the bullshit. What's the weapons' policy of Spain? Are we good to secure ourselves or what?"

The Sarge said, "Let me get Mr. Amazing back here. As I was walking down the aisle, I noticed that every woman on this damn plane is pregnant except Courtney, Ava, Carla, and Monica. I hope we don't have to depend on them to defend us."

"You know, Sarge, Monica is taking our missed opportunity pretty bad. She wants to be a mother, but natural mother time, is against her and me as you all know."

Jilkes said, "We're going to a damn monastery where people drop kids off, they don't want or can't afford. If she is that concerned Mallory, you guys should adopt one or two. It won't be because you can't afford them. According to our last encounter with numbers, we all should have about one-quarter of a billion dollars in assets. I mean between Amazon, Facebook, Netflix, and Alibaba, we have made a fortune and we're still making money hand over foot. We made $176 million on FB alone. Adopt an entire fricken village. If you want to live quiet and simple, John Lee and I have plenty of property. I never thought about adopting, but if Yeshida wants to think about it, then I'm on it. I, however, prefer to adopt from an American agency because I'm an American."

Jong walked into the galley and said, "I didn't do it. It was that guy's fault."

The Sarge asked, "What guy are you talking about?"

"That guy."

"What guy?"

"That guy."

"You say it one more time and I'm going to shock you like you did me. Can you handle it?"

"Anyway, why are you trying to oppress Asian Americans?"

"Jong, can it. What's the weapons' policy in Spain?" the Sarge asked.

"If you get caught with a weapon, you spend the balance of your life in jail. Carrying a weapon is a privilege and not a right. The country's policies are very restrictive."

"How did you know that was what we were going to ask you?"

"That's why I'm Mr. Amazing and you're just, well, Sergeant Beckmire."

"I love you so much, man. We can't just walk around the country without weapons. Oh shit, my new son-in-law to be is from here. I'll get him," the Sarge noted.

When the Sarge walked back and saw a sleepy Juan and Carlos, he said, "Gentlemen, we will soon be guests in your country. What's the weapons policy?"

Carlos said, "Ava's people are going to meet us at the airport, and I think she's going to have something for everyone to carry, if you know what I mean. The laws are a little out of date, but we can probably manage the situation."

"Carlos, you know how we feel about strangers having responsibilities for our group."

"That is why her oldest family members are picking us up. I would lay down in the road for these people. We will be blanketed by friends the entire time that we're here. There are too many of us to stay at her villa, but we have a resort that she partially owns that is receptive to hosting us. It may be another one of those situations where you can keep the wolves away, make an investment, and help someone hang on to their life's work. She could afford to do it, but it would consume a lot of her resources. Just a hint at an opportunity for our group," Carlos announced.

"Carlos, you and Juan do know that you're a part of our group. Right? And as such, you have been inuring to the benefits of this group, in a monetary nature. Correct?"

"Sarge, here is how we do this thing. Wherever Ms. De Lombardo goes, I go. Juan and the others must make up their minds now that they're returning home. It is going to be a tough choice for some of the guys because their wives have been philandering around with neighbors and cousins. They will make their choices, but I'm about to marry Ava, Juan is engaged to your daughter, so we're good to go. Listen, this has been the best time of my life. I've been places that I didn't know existed. I have had food that should have made my stomach turn. I have met my employer on another level that allowed me to exclaim my love for her. Thank God, she felt the same way. If I have a vote, we buy a place near John Lee and Jilkes, continue to enjoy the adventures, even though they're at times life threatening."

"Juan, you don't need to say anything. I have you by the balls. And I must warn you, my daughter is as feisty as they come. She will put a hurting on your ass if you screw up. I'm just saying. So, if this thing is a little too much for you, then I suggest that you disappear once we land."

"Mr. Beckmire, I think you're missing a few points. I desperately want to be with Rashida because she is smart, attractive, and a no-nonsense kind of person. I love LaGina and I love Rashida. I have never known a family before and that's why I promised Rashida I would pull out rather than spray my essence into her fertile garden. I guess that didn't work because I wanted to impregnate her, to show her I am, and will be there for her, LaGina, and our new child until the day I die."

John Lee said, "It don't get no clearer than that."

The Sarge looked at Juan and said, "I'll never underestimate your objectives again. Please, forgive me if I have ever offended you, Son." He reached out and the two men hugged and whispered they loved each other.

Mike saw what he considered the brain trust in the galley. He thought to himself now was as good as time as any to propose a project. He unbuckled his seatbelt and walked towards the galley. Bernstein and Brown instinctively jumped up. Brown said, "You're still a passenger. You don't have full movement."

Mike said, "You're right, but what I have to say is worth a shit load of money to everyone, including me."

Bernstein said, "Hold here, until I clear it with the Sarge."

When Bernstein returned, he said, "I guess you got another level of clearance we didn't know about."

As Mike entered the galley, the conversation concluded. He thought it was about him. He said, "I have some information that is critical to your mission and hopefully, my mine. Listen, Allen was a piece of work. He violated every code of conduct one could as a government employee. On a personal level, he mandated favors from his staff of a sexual nature, in order for them to remain employed. Mr. Beckmire, he trusted you more than any human being he had met. He stated one time, that with you, there is no need to guess. If you come for him, he will find a way to come for you. I, on the other hand, was just a worker bee until Allen realized he couldn't trust anyone except you and me. I say all of that to say, I have three locations that are ripe. Allen couldn't move money because the airwaves were always looking out for a hint of his existence. I'm talking about sites that Walter did not know Allen knew about."

Mallory asked, "Why are you coming forward with this kind of information at this point in time?"

"Because Allen asked me to make sure that he was dead before I gave this information to Beckmire. You know, some spies, have a way of reincarnating and he wanted me to be sure that he was dead, dead, and dead, before I gave you this information."

"If it's about money, why didn't you just keep it for yourself and enjoy the spoils?"

"I don't do stupid. I fought alongside you guys. When he gave me this information, I asked him, "What makes you think you can trust me?" You know what he said? That guy said, "After living in the alleys and sewers, I now know what it means to look after your brother. Ben Beckmire and his merry band of bad guys are true warriors. They don't demand ransom or payment. If you find people who have a common mission and who don't demand money for it, then they are principle driven. Those guys are the true patriots because they don't do what they do for a fee. They have honor and that is why they kicked the shit out of every living soul I sent to kick the crap out of them."

The Sarge said, "We're not profit driven, but I must admit, we did find a few cases full of money along the way. I have a simple question for you, Mike. Why didn't you go for this venue alone?"

"Sarge, I'm a worker bee. I can't lead the charge nor institute the correct notions to get around the problems when all goes bad. I shot people trying to kill you guys and me. I'm on your cousin's hit list. I have people within the agency calling me a traitor. I don't have many places to sleep, or many friends to give me a hamburger and fries. I'm in love with your pilot, when this thing is all said and done, if you think I deserve a portion of what is behind each of the three doors, then I say, help a brother out. I'm not treacherous and you can depend on me. I have never offered you an untruth. Think about it! I have been on the up and up and it's my naivete that found me in places or camps that seemed like I'd been compromised. I bring you three olive branches and a request to pursue your pilot fully and actively. I love her, I want to make her pregnant and my wife at the same time."

"Well, hell, Son, I hope you marry her first and then consider a family. Listen, she's my pilot-in-command and not many people can play the games that she does with this aircraft. We are all adults. I have no control over what my pilot-in- command feels and does if it doesn't place my friends and family in harm's way. Exactly what do you want for this information in terms of assets?"

"Listen, you made it possible for me to survive in the sewers. You always asked if I needed some coins. What I now need is a package that will allow me to offer that wonderful woman flying this plane a stable life. I need to have a cut. You decide the value and I'm okay with the result."

"Mike, I'm going to say this in front of my people. I don't know your worth other than that moment in Virginia when you made that shot and rescued us from a precarious situation. We don't care about money, but if the other person does, then we try to make a statement by taking what is theirs. If the information you have is credible, and I suspect it is, then we will make you whole from that point forward. It's like pre-nuptials. What's mine is mine until we marry, and from that point forward, what's mine is ours. Do you buy into such an equation?"

"Absodamnlutely! That's as fair as it gets."

Surprisingly, Ava entered the galley and said, "Oh my! Hell, hell, the whole gang is almost here. Ben, I need to make a call to make sure our entrance doesn't cause problems. I need my people in position in the next two hours. My question is, can I use one of the non-descript phones?"

Ben Beckmire said, "Mallory, lend Ava your phone. Oh, Ava, am I to assume your people will be providing us with transportation to a secure location?"

"Ben Beckmire, I made one monumental mistake with you. I assure you—it won't happen again. And by the way, I am loving every moment of this adventure. I think I might have another business venture for our group, if you guys would entertain a conversation with a friend of mine whose business is tanking."

Mallory said, "Ava, you set it up. We'll give it our scrutiny. You're a part of this team, and as such, you should be adamant about what you want the group to consider. You have carried a weapon and have killed to protect us. Your notion is as important as anyone else's."

Ben Beckmire turned to her and said, "I wouldn't have said that, but he's correct. Your suggestion is as important as the next person. We're a democracy and no one, including me has any privileges that overshadow the others, except in the event of armed conflict, that's when I become the despot!"

She instinctively reached out and hugged the Sarge. At that precise moment, Courtney entered the galley. She looked at the Sarge, and then Ava, and asked, "Am I going to have to kill you both?"

The Sarge said, "Honey, that was as innocent as can be. Right guys?"

Ava said, "Ben, stop being so defensive when it comes to me. Courtney knows I don't stand a chance and that I'm I love with Carlos. We need to stop that bullshit about the past and focus on who and what we're interested in now. That clock you're talking about has already turned to another era and that boat has left the dock."

"Honey, why are you looking at me like that? Ava made it perfectly clear. Listen, Ben, we, meaning Ava and I, have already had this conversation. She knows that if she messes with my man, I will surgically remove her head from her body, and by the way, she agreed to that."

"I guess I'm not the stud that I thought I was."

"If you were that stud Ben, then I would be sharpening my tools, hooking up my wires, to create me a new 'Beckmirenstein'."

"Jesus, can everyone in here stop trying to kill me? I have enough people on the ground who want me dead."

The entire séance was interrupted by the pilot coming on the intercom system. She said, "People, we are less than one hour from landing in Valencia. I need you frequent flyers to begin to prepare the cabin for arrival and Mike, you big seductive hunk of cheese, I need you to act like my attendant and make sure that the plane is ready for landing."

Her copilot asked, "Is that for real?"

"Is what for real?"

"Don't play stupid. Are you two an item?"

"Not yet, but I'm working on it. He's really a shy guy with little experience."

Mike turned beet red and the Sarge said, "Damn, she has your number already. I hope you at least had a moment of pleasure with her."

"That wouldn't be your concern, Mr. Beckmire, now, would it?" Courtney stated.

"And by the way, I'm looking forward to our date at the McDonald's that you have made so famous. Luvu."

CHAPTER TWO

As the plane began its descent, the captain pointed out historical sites and areas on both sides of the plane. Ava had the aisle seat and reached forward and portside to where Zanthius was sitting and said, "I have this old map of Spain that lists some of the monasteries. Take a look at it and see if there is anything that gives you a clue. I'm hoping there is some indication it's one of the Route of the Five Monasteries. Before we go marching in, I think we should do a little surveillance and see if we can find out any information."

Asiram said, "I'm sure Helga left a clue, because I can't imagine her wanting her child raised in a monastery. Honey, there must be something that reminds you of your time and conversations with her. She's methodical but not predictable. Just scramble your thoughts and see if you can come up with anything."

Asiram asked, "Ava, are we going to have time to go to your place or places while we're here?"

"Asiram, that's my intention, but you have to convince your father-in-law we need to stay awhile. We can't say the baby is sick because he doesn't budge once this thing takes off unless he's hungry or needs changing. Talk to Courtney. We need at least a week in Spain."

#

As the wheels of the plane touched down, everyone breathed a sigh of relief. Once in the terminal, everyone was given immigration forms to fill out. Ava, Carlos, and their men walked through the lines like royalty, and everyone watched in awe. They were showing off that they were citizens, didn't have to stand in line, and be examined. They sat on the other side of immigration and waited until everyone was through.

John Lee was the only one who drew attention because he was nervous after his encounter in Asia. Jilkes told him to breathe deep, focus on that pretty and pregnant lady of his, and he would be alright.

Once through immigration, their bags were scanned, and they were on their way into the private terminal. Once in the terminal, it seemed like a small army had amassed to welcome them. It was a combination of family, friends, and Ava's security team. Once they retrieved their bags, they exited the airport and entered a series of vans, SUVs, and limos. Ava had informed the group that the vehicles were armored. She assigned four of her people to provide around the clock security for the plane along with the pilots doing their rotation.

The captain told the Sarge she was going to stay with the plane because she wanted to have it refueled immediately. He told her when she was ready to spend time in town to give him a call, and he would send a vehicle for her. The captain said, "Mr. Beckmire, you know Mike is going to be here with me. Is that a problem?"

The Sarge called Mallory and Jong over and said, "The captain and Mike have some exploratory things they are trying to decide upon. Do we leave him here with her? Do we trust him?"

Jong said, "He's one of us."

Mallory said, "I agree. He killed for us, he defended us, and that kind of makes him one of us."

The Sarge said, "I agree with what you both say, but there are certain circumstances that I don't like to compromise."

The captain cleared her throat and said, "I'm sorry to create this much drama. I need to remember that I'm the captain first, and my sole mission is to fly and maintain this aircraft for my employers. I'll speak with Mike once we have completed our checklist and maintenance requirements. Sorry to involve you in a frivolous moment of mine."

The Sarge said, "Thanks for making this one easy for us. We have a few concerns, we need to know our planes are safe, and haven't been compromised. We all expect to take-off and land safely. Is that too much to expect?"

"We're on the same page. Never again will this kind of an inconvenient notion, require your time," the captain stated.

"Listen, you're a part of this family. Mike has worked for some unscrupulous characters and until we have a better sense of what he's been up to, I prefer separation. Thanks, and never hesitate to bring your personal issues to me or one of the others. Your mental wellness is also important to us. This is not just a job, Captain, this has become a damn adventure."

The Sarge whistled for Mike and told him until they amend their protocols, only their crews are allowed alone on the planes. I know we might have to make an exception in your case in the future, but for now, we have SOPs that we must adhere to."

"I understand and respect that. But I have a deeper issue I need help with. I want to make a move on her, in a gentlemanly manner, but I don't really know how to talk about what I want to do with a woman. I think she trusts me, but I don't want to do something, or say the wrong thing and then blow my chances with her. I mean I live, sleep, and eat that woman. Not literally, but you know what I mean. I kissed her, and it was a bit awkward. I didn't know if I did it right or what. Once we get settled, can we talk, and you not make me the laughingstock of the group?"

"Mike, if you want me to do that then it's necessary that I ask you a question. Have you had sex with her?"

"Absolutely not. Oh, my God! I want to, but I think I'm looking for a bit more than sex from her. That's why I don't want to blow this. Have you ever seen a woman and your heart fell from its position, moved down to your feet, then rushed to your brain, and then back to its resting place?"

The Sarge looked at him and said, "I know exactly how you feel. It will be my pleasure to have a drink with you as soon as we get settled. And, Mike, I won't tell if you don't."

# # #

The Sarge and Mike were the last two to enter the vehicles. The caravan left the airport and headed thirty miles to a resort that was in disrepair but sat on top of a majestic hill overlooking Valencia. Unsuspectingly and fortuitously, certain details about the group's quest would be found within this establishment.

Ava walked through the oversized front doors and was welcomed as if she were the Queen of Spain. She was handed a bouquet of roses. As she spoke to an elder gentleman in Spanish, it was obvious that the two were talking about the state of the hotel. Ava said, "I brought my American friends here to stay, and I was promised the place would be ready and pristine. Don Carlo, I'm not sure we can stay here."

"I beg of you to give us a chance. Business has been slow because that swine down the hill from here, has spread rumors about my hotel."

"Don Carlo, how much longer can you survive in this business? Don't tell me about your plans, tell me why you have no clients. How long can you keep the doors open?"

"Senora, that is why I wanted to talk to you. I need you to invest in my place by paying the bank the five-months mortgage I owe along with the penalties."

"What happens after that? You can't attract anyone here, even though you have the best view in all of Valencia. If the bank doesn't take the property, those people from the other side of the law certainly will take it from you. How much do you owe the bad guys?"

"I owe the mob, 20,000 euros in principle, but 200,000 in penalties and interest."

"Two hundred and twenty thousand? What do you owe the bank?" Ava asked.

"I owe the bank € 175,000," Don Carlo stated.

"How much longer can you stay in business?"

"I was going to take the profits from your visit, shut the doors, and leave Spain. I can't take the threats anymore. They set my house and car on fire. And they told me to sign the paperwork or the next thing that will burn, would be me."

"Suppose I want to invest further in your place, payoff your bad debts, and rearrange the mob's numbers to something reasonable? How about if I also gave you a job for life, a new car, health benefits and a profit-sharing plan. What if I also said that we would gut the building, and restore this place to its original grandeur? What if I offered you all of that and left you with 30 to 35% ownership? What would be your answer to that?"

"Ms. Ava, I currently stand to lose everything and perhaps my life. I need help and most of all I need to have those mob guys leave me alone. They come to my house, make noise all night long, then they show up here, eat and drink, and then charge the bill to me. I'm desperate."

"Let me introduce you to my son's father and his wife. You've known Zanthius since he was a child, this is his wife and baby. That woman over there is Monica, our lawyer and her husband, Mallory. Now, Ben Beckmire is Zanthius's father and oh, you remember Carlos who worked for me? Well, he is my fiancé. Oh, that Asian guy is Mr. Amazing. If they think we can help you, then we have a deal. Is that a fair assessment, Ben and Courtney?"

Courtney looked at Ben and nudged him who said, "Ava, is a member of our family, if this is an idea that she thinks helps you and other good people, then we're all in. I suggest one thing, I want you to invite the mob types and their boss for dinner, tonight, so we don't have any issues. Can you make that happen? My grandson and other grandbabies are in the house. I don't want anyone to have an explosive attitude or thought. In the meantime, Ava, I'm going to need someone to follow whoever shows up for dinner and get me close to who heads this group. I prefer not to kill anyone, but if we must, then it is what it is. Don Carlo, I need you to make sure whoever you communicate with is at dinner. I have people who can do the unspeakable and make people divulge anything, and I do mean anything."

Don Carlo replied, "Perhaps it is better if we meet at the *Casa Romana* restaurant, another place they have acquired through harassment."

Ava exclaimed, "Small minds, little crooks, with big ambitions! Let's move the venue to there. It is much more aesthetically pleasing than the hotel that has nothing that I would eat."

Ava walked over to Ben and Courtney and asked, "Did I overstep my boundaries?"

Ben said, "You were speaking in Spanish and not many of us can do that. Listen Ava, we're here to find a grandchild and/or be prepared for some sick engagement by Walter. Stop second guessing what you do, we're in your house and as such, we need you to guide us. The one thing I want you to do before we check in is to obtain us some small weapons. Is that possible?"

"Oh, I'm sorry. I had my people bring them in a suitcase. Once we get settled, I'll have them sent to your room and you can disperse them. Courtney, Monica, Rashida, Asiram, Marisa, the three Asian ladies, Mary Alice, and I, already have ours. Catch you later."

"Oh, Ava, Rashida wants to have a small wedding here in Valencia with our group as the only guests. Do you have connections with a church that could accommodate the ceremony?" Courtney asked.

"I'm a good Catholic woman. I know a priest, but I should go to confession first and that might take a week or two. Just kidding, I will make the arrangements tomorrow, if that's okay with them."

"Why don't you touch base with them and check it out?"

Ben Beckmire asked, "Courtney, do you have a weapon on you?"

"Honey, of course I do. Do I look stupid or something to you? Ben don't bother me with details. I like Ava, she looks out for us, and I look out for her. You brought us together, so let us figure out how we roll with each other. She loves Carlos, but she is in love with my man, and I don't blame her. My man, is the Man!" Courtney exclaimed.

Jong walked over and said, "Are any members of our group Muslim?"

The Sarge asked, "What's up with you?"

"Well, our new president just signed an executive order banning all Muslims from five or six different countries."

The Sarge asked, "I wonder who's next?" He looked at Jong and whispered, "Look at this place. Look at that ceiling. It looks as if it could fall down on us at any minute. Once we figure out the whereabouts of the child, we leave Valencia immediately or try to find a place that can house all of us."

# # #

Less than an hour later after arriving to their room, there was a knock at Beckmire's door. It was Carlos. The Sarge invited him in and noticed the suitcase he was carrying. Carlos said, "My wife to be, is concerned about your inviting the mob for dinner. As such, she has asked that everyone be in the dining room and all of our people have weapons."

Carlos looked at Courtney and snidely remarked, "I hear some people already have weapons. I'm here to make sure I can offer the rest of our shooting family something. Your call, Sarge."

"Carlos, are we expecting a full-scale battle or something? Did I miss something in the translation?"

"Sarge, Ava feels if we present them with an option tonight it ends at that point. She doesn't want to get into a back and forth, pissing match with them because of the possibility of collateral damage. She feels we should engage them and extract the names of their leaders. You may not know this, but she has been in a quiet battle with the mob for years over the import and distribution of drugs. She hates them, but they respect each other. In my opinion, if we go through with this dinner, we had better be prepared to waltz into their bedrooms and offer them their last rites. There can be no backing down from this."

"What the hell did we walk into?" the Sarge asked.

"Sarge, these guys are petty and look for any opportunity to steal from or bribe someone. They are small time but will also exact damage on anyone who screws with their income," Carlos stated.

"Carlos, is there a place where I can meet the person in charge and attempt to minimize the notion of battle? I mean I don't know these people, and I sure as hell don't want to kill someone over a bad deal made by another adult who I happen to have no loyalty to," the Sarge proclaimed.

"I could take you to where the person I know who calls the shots is, but it could turn out to be a mistake, one that might eliminate my potential for marrying the woman I love," Carlos declared.

"Coerce her into a car, Courtney and I will join you with Jilkes, John Lee, Yeshida, Somara, Mallory and Monica in another vehicle, armed. I'm trying not to immediately kill people on my first day in a new country. Can you put this together?" the Sarge inquired.

"Sarge, you know Ava doesn't do well with surprises. I can't get her out without details."

The Sarge asked, "Courtney, can you make this happen?"

"Honey, I'll make it happen, but we ain't going to dinner at the mob's hangout with just a few of us. I think I want our people covering every aspect of the place if Carlos can arrange it."

"Honey, Carlos isn't arranging anything. He knows where they hang out and we're going there for drinks and perhaps a coup d'état. I just don't want to kill anyone else. I want to save all of my rage for my cousin, Walter."

Courtney said, "Carlos, get Juan and alert Mallory about what we're considering. Carlos and I will have a word with Ava and hopefully we'll all agree on this non-violent strategy."

## CHAPTER THREE

The mob had recently swindled their way into the '*Casa Romana*' restaurant. It served an eclectic variety of Mediterranean and French cuisine. When the group arrived in shifts, everyone was impressed with the view and the menu. Carlos walked in, scoped out the place, left, and returned with Ava, Ben, and Courtney. Standing behind them in an unfriendly fashion were Monica and Mallory. Monica appeared to be at odds with Mallory, which was a part of the ruse that was being offered. When the initial group was escorted to their table, a tall and elegant looking man stood up and said to his compatriots, "That's Ava De Lombardo. What the hell is she doing here?" He walked over to where she was sitting and said, "Ms. De Lombardo, welcome to my restaurant."

Ava, without ever looking up at the man, sternly asked, "When did this become your restaurant?"

The individual said, "Ms. De Lombardo, there is no need to entertain questions of that nature. I just want to welcome you and your guests and hope that the meal meets with your exquisite standards."

The guy looked at Beckmire and asked, "Have I met you before, *Senor*?"

Ben replied, "Unless you live in the States, then I don't think so. This is my first time in your country."

Ava looked at Ben, then at Courtney, and didn't bother to introduce the man talking, but rather insisted they look at the menu and order drinks. As the man walked away, Ava said, "I think his father was a part of the group that killed my father. I can't prove it, but I feel it. Don't look now, but Jilkes and the rest of the crew are entering the place."

Courtney said, "That guy looked a little frail. Is he the one we make first contact with?"

Ava said, "Believe it or not, I think he is substituting for the person who runs this entire area. The guy sitting to his left is his lieutenant and hitman. Brutal and rumored to be his lover."

The Sarge said, "Oh, my! This seems too easy. Do you want to do this here and now, or wait until we get full information on who is watching who?"

Ava said without looking around the room, "They have let their guard down. They are so accustomed to being in control, they can't imagine someone moving on them in their own place. This would be an opportune time to scale the fish, Sarge."

# # #

John Lee stood up and said, "I be needing to find the men's room."

From a not-too-distant table, someone said in broken English, "Try the ladies playground."

John Lee stopped in his tracks and thought to himself, "I must be doing that hallucinating shit or something going on."

Jilkes jumped up and walked over to the table where the slight came from and said, "My friend is sensitive. He has that post trauma syndrome or something crazy like that from being over in the Nam years ago. Please don't set him off. An apology would be in order."

One of the guys said, "Retardo, screw yourself."

Jilkes reacted immediately by hitting the man in the back of his head. The blow almost broke his neck. As his friends pulled out their knives and little pistols, within the entire restaurant, one could hear the sounds of, click, click, click, many times. John Lee walked over to the table and asked, "Why you break his neck?"

"I didn't mean to hit him that hard, but I'm not fricken retarded. Okay, assholes, you want to insult us, then let me tell you who we are first. We are not nice people. When we get involved, the only possible outcome, is a terminal one."

Jilkes walked over to where the alleged owner of the restaurant was and said, "You must be the owner and you must be his lover. As the person who was the alleged lover rose from the table with a machine pistol in his hand, John Lee hit him in his solar plexus and basically crippled the man.

Jilkes said, "I hear you're buying up properties at a better than discounted rate because intimidating people and killing their family members is the way you operate. This is how this is going to go down. I know you are a tough guy, and you didn't get to this position by being a patsy. So, I'm going to give you respect and ask you two questions. Your answers will clearly dictate the amount of pain we're going to inflict on your ass. Are you ready?"

The guy in the white linen suit said, "I don't know who you people are, but you really don't know who you're messing with."

Jilkes violently approached the man, swung his left hand at the man's face, stopped short of hitting him, and with his other hand, grabbed all that was essential to the guys existence. After fifteen seconds, the individual receiving that experience collapsed on the floor.

When he awoke, Jilkes said, "How did you like that? I guess you don't remember. Let's try that again, and again, until your heart stops. You can't be revitalized from the trauma I'm going to inflict. I'm going to ask you one question. If you want to debate the efficacy of the question and not answer it, I will crush your damn balls with my hands. Are the rules clear? Oh, you still seemed dazed from the first go-round. I'm going to be compassionate and give you thirty seconds to get your shit together."

At the fifteen second mark, Jilkes asked, "What's another fifteen seconds? Who is your boss and where can I find him in the next thirty minutes?"

The guy looked at Jilkes and said, "Are you the leader of this group?"

Jilkes responded, "That's not the answer I sought to the question I asked." He forcefully increased the pressure on the guy's testicles for twenty seconds that seemed like an eternity to the guy.

He said, "I'm going to ask you the same question again. If you pass out, then I'm going to wait until you awaken and then squeeze the living shit out of your testes."

The guy attempted to say something and Jilkes said, "Okay, you can waste your time attempting to threaten me, but I'm determined to make sure you never experience another orgasm unless your mind is extremely virtual. I don't want to be redundant, however, you know the question so, here we go again. I'm going to give you thirty seconds and then I'm going to go to work to make sure that the last orgasm you had, will be the only one that you remember. I'm going to crush your nuts, dude. The clock is ticking."

Less than five seconds after the clock started to tick, the guy in charge said, "Open my phone, select the letter 'F', scroll down and select, 'Flohr'. He's the man and he'll be here in less than an hour with five of his guards."

Jilkes said, "How the hell did someone named Flohr become the boss of bosses in a damn Spanish town?"

The guy barely audible replied, "That is not his real name. That is how I have him listed in my contacts. His real name is Franco Jorge De Frisca. He, and his associates, resurrected a good after market economy in terms of the fish industry and continued to move up the food chain by terminating their competitors one night in a complete purge. He and his people eliminated thirteen people in the same night, but it never made the news. He's now suffering with a disease or a condition that you people call dementia. He's a member of the Tea Party and a loyal supporter of your new despondent president. His natural state of demise is imminent because he has several conflicting viruses."

Jilkes said, "What the hell does that mean?"

"He likes little boys and little girls, but he is attracted to big boys and big girls too. He doesn't know it, but I know that he's dying from a variety of venereal diseases. I intercepted his last medical report and it indicated that he was infected with several viruses, as well as his third, fourth, and seventh wives."

"Why aren't the first, second, fifth, and sixth wives infected?"

"They are women from the north who knew he was a permanent freak and knew that sex was not what he wanted, at least with them. Their motives were financial."

Zanthius walked into the restaurant and went over to his mother's table. He said, "Mom, that guy in the white suit, is he that freaky person who played tough, but loved men?"

Ava said, "Sit down, Son. Jilkes has pretty much crushed his cojones. He passed out the first time, Jilkes woke him up, and started the process again. You might not want to watch it, dear. It seems awful painful."

Zanthius looked at what was going on, and then decided to walk over to where Jilkes and John Lee were and said to the guy, "I know you. We attended the same school at one time. Is that, right?"

"Zanthius, everyone knows who you are. Are you with these crazy people, the guy barely whispered?"

"I'm afraid you have just met the world's best assassins. I know these guys and they are associates of my father. Do yourself a favor, just give up the world, let them send you somewhere far, and be done with this mess. I saw that big white guy gut a woman. Think about it. He gutted a beautiful woman from her vagina to her brain, then took a bite out of her beating heart. I don't know what you're into, but I do know you don't want to screw with these nuts," Zanthius announced.

Without further ado, the guy began to talk in detail. He told Jilkes that two of the men escorting the boss, were going to go to the upper level first, to cover him, and everyone else was going to spread out without ever taking their eyes off their employer. He asked Jilkes if they had plans to eliminate his employer, and Jilkes told him they weren't there to kill people, but to make sure that the little guy, the small businesses, had a fair chance without some intimidating asshole standing over them.

Jilkes asked, "Why are you sashaying as the owner?"

"That's one of the things we do when we encounter strangers. I play him until we determine there is no threat."

On schedule and according to plan, two men walked into the restaurant, scanned the environment, and headed upstairs. Four or five minutes later, the boss walked in, was led to his table, and his people dispersed throughout the restaurant.

When he sat down, he saw Courtney. He thought to himself that he would like to meet her. He signaled to one of his men to come to his table. He whispered something in his ear. The man walked towards the table where Beckmire, Courtney, Ava, Zanthius, and Carlos were sitting. In his best English, the man said to Courtney, "Pardon me, but my boss would like to offer you stimulating conversation and champagne. He would like your company at his table."

Ben Beckmire was about to throw the guy through the roof, when Courtney said, "I would love to join your boss. We're all just friends at this table. I would love to have some champagne and stimulating conversation."

Beckmire said, "I thought you were going to hang out with us tonight."

"When in Spain, do as the Spaniards do," Courtney stated.

When Courtney arrived at the table of her host, he stood and said, "I am Franco Jorge De Frisca, and this is my restaurant." He reached for Courtney's hand and kissed it.

Ben Beckmire, witnessing this, attempted to get up from the table, but Zanthius said, "Pops don't blow this. Be the bigger man. Take one for the team."

Franco asked, "Is that Ava De Lombardo at your table?"

"Courtney said, "Oh yes! That is Ava. We are her guests. How on earth do you know Ava?"

"I did business with her papa when he was living." He looked to his right and saw that his man seemed to be in a stressful situation. He motioned for him to come over to his table, but when he looked back at Courtney, she had her weapon out, cocked, and placed in his side. He said, "What is going on here? Who are you people?"

Ben Beckmire walked over to the table and said, "That woman is my wife. Your man insisted she come and have a drink with you. Now, this is how this is going to go down. Call your people from the balcony down and keep both of your hands on the table. Any false move and you will truly see how much this woman loves me. Are we clear?"

"You Americans think you can come to our country and just abuse us? What is this about anyway? Did that mental patient create some false narrative about me killing her father?"

Beckmire said, "I don't know anything about her issues. What I do know is you have been stealing property, and you're trying to take a place that we like. The question is whether we take you, and feed you to the fish? That resort, on the hill where we're staying, I hear you made the owner an offer that he couldn't refuse. How about we offer you the same kind of deal—that is, one that you will not be able to turn down?"

Franco said, "You must be out of your mind to come to my country and try to tell me how to do business. What do you think will happen to those who refuse to cooperate with me once you leave? Do you think you can make a threat that will not allow me to fortify my position with my people? This is no good deal for anybody. I think we can dismiss the bravado and call this a draw as you say in your country. You cannot win here, and those who have confided in you will certainly have to pay more for bringing in outsiders to interfere with internal issues. That resort, for example, has no intrinsic value to me or my people. We think it's a national disgrace to let your property slip into ruin because you can't afford to take care of it. We're doing him a favor. What happened to his home has nothing to do with me or my people. Such a tragedy, but those things do happen. We are like his guardian angels."

"Franco, you talk a lot and say little in defense of yourself. You stole this place, and you're about to steal the resort by extortion, torture, firebombs, and kidnapping. Here is the situation as I see it. You don't have enough manpower here to deter us from just slitting your throat and dropping your corpse in the ocean. That's one consideration. The other is, you make a few dollars by selling us the properties at, lets' say, a 10% fee. That's on top of what you put into the place which is nothing because you threaten people and their families. So, that's the 10% we're talking about. How much money have you invested in the restaurant?"

Franco was about to say something when Jilkes walked over and said, "Sarge, he paid nothing for this place. Why are you offering him 10% of nothing and then we have to take out a $250k contract on his ass with our friends in Northern Africa who have a beef with some mob types up here anyway?"

Hearing the reference to Northern Africa and a contract, Franco knew that he did not want to be involved with anyone from that area. He said, "Perhaps we're getting ahead of ourselves. Who are you people and what is your interest in the resort and this place? Are you looking to invest or own outright? Perhaps we should consider a partnership. That seems a lot better than you slitting my throat or me trying to figure out if my other men are going to show up here and start shooting the place up. I must admit, this is a recent acquisition and one that I'm not prepared to die over. Now, is there any room for negotiation? I don't want you to kill me, and I don't want to have to kill you or anyone else. I mean one of my former associates got a little crazy when he misinterpreted my commands. I said, 'rough and a little hurt'. I never said, 'dead'. I did say start a fire, but I didn't say engulf the entire place with flames. He's no longer with us. Listen, our organization brings stability to the area, it is a needed commodity. How can we settle this thing amicably?"

The Sarge looked at Franco and said, "Your business tactics lead me to discount your words, and I have less than 10% faith in thinking that we can work out a relationship where you don't kill me, and I don't kill you. You're a mob boss, and basically a person who strong arms the little guy or even kills them if you don't get your way. I don't know how much faith I can put in a relationship with you. Let me talk it over with my guys, but I can assure you, they are going to want to kill you, or take a contract out on your ass."

Franco said, "Listen *mi amigo* this thing need not get any bigger. We can seek opportunities elsewhere."

"See Franco, that's the problem. You leave a few families alone, then you move on to another person that can't refuse your offer like a rat procreating and starting a new home. We're against people who take advantage of others. You're a carpetbagger to us, and we don't like them at all. The problem is if we don't end the conflict here, it may appear somewhere else. Why can't you just go legitimate and help people by truly investing in them as opposed to taking advantage of them when they miss a payment?"

"So, ah, what is your name?"

"My name is Ben Beckmire."

"I heard one of your associates call you something else."

"He called me Sarge."

"Are you people ex-military? It doesn't matter. Franco looked around the room and said, "You came into my house and captured it without firing a single shot. Your earlier statement is so altruistic. What is your potential gain from investing in the resort and the restaurant?"

Franco looked at Courtney pointing the cocked weapon at him. He politely asked, "Mrs. Beckmire, I promise not to do stupid, will you please remove that weapon from my ribs?"

Ben Beckmire nodded at Courtney to remove the weapon. He said, "To your question. Honestly, I don't know. We came for dinner, some information, and found out you were swindling these people out of their business. I can tell you this without going into any details, we would probably gut the building, rebuild from the ground up, and appoint the place with modern fixtures and amenities. We would offer the real owners a salary, a percent of the profits, a repurchase option, fringe benefits, and 30 to 35 percent ownership."

"Seems like you people are angels. Where is the hustle? I mean when do you start asking for fees, construction costs, on and on and on?"

"We rebuild in a third of the time that it takes most places to reconstruct."

"How on earth can you do that?"

"We hire local labor from the community, and we run three full-time shifts, six days a week."

Franco looked at the Sarge, paused, smiled, and said, "Are you for real or are you blowing smoke up *mi culo*? I mean, I see an opportunity for us to help you and you help us. You might just be on to a new paradigm."

As the Sarge looked around the restaurant, he could see that the hostilities had subsided and that his people were eating. He said to Franco, "What do you mean a new paradigm?"

"I simply mean that your notion of creating structures in a third of the time using three shifts could be expensive but cost effective when you consider the amount of time it now takes to construct a building. Now, this is where I can come in, and help you with a legitimate offer, and a guarantee of no strong-arming or intimidations. Let me and my organization be responsible for selecting the locals and developing training programs. I'll charge you a fee, me and my people will act as your on-site managers. It's all straight up and above board. No hustle, real inspectors, and that way I don't try to kill you and you won't have to kill me."

The Sarge said, "Franco in the last ten or fifteen minutes, you and I have found ways to not kill each other. Why can't our leaders realize the value of conversation? Let me think about this a minute before I call my business types over. I would first like to order something to eat. What do you recommend?"

"I have not had the chance to eat here, but my people tell me the food is amazing. Before I make a recommendation, can we agree to not kill each other or take hostilities to the next level tonight?"

"You're about to invite me and my wife to dinner. Do you plan on trying to kill us as your guests?"

"No, *mi amigo*. I would love the pleasure of her company and you may hang around to make sure that I don't swipe, or how you say it, ah, 'sweep her on her feet'."

"No, my friend. It is 'sweep her off her feet'."

# # #

One hour and a half later, Franco, Courtney, and the Sarge were drinking wine and telling stories. In the middle of biting into a piece of Mediterranean style chicken, Courtney said, "I don't know how we ended up on this path. We're here searching for someone in a monastery."

The Sarge nudged her under the table. Franco after hearing this information, tilted his head, curiously looked at Courtney, and said, "Many people from your country come to our monasteries. Rarely are they seeking someone. On the contrary, they leave their unwanted sins for care." Franco paused for a moment, thought about the hypocrisy of his statement, and realized that there could be another kind of interest in play here. He said, "If you will indulge me, I would like to tell you a story of one such case that occurred a week or so ago." He hesitated and asked, "Is that okay with you?"

The Sarge responded, "By all means, tell us a bedtime story."

Franco smiled and said, "Just a week or so ago, a young woman, who had a strong European accent that resembled a dialect that was Russian, stayed at the resort where you people are staying. It was said that during the night, a child could be heard crying in her room. No one seems to remember her leaving, but some did see a nun from a monastery enter through a rear door and within a few minutes, she had a basket in her hands."

The Sarge asked, "Tell us more about this encounter, and what makes it so suspicious that someone would tell you about it?"

"I am considered a religious man, despite my shortcomings and my never-ending appreciation for women as beautiful as your wife. I happened to be at the resort on that given night with a couple of friends. I walked out on the balcony to smoke a cigarette, and that is when I saw the figure appear out of the dark and hastily move towards the back door of the resort. I did not think anything of it because I, too, was in a place that I shouldn't have been. As I continued to watch, I saw her retreat, with a basket in her hand. The night was young, and the air was still. I did hear the sound of a baby. I just said to myself, 'Another sinner giving their wickedness to someone else'."

"Franco, you weave wonderful stories. You should write such things down as fiction and try to develop a legitimate business model for weaving tales."

"Ah, perhaps you are correct, *mi amigo*. However, I'm not through with this story. As hastily as the woman disappeared into the night with the basket, another development began at the resort. There were two men and one woman dressed in police uniforms who attacked one of the doors in the resort."

"What do you mean by 'attacked one of the doors'?" Beckmire asked.

"*Mi amigo*, you must learn to listen to the full story before you interrupt and/ or threaten to drop people in the ocean."

Franco paused, took a sip of his wine, then continued. "As I was saying, this didn't make sense to me because the woman spoke in Spanish and the men spoke in Russian. The room that they attacked was a decoy, the real room was across the hallway. As the makeshift alarm went off, the people in the uniforms made haste and disappeared into the night. They were not Spaniard, they were Russians. Now, you may ask me the question that is burning in your brain, but you're not sure what you might have to give up for the information that I might, just fortuitously, possess about a certain male child."

"What makes you so sure I want to ask you questions, and if so, why about a male child?" Beckmire inquired.

"As I was spinning my tale, I could not help but notice the attention you and your lovely wife gave to my story. *Mi amigo*, could there be a reason for you and me to have further dialogue about our relationship? Is it possible I might be able to direct you to the correct monastery or let you wander around Valencia and Barcelona endlessly, asking extremely perplexing questions? I think it is time for you to invite your business partners over so that we can discuss that new paradigm. Oh, my goodness, this is truly an opportune moment. What do you think?"

The Sarge looked at Franco and said, "You my friend are one silver tongued charlatan. I have never known anyone like you and hope to the heavens I never do again. What I will divulge about all of this, is perhaps the woman is the same one we're seeking, but more importantly, we seek the whereabouts of the child. It has been purported my son is the father of the child we seek, and his mother is a Russian spy who the entire world is seeking. If you think we're some bad hombres, then try to weave this into a story once we give our Russian contacts your information."

"I don't like Russians and, therefore, there is no need for me to have any conversations with them. However, I would like to share all that I know about the situation. I could perhaps, give you a ride to the monastery that is holding the little fellow. I also know who is in charge and could probably cut through a lot of red tape."

"Franco don't bullshit me. The price you would have to pay is too high, in this case." Ben Beckmire hesitated and exclaimed, "I'm seeking my grandchild! Not a deal or a bargain!"

Franco looked at the Sarge and Courtney and stated, "You're right. A child's life is not a thing to bargain with. Let us finish our meal, and we all can proceed to the monastery."

Courtney exclaimed, "Really! You want to finish eating?"

"I'm sorry. I meant to say, I'm ready to go, right now. Will we be traveling with all these people?"

"Me and my people never separate. After I make the call, there will be more of them joining us. How about your people?"

"We don't exist in a world where people fly in from out of town and take over our businesses in a matter of minutes. What's more, we do weekends off. Have your people follow me."

# # #

Forty-five minutes later, a caravan of vehicles proceeded up the road towards the Route of the Five Monasteries. The Sarge said, "I'm placing a lot of trust in your hands. I'm not sure you've earned it. Just remember, my wife or her associates will place a round in you without hesitation."

"*Es stop it*! We're beyond that kind of activity. We're on a search for the Holy Grail, or the child that's so important to you that it seems like the Holy Grail. My interest is beyond what you seek. I think this opportunity is big, expensive, and therefore, where possible, I want to be a part of the equation. I want to make sure I do whatever I can to secure the 'diamond child'. After that, it becomes a notion of opportunity."

"Franco, there are over five hundred souls in the last few months who have searched for an opportunity. We are the people who sent them to hell. I suggest you concentrate on being righteous and leave all seemingly good opportunities alone. I like you and I would hate to add you to the list of the dead and greedy. Let it go, my brother, or you might have the wrath of all of us upon you. Let's move on and don't lie to me. Are you the full owner of the resort and the restaurant, or are you fronting for someone?"

"Why would you insult me with a question like that?"

"We don't really have a lot of time for bullshit. If the two properties are yours, what would you want for them? They're both in disrepair. One much more so, than the other. They both appear far from being up to code, structurally and crumbling down at the corners, and not nice places in general."

Franco looked at Beckmire and said, "I'm going to reserve my answer until I know what your intentions are."

"We're going to offer the owners a significant portion of the ownership, salaries, benefits, and other things that my people handle. For that, we take a controlling percentage of the properties, we get the titles back from the bank and place them in their hands. We then gut and refit the entire properties," Beckmire stated.

Franco, after lowering his head for approximately ten seconds or so, said, "I am not the owner. However, I am the front man for a person at the bank who sees an opportunity. I also didn't purge 13 people during a night raid. I watched those who conducted those hideous assaults, enter a van, I assume someone accidently discharged their firearm, the bullet hit a case that had dynamite in it, and blew the vehicle to bits. I saw an opportunity, and I never looked back."

Wow, Franco, that's some story. After we deal with the monastery business, will you gather the owners, march them and me into the bank, so that we can have a discussion with the owners and let us settle this business, so that you earn a fee, instead of a bullet?"

Zanthius said, "You seem to have your hands in a lot of different businesses. You're a true entrepreneur. What makes you so sure this is where we will find the child?"

"You mean, your child, don't you? Of course, I'm not 100% positive, but if I had to make a bet, given the circumstances of a few weeks ago, it would lead me here first, and then I would fan out after that. There was much too much chaos happening that night when I was at the resort. Plus, the fact that there were people in Spanish police uniforms speaking Russian. Well, I wouldn't consider that a coincidence. Now, that's what made me suspicious. Then, you people show up and the word monastery is mentioned. I

like to think I listen well, deduce, and reason even better. I
hope I'm correct about this one. And Mr. Beckmire, what's
wrong with doing good and hoping that an opportunity
presents itself?"

# # #

As the caravan proceeded towards the first of five
monasteries on the route, Franco told the driver to slow down,
douse the headlights, and use the running lights. Nearing the
gate, he instructed the driver to turn on his headlights and the
old gate began to open.

When the caravan pulled up to the main door, it opened
and there stood a little lady in her nun garb. Franco displayed
his soft side and began to have a conversation with the nun in
Spanish. Ava and Carlos knew exactly what was being said
and listened for any signs of treachery. The conversation
proceeded well, and then suddenly, Franco asked in a stern
manner, "What happened to the bambino who was brought to
the monastery almost two weeks ago? He pointed to Zanthius
and told the nun that he was the father and was here to claim
the child. The nun indicated she did not know what he was
talking about, and that he would have to speak with the sister
in charge.

Approximately ten minutes later, a nun approached from
across the court and spoke to Franco as if she knew him. He
asked her about the *bambino*, and she asked him, "Since when
did he start caring about babies?" The conversation continued,
and the nun turned to Zanthius and asked, "What is your
name?"

He replied, "My name is Zanthius Beckmire De Lombardo, and this is my father, Ben Beckmire and my mother, Ava De Lombardo. That is my other mother, Courtney Beckmire."

"You seem to have a lot of support." The nun spoke in accented English. She studied Zanthius before asking, "Are you married, and do you believe in Christ?"

"I am married, and I was raised here in Spain, as a Catholic," Zanthius replied.

"Where is your wife and what is her contribution to this event?"

"My wife and I recently had a child. I did not know that I was expecting a child by another woman."

"There is a word for such an act, but I'm not here to judge you. May I ask the name your wife goes by?"

Zanthius replied, "Asiram."

"Ah, when spelled backwards it is Marisa. Helga indicated to me you would come for your child and that you and your wife would love this child throughout eternity. Is that correct Zanthius Beckmire De Lombardo?"

"That is correct. It was my wife who insisted that we come to Spain immediately and claim our child. She knew that Helga would probably not survive the onslaught of the people searching for her."

The nun said, "Please wait here. There is something I must retrieve that you must sign. There will be no formal transfer of the child because Helga never wants him to know he was without parents. She has supported our monastery for many years and has endowed us handsomely. She also left an endowment that our order will oversee as well as some starter money, as she called it, for the child." She then looked at

Franco and said, "You should be in confession. You must stop your foolishness and become the person God intended you to be."

"I am truly working on that, Sister, with the help of some people I just met. I'm truly considering a new line of work."

"I will pray for you and believe it when I see you no longer involved in petty things that only hurt people. I will pray for you."

The nun left the reception hall and disappeared into the night across the court. Twelve minutes later, she returned with a briefcase and said to Zanthius, "I was told you, and only you, could open this briefcase on the first try. Please show me."

Zanthius looked at the case and said, "I've never seen this briefcase in my life."

The nun said, "Unless you focus, and fast, you will not find out where your child is being cared for. That information is contained within the briefcase."

Zanthius looked at it and said, "Please set it on the table." The nun responded and did what he asked. Zanthius walked over to it, studied it closely, and finally dialed the number 2 on the left, and 34 on the right dials. He pressed the plungers and the case opened.

Ava looked at him and said, "You are amazing. God is always watching over you even when you do wrong, Son."

Once Zanthius opened the case, he found an envelope with a passport, other kinds of ID, and a series of numbers that essentially stated that the baby's DNA matched his

99.999999%. He stated, "I guess you can't get any closer than that?"

The nun said, "Come, let us pray." They entered a small sanctuary, and she began to pray for the child, for his safety, as well as for the safety of all the adults. In conclusion, she said, "Dear Father, change the wicked ways of Franco and show him the way to the right path."

The nun turned to Zanthius and the rest of the group and said, "I'm Sister Mary Marisa. Helga was a friend from another life. She did not name the child because she felt that it was the responsibility of those providing care for him. I would now like to present you to our 'diamond child' as he has been termed."

The Sarge looked at Franco and asked, "How did you know that was what he was being called?"

"In the house of our Lord, I tell you I did not know what the child was being called."

Sister Mary Marisa said, "He could not have known. It was only I who called him that."

Franco looked at the Sarge and said, "You should trust people outside of your world, on occasion. You're missing a lot of intelligence that might help you in the long run."

#

Mallory and Monica walked into the monastery. Monica said, "I want to take one or two children home with me. Is that possible, Sister?"

"In God's house, everything is possible. It's only the ways of man that prevent us from doing the honorable things that we want to do."

"Sister, I'm serious, and so is my husband. We might be a little old, but we are still capable of rearing children—we just can't conceive them."

Sister Mary Marisa looked at Monica and then at Mallory. She was looking for the one who was hesitant about this lifelong commitment and she did not see it reflected on their faces. She said, "If you two are serious, I will entertain your notions at lunch tomorrow, here at the convent. Please bring references with you."

Zanthius asked, "When will my son be presented to me?"

Sister Mary Marisa said, "I thought you would never ask. Those were the magic words, Zanthius." She rang a little bell. A baby and an attendant literally walked out of a picture of Christ, which was painted on the side of the wall that was a hidden passage. The child was turned over to Sister Mary Marisa who fondled him for a few moments and presented him to Zanthius and Ava. Zanthius looked at his son and began to cry. Ava held his fingers, he smiled. Courtney kissed his forehead, he continued to smile. Ben Beckmire smiled at him, he started to cry.

Ben asked Sister Mary Marisa if he could have a private word with her. The two walked into another room where Ben Beckmire asked for her help on a local matter.

CHAPTER FOUR

Back at the resort, an anxious Asiram waited for a knock on her door. Since they had split their resources, Brown, Bernstein, McArthur, Whitmore, Gladstone, Jong, and Montomie were armed and watching over the suites where the pregnant women had converged with their pistols. Asiram kept waltzing and feeding her Ben. She said, "I'm not good at this waiting. I think something went wrong. She opened the door and said to Jong, "Make the call, damn it. Check to see if all is okay."

Jong said, "You know we're on radio silence. Give them fifteen more minutes, then we all pile into the van and head to monastery."

Asiram looked at her watch and engaged the timer. She said, "With or without you—in fifteen."

Jong said, "You put too much pressure on me. I must do what they say, now you try to tell me what to do. I no like yen and yang bosses. One or the other or I quit."

"Stop your bitching. When that woman of yours comes to term, you're going to be calling me for help. Just wait and see, Buster."

"Another promise of a threat. I no like overseeing you."

"Anyway, the clock is ticking. I, or rather, we, expect you to honor your word," Asiram said.

#

At 0400 hours, there was a knock at the door. Asiram opened it thinking it was Jong. She said, "We're leaving here—in—five—minutes. Asiram exclaimed "Oh my God! Honey." She saw it was Zanthius holding a beautiful baby boy. I was coming to look for you. Let me hold him. What's his name? How old is he? When can we take him home? I have a million questions. Oh, he's gorgeous. You now have two wonderful looking children, and they will probably be equally as smart. What's his name?"

"Helga left that task to you and me. His passport reads Z. A. De Lombardo. I don't know what that means, but that's what his papers state."

"She named him Zanthius and I'm assuming that instead of Asiram, I suppose she wanted his middle name to be something out of my name. I'm so happy. I just had a baby, and now I have two, and one without the pain. How about Aram? I like that. How about you?"

"Asiram, are you sure you're alright with this?"

"Zanthius, the baby is here and is depending on us to care for him. I'm not going to say, 'his eyes are green' send him back'. I don't give a shit about nothing except that he's yours and you're mine. Unless that's not the case, then I don't have a problem."

Ava announced, "Asiram, I'm here to help. Courtney and I have agreed that we can take turns providing care and helping. We thought about getting help, but we have a lot of pregnant women to help along the way. And, until we complete the puzzle to that Carbon shit, we're going to be together for a long time. We should seriously consider turning those last eight rows of the plane into a nursery."

"Now, that's a great idea. I want to conclude our business here so we can get home and get his paperwork in order. I'm not feeling comfortable here, especially knowing that the Russians were, or are here looking for his mother and perhaps him. Right now, everything is a little shaky. I am going to ask my father to consider leaving here asap," Zanthius said.

Courtney said, "Mallory and Monica have a date with the head nun about adopting a child and Rashida and Juan are supposed to get married tomorrow. I think she would rather marry at The Sanctuary. I will speak to Juan and Rashida and suggest that they hold their wedding in abeyance until we are back on the other side of the world. Depending upon both outcomes, I will broach the subject of the marriage license with her and see if my assumptions about my daughter are correct."

Courtney went on to say, "Look at him, he's sleeping with the angels. We're lucky. You're lucky and smart to take this baby as your own and love him."

"Zanthius is now perplexed about his situation with you and is wondering when you're going to put the other foot up his ass. Never play him against the babies. Never bring them into your disagreements. Love the children because they did nothing wrong. Keep your mind open and treat them fairly. Love them or leave them. If you can't come around to fully loving this child as your own, then come to me. I will make a home for him somewhere in our group," Courtney stated.

"Courtney, I already thought about that. I'm good. How about you? I expect you two ladies to be my associate baby's mammas. Listen, I love my husband, his wacky family, and their associates. This child is mine. Way before Helga and I became enemies, we were secretly friends. We always discussed having children and being each other's protector. I just didn't think we would have children by the same *conjeo*, at the same damn time. Truly, I am happy and know the value of this life. I can't really tell them apart."

Asiram paused, smiled and continued, "Ladies, Zanthius and I met under precarious circumstances where it was designed for him to meet his death. I fell for him and so did Helga, and damn, we both got pregnant by the *conjeo*. He's probably feeling terrible at this moment, but I'm happy we found this child and removed him from the monastery. He's a Beckmire/De Lombardo, and we don't do monasteries for our own or our friends."

With tears streaming down her face, Ava said, "I will be here for you. When you need to take that walk in the park alone, and you will need to do that, I'll be here."

Courtney, not to be outdone said, "When you want to have a drink, I'll be there for you while Ava watches the boys." They all laughed.

Zanthius walked into the room, immediately kissed Asiram on the forehead and looked in on both of his boys. He announced, "I am confused, anxious, happy, sad, and thankful. I'm so happy I have you people in my life."

He walked over to Ava, put his arms around her, and said, "You saved me from myself when I had slipped into the darkest corners of my mind, and when the solution I sought was permanent."

He then walked over to Courtney, placed his arms around her and said, "I thank you and my dad for showing up, and in a big way. There is no way any of us in this room would be alive without you, him, and his friends. What a group of great and dedicated people."

He walked over to Asiram and kissed her dearly and seductively. She said, "Slow down, big boy. I'm not ready for a third one yet."

"I just want to show you every day how much I love and appreciate you. You saved me and you saved us all by offering your homes that were all destroyed because of my dad." Everyone broke into laughter. Zanthius continued, "On a serious note, we have embarked on a wonderful journey with an immediate family. I pledge to understand and appreciate all that you do. I will help you every minute of my life to raise our sons. I love you, my darling."

# # #

The following morning, Monica was up, dressed and prancing around the room waiting to head to the monastery.

Later, towards noon, Mallory and Monica met Sister Mary Marisa for lunch, and she told them about her association with groups in America. She said, "Sometimes people are hoodwinked into thinking they want to embark on a certain path because someone close to them has. After talking to you two, I'm convinced this is not the case. There is a genuine desire to help someone and care for them. As such, I have decided to give you the phone number of a friend of mine in America who will help you fulfill your desires. It is not often we find people such as you two, and we thank Christ for sending you, our way. But we feel you can do a lot of good in your own country."

Monica began to tear up, and Sister Mary Marisa said, "My dear, when you make that call, everything you wish for will come true. Having that telephone number indicates to my friend, I have prayed with you, over you, and I feel that you are prime candidates. Don't cry and don't disappoint me. When you get home, make the call, and you will be blessed. God be with you two."

# # #

Franco was invited to the resort to have a serious conversation about conducting business with the group. He traveled alone and was greeted by Jilkes who said, "I didn't mean to hurt your associate, but it was either squeeze his balls or put a bullet in him."

"You may have thought you hurt him, but the only thing you did was to stimulate him. That's the sort of thing he secretly likes. Is Mr. Beckmire available? I have an appointment with him."

After patting Franco down, Jilkes led Franco in the dining area where Beckmire, Mallory, Monica, and Jong were sitting. Franco said, *"Buenos Dias Senora and mis amigos. Como estas? Que pasa?"*

Beckmire replied, "Hey Franco, what's up?" He quickly reintroduced the other members of the team and jumped right into the nature of the business. The Sarge said, "Franco, we know you're a crook, but we're going to do business with you and pray we don't have to have parts of your anatomy removed for being *estupido*. You screw this deal up, and you're dead. Am I clear?"

"*Mi amigo*, why do you insist on threatening your business associate? We got through all of the ways I wanted to kill you, you wanted to kill me, settled on not killing anyone, and doing a project that is legitimate and makes sense."

"Do you think we should take on both projects at the same time or do one and then the other?" Beckmire inquired.

"*Senor Beckmire*, if you do both at the same time, there are economies of scale to be had. I mean some of those economies might be available with a promise or two, but it would be good business sense to demolish both places and start anew using the same companies to provide cement and other materials. I think your idea of working around the clock, except on the Sabbath, is a marvelous idea. I mean I can get the labor. I can have them trained, and I can monitor them. However, we will need some seasoned artisans who know what the hell they're doing. I have an architect we can use, but I will defer that part to you. Also, all contractors will be selected by a bidding process and handled by a panel you can select from afar."

Jong said, "Okay—let's head to the bank and conclude this deal. Are all of the property owners here?"

Beckmire looked at Jong and dismissed his comment before replying, "Do you know how to do video conferencing and how are you going to do this? Are we picking up the owners of the restaurant and then proceeding to the bank or what?"

"My friend, they're already at the bank without any knowledge of what is about to happen. The owner of the resort is also unaware of what's going to happen. It's going to be a glorious day, and hopefully, a business opportunity for me. Can we go now?"

# # #

On the way to the bank, the Sarge said, "Get us an architect and let us see some plans, immediately. First, have a survey conducted of the properties with all their boundaries, so we can see if there is room for expansion. Franco, I want to see the side of you Sister Mary Marisa knows. I want to, or rather, we want to, see something spectacular. Not just a building being razed, and another built in its place. We also need to know how many people are working at the resort and restaurant and give them some sort of unemployment payment when they are unemployed if they're good workers. Also, why can't they do other labor if they are so inclined, and earn a salary? Just a few issues for you to think over and report back to us on. In the meantime, I suggest you go back to church and speak with Sister Mary Marisa. We left her in charge of the funds. One million dollars to be exact. We think that amount will pay for the initial costs.

"On a personal matter, it is doubtful you consistently make $5k per month. In any event, your monthly salary is going to be $12k per month, until you show us what you're made of—meaning things are up for negotiation once we see demolition and construction plans. We're serious about the three shifts. We want to spread the employment notion. We would be upset if one man or woman, worked two shifts. That's not what we want. We want to hire the community and employ as many people as possible. That would be a deal breaker if that edict isn't in place."

Franco held his head down and said, "A little conversation goes a long way. I'll show you my mettle, conduct this position with integrity, and account for every penny. I would also like to hire my people, to get their hands dirty, so to say, and learn a useful skill. I will send you a list of what we pay each person and the payroll for each month. This will be a squeaky-clean operation."

# # #

At the bank, Mallory, Jong, and Monica were the architects of this deal and they did their due diligence. Jong wired the funds to honor the outstanding mortgages for both businesses. During the process, Monica spelled out the conditions to each owner and told them they had the right to terminate the agreement for cause at any time without penalty. She said, "If Franco gets on your nerves, cancel his contract, and a new one immediately goes into place that will terminate his ass."

Franco sat quietly, and briefly pondered why he was suddenly the errand boy. He then remembered it was a lucrative arrangement with greater potential. He knew and recognized that these dealings were to be above board.

CHAPTER FIVE

On the plane ride back to St. Thomas, Zanthius Jr., was crying his little head off. Ben Beckmire De Lombardo was gracious enough to share his food supply with his brother. During one of her breaks, Asiram walked up to Monica and said, "You want to do duty for a while to make sure this is the decision that you want to make?"

Monica said, "I'll come back and keep you company. I'm not sure I want to be left alone with them because I don't know much about babies. Perhaps I can be your understudy as you embark on trying to figure this whole motherhood thing out."

"That sounds like a plan, Monica. Come on back whenever you want. I'll be there. I ain't going nowhere."

Mike strolled up to where the Sarge was sitting and asked, "May I have a word with you in the back of the plane?"

The Sarge said, "I'll be right there. Grab us a couple of beers."

Five minutes later, the Sarge entered the galley and saw Mike. He said, "So, what's up?"

Mike said, "I got a text before we took off." He pulled out his phone and showed it to the Sarge, who said, "Well, that's not possible. Is someone masquerading as him?"

Mike responded, "I don't know, but what I do know is he's dead, dead, and probably completely devoured by sea animals. Do you think his wife put her lover up to trying to impersonate him?"

"That's a strong possibility. I knew he wasn't broke, he needed money, but didn't want to be traced because of bank transactions. This could be complicated. How can you walk into a bank and withdraw $250,000 in cash, especially, when I know you were murdered, and I assisted people in the disposal of your body? Someone is doubling down on this one," the Sarge stated.

"Okay, that was the first text. Look at this one," Mike said.

The Sarge began to visibly turn colors. He asked, "Walter was seen having lunch at the Palm Restaurant in Philadelphia?"

"According to my street associates, he got out of a car with three other guys and acted as though he didn't have a care in the world. He entered after four other guys staked out the place. My source said there were two guys pretending to be homeless and begging, but he could tell they were a fraud. Do you think he has regenerated himself, his forces, and is ready to make a final push at you?" Mike asked.

"No telling what's on his mind. Allen and I had planned on having a conversation about a place where it is said that Walter keeps a lot of cash. If I keep robbing him, he can't pay people to come after us," the Sarge indicated.

"Allen and I probably talked about that place. I told him it was too fortified and would require some real tough cookies to handle that kind of job."

As if he had an epiphany, Mike screamed, "Oh, my god! He had you guys in mind. He told me we had an opportunity to make a few extra dollars. I didn't put it together until now."

The Sarge smiled and said, "How tough could it be? When we get back, why don't you stake it out overnight and design a plan for us to review?"

"I could and would like to do that. I know you and your people are weary of strangers, but I'm out in the cold. Especially since the demise of Allen. I didn't consider him a friend, but we had one thing in common—your crazy ass cousin was looking for us. Yes, I want to do that and one more thing while I have your ear. You know me and your pilot-in-command are having serious talks about our relationship. I mean, we haven't gotten intimate or nothing, but we're moving in that direction. My question is, do you have a problem with me seeing her?"

"What if I did? What would you do differently, based upon the way you feel about her?"

"Honestly, I would have to tell you I was going to continue to see her regardless of how you felt."

"There's your answer. Good luck with that one."

# # #

Once the Sarge was back in his seat, Courtney asked, "What was that all about?"

"Guess who was seen having dinner at the Palm in Philadelphia?

"Are you kidding me. Walter is openly having dinner in Philly?"

"I can't confirm the fact, but Mike's sources said he and his new henchmen were seen having dinner in the restaurant."

"When will we be rid of that vermin?" Courtney asked.

"After we relax for a few days, or so on the islands, I'm going to call a meeting of my people to figure out our next steps in relationship to him."

"Ben, why do you continue to make that mistake?"

"Honey, what mistake?"

"You're going to call a meeting of your people. What happened to Rashida, Okema, Mary Alice, Somara, Monica, Yvett, Yeshida, Carlos, Ava, and the rest of the group? Your people and this group are no longer stand-alone units. They can't operate without each other," Courtney advised.

"Damn, I'm sorry. You know I realize everyone is important to our safety and our mission. I will try not to forget that again. However, you must recognize that my people usually carry the heaviest loads."

"Ben Beckmire don't make me send you to the back of this plane. Your people are lost without their new-found mates. I mean, you mean the world to them, but you ain't got nothing they want late at night or first thing in the morning. So, get over that 'BS'."

Courtney smiled and continued, "That scoundrel was charming, wasn't he?"

"Are you referring to Franco? If you like that kind of 'BS'. I mean, he was smooth, loquacious, and I could definitely see him seducing a lot of women who are weak," Ben Beckmire said.

"Why would a woman have to be weak? Why couldn't she be strong and desire the kind of flare he was shooting off?"

"Okay, Mrs. Beckmire. Where're you going with this one?"

"Ben, I just thought he was smooth and entertaining. Nothing more and nothing less. It would not have mattered if

I had to shoot him. He talked about compromise rather than trying to find ways for you two to kill each other. After it was all over, he got his way, a business deal, and a new source of revenue. Damn smooth if you ask me. Wouldn't you agree?"

"Whatever, I hope he lives up to our arrangement."

# # #

Elsewhere on the plane Zanthius was rocking his son, Ben, to sleep. Asiram said, "I only have one request of you in relationship to our new baby. I don't trust Helga. She has always been full of surprises. I mean this child is ours and there is no giving him back. I just want to know if he's yours. Will you privately do a DNA test for me?"

"Of course, I will. As soon as we get back to the States, I'll get with Courtney and have her order a kit. I was thinking how slick she is as well and wondered myself if she was just tricking me because she realizes we are connected, and my family is strong. It happened too quick to be real, but like you said, this child is ours and we're going to love him regardless. I saw the DNA results in the briefcase, but I don't trust the source."

"This is like a fairy tale. I saw you in the airport and felt my heart melt. I saw you with Helga and wanted to cut your balls off. We made love, a thing I was not accustomed to. I was more familiarized with abuse. I never knew two people could enjoy each other with so much passion. You treated me with such tenderness and affection. I can still recall our first time together. Look at us now—two new babies and still in love."

"That was a pleasant memory. However, I saw you first and decided I had to introduce myself to you. It doesn't really matter who saw whom first, all that matters is it wasn't a fling, we're married, with babies, and a we have a tremendous group of friends and family. By the way, do you think we should build a small place down there where John Lee and Jilkes are building, and where my other mother wants to build as well?"

"Honey, do you think you'll ever get tired of these people?" Asiram inquired.

"Honestly, hell no. I love being around everyone here. It's so positive, entertaining at times, and plus, they're all family. This can't get no better. Think about it, no drama, no wives from the last frontier shit, just family and friends not concerned about money, just their mates and friends."

"Then, we too shall inquire about space, an architect, and a builder if you like. Do you think we should sell our place in the Midwest?" Asiram asked.

"Honey, why on earth would we do that? I love that place, and we all love it. Why would you consider selling?" Zanthius inquired.

"How many different places can we live in?"

"Why don't we keep adding to the list and decide in twenty years when our boys will be heading off to college." Zanthius stated.

"Wait a minute, boyfriend! We're supposed to be trying for a little princess. Did you forget?" Asiram asked.

"Honey, we have enough support to try and have as many of them as you would like. I want a whole army of children because we have the best support mechanism in the world."

# # #

In another part of the plane, Ben Beckmire's cell phone rang. He looked at the number but didn't recognize it. He decided to answer it. It was Franco who started out by saying, "I kept wondering why I never saw the face of Sister Mary Marisa and just her shadow as she came and left. The person who made the transfer to you, was not Sister Mary Marisa. The other nuns found the real Sister Mary Marisa unconscious and in a confessional. We don't know who made the transfer. If I, were you *mi amigo*, I would check everything that is connected to the baby. Good luck, *mi amigo*." Franco hung up.

Ben Beckmire walked to the back of the plane where Zanthius and Asiram were sitting and said, "Franco called and said the real Sister Mary Marisa was found unconscious in a confessional. He wasn't sure who made the hand-off of the child."

Asiram asked, "Honey, what did you bring on this plane from the monastery?"

Zanthius replied, "I brought only the baby. No basket, no bag, just the baby." He looked around realizing the urgency of the question and said, 'Did anyone receive a package from any of the nuns that was for the baby?"

Asiram stated, "Helga might be a *bruja*, but I'm sure she didn't sign on to kill babies—especially one that she mothered."

Meantime, Beckmire received a text on his phone that read, 'Please forgive me. I left you thirty times or better the amount I will use from the money you left. I couldn't access my funds without drawing suspicion, so I used $250k of yours and will use the rest later. Tell Zanthius to t

After reading the message aloud, Asiram said, "I told you. That woman is indestructible. I just hope she doesn't think she can waltz back into your lives or mine and claim this child. It ain't going to fricken happen. This baby is mine!"

CHAPTER SIX

Upon arrival in St. Thomas, Mr. Christopher Carter was standing at the gate with his crew to welcome the group. He walked into the arrival lounge and had a glass of the airport's signature rum punch. When he saw the jet taxi to the private terminal, he got into the van and headed towards the reception area. He saw the doors to the plane open and knew the group would be heading to customs. He also saw two people with earpieces talking to their watches. He dismissed it at first and surmised the rum punch was probably creating a case of paranoia in him. As he looked closer at the bulge in their coats, he knew that all wasn't right. He texted Beckmire (who never cuts his phone off) and said, "Do not exit the plane. Do not exit the plane."

Beckmire saw the text and shouted to the group, "Freeze!" Chris Carter is texting me not leave the plane. There must be an obvious threat. I need two people to volunteer."

The captain came out of the cockpit and said, "You people love my flying that much you don't want to leave?"

Beckmire said, "I just got a text telling me not to exit the plane."

The captain said, "You have four pilots on this plane who are effective at what they do and what you don't see them do. Let us act as if there is a problem while two of us slip right out of the tail portion of the plane that is backed into the hangar."

The Sarge looked around and considered the plan but instead selected the copilot and another reserve to exit the plane along with Mike.

As the three men exited the plane from the tail, they went out the back door and through customs. Two of the men flashed their pilots' credentials and indicated that Mike was their mechanic. Everything seemed in order to the agent, and there was no need to hold them. As they entered the terminal, they saw Mr. Carter, and he pointed out the two men in dark suits and glasses. Mike walked close to them and saw their gadgets. He thought that they were DEA. He was correct. As he purchased a paper from the newsstand, they took off in a hurry running towards the entrance to the airport. It was there they intercepted a man and a woman. They were placed in handcuffs and led out of the airport.

The three scouts reentered customs and made their way back to the plane. After boarding, Mike told the group about what he considered was a drug bust by DEA agents. They placed a man and a woman in cuffs and led them into a SUV.

After disembarking and entering customs, a slightly disoriented Mr. Carter walked over to the Sarge and said, "You guys really should follow me to the main arrival gate and enjoy some rum punch. It's wonderful."

"Well, after we're all accounted for, why don't you walk us over so that we can feel the effects that you're displaying? Is the rum punch here different than what you serve at the resort?"

"I'm not sure, what's in it and they won't divulge their secret. All I know is that whenever I get a chance to come to the airport, I take a moment to enjoy the rum punch."

"Why don't we do a taste test amongst our group? We'll let them all try the rum punch from the airport, and then measure it against the drink at the resort. Let the numbers decide which is better. By the way, you're not driving, are you?"

# # #

The Sarge saw Jong and said, "Mr. Amazing, I would like to ask you and Corporal Mallory a few questions. Oh, and please invite Mrs. Mallory as well."

"Should I bring Mary Alice?"

"We're not having dinner together," the Sarge stated.

Approximately ten minutes later, after having the "Welcome to the Island" rum punch, Mallory and Monica plus Jong walked over to the Sarge and he said, "We'll have this conversation another time. We can't do business when the entire leadership is intoxicated. Let's go back, have another, and then one for the road." When they got back to the welcome counter, his entire group was there having a wonderful time. Those who were pregnant shared in a single drink.

The ride back to the resort was full of singing and storytelling. When they pulled into the cul-de-sac that lead to their properties, it was clear that work had begun on the properties of their new partners and members. Signs were visible indicating that both places would become resorts, focusing on fishing, diving, and marine biology. When the lead vehicle pulled into the circle, the Sarge asked the driver if he would stop for a minute so that he could have a word with their new partners. The vehicle stopped and the Sarge got out of it and saw his two new partners, Mr. Wilson, and Mr. Smith, sitting under a tree having a beer. He walked over to them and said, "I'm so glad you guys didn't assassinate me when I showed up at your bars. I think this is a wonderful partnership and you can only grow. Before you were stuck in the mud. This way, you guys and our other two partners, own this place. It's going to be a great venue. And just think, you get a new place, a helluva job with benefits, and you still have ownership in your business. Now, I'm going to insist on making you knuckleheads go to training to update you on some basic shit like the purpose of the internet, cellphone towers, and giving a customer whatever he or she wants. I stopped here to thank you for not shooting me. Catch you later. We're going to be here for a few days, but then we have to go and try to find the devil walking amongst humans."

One of his partners said, "Ben Beckmire, you keep thanking us, and it's we who should be thanking you for keeping that damn bank from taking our properties. You say it Man, we do it. Nowhere on earth man, could we find a deal that is fair like this one. Man, you, and your people come from the heavens. You no take nothing, you no ask for nothing, you just make deals that make people keep what they worked hard for. We be thinking how much we love you and your people. We figure we going to do more to build up this island, so everyone thinks like you people. Man—help people help themselves!"

The Sarge said, "Once we are sober again, I hope you can come down and have a conversation with me and mine about what we're trying to do here. It's fabulous, and you guys are going to be the kings of the mountain."

As he stumbled back to the van, Courtney said, "Oh, my! I've never seen him miss steps like that. Look at him, that's so funny. Look at how he favors that right foot. That's amazing! He's intoxicated from the punch. Perhaps this way, I can get him to get some much-needed sleep."

When they arrived at the resort, the Sarge said, "I want to take a nap. Honey, do you want to take a nap as well?"

The Sarge and Courtney entered their room, he went directly into the bedroom and hit the bed like a brick. It would be twelve hours later before he would utter a single word.

Mike made a few calls to a few of his friend in the sewers of DC, with one specific request. He was interested in people staking out a certain property on K Street, Northeast. Mike indicated he did not want the property breached, but that he did want photos of who went in and who came out. He stated that he wanted a view of the property from the front and the rear. He said he would accept bids for sneakers, coats, hats, but no druggies were to apply. One of his friends reminded him, "We all have our drugs, define what you mean"?

Mike informed him he needed reliable sources on this one and not people who would close their eyes and place a needle in their arm and couldn't be counted on. He was told that it was such a conspicuous area because there were restaurants two blocks away and that a lot of homeless people were trying to find a place to start a fire and keep warm throughout the night. Mike was about to say something else when a hand was placed on his left butt cheek. The pilot-in-command said seductively, "I'm getting tired of you promising me a grand relationship and wedding. I want to be married here and now on this island. Can you manifest that?"

Mike said to the person on the phone, "I just received an offer that I can't refuse. Please put that thing we talked about in motion with extreme discretion. Catch you later."

He looked at Carla and said, "That was a surprise. More important is the fact that you felt my ass and demanded a ceremony on this island. I want it to happen soon. I want to caress you and love you without violating you. I want you to be my wife."

"Mike, are we doing this for the sake of sex or love?"

"Carla, to me that's an unfair question. I must first tell you I'm not the world's greatest lover and, therefore, I can't hardly see anyone going bonkers over me for sex. I want to learn and teach at the same time. I know this is happening at lightning speed, but I have never felt this way about a woman. Everything about me tingles when you touch me. Anyhow, if the marriage doesn't work out, we can have it annulled."

"Now, that's for sure, but why start with the idea that it's not going to work? I'm madly in love with you, and you profess to be deeply in love with me. We must communicate in positive terms and leave the negatives to those other people who are not sure of what they're doing. I know you're the man that makes me 'happy, healthy and horny' and not necessarily in that order. If you have any doubts, then you need to work through them, and we should hold this event in abeyance until we know what we're committing to. Don't get finicky on me now, Romeo. I told you I play for keeps and I don't do games! I'm not really experienced in the art of romance either. I've had sex with people, but I don't feel as if I have ever made love to a man. It felt more like an invasive medical procedure than something I should remember and cherish. I never really got anything out of my experiences."

"Carla, this isn't about sex to me. I want to be around you, with you, smell your aroma, feel your touch, cherish your smile, and love your kiss. I think if we both think about the same thing then it might bring us to that nirvana that we both seek. I just know I want you in my life. That thing called sex is something I guess two people love, learn, create, or indulge in and feel momentary happiness. I want eternal enjoyment and contentment. I'm not looking for a short-term solution to some biological and natural notion that doesn't seem important to me. I like the spiritual nature of what I feel for you. I know if we can conquer that, then the physical will be a walk in the park."

"Mike, let's go find the Sarge and inform him of our intent to join as one."

#

Around dinner time, Mike saw Courtney and asked, "Where is the Sarge?"

"He's out like a light."

Mike said, "Of all nights, when I really need him."

"What's so perplexing that Mallory and/or I can't handle it?"

"I wanted to ask him to help arrange my marital ceremony with Carla, the captain of the plane."

"Oh, hell yeah. That's going to happen if you two want it to happen. My husband is getting much needed rest. I will present it to him and then from there, you two and Mr. Carter can plan the when and the where. Just remember this—I heard him state we would only be here for a few days, then we would head to the states to hopefully end this situation with the Carbon Factor formula and his cousin."

"I might have some intel coming in tomorrow about both issues, plus info about a stash house right in front of our eyes that has a boat load of illicit funds stolen from dealers and the government. Those illicit funds are used to pay and enrich crooked politicians—what a ruse."

# # #

In the morning, Courtney put together a list of things for Ben Beckmire to do, sort of a, 'honey-do-list'. She handed the list to the Ben, and he asked, "What on earth is this?"

"This is a list of things I need you to attend to today, and hopefully, all in the morning. I also have a naptime schedule listed in red for you, and this is the thing that is going to make me happy the most. First thing on that list is Mike. Mike wants to marry Carla, she wants to marry him, here and now. I told him the plan was to stay here for a few days and then head back to deal with your cousin. Oh, and by the way, he said, he had some new information about the Carbon Factor formula, a cash safe house that is right in the open, and possible leads to Walter. Finally, I am sure our daughter wants to wed Juan. Remember I asked them to postpone that until we got out of Spain.

"Honey, can we go to breakfast and relax for an hour or so before you put me to work?"

"Okay, that's a deal. But when I say it's naptime, don't try and develop amnesia on me, and act as if you don't know what I'm talking about because I will go colored on you."

"Sapphire, I mean Courtney, I'm not mentally challenged. I know who to listen to."

#

Mike walked into the restaurant without Carla and the Sarge said, "Oh shit, I guess we can scratch one event off the list. Look at Mike, he looks as if he has lost something valuable."

Mike saw the Sarge and Courtney and since they were eating, he decided to walk down to the water and chill out.

An hour later, as the Sarge walked on the deck, he saw Mike sitting on the beach with his head hung between his legs and said, "Hell, I can't let him sulk like that. Honey, I'm going to go and get him."

"That's why I love you so very much, man. You're so good to everyone. Yes, please get him out of that funk."

#

On the beach, the Sarge said, "Hell, man, the whole world knows you just lost your woman. Do you want to announce it more and hire a plane to skywrite it?"

"Sarge, I haven't lost my woman. She wants to get married and so do I, but I realized that I'm a wanted man and I have $300 bucks to my name. I don't have enough money to rent a hotel for a week or pay for the wedding expenses. It just hit me."

"You're a part of a wonderful brotherhood and sisterhood. You have provided me with valuable information. I just want you to tell me what you need, want, and I will make it happen."

"Sarge, I'm not looking for handouts. I'm looking for a way to support my wife."

"When Allen was alive and asked me to send some funds to his family, I asked you if you needed anything, and you said no. I owe you for a couple of jobs. I'm not going to give you a handout, but I will pay you for your value to this team. Here is the deal—you will get in a van with a few of my people, you will go into town, and buy my captain a wonderful size engagement ring and a wedding ring. I'm thinking a full carat or better. What are your thoughts?"

"How about a sparkle? That's all I can afford and plus, I don't have a credit card."

"Hush! Don't talk about such things when it comes to love. Love is the kind of thing that makes you spend your last dime on the woman or man you love. Now, I'm going to say we owe you at least $1 million. If the thing Courtney spoke to me about that you told her pans out, then I'll give you the finder's share which is usually around 5% of the take. For example, if it were $50 million in the stash house, your take would be $2.5 million. So, therefore, you have already earned a million and if the DC thing works out, it will be a total of $3.5 million, plus a buy-in to our foundation that provides you with handsome monthly retirement benefits. So, as I see it, you need to take a shower, find Jong, beg Jilkes, John Lee, and Larry to accompany you into town. Oh, by the way, find Juan and see if he needs to make a trip as well. Tell him that we got him covered."

The Sarge saw that the guy was crying his eyes out and said, "I think I see that pretty lady of yours, do something stupid, kick your shoes off and dive into the water. Don't let her see you like this because she'll only think the deal went south."

Without further ado, Mike walked into the water with his only pair of shoes, and dove under and came up and yelled, "I'm a lucky son-of-a gun". As he walked out of the water, Carla said, "Baby, are you okay? You know you don't have any other clothes."

"Sweetheart, I'm better than okay. I'm in love with a wonderful woman who makes my heart skip beats. Listen, I must speak with some of the guys about a thing the Sarge needs me to do in town for him. Perhaps, I'll pick up a few things. Do you need anything? Oh, will it be alright if I just gave you a band for now, until I get on my feet?"

"Dude, place a damn string on my finger, just make me yours." Soaking wet, Mike grabbed her and kissed her. They both fell to their knees, and he said, "I have never been an impetuous person, but if I don't marry you ASAP, I'm going to go crazy. I love you, Carla."

# # #

On the ride to town, John Lee asked, "So, you be marrying that pilot of ours soon? Ain't that a little bit in a hurry?"

Jilkes looked at him and asked, "How long did you know that woman you call your wife and soon to be your baby's' momma?"

"Why you always got to be up in my business, African American?"

"Because you need me. You know you ain't too bright."

"You're right. I need you, but not for no brain activity. I need you to make sure that your fellow brothers don't mess with my white ass."

Mike asked, "Do you guys always go at it so hard?"

"Naw, just lately because them new wives be pregnant and all, and we ain't getting that special treatment no more," John Lee announced.

Juan asked, "Do you guys even like each other?"

John Lee emphatically stated, "Fuck with him or me, and see what happens next!"

Jong looked at Mike and said, "We're going to take you to Mr. Bassman's place. He makes good deals for us and as a matter of fact, I need to get Mary Alice a new ring as well. Jilkes looked at John Lee and said, "I'll be damn. Do you think this could be the issue?"

"You be one smart colored fellow. I'll bet you a dance with my favorite pig if we show up with some sparkle, we'll be taken care of as much as we want."

"You don't have a favorite pig anymore. You have a favorite wife, my country ass brother."

# # #

Mr. Bassman saw the writing on the side of the van and knew the resort had recommended people to him for business. When John Lee opened the door, Mr. Bassman said, "I was hoping you were bringing me customers. What do you blokes want?"

Jilkes said, "We are your customers, and we want to make sure we get the 10% off as annotated in your brochure and another 5 to 10 % off for bulk purchases."

"What are you referring to?" Mr. Bassman inquired.

Jilkes stated, "We all need rings for our ladies, and we don't want them to look alike. What can you do for us?"

# # #

Two hours later, as the group exited the store, John Lee said, "Now, that was some expensive ass bonding. Mike, your broke ass self, had to have at least a full carat. What happened to ½ carat? You can still see it."

"I would say that I love my woman more than you guys love yours. But that wouldn't be fair. I'll say this, those things you guys were looking at were throwaways. We have to make a statement. Our women are special because we love them. Listen, 1.75 carats is a great way to say, 'I love you'. I'll bet you everyone with something smaller is going to have to run their asses down here tomorrow to keep up with the Jones. I mean, I don't know diamonds and that guy could have sold us plate glass. It doesn't matter to me because I feel great about being able to give something fabulous to someone I love. Guys, you must realize, I have been living in alleys, sewers, and abandoned houses. I feel damn free, and I love that woman with all my heart." There was a silence in the van as the men reflected on Mike's statements.

When they got closer to the resort, John Lee said, "I think we should have a special ceremony when we give them angels these expensive pieces of glass."

Jilkes said, "I don't know if I want to be a part of that. I think if we grandstand, we might embarrass some of our brothers. This needs to be done privately."

John Lee said, "Mike, now that be why I like his black ass. He's smarter than all my pigs put together."

"How did you two survive the Nam? You seemingly hate each other."

"Nope! I love him as much as I love my woman. He loves me the same way. It would be a sin and a death wish to come between him and me!" John Lee proclaimed.

Mike looked at Jilkes and knew that what he was witnessing was greater than any piece of jewelry. Jong sprung out of his silence and said, "Why no one loves Mr. Amazing like that?"

Jilkes said, "Because everyone loves Mr. Amazing because he's astonishing. We can't function without him. His love for us and our love for him is like the blood in our veins. We have all bled for each other. When Jong was felled by bullets and shrapnel in the Nam, the Sarge, walked into the enemy's camp, stabbed people, broke their backs, picked Jong up and carried him out. He killed six to eight people by himself. He said, 'I'm not leaving my little brother. I'll kill every living ass down there'. We had no more bullets, and we were bleeding all over each other. This thing we have between us, well, it's insane. You mess with one of us and you inherit the wrath of us all."

John Lee reached over the front seat and grabbed Jong by his shoulder and said, "I know we don't usually talk about that time, but I be thinking that Mike ain't got nowhere else to go, he's going to be here with us, and we just might have to depend on him like we did at the farm. I'm sorry man. I know you hate to hear that shit. I'm sorry."

"I no hate to hear it. The Sarge had no choice, but to rescue me. Who else could lead this group without me? He knew what he was doing."

Jilkes said, "Ah, shit. Now you've unleased the creature."

John Lee asked, "So, Mike, what's it like living in alleys and abandoned places?"

Mike turned around and said, "It's a thing I would like to forget. Please forgive me if I don't indulge your question. I want to focus on where I'm trying to go and who I'm trying to go with."

"I feel you, Brother. I feel you. Sorry for the insensitive question," John Lee stated.

As the group rounded the bend that led to the resort, Jilkes said, "If this place is marketed properly, it will yield a fortune for us over time."

"I be agreeing with you. It be private, not too far out of the way, but boxed in. It be like a sanctuary. Once you enter, you never want to be leaving."

Jilkes froze for a moment, digested what John Lee had uttered, and yelled, "That's it. That's the marketing slogan we need. You're absolutely brilliant, my dumb ass white friend."

"What you be talking about, man?"

"I'm talking about our marketing strategy. You just nailed it to the door. You are absolutely, transparently, brilliant—private and not too far away, but boxed in—The Sanctuary!"

When the group arrived at the resort, Jilkes grabbed John Lee by the arm and when he saw Mr. Carter, he asked, "Have you seen the Sarge?"

He responded, "Mr. Beckmire is taking a nap and is not to be disturbed for the next 1.5 hours, per his wife, Dr. Beckmire's instructions. Would you like to go against her word?"

Jilkes said, "We'll catch him later."

John Lee told Jilkes he had to speak to his wife and present her with the ring. Jilkes responded, "More important than the ring, is the presentation of it. Just don't walk in there and say, 'I bought you a ring'. Fall to your knees, tell her how much you love her and that you're so happy she's going to be the mother of your child. Don't do stupid on this one. Be as brilliant as possible and make your presentation regal'."

"You mean like royal?" John Lee asked.

Jilkes exclaimed, "Yes!" With a touch of class and elegance. Make it special and don't talk about no damn pigs," Jilkes suggested.

# # #

Later, each man made a monumental display of his undying love, affection, and commitment to his woman throughout eternity. Mike asked Carla to meet him on the beach where Mr. Carter had erected his testament to love and marriage—a dazzling gazebo. Mike spoke plainly, promised Carla fidelity, loyalty, understanding, partnership, friendship, and love. He asked her to not measure him against other mortals, but to honor him for his undying love and devotion.

The ladies were impressed with the new shiners and were thrilled by the magnitude of them as well. The entire group walked down to the beach after Mike had his private words with Carla and congratulated them. They had flowers and engagement gifts. Ben Beckmire said to Courtney, "I didn't know engagement gifts were given. Did you?"

"Honey, I'm here to make sure you're okay health wise and that all of those other little things you don't know about, are taken care of."

"What did we give them?"

"We gave them a $30,000 promissory note, to get them started."

As the group returned to the dining room, Mr. Carter placed a headset and mouthpiece on and watched as the servers provided the first course. As people talked and enjoyed the moment, a booming voice suddenly came over the eighteen speakers in the dining room and said, "This is a night for you to remember." There was silence throughout the dining room. Mr. Carter announced, "A group of people came to my resort some time ago and realized it was not the place it could or should be. What did they do? They took it from the bank that was going to take it from me and my family. They gutted it, they rebuilt it in record time, by using around the clock labor consisting of our friends and families. Another member of our community was in the same bad shape as me, and what did they do? They rescued him from the same devils at the bank that were about to take his life-long work. They gutted his place and used the same techniques to rebuild his place in record time. We thought, 'These strangers must be rogues or demons from beyond the pillars of hell'.

"Those same rogues or demons dropped in on our feuding neighbor's places and realized that the same bank was about to take from them all they had worked for. What did they do? They marched our neighbors down to that stealing ass bank and purchased their overdue loans. They recently began the demolition phase of those two properties. We, or those of us who were about to lose all that we had worked for, asked ourselves, when will the fine print surface and we find ourselves at war with these demons? Mr. Smith and Mr. Wilson agreed on the fact, 'that you can tell the kind of demons people are by the women they surround themselves with'. We realized you people were not demons, but people who believed that people should help people help themselves. We took our agreements, albeit loosely written to our local university for analysis. The five people who reviewed them said, 'we have everything to gain, and they have everything to lose'. We can turn your language against you and take complete advantage of the loosely written agreement. But the question remained, why would that smart woman attorney not perform due diligence with a group of strangers?"

Beckmire stood up and yelled, "Because we believe in people, and not banks."

Jilkes began to slowly clap, and the entire group joined him until it entered the crescendo stage.

Mr. Carter stated, "That's exactly our point. We're here for you and yours. We want to call this resort, The Sanctuary. A name that was crafted by none other than John Lee."

Jilkes stood up and yelled, "Yeah!" He pointed to John Lee and said, "You are a powerful human being. I love you man."

# # #

Later, the Sarge had dinner with Mallory, Monica, Jilkes, John Lee, Yeshida and Somara. He saw Jong and beckoned him over. Jong said, "I need Mary Alice to join us too. You big people, squeeze in so we can fit."

The Sarge said, "You don't have to stay, I just want your advice."

"You no invite me and my wife to dinner? You want my advice? I give you advice after dinner."

The Sarge said, "My wife isn't here. She's over there with Zanthius and Asiram."

Jong said, "Okay, but I need my wife. She makes me smarter."

"Whatever! Can you do whatever you're going to do so that I can discuss this small issue of timing?"

"You need more rest? You grouchy! I just kidding."

A few minutes later when Jong and Mary Alice returned, the Sarge said, "Anyway, I called you people over to discuss when we should depart and where we should go. Personally, I think we need to go to Virginia, because I think our person of interest is floating around there. Also, Mike is convinced that there is a stash-house on K Street in DC. The one thing we must consider is the fact that our captain wants to marry Mike, Carlos wants to marry Ava, and Juan wants to marry Rashida here on the island which will add another day to our stay. Plus, Mike indicated he has some new information about the Carbon Factor formula."

Jong said, "Perfect. We stay today. Mike, Juan, and Carlos marry tomorrow, and we leave on Sunday. Anything else?"

"No, Mr. Amazing. The rest of the group may have a word or two to say about the arrangements. Any additional comments from anyone?"

No one had anything to add. The group continued to eat, drink, and tell old and stale stories until the wee small hours of the morning.

# # #

The next morning was Saturday, and the ladies were prepping Carla, Ava, and Rashida for their afternoon weddings to Mike, Carlos, and Juan. Mr. Carter and staff had baked a wonderful cake as well as created a makeshift canopy for the guests. The Sarge was discussing costs with Jong and Monica when his phone rang. He answered it, and it was Franco who said, "Is this a good time to have a conversation, *mi amigo*?"

The Sarge said, "Give me a minute." He walked away from the group and asked, "Franco, what's up? Is everything alright?"

"On the business front, all is okay and moving ahead on schedule. I'm so excited about doing something legitimate that I can't sleep at night. Oh, by the way, there are nasty rumors floating around that I have dementia, several venereal diseases, many ex-wives, and that my henchman is my lover. None of that fiction is accurate. On the other hand, there is good news and bad news that I must present to you. Which would you like first?"

"Give me the bad news first."

"The bad news is, and I've discussed this with you before, the woman who paraded around as Sister Mary Marisa, was not her. I couldn't tell because I never got a close look at her face and besides, I didn't remember a Sister Mary Marisa. I wasn't going to challenge her in the monastery. The second part of the equation is that the $1 million dollars you left can't be found, and people are looking for payment. The real Sister Mary Marisa, as I stated, was found in a confessional tied up. My question is, do you want me to suspend operations until we get clarity on the money or what?"

"Now, that's some funny shit. I don't want you to suspend anything. I want you to call me from the bank when it opens in the morning, and I will have my guy wire two million dollars to an account that you will open under the name, 'Sanctuary II'. You will temporarily be the only signer. Do I have your word we're good with this decision?"

"*Mi amigo*, you did not threaten me. I'm happy you didn't kill me, and I didn't try to kill you. We have an opportunity to do some great things in Ava De Lombardo's back yard and I'm interested in leading the charge. I will disseminate the funds and you will see how the funds are dispersed from the monthly bank statement. God, bless you, *mi amigo*. There will be no chicanery on my part. I will call you in the morning. Oh, oh, and one more thing, the woman parading as Sister Mary Marisa left a flash drive and a note for me. It read, 'And once again, someone I don't know, is threatening me. Get this information to the 'idiot spy'. *Mi amigo*, I don't know anybody named the 'idiot spy'."

There was a long pause on the phone. The Sarge finally said, "Franco, I want to ask you a question. Do you guys have private jets for rent in Valencia?"

"How I dislike the association of my country with third world countries. Of course, we have private jets for rent."

"Franco, where are you right now and who are you with?"

"I'm at the restaurant making amends, with four of my associates."

"Franco, go to the airport and stay there until you hear from me. I'm going to send a plane for you and your associates or hire one if possible. I know you don't walk around with your passport. Can you send one of your associates to your house to get your passport and have them pick up theirs?"

Franco asked the Sarge to hold on. Two minutes later, he came back on the phone and said, "I sent him. He's on his way."

"Good. I'm going to have my man find you a plane and fly you to the US Virgin Islands. Don't do stupid and bring weapons to the airport. When you get to the airport call the police. Have them guard you because someone is going to try to kill you tonight."

"I thought we were beyond that?"

"Franco, it's not me. Get to the airport and stay close to security."

"I have to pack first."

"Franco, go to the fucking airport, run inside and hide! I will either send a plane for you or hire one from your country to fly you to me. That disk you're holding, well, *Mi Amigo*, is the key to your death. Don't screw this one up buddy, or you'll be made real dead by those Russian thugs."

"Understood. Me and two associates are going to the airport and two others are going for passports." He hung up the phone, walked over to the owners of the restaurant and said, "Once again, this is going to be great for all of us. I must leave for America now to consult with our partners."

Franco whispered something to one of his people, and he hastily ran outside. A minute or so later, the sound of a car engine could be heard, Franco walked out of the restaurant, entered the car, and the two men headed for the airport. Franco cautioned his associate about entering the airport with weapons. He suggested that he wipe them down, break them down, and scatter the pieces.

Franco and his man entered the international terminal. That was not where they should have been. In their haste, they miscalculated. They needed to be in the private terminal for small jets.

His associates returned with their passports, went to the right area, called his employer and asked, "Where are you? We're at the private terminal and you're not here."

Franco responded, "Shit, we're at the international terminal. We are fifteen minutes away. We left my car at the entrance. Hopefully, we can get it and come to you."

The two men looked and acted suspiciously and drew the attention of the airport security. Even so, they politely walked out of the terminal, got into the car, and drove to the parking lot of the private terminal without a problem.

In the meantime, and on another continent, the Sarge summoned Jong and told him he needed a plane to pick up five passengers in Valencia in the next hour. Jong started to say something flippant but saw the look on the Sarge's face. He opened his laptop and immediately got to work. The Sarge requested the bridal party to delay the wedding for thirty minutes because of an emergency.

Twenty minutes later, Jong ran to the Sarge and said, "I found a local Spanish company that flies their high-end clients around the world. Do you want a slow jet or a G5?"

"Jong, I need the passengers here like yesterday. All that we are, is dependent upon this mission. I need you to do this and have them in the air in the next thirty minutes."

Twenty-minutes later, Jong called out to the Sarge and said, "They're good to go. Here are their reservation numbers and the plane that will fly them here."

The Sarge said, "You call them, tell them the airline and where to go."

Jong used the Sarge's phone to call Franco, told him the hangar, the name of the plane, and the captain who would attend to them and ferry them to St. Thomas.

CHAPTER SEVEN

In St. Thomas early in the afternoon, is when most people who are interested in tanning, lay out in the sun, and try to gain a different hue from the Sun God. Mr. Carter constructed a canopy that would shade the attendees to this magnificent event from the powerful rays of the sun. Ava, Rashida, and Carla stood in the resort admiring each other. Ava said, "Rashida, if someone hadn't tried to kill me, your father, and mother, none of this would be happening. I'm not saying I'm glad someone tried to annihilate us, but I'm damn happy they didn't succeed." She reached over and kissed Rashida on both cheeks.

Rashida said, "I used to think you were a little stuffy until that time in Virginia when we both lost our virginity and blew those mercs away. I used to have nightmares about killing them, but then I realized that they were there to kill me, my child, you, and everyone else. I'm happy we're connected, and I absolutely love you. My dad is the luckiest man on earth. He has a masterful son by you and his love for my mom is in the stratosphere. And we all like each other and get along together. Now, as for our pilot here, captain-in-command, our main concern and connection, is perfection in what she does." Rashida stared at Carla and said, "I think Mike and you are going to require us to get another female pilot. You look as ripe as hell."

Carla looked at Rashida and said, "I can still fly a plane while pregnant."

"Carla, I'm only kidding. My dad will never replace you. You'll have to replace yourself by doing some deed that is not looked upon favorably by this group. As I see it, you're here until we all give it up. Anyway, this is our wedding day. Let's have fun and give them a show."

As the local minister looked at the group, he said, "Now, these are some good-looking women. You guys look okay, but I'm more in tune with the brides to be."

Later, after remarks, and describing the adventure of marriage, the preacher was about to make his final statement, when the Sarge's phone rang. It was Franco and his entourage. They were safely aboard a private jet and headed for the US Virgin Islands.

The minister concluded his performance by indicating that the grooms could kiss their brides. Each man with purpose, kissed his new wife.

After the official ceremony, Beckmire signaled to Mallory, Zanthius, Jilkes, Jong, and John Lee to meet him at the bar. When they all assembled, he said, "Zanthius, my Son, it appears that the 'idiot spy' has been resurrected. The woman that we engaged with in Valencia, Sister Mary Marisa, was not the real one. Apparently, Helga is still afloat and on the move. Jong, she, by the way, hustled us out of a million dollars."

"Not so! Jong exclaimed. "In the papers with the baby, that everyone ignored, she left Zanthius and Asiram, eight million dollars in two accounts. Therefore, we only lost one million and gained $7 million. Not bad business if you ask me," Jong confidently announced.

"Oh, I missed that little detail. We're going to have to meet about protocol and the sharing of information once we get settled. By the way, are you thinking about buying land near John Lee?" The Sarge inquired.

"I no think? I buy land there to build Mary Alice a house."

# # #

In another part of the world, Franco and his henchmen were enjoying the amenities of the private plane. Once the plane was airborne, they began to freely imbibe on the stash of vodka that was present. At first, they did two shots each, and then they turned their attention to martinis. The plane was not serviced for food, and therefore, they would only enjoy peanuts, pretzels, and chips for the remainder of the flight. One of Franco's associates asked, "So, boss, what's so important on that little disk you have? It must be really crucial for them to hire a jet and fly us all the way to the islands."

"Piero, you're probably correct. However, I'm not interested or concerned with its value. We are providing a service to our partners who will place two million dollars in a bank account that I will set up under the name, 'Sanctuary II', gentlemen. We're going to go legit and stop hustling nickels and dimes. However, I will tell you what my new partner said about the disk. He told me the disk was my highway to hell. He said the Russians are looking for it."

"Perhaps, you should dialogue with our Russian associates to ascertain the value of it," Piero commented.

"Piero, you don't get it. Those people dropped you guys like flies. We made a deal. Sometimes it's best to get a little and live, than to get a lot and look over your shoulders knowing that someone is coming for you. No more such talk. We work for the Yankees. I think they have been fair. I am going to stretch out and go to sleep. I suggest you guys do the same."

# # #

At 0800 hours, Franco called Ben Beckmire and said, "We should be on the ground in one hour. Will we have the pleasure of you meeting us?"

"You shall. Let me round up a few of my guys. I'll head out to the airport in thirty minutes. I want you to have the captain keep the doors locked until me and my people get there. Perhaps you should ask him to circle a couple of times to make sure I get there before you get off the plane. We don't want any messiness at customs. See what you can arrange. Tell him that his tip will be good."

Sometimes it is better to sit down, face your enemy and expose your hand, as opposed to shooting him on sight. Franco and Beckmire made the choice to coexist. The fruit of that decision was about to pay off for both parties. Franco, a small-time pirate had his fingers in a lot of different hustles in Valencia and Barcelona. He knew that you couldn't get juice from a rock. His transition into the resort and the restaurant business was a function of a relationship with a devious banker. He had no money to invest in the two properties, but the banker had developed a scheme to use him and his name to create problems for the two owners.

# # #

The Sarge roused Jilkes, and John Lee, Bernstein, and Brown. He told them that he needed them dressed and prepared to leave the compound in twenty minutes. As if they were still enlisted men, each jumped up, bird washed and dressed in a hurry.

Yvette asked Bernstein, "What the heck is going on?"

"The Sarge called. He said he needed me to accompany him to the airport."

"Do you want me to come with you?"

"Damn, that's precious." He slowed his movements, sat on the side of the bed and said, "You remember when we met? Of course, you do. I saw you from the car window and my heart began to pound. I had no right interfering in that event, no more than the man on the moon, but I was directed to your assistance and I'm so damn happy I did what I did. I love you more than life. Look at us, we're about to become parents. Oh, you know what, we should decide on where we want to live. A lot of people are moving near John Lee. You might want to have a conversation with Yeshida or Somara and see if it might be a place where we can raise our family. I hate to go, but duty calls baby. Love you."

# # #

The Sarge looked around and said, "This looks a little thin to me. Is anyone else up?"

"Juan, Carlos, Rashida, and Ava are having breakfast," Jilkes stated.

"I need those two guys. Jilkes, ask Mr. Carter if he could give us a ride to the airport along with another vehicle for our guests?"

The Sarge approached the group, and instinctively, the two men began to look defensive. Before the Sarge could open his mouth, Juan said, "What's up Sarge? You need my help in any way?"

The Sarge said, "As a matter of fact, I need you and Carlos. I must pick some people up at the airport and I don't want to be compromised in the process. Ladies, if you have other more pressing tasks outlined for your men, I can make a few other calls."

Ava said, "Turn around. Unless you recruited some new people, all of your people are accounted for."

The Sarge jerked his head around and saw Mike, ten previously enlisted men, his sons Larry and Zanthius, standing ready to leave the compound. He looked at Mallory and said, "Damn, I'm happy we had that drink on that mountain that night. Divide our forces and put everyone on alert including the resort staff. You know Franco and his group are landing in a few minutes. I don't know who the hell they're bringing with them."

Mallory said, "I thought you trusted him?"

"My brothers are in front of me. These are the people I trust. Everyone else has to burn the candle with me before I go blindly into the night."

"Now that there be some new kind of poetry shit. I like that Sarge," John Lee bellowed.

# # #

Ten minutes later and on their way to the airport, the Sarge looked at Mr. Carter and said, "You look weary. Is there a problem?"

"Nothing I care to bother you with, Mr. Beckmire."

"Come now, we're beyond secrets. What's going on?"

"We need more personnel, and I don't know how to justify it?"

"Mr. Carter, when we get back, if possible, let's you, me, Jong, and Monica sit down together to discuss your needs."

"Sarge, I want to add more security. I saw one of our guests making a deal with a local dealer."

"As I said, when we get back, you give me his name, whereabouts and we will go and tell him if he shows up near, or on any of our properties in the cul-de-sac, we will kill him, his dog, his wife and everyone who has the same last name. You make a call to any dealer that you know. Spread that word and by God, if anyone wants to challenge The Sanctuary, then they just made a reservation to see hell."

"Who are you people? You don't do drugs and I can't think of any other hustles that would afford you people the kind of lifestyle you live?"

"Mr. Carter, we are on a quest for broader justice. We don't like to see people get hurt and big institutions benefit," Beckmire stated.

"Are you expecting trouble at the airport?" Mr. Carter inquired.

"Not sure. We're meeting someone who we thought we were going to kill, but instead he turned out to be instrumental in us finding my son's baby. However, he is a person who looks for opportunities amid current relationships. In other words, I don't know him that well. They're traveling on a private jet, so we need to wait outside of customs. By the way, how is your son and his mother working out for you?"

"It has finally hit my son that he involved his sisters and mother in a crime against a human being. He feels guilty and can't sleep because he keeps seeing the man's eyes at night. He works ten hours and tries to sleep for a few hours before he does security work. Anyway, he's working out extremely well and is studying management at the university on the masters level. He says he wants to get another degree in hospitality. I ask him for what and he told me that I should study with him to learn the modern ways of doing business with humans."

"You know he's right. It is never too late to learn, and learning should be a life-long process. When we return to the resort, tell him I'd like to speak to him when he has a moment."

# # #

At the airport, members of the team got out of the vehicles at varying points and hustled their way into position, both defensively and offensively. The Sarge said to Mr. Carter, "If there is a problem, I need you to step up and rescue my people from any danger if you can intercede. Are you capable of doing that?"

"Your people are my bloodline—I got your back. Tell me where to be and when to leave."

#

The Sarge called Franco and said, "I'm waiting for you outside of customs. What's taking you so long, my friend?"

"I would have called you, but they don't allow the use of phones back here and they are so intense. They want to know where we're staying, and I didn't have an answer, so they held us all up."

"Tell them you're Mr. Carter's guests at The Sanctuary. Tell them Mr. Carter is here waiting for you."

Franco relayed the information and the custom's worker said, "Why the hell didn't you just say that? Guys, stamp their passes, they're guests of Mr. Carter."

Franco waltzed through the doors with his coat draped around his shoulders and said, "*Mi amigo. Como estas?*" He walked up to Beckmire, kissed him on both cheeks, and said, "Damn, I thought they wanted to examine my poop. How are you, *mi amigo*? I must admit, we're hungry. Do you have some place close we can eat?"

The Sarge looked at the group and asked, "What do you want to eat?"

Peiro said, "Food. Nothing fancy, simple good food."

"Do you want breakfast or dinner?"

"We want to eat dinner food, Mr. Beckmire because it is our dinner time." Beckmire summoned Mr. Carter and asked if his people could prepare a buffet of dinner foods for some really hungry Spaniards?"

On the ride to the resort, Beckmire asked Franco, "I want to ask you a few questions, my friend and I hope you indulge me with the truth. Franco, I know human nature. I know greed and I know betrayal. Did you wonder what is on that disk you're carrying?"

"But of course! I mean out of the blue, you call me, send a plane for me and mine, after you find out that I have a certain disk. Pretty powerful stuff if you ask me. Why are you asking me these almost insulting questions since I'm here and here is your disk?"

"Did you think that this disk is so important that you might want to check with another group to ascertain a negotiating position?"

"*Mi amigo*, we did that and been there, as you say."

"No, we say, been there and done that."

"Oh, I see. Why are you still challenging my loyalty?"

"Please, indulge me. Did anyone one in your group ask you to consider options relative to the disk?"

Franco paused for a moment and responded, "Ah, well, yes. I did have that kind of discussion with Piero, and I told him that you told me this thing was my gateway to hell."

"He's your weak link. Unbeknownst to you or him, a friend of ours approached Piero, asked him to keep him informed about our mission, and relationships. They paid him $25,000 in cash and promised him up to $2 million more if he would provide them with strategic information about the Carbon Factor formula. He's on the phone now with our contact. Look over my right shoulder."

Franco looked at Beckmire and sighed, "My friend, I suppose you're going to kill us all, and rightfully so."

"Franco, I nor none of my associates are going to do such a thing. As we see it, it's your problem, and we leave the associated punishment up to you. We set each of your people up in the same fashion and sorry to say, Piero was the only one to bite."

"Thank you, for being compassionate," Franco replied.

"Now, we can take care of this business for you as a courtesy. However, you must sanction it. You ever see the movie the *Godfather*?"

"Of course, all aspiring rogues watched that movie," Franco commented.

"You remember the part when Michael had his brother taken on a fishing trip?" Beckmire asked.

"I so clearly remember that part," Franco acknowledged. Franco continued, "Can you arrange such a trip, and the tool necessary to complete the job? That is the only recourse I see, but first, I want to complete my task for coming here. This is the disk that I swear to you was never opened or touched by any human hands, other than mine. It too is clean. I just can't believe that one of mine would fall for such a set-up. I will speak to him first, then present the information and ask him for the truth. I'm not into terminating another person's life. However, if the facts warrant it, then I will complete the task. I'm not sure about the time difference, but I'm extremely sleepy. On another matter of concern, how does the missing one million dollars affect our plan?"

Beckmire replied, "It doesn't, Franco. We do business with a bank here on the island and we can set up a staging point from here. I will have Monica and Jong, plus a few security members escort you to the bank, open an account, and have them develop a relationship with the bank in Valencia. Jong will make the transfers to Valencia and you can extract funds, subject to approval in Spain by the real Sister Mary Marisa. So, before you catch that plane back, minus a key player on your team, Jong and the others will go to the bank and make this happen. Have you found a suitable architect?"

"I have the prime candidate. Mario has been called retardo, as well as moron. I think his designs are way ahead of our times and I would like to at least give him a week to sketch his rendition of both places. Believe it or not, I will have both places shut down by this coming Friday and provide the staff with the kinds of things I expect to happen in the interim. For example, I plan to keep them on the payroll and have them conduct a house sale of sorts. I would like to conduct a flea market and sell everything in both places, take the proceeds and begin to figure out how long that will pay the staff until they are added on the reconstruction payroll."

"Franco, just remember, you have little to say in the design of the resort and the restaurant. You are the facilitator. You make shit happen. Please remember the current owners have final input and approval."

"*Mi amigo*, I see what you mean. I will present the plans to them first, but I will attempt to sway them by providing them pictures of modern restaurants and resorts as well as the amenities. I will just provide them with information. I have no hand in the decision. My hands are to make sure their wishes are my command."

"Now, you're talking. Attempt to sway them, but remember, they don't really like you and are suspicious of you. Perhaps, you could have your meetings at the monastery and have the real Sister Mary Marisa oversee and pray for the designs. I'm just trying to get you back into their good graces. After all, it was your man who set fire to their home and killed a loved one. Damn, here's an idea. Why don't you figure out a way to help them cover the expenses of rebuilding their home? I can help you, but it will cost you a few thousand per pay period."

"That's an excellent idea, one that I don't have to think about. Please, *mi amigo*, take the funds and I will offer them a goodwill payment of a couple of thousand dollars per month, realizing that the real costs and human costs far exceed my little goodwill payments."

Ben said, "So, you like the idea, and you're willing to give up a part of your salary to help those people rebuild?"

"How many times would you like me to say this thing? I said it and I mean it," Franco affirmatively stated.

"If that's the case, then I will increase your salary so that you can continue to do the right thing and make us all feel good about our relationship."

"*Mi amigo*, I could say something dumb like you don't have to do that. However, I accept your generosity and will thank you in my prayers. I will say this, I don't want you to subsidize my problems. I need to do this by way of good spirits, with earned and not hustled money."

"Wow, you continue to surprise me. Get some rest and I'll see you at dinner time. Try not to take care of that other situation until you are absolutely, certain. Keep smiling and acting normal." The Sarge handed Franco a case and he knew what was in it.

As the Sarge was walking towards the dining room, he saw Mike throwing stones into the water. He walked down to him and said, "You're up early on your first legitimate day as a new husband. What's up with that?"

"Sarge, we talked the entire night, and we never consummated our marriage. She started her woman's thing, and apparently, it's both painful and messy."

"Do you think I should have my wife look in on her?"

"Sarge, I don't know anything about this situation. I feel useless as she continues to cry from pain and the emotional trauma of not being able to love her husband on their wedding night."

"I'm going to have Courtney look and see if there is some over-the-counter stuff she can recommend. Dude, you got to take the good with the bad."

"Oh, I know that. She's asleep now. I told her I was going to go for a run on the beach. My melancholy mood is because she seemingly is in a lot of pain and I don't have the slightest clue as to what to do."

"Listen, a few more of these, and you'll know when it's coming and how far to run away. Just kidding. I'll have Courtney look in on her."

As the Sarge started to walk away, Mike received a text. He asked the Sarge to take a moment and read it. It stated that the alternative property on K street had only two visitors in four days with two other guys showing up who seem to work there on 12-hour shifts. The same two guys who came with cases, leave with heavier ones. The final text read, "I think the stash house is ripe."

"Good news. Once we finish with our Spanish friends, we'll talk to Jong about when we can leave the compound. Go and check on that wife of yours. I'll send Courtney in a few."

Further down the beach, the Sarge could see a group of over-dressed people sitting on the beach in a circle. He decided to walk towards them. Mike saw the group as well and said, "Do you want me to get some assistance?"

"Naw, I think I can handle this one. As the two men got closer, he saw that it was Franco and his group, with Piero sitting in the middle. The Sarge said to Mike, "Let them handle their business. I just wasn't sure who it was. Let them do their thing." He walked back to the resort and saw Mr. Carter yelling at his son. The Sarge stood a respectful distance away. When he was acknowledged, he walked slowly and methodically up to the two men. In an exceptionally soft tone, he asked, "Mr. Carter, do we have a problem?"

Mr. Carter announced, "I'm not sure this guy is going to work out. For the last two days, he has been respectively, five and seven minutes late for work."

Ben Beckmire smiled and said, "The way you were yelling at him, I thought he stole the entire bank or something. Did you ask him why he was late?"

"These young people have nothing but excuses."

"Give it a try. Ask him why he was late?"

"Why were you late for work two days in a row?"

"My mom, your ex-wife, is sick. I've been attending to her all night."

"Who's been cooking the food?"

"Dad, I've been cooking, serving, cleaning, checking supplies and making sure everything is in order."

"You've been doing all of her work as well as yours?"

"Yes, because she didn't want you to think you made a mistake by hiring us. We like being here and we like working for you even though you don't communicate well or often. So, we work, and she no have to see you or hear you scream."

"How sick is she?"

"Your daughter is there with her now. I told my sister that I couldn't takeoff. I needed her to help me out."

"Wow, you people are doing that to cover for your mother? That's admirable. I need you to handle the resort,

I'm going to visit your mother and see if there is anything I can do."

"I think she needs a doctor, but we're still trying to get our act together."

Beckmire interrupted and asked, "What does that mean. Don't you have insurance for all of our workers?"

"Mr. Beckmire, these things are all new to me. I have been checking on it, but it seems so expensive."

"Okay, your daughter is a CPA, right? Have her drive to the resort so that I can talk to her and your son about some of the other things we need here such as health insurance, risk insurance, and all kinds of stuff to protect us from simple lawsuits. And you, young man, I might have another mission for you subject to the approval of your father," Beckmire stated.

Beckmire pulled Mr. Carter aside and said, "I may have a situation like the one that I bailed your family out of. It seems that our Spanish friends have a traitor in their midst, and they want him to be fish bait. Do you have a problem if I put your son in charge of that duty, since he's proficient at it?"

Mr. Carter smiled and said, "He be a grown man. He's happy here and I'm happy that he's here. He has made so many improvements that I can't name them all. This wi-fi stuff, whatever that is, is available anywhere on the beach. He's incredibly good for this place. His other dealings with you is not my business and, therefore, what I don't know, protects the ones involved."

"Okay, go check on your family and see if your daughter can come and have a meeting with me ASAP. We need to have insurance for our people, also in case a guest falls from being drunk and tries to sue us."

He walked over to Mr. Carter's son and said, "I might have a situation that requires a few of your special skills. My Spanish friends have a significant problem in their ranks. Would you be willing to take a rancid fish out for a final ride and deep six it?"

"I will not do such a thing. However, I will take a large rotten fish that is wrapped and weighed down, so that the other fish can feed." He threw out his hand and received the massive hand and the strength of Beckmire. Beckmire said, "I'm not sure they're going to resolve it here, but in case they do, please handle that rotten fish under the gaze of the moon. I will be indebted to you for all time."

"No, Sir! It is me and my family who are indebted to you. What you have accomplished in this cul-de-sac is beyond words. They all were going to forfeit their places. You came along rebuilt, rekindled their spirits, and gave them hope. No, Man, I owe you."

# # #

The Sarge felt that he and his people were probably not going to heaven but stood first in line to help people. He walked into the resort's restaurant and yelled, "Good morning, my friends and family." He walked over to where Courtney was having oatmeal and kissed her seductively. She said, "What on earth have you been smoking?"

"I've been smoking life. Oh, and by the way, I need you to check on Carla. Mike said she's in pain—emotionally and physically because she is having her woman thing and because she couldn't make love to her husband on their wedding night."

"Oh, my. Now, that would make me cranky as well. What room are they in? I'll go up now and see what's going on. And from now on Mr. Benjamin Beckmire, when you see me in a restaurant, you had better bring your handsome ass over and kiss me like that. This is the new standard for kissing me, dude."

The Sarge reached into his pocket and said, "Oh My God! I completely forgot about the damn disk that Franco gave me. He looked around the room and saw Jong and said, "I need to see you, Mallory, Jilkes, John Lee, Gladstone, and Zanthius. I need to see you people, now."

As the members of the team assembled, he said, "I've been so distracted this morning, I forgot what got us here— The Carbon Factor formula. Franco delivered to me this disk from the fake Sister Mary Marisa, who, by the way, I think is Helga. Mr. Amazing, open that damn computer that you never put down and see what's on this damn disk."

Jong engaged his unit and inserted the flash drive into it. Once the drive was recognized, it opened in a format that was not recognized by Jong. It gave him two options to open it but stated that successive failures would result in the erasing of the information on it. Jong said, "I do not know what this means. This is not standard."

Zanthius, looking over Jong's shoulder, instructed, "Type 234 and enter." Jong hesitantly typed 234, hit enter, and bingo! It appeared that the disk contained information that was related to the Carbon Factor formula.

No one could ascertain or deduce the meaning of the formulas. Zanthius said, "I don't know chemistry, but there are several references to carbon in this stuff."

The Sarge said, "I hope this gets us out and away from some extremely dangerous people. The question that remains is, who do we give it to? We all know the senator is a fraud and was connected to Allen and Walter. No way in hell can we give it to the reigning lunatic because he might send a copy to his Russian lover. However, people are still under the impression we control the damn information. We need to make sure and explicitly state, we turned the information over to the senator, even if it's a lie. She lives and works by alternative facts. I know she can weave a story denying the very existence of the Carbon Factor." He looked at Zanthius and asked, "Son, can you, secure access to the farm in Virginia?"

"Dad, we're family. All that is ours, is yours to command."

"Jong, when can you have the group prepared to leave paradise?"

"Give me three hours, and I can make sure we have circled the wagons."

"Circled the wagons. What the hell are you talking about?" the Sarge asked.

"I don't know. I just heard that from a movie. I thought it was special. I guess not."

"I have several things to deal with. I need to make sure we have some cash around to tip the pilots, and make sure that Franco and his group are covered. Also, there is the potential disposal of a dead fish. Did you pay for the plane roundtrip?" the Sarge inquired.

"No, Mr. Sarge. I wanted them to get stuck here on the islands—duh! Of course, I did."

"You're one smart man, Mr. Amazing, and I want to say publicly, I wouldn't be able to do this work without you."

"There is no public here. Why you blow smoke up my ass?"

"Because I love you. By the way, our captain is incapacitated. Who is going to fly us out of here?"

"We have three more pilots capable of flying our aircraft. That is not a problem."

The Sarge said, "Let me know the timetable. It's probably better that we plan to leave tomorrow. I have a funny suspicion our business in Spain is going to keep us here until tomorrow. By the way, what's your opinion of Franco?"

"I like him because he's trying to do the right thing and he favors us. He's trustworthy and will be a good manager for those properties in Spain. Although, I don't like bringing in new people. Never know who to trust. Is there a question about one of Franco's men?"

"You're clairvoyant. Yes, there is, and I guess I must make sure he's attended to properly before we leave the island. Just another thing that I must address. I can't save this guy because he believed he was in communication with the Russians. He tried to seduce his employer to opening a dialogue with them. It's not our affair and I have no say in the outcome, but I must admit, I didn't like his ass from the start. In the restaurant, I just saw an individual who was attempting to figure out how to get rid of his employer and take over his legacy. Greed kills!

# # #

Courtney saw Carla and gave her the name of an over-the-counter medication. She also examined Carla, through a series of touches and probing. Courtney deduced that she had a few female issues that needed addressing. She suggested to Carla to see a specialist when they returned to the mainland and expect to be laid up for a few days. Courtney also suggested that Carla should have any procedures done in Virginia, near the farm. Carla asked, "If I take this medicine, will it preclude me from handling my responsibilities as the captain?"

"Young lady, isn't there a jump seat in the cockpit? I suggest you operate from there and assign full flight responsibilities to one of the other three pilots that we have on board. We're probably going to leave tomorrow, but until then, I don't expect you to do any dancing or trying to honor your wedding vows. Mike understands and is patient. I want you to see a specialist before there is any further probing in that canal."

"I must admit, my previous lover was too big for comfort."

"I can tell, honey, and that's why I want you to see a specialist. I'm surprised you haven't had to go to the emergency room. My initial prognosis is that your uterus may be misaligned. That's the reason for all the pain you're feeling. Now, that's my opinion without invasively checking you. Get some rest, call me if you need me."

"Please keep this between the two of us. I'm so ashamed," Carla emphatically stated.

"Why? That was another time and another person. Hopefully, you upgraded with this new one. By the way, I like him a lot. He's dedicated and concerned."

As Courtney exited the room, the ever-attentive Mike asked, "Is she going to be alright?"

"Oh, yeah! I want her to see a specialist when we get back to the states. I just think she has some minor female issues that she has neglected to attend to. Don't worry. Just be supportive and understanding. The female body is a complicated device, given the fact we can produce life. Can you, Mike?" He smiled.

"Ah, didn't think so. Let her rest and don't worry her with nonsense. Don't keep asking her if she's alright. Women hate that. Catch you later."

Courtney thought she had covered her tracks well. She felt there was no need to address the pounding that Carla's special place had been subjected to. She thought to herself, "Love and passion will make you do things that hurt in more ways than one".

#

As the day prepared to roll into night, the sound of a small caliber weapon being fired could be heard. Much later, Mr. Carter's son, Michael, placed the lifeless body into a bag that would eventually dissolve over time and allow small, medium, and large sea animals to feast upon the remains. The body was carefully loaded in the dingy and off into the night, Piero was heading on his final voyage.

Franco said to Michael, "I don't know you, but I trust you because the people here trust you. I left Spain in a hurry. I will borrow from my friend and leave you a package for assisting me in getting rid of a traitor. Thank you very much."

As Franco and his crew entered the lounge, Ben Beckmire, Jilkes, and John Lee stood at the bar with shots of Cruzan rum in front of them. Zanthius walked in and said, "Pops, I heard the sound of gunfire." Zanthius looked at Franco, his crew coming in and realized that someone had become fish food. He said, "Pops never mind, I guess I'm hearing things. Catch you later."

"How are the babies doing?"

"Pops, these women won't let me hold my own children."

"Son, it's now or never. Don't let them start this or it will never end. Give them visiting hours and be done with it."

As Franco and his crew walked in, they had solemn looks on their faces. He said to Beckmire, "Piero confessed to several crimes and plots including kidnapping the baby, capturing the 'idiot spy', blackmailing you for the disk and the complete files, for $50 million."

"Your man was going to put all of that in play? And what were you going to be doing while this was all happening?" the Sarge asked.

"Oh, sadly, he was going to kill me and offer these guys a deal that they couldn't refuse."

John Lee said, "Well, hell. That there guy was a problem and had no sense of loyalty like we be having. None of us would think of killing the Sarge. Ain't that right, my African American friend?" He winked at Jilkes and began to laugh.

The Sarge said, "I asked Mr. Carter's son, Michael, to assist you. I hope that wasn't a problem for you."

"No, no. I figured he was trusted by you, or you would never have asked him to assist in such a dastardly deed. Which brings me to another point. We left in such a hurry, all we have is a few euros between us. Is there any way you can front us some funds?"

"Absolutely! Beckmire exclaimed. By the way, I thought we would be around for a few days. Unfortunately, we're leaving as soon as possible. I need you to stay here until Monday morning because you need to sign papers at the bank. I will arrange for Mr. Carter or Michael to escort you. On another topic, you guys have acted like real partners on this trip. Therefore, we're going to give you a special gift. For your time and trouble, as well as discovering a traitor, I want to give you $40k Franco, and each of your men, $20k."

"What do you mean by that?"

"Jong is going to give you debit cards that will be worth that amount of dollars for your troubles. I'm also going to give you $10k for Mr. Carter's son, Jong will take care of the pilots. Give them a head's up on when you plan on leaving, so that they can file their flight plan."

Jilkes pardoned himself and said, "I need to have a private word with you guys—I have an idea."

The team walked away from Franco, his people, and huddled in a corner. Jilkes said, "How funky would it be to have these guys pull off that job on K Street. That would surely draw your cousin out because he won't have a clue as to who these people are."

John Lee said, "Now, I be liking that. My African American associate is brilliant. That action would give us a few days to get accustomed to killing people again. We do the back-up. If there is anything to haul, they carry the load."

The Sarge looked at Franco and his group, then at his guys, and said, "I think they're a bunch of novices. I would hate to be the cause of their deaths."

"Let's ask them about their experiences," Jilkes stated.

The group walked back to the bar and the Sarge said, "You know sometimes people exaggerate how bad they are and what they've done. Are you guys like that?"

Franco looked for the hidden meaning to that question and stated, "I don't understand what you're implying. We never said we were bad, nor have we bragged about what we have done. Your question is perplexing, *mi amigo*."

John Lee said, "We be needing someone to rob a bad guy. We want to know if you people can do that without killing a lot of people, getting killed, or getting caught."

Franco said, "You speak plain sometimes, but other times I have problems translating what you're saying."

Jilkes jumped in and added, "Do you people want to earn some real money? I mean a percentage of what we take from Ben Beckmire's cousin, Walter, who has been trying to kill us, and we him, for years?"

"What do you call real money, Mr. Jilkes?"

"Let's say, and Sarge, can I address this hypothetically?"

"Absolutely—this is your play."

"His cousin, our enemy has stolen money from the government, blackmailed people and keeps millions of dollars in what we call his stash houses. Let's say, hypothetically, in a house, he might have 20 cases of money or approximately, $50 million. Now, his problem is those who know of the houses would never betray him because he would kill all people with like names and kill them last. He is ruthless, cunning, a thief, politician, and has the current president in his pocket. If you guys did the job, he would be looking for ghosts because you would be on that plane heading back to Spain with a shit load of champagne after the heist. We don't know how much is in the place, but do you think you have the balls to try this one?"

Franco looked at his people who were not accustomed to hearing the kinds of possibilities that were being thrown out before replying, "*Mi amigo*, we are professionals. Give us the relevant intel on the situation and we will do our analysis and schedule an appointment."

The Sarge looked at Jilkes and said, "Give Mike a call. I'm sure he's going to want to be in on this one." The Sarge looked at Franco and said, "This is not your ordinary strong-arm-tactic, situation. There are a few guards that we do not want to hurt, do you understand? No trigger-happy responses. Just an-in-and-an-out function, with lots of cash. We'll perform back up and security for you."

"Why pay the extra premium? Why not do it yourself?"

"Oh, we've hit him hard before. We need to watch who comes and goes. He's the cause of over 300 souls wandering around hell looking for me and my guys. To recognize our impact, you must add that number to the thousands from Vietnam, Boston, Australia, Europe and on and on, who are also searching for us. In other word's Franco, we're a killing machine, but we can't catch my devious ass cousin. Each of my men from Nam, has killed close to 300 people each. If we use you for bait, he'll come out, want to know who this new group is, how they knew about where he lives, and his stash house."

"*Mi amigo*, I have, or we have, embarked on a new level of trust and relationship building. We never talk about the kinds of numbers that you people take for granted. So, my friend, what would, in your estimation, be our take if, in fact, we walked into a place, came out, with, say $50 million? What would our recompence for such an endeavor be?"

"I would probably offer you anywhere between 5 to 10 percent. If 10 percent, it would be $1.25 million per man. That's a lot of money."

Franco said, "*Mi amigo*, we would like to help you because we want to work with you in the future. We will do this thing to assist you. It is not about the money. Is that clear, *mi amigo*?" Franco looked at the Sarge and said, "Now, please do not believe that bullshit. This is all about the money."

The Sarge said, "You're a funny man." He turned to Jong and said, "I need the jet that they came in on to take them to Miami. They will land for fuel, then they will board our plane to Maryland, and begin to strategically plan to gut my cousin's places on K Street."

Franco asked, "Why not fly our plane all the way to Virginia?"

"My cousin is connected in high and low places. He will track your plane, know how to find you, and mercilessly execute you. Before you start counting money that may not be there, you should remember my cousin will kill your unborn children. He placed suicide vests on my grandchildren. He is ruthless and will kill all that matters to you to get to me. Please, consider the downside to this equation."

Franco replied, "We considered it, we have faith in our new alliance, and partnership. We will flawlessly plan and execute this job without the loss of life. Mario, here, is excellent at producing disguises. We will create another layer of confusion and speak in Arabic, perhaps? Not sure of that one, but we will plan it and let you know."

The Sarge looked at Jilkes and said, "This is your play. What are your thoughts?"

Jilkes looked at John Lee who urged him on. Jilkes stated, "My main concern is for everyone's safety and, as such, I need you to prepare a plan based upon the sketchy information that Mike, who just showed up, is going to give you. Sarge, you're correct, we do have a plane in Miami. Their plane flies into Miami, they board our plane, and fly to Maryland. This gives us some distance, and we will begin to figure out how to access his place from the front and the rear. By the way, we have three planes. Are we going to keep them all?"

"I don't want to deal with that now. It does not hurt us to own them and, plus, we employ people to fly them and keep them functional. It's a good thing. Right?" the Sarge inquired.

"I think everything we do is good and you're the brains behind it," Jilkes stated.

"Okay, Franco, you should stay until Monday so that you can sign some papers for the work in Spain. You will do that early, then fly to Miami where you will go through customs, and we will have one of our pilots meet you," the Sarge announced.

Jilkes looked at John Lee and said, "Get the names of the pilots in Miami. Have Jong contact them and tell them about their new pick-up," Jilkes stated.

Jilkes looked at Franco and said, "Once you're in Miami, let our pilots guide you through the process. Don't second guess them, do as they say, and all will be okay. Remember, don't even think of bringing weapons or any contraband aboard our plane. Whatever you need will be provided for you. Also, Mike, I'm going to need you to stay here until Monday. Is that going to be a problem?"

"I don't think so. It depends on how Carla is feeling and whether I feel comfortable being away from her when she's sick."

"Why don't you check with her and get back to me. My goal is to breach K Street by Wednesday and have these guys on a plane back to Miami and then on a continuing flight to Spain, all in the same day. Let me know if you can do it and want to be a part of this. How about this, can your people on the ground send pictures? If so, you can go over the general topography from here. Now, that's a better solution. I mean we're not trying to get the details of the property; we're just trying to get an idea of traffic flow, the closest law enforcement establishment, cameras, and general things that burglars consider."

Mike said, "Let me send a text and see what I can come up with. I'm sure I can get some pictures of the front, the rear, as well as the street, and escape routes."

"Sarge, we might need Jong's people to lend assistance on vehicles and drivers on this one," Jilkes acknowledged.

"Mr. Amazing can your family members accommodate us and wash the money as well?" the Sarge asked.

John Lee asked, "Do you guys have any questions of our alternate leader? If not, let's have a drink and be done with this here meeting. My wife is on my butt about something called, 'a lack of attention' since she done got pregnant."

CHAPTER EIGHT

Carla sat in the cockpit and essentially allowed the pilots to earn hours on the equipment under the supervision of a certified captain. In the cockpit and as the plane taxied towards the runway, the acting captain asked Carla, "Do you have any questions or suggestions for us?"

Carla replied, "Yes, I do. Point this thing down the runway and blast into the sky without hitting that little mountain in front of you."

A few minutes later, the captain-in-command, while engaging the breaks and moving the throttles forward, received the response he was anticipating, disengaged the breaks, and the plane headed down the runway. As the plane rose into the sky, everyone breathed a sigh of relief.

#

That evening at The Sanctuary, a group of fashion models checked in for a scheduled filming session. Franco and his guys were being transported from town where they purchased leisure clothes that were appropriate for the tropics. When they entered the lounge of the resort, they saw magnificent young female specimens. He suggested they shower, shave, and meet in an hour in the bar for cocktails. He looked at a redhead who acted like the den-mother, and said, "That one is going to marry me. I love that woman."

Mario said, "Boss, you say that about all women."

"See you guys in the bar in an hour. We should figure out what we have to do for this caper before we begin mesmerizing, lovely young ladies."

Meanwhile, at 30,000 feet in the air, Carla came out of the cockpit, sweating and dizzy. Mike was asleep until he heard a thump. It was Carla who fell to her knees because of excruciating pain. Courtney instructed Rashida to get a portable oxygen tank and a plastic cover.

When Rashida returned, Courtney immediately placed the cup around Carla's mouth and slowly increased the flow of oxygen. She gently rolled Carla onto the plastic sheet. No one quite understood the purpose of it, but it made moving Carla easy. Courtney single-handedly pulled Carla to the back of the plane. She asked Rashida to get her lots of ice. They placed bags of ice on strategic places of Carla's body to decrease the apparent fever. Mike, not having a clue asked, "What can I do?"

"At this point in time, I need you to give us space and stop blocking the flow of air. I'll call you if I need anything."

Rashida said, "Mom, I know these symptoms. Am I correct?"

"Honey, you should have gone to medical school. You're guessing, but you're close. I'll give you that. I guess having been there and done that, you can recognize it anywhere. What's more important is that she's a recent bride. Don't let this conversation go any further than you and me. Okay, Baby?"

"You know, I ain't got a lot to say."

"Okay, I need you to get my bag, we need to get her hydrated. She's lost a lot of fluids and I'm going to need you to close those curtains and massage vigorously the places that I point to."

An hour later, Carla was stabilized and receiving fluids from an IV. Courtney walked into the cabin and said, "Our newlywed is having an anxiety attack. She is dehydrated, and we're taking care of that. I don't see a need for us to make an emergency medical landing. I will stay with her and I suggest that if you need to use the head, use the forward ones, thanks."

Mike walked to the back of the cabin and asked, "What's going on with my wife?"

Courtney looked at him and decided to give him a complicated scenario that would be the truth for her, but uninterpretable by him. She dove into her medical dictionary and provided Mike with a series of potential issues that Carla may be facing. She continued to ask him about any seafood he had seen her consume and expressed that some bodies can't handle certain types of seafood that lodge in their digestive tracks and creates havoc. At the conclusion of the presentation of bullshit, Courtney said, "I will go with your wife to the hospital and have them conduct an allergy test as well as check her digestive system for blockage." Mike looked at her and said, "If I didn't know any better, I would think you are simply saying that you don't know what's wrong with my wife."

Courtney looked at him and said, "You're too damn smart, Mike. I'm only giving you estimates of time travel. I have no idea how you manage her issue without an invasive examination." He looked at Courtney and then kissed his wife on the forehead.

# # #

Jilkes walked over to the Sarge and said, "You, know, I don't think we've ever landed at this airport. I think we need to head to Maryland. I like our cover and the fact that the NSA types monitor flights that come in here from out of the country."

"Are you trying to take my job?"

"I didn't know there was the possibility of such a thing happening. Let me get back to you on that one. Anyhow, I don't like our exposure at this airport. Feds are always around."

"You're right." The Sarge turned around and beckoned for Jong to come over. He said, "Have our pilots divert this thing to the Maryland airport. This place seems to be the hub of eyes watching who comes and goes. Once we're on the ground, I will ask Courtney if we should take Carla to a hospital in Maryland."

# # #

In addition to diverting their plane to Maryland, Jong made a call to his cousin and told him he would need a large vehicle for a lot of people. His cousin asked him if he thought he was a school bus driver or something. Jong told him to make it happen and to pick them up at their favorite place.

Approximately one and a half hours later, 6 ten-person vans were parked outside of the airport. After a brief discussion with the local customs officials, the group disembarked from their plane.

Shortly thereafter, the group boarded the vans and were on their way to the farmhouse in Virginia. Jilkes indicated to the Sarge that he wanted to ride in the van with John Lee, Chakes, Montomie, Gladstone, Larry, and McArthur and that he wanted the rest of the caravan to head into DC and hang out at the McDonalds on New York Avenue and Florida Avenue. He and his group were going to ride past the K Street area and check out the location.

As the group entered the DC boundaries, the main caravan continued on New York Avenue and Jilkes and his crew made their way towards the target area. Jilkes said to Larry, "You and I are going to walk past the houses between 9th & 10th on K Street. John Lee and Chakes will take the North side of the street, Larry and I will take the South side. Montomie, you, Gladstone and McArthur will take active video of the street with your cameras. Nothing fancy, but a lay out of the houses. At this point, I do not know which one is the stash house. Mike will have that information for us later tonight. Do nothing suspicious, but keep a mental picture of what you see, but don't stare at any particular property. As soon as you get in the van, write down your recollection of houses, colors, and what distinguishes one from the other."

# # #

Some things are truly remarkable. When a horse loves you, and you love it, the animal will confirm the fact. Asiram barely exited the van when the horses started racing towards her and prancing around. She had Ben in her arms, and turned to Courtney and asked, "Will you hold Ben a moment? I would like to say hello to my horses. Ava, are you okay for a few minutes with Zanthius Jr?" She gave her baby to Courtney and proceeded towards the alpha, Rajz. He backed up and snorted, backed up again and snorted, finally dropped his head and eased up ever so gently next to Asiram. Within moments, all the horses surrounded her. Zanthius bellowed out, "I don't like this. I need to go and get my wife."

Ava calmly said, "You will spook them, and you might cause them to inadvertently harm your Asiram. Let this one be. She's fine, and they all know and love her. Look at them and she's not even offering them treats. They are bonding."

# # #

Asiram's caretaker, Jude, drove up in his mule and welcomed her home. He told her that the food in the freezer and refrigerator had been rotated two days ago, and that everything was fresh. She thanked him and asked about the general health of the horses and the farm. He indicated that Grey, was having some dental issues, but other than that, everything was okay. She asked about the security system and he told her that he uses the simple format daily which limits his access and ability to go into certain areas of the house. He told her the observation system was functional and that it captured rabbits, snakes, and rodents. He told her he liked the fact it could classify or discern a human from animals.

This was the first time the group had been back to the farm since its full restoration and modification. Asiram asked Courtney and Ava if they could handle the boys for a moment while she checked on a few security issues.

Asiram smacked her husband on the butt and told him to get his father, Jong, Larry, John Lee, and Jilkes and meet her in the tunnel.

A few minutes later, as the group gathered, she told them she wanted to check on their assets, especially since prior to their engagement, she had several millions in the safe. No one could recall what was left and what the division of the assets were. As she entered the code numbers, Jilkes asked, "Why are we here? We don't have a clue as to what was in that safe."

Asiram looked at him and John Lee and said, "You two mean the world to me. I love all of the people up top, but this group is where I confide all of my issues."

The group entered the safe, and suddenly, things became crystal clear. Jong said, "That's right. The safe was protected from the explosion and the fire. Access was denied because of the collapse of those booby-trapped walls. Does your caretaker know about this aspect of the house?"

"I'm afraid he does, but he also realizes the house is booby-trapped. He enters the house with only a simple password. If he had entered this area, then a text and email would have been sent to my discrete phone." Asiram placed her hand on what appeared to be a wall panel and the vault lit up. Another vault appeared from the rear and all their assets were sitting in front of them.

Zanthius said, "There must be $50 million dollars in this vault."

Asiram said, "No, my love. There's approximately $80 million. If I remember correctly, $5 to $10 million was there before we started emptying your uncle's places, not to mention the funds we captured from the mercs. I'm just guessing from the stacks, width, and height of the money."

The Sarge said, "This is absolutely unacceptable. Mr. Amazing, I want this money moved out of here and into our various banking systems on Monday. I do not think that we will ever need more than $5 to $10 million. What's your thought on that, Asiram?'

"Daddy-in-Law, I agree with you, and besides, we should open a few debit accounts that will afford us up to a quarter of million dollars each. That won't be hard to do, especially, if we asset back each account."

Zanthius said, "Honey, what is the possibility of some stranger breaking into this place and over time, carting all of this money away?"

"Baby Boy, this is a time-bomb. You can't just walk into our safe. Each time the sensors detect the slightest vibration, another vault kicks into place. That can happen four successive times. Look at the thickness of each vault wall. If you come for this place in the future, you had better come with the Lord Jesus Christ leading you. This place can explode and drop our funds down another level and that can happen four consecutive times. The last thing I worry about is the security of our cash."

The Sarge asked, "Are we just a wee bit paranoid, my love?"

"I don't think so. Remember we can exist in the vault for over a month. And besides, I am paranoid about the kinds of people who have come to end our lives."

"I didn't mean it that way, Baby Girl. I'm thinking we don't need a bank." He looked at Zanthius and said, "Son, what are your thoughts?"

"I prefer a bank because it gives everyone access to the funds. If McArthur needs several millions, what would he have to do, come here, and make a withdrawal? We need to have most of our assets in financial institutions where we all can monitor them."

John Lee said, "Most of us have plenty of money on hand to do whatever we want. I still believe in banks and although this here place is sophisticated, I think I want my life protected and everyone else's rather than the money. The question be, how we just going to waltz into a bank and deposit sixty million or so dollars?"

Asiram said, "Now, that's a great question. I think we secure and pay for our expenses first. How many houses are being built in your neighborhood, John Lee?"

"I think so far it's just Jong, the colored fellow, and me."

"No! I heard that Courtney, Brown, and Bernstein are looking to relocate to a small southern place, in addition, Zanthius and I have discussed it with Juan and Rashida, Larry, and Marisa. You have that much land?"

"Well, hell yes."

Jilkes butted in and said, "We have that much land."

John Lee paused and recalled the transaction and said, "Oh yeah, we did buy that other parcel of land as partners. My bad."

"Anyway, I'm thinking it's going to cost around $2 million each to build and furnish. That's damn near $20 million off the top. We're going to need cars, trucks, tractors, and other farm stuff. Jong, you, and Mallory have the banking relationship with those guys on the island. Why don't you give them a call and see how we can legitimately work with our cash assets? They like working with us and may see a way to assist us with this minor problem," Asiram stated.

#

Later, the Sarge indicated to Asiram and the group, "I need to give Franco a call and make sure he and his people are on for tomorrow. It's going to happen tomorrow, is that right, Jilkes? And by the way Asiram, what are we going to do with all that property we got from the ex-senator? If you look around us, we're running out of space here and we need a community place. Now, the bigger question is, do you and Zanthius want that property exclusively for yourselves or do you want to expand our housing options, so that we can co-exist comfortably without having to share a room? Expanding the other place would be ideal, but this is your home and I've destroyed a few of them in my day. Just a question."

"Daddy-in-Law, I have an architect coming out here tomorrow to assist my husband and me in developing that property for the entire group. As I see it, this is how we roll. I see us constantly in contact and near each other at all times."

"Thanks, Asiram. You're the best."

Jilkes said, switching the subject, "Sarge, I was thinking it would be better if we gave Franco and his crew time to rehearse first, then execute on Wednesday morning. After that, they're on our plane and out of here Wednesday afternoon."

"The burning question I have is what are we going to do with all of this cash? We need to get Monica involved in this as well as Brown, Bernstein, and Chakes. Actually, ask everyone if they would like to join the committee to work on this issue."

#

Jilkes said to John Lee, "I'm hungry. How about you and me starting those grills out back and doing some cooking?"

"I like that idea. Hey, is your woman acting strange?" John Lee inquired.

Jilkes smiled and replied, "They're pregnant and this is their first. They are scared because they want to bring into the world healthy, happy, and smart children for us. You're going to sit there at night and tell soothing stories to her and always rub her belly."

"Why would I be rubbing her belly?"

"You're communicating with your child. You know what, you dumb red-neck, we're going to sign up for parenting classes, or at least ask Courtney to conduct and help us understand what the hell we're supposed to be doing to support our women."

"Before we cook, can we find her and ask her about it. I'm lost in space on this one. I don't have a single clue as to what's going on, other than the fact, she be getting bigger and moving slower. I asked her, how can I help? She bows and says, 'you already did'."

"John Lee, do you truly love your woman?"

"Why you be asking a dumb-ass question like that? You know I would kill all humans for her."

"Dude, I know you trust me. Listen, go to her, and tell her you love her with all your heart and that she means the world to you. Then say, 'you're pregnant and I don't know what to do. I want to love you and hold you, but I feel I may hurt the baby'. Listen, dude, tell her you need to play a larger part in the birthing process and then ask her, what can you do?" Jilkes said.

"Oh, I see. I ain't been loving or showing love. I need to be there, be soft, and gracious, right?" John Lee replied.

"That's the general idea. Listen hold her hand, rub and kiss her belly, dude. It goes a long way towards having a wonderful relationship. John Lee, this is different from a lot of things we have done in the past. These women are pregnant by us. Therefore, they are having our children. We have to show them more love now than we did when we so-called conquered them."

"I be feeling you. You know I just lay up and say, do you need anything, and we rarely have real conversations," John Lee acknowledged.

"Don't screw this up. Tell her you are new at this thing called love and parenting, you need her to guide you through this thing, and make sure she is satisfied with her choice in a man. Make her honor and respect you for being the person you are, John Lee. Don't pull that macho shit on her, get on your knees, and kiss that belly and tell her you want to learn her language. How about we do dinner tonight in the field and when they start to talk in their language we say, 'hold up', we want to learn your language and we want you to speak our language when we are out socializing. That seems fair, doesn't it?"

"Damn, I'm glad you're my friend. I learn so much from you. I'll never admit it in public, but you're a wonderful human being. I mean, I taunt you with racist bullshit and you just love me more and help me all the time. Damn, you be a good man, Jilkes, and I love you. Let's burn up them there grills. I'll bet you $5 that everyone in this place is going to want to eat chicken or beef today and forget about that 'veggie' bull crap."

# # #

The Sarge called Franco just to check up on him and his people. Franco told him a group of models checked into the resort and that he and his men were having the time of their lives since they were the only single men there. He told the Sarge that the lead woman was a stunning, well-sculptured, middle aged, red-head, and that he was in love. He added that she wanted to get married on the spot. The Sarge suggested to him that he at least wait until he was sober to consider such a permanent and expensive arrangement. The Sarge reminded him to be at the bank when it opened, and to have Mr. Carter or his son get them to the airport. He told Franco that they would be in his area on Monday, to enjoy the farm and they would be on their way after the event on Wednesday. Franco indicated that he was interested in touring the area, but the Sarge told him that this was not tourism season.

# # #

Jilkes and John Lee fired up the grills, donned some aprons, and started churning out the food. They cooked steaks, burgers, chicken, salmon on two of the grills, and on the third was a vegetable medley. Members of the group told them they liked the way they cooked, without regards to calories, cholesterol, fat content or anything else.

John Lee saw his woman lingering in the background, snatched his apron off and said, "You belong at the front of the line. Why you be hanging back here? I be the cook and you be my wife. You be eating first, my lady." In front of all eyes, he got on his knees, embraced her belly, and kissed it. He looked up and told her he loved her more than his favorite pigs. What a guy!

That night, John Lee found out exactly what his woman was missing when she told him, 'She no need words, but action!"

From a less than aggressive position, he fulfilled his woman's needs as well as his own. Afterwards, as the two panted from exhaustion, John Lee said, "I didn't know you could do it after you were pregnant. I guess there are a lot of things I don't know." They kissed and fell asleep in each other's arms. The art of communication had been resolved and from that day forward, the stress reduction function would be in play.

# # #

When Courtney, Rashida, Carla, Mike, and few support staff, arrived at the hospital, the resident doctor said, "Oh my, these are the people who contributed to our hospital. Dr. Beckmire, how can I assist you?"

In scientific and medical terms, Courtney laid out the scenario for the doctor, what her prognosis was, a suggested procedure that would correct the misalignment of the uterus subject to his confirmation of the problem. The doctor told her he would prep her and get his nurses ready as well.

Much later, after Mike resurfaced, everyone wanted to know how Carla was. He indicated she was under the expert care of Courtney and Rashida and should be up and about in the next day or two.

#

In another place and time, Franco and his men were reeling from an explosive influx of beautiful women. He told Mario, "I don't think I want to go to DC and earn money. I prefer to earn love—what about you?"

"Boss, this is paradise, and these women are spectacular. However, I don't think we need to be so free with this group. They ask too many questions and only flirt. I don't trust them."

"Mario, you never trust women. Anyway, I like your instincts. I too noticed they're full of questions about how we got here. We got here by plane that was my answer. The redhead did say to me some things never seem to be what they really are. I found that puzzling but continued to drink. All of us indicated that we are here on holiday. I hope no one discussed the new partnership arrangement we have in place. Actually, get everyone here for a quick meeting."

As the group assembled, Franco said, "It seems like we're the only men on earth. However, Mario made a point that I agree with. He thinks the beautiful ladies ask a lot of questions. Do you guys get the same feeling?"

His men agreed with him. He then said, "Did anyone discuss our relationship with the owners of this place?" Everyone remained silent for a few seconds. Finally, one of his men spoke up and stated he had mentioned they met some nice people here, but that was the extent of it. He assured

Franco he didn't disclose any information about them or their
partners.

Franco said, "I think their true colors are about to show.
Stay focused, admit that you're married, and just looking for a
good time. If they ask you about the ownership of this place
or anything else, don't indulge, deny everything. I don't know
what they're looking for, but I don't want anything to get in
the way of that job in DC. Is that clear?"

## CHAPTER NINE

At 0900 hours, a weary looking group of men met in the lobby of the resort and Mr. Carter said, "I took the liberty of making ham, egg, cheese, sausage and bacon sandwiches. There is plenty of coffee in the kitchen, make yourselves a cup, and I'll meet you outside in ten minutes. You can bring your food with you if you like."

On the way to the bank, Mr. Carter said, "Did you guys have a good time last night? Those ladies wanted to know where you were from, where you were going, what were you doing here on the island and whether there was another group here with you?"

Franco coughed and asked, "Mr. Carter, are you manufacturing information or is that the truth?"

"Oh, no, Sir. That be the truth. My people are smart enough not to speak about guests. I told them you guys were here on holiday and that your wives are on another island. I was offered $500 for any information about you and my partners. I sure hope you people didn't let your small brain do your thinking last night. If you did, you should call our friend and tell him you may have been compromised. I don't know their business, but I do know our friends don't do stupid."

Franco inquired, "What does that mean, Mr. Carter?"

"That means, if you blew their cover, and it becomes a problem for them, then I hope you can hold your breath for a long time. They're purely professional and don't like dumb."

"Mr. Carter, you referred to stupid and dumb. One or the other is enough."

"Mr. Franco, I'm just saying, this would be a great time to reflect on your shenanigans of last night and attempt to deduce if you let information about your partners out. Now listen, if you're not sure, I can play back the recordings from your rooms and let you know if you should hop on that jet of yours and fly the hell back to Spain. I'm just trying to protect you, me, and our partners. I wouldn't have this 6-star resort without them. They don't bother me and let me run the place according to my wishes. They now have my son involved and he's suggesting alternative ways to operate the resort. I mean, we're booked for the next two years. If they want to come here, we vacate the place and send people to the Four Seasons and the other fancy hotels at our cost. So, I want you guys to leave here safely, but don't screw up our relationship over some pagan acts."

"Mr. Carter, everyone threatens us. Let me tell you a few things. We have signed on with our mutual friends, and, just last evening, I cautioned my comrades to close their mouths. We concluded that those ladies were too inquisitive and, how do you say it—gossipy. We met and decided we would not discuss our partners on any level and only say that we were married men looking for a good time. That, Mr. Carter, would be the end of our involvement, ah, and conversation."

Mr. Carter said, "Mr. Franco, I'm glad to hear that. My instructions are to take you directly to the airport, give you this envelope, and tell you to wait for a call. This is the conclusion of any imaginary or real relationship plus $75K. Now, giving me alternative facts would not be in your best interest since your rooms were bugged and I had people listening to the transmissions. Just for your own edification, this group is highly organized and connected. Their foundations give away millions of dollars each year, so you can bet your last dollar, they're not going to let loose lips sink their ships."

"Mr. Carter, I do not recognize that colloquial statement. Can you embellish it for us?"

"It means keep your fucking mouth shut or learn to hold your breath for a very long time."

###

On the way to the bank, Mr. Carter said, "These guys are going to try to sell you insurance, this, that and the other. Tell them you want a seamless way of using their bank to make construction payments in Spain. Oh, also tell them that Mr. Jong and Mrs. Mallory will eventually sign on this agreement and are to be copied on all transactions. So, in the meantime, you could take the money and run, but when they find time, they will come and get you. Your choice, you're in control of $2 million that's going to be transferred and the salaries that were agreed upon started when your plane landed. Oh also, I'm going to give you guys debit cards in the amount that was promised. Are there any questions?"

Franco looked at Mr. Carter and said, "Are you a relation of theirs?"

"I am not. I am their partner in the resort. There are three other partners that round off the properties in that cul-de-sac."

"By the way, the resort is immaculate. The attention to detail is incredible. Who was the architect and is it possible to use him in Spain?"

"If there was no breach in protocol, ask Mrs. Mallory and Mr. Jong when you arrive wherever you're going this afternoon."

"You seem protective as well as honored to be associated with these people," Franco announced.

"Mr. Franco, if you have larceny in your heart, then these are not the guys you want to partner with. If you appreciate a second chance or any chance, then you will feel honored because they are simple folks who respect others and have a simple mission; 'to help people help themselves'."

"I know they are incredibly stealthy, and you don't suspect that they are together, when they are all colors and races. They waltzed into what I thought was a heavily armed restaurant and took it over without drawing a weapon. The big guy threatened me a lot, and then I finally asked him to have a conversation without the threats. We did, and bingo. I, of all people, was privy to information concerning a relative of theirs. It was absolutely amazing that this meeting went from 'who shoots who first', to I know someone who may have the necessary information that you seek."

Mr. Carter announced, "I gave you a head's up on dealing with this group. Don't throw me under the bus."

"Mr. Carter, why would I throw you under a bus?"

"It's a Yankee saying Franco. Just a simple saying meaning, not to give me up for the information that I gave you. Let's go in here and do this thing. I'm convinced that you're legit, therefore, I'll sign off on this agreement."

"Mr. Carter, what does that mean? You'll sign off on this agreement."

"Mr. Franco, I'm in charge of this transaction. I have the power to agree or disagree. I also have the power to take you to the bank or to the airport. Let's make this thing happen. Oh, and by the way, I had them stock your plane with good island food for lunch for your short trip to Miami."

#

In Miami, one of the group's pilots was waiting for the foreign plane to land and its passengers to disembark and go through customs. The men walked through customs in clothes that totally identified them as tourists. The copilot looked at them and said, "Hi, I presume you're Mr. Franco."

Franco said, "How did you know that?"

"I can tell by the clothes you're wearing. Listen, you guys stick out like Santa Claus in July. We're going to take a little ride into town and outfit you guys with some inconspicuous clothing. Do you have luggage?"

Franco barked, "We left Spain in a hurry."

"It's okay. Let me make a call, and then we're off." The pilot called Jong, told him he had the packages, and was taking them to town for some needed provisions.

The group exited the airport and entered a black SUV that would take them to a few stores of fashion. On their way to town, the pilot said, "I need you guys to focus on denim pants, shirts and dark jackets. Also, look for hats that are normal not flashy, like baseball caps. I don't know your mission, but think about it this way, if police scanners state that the perpetrators are wearing white suits, pink shirts, red hats, and blue shoes, easy to identify, right? Okay, how about blue jeans, brown shoes, black caps, and dark shirts—that's everybody, right?"

The group smiled and laughed. The pilot saw the Target sign and said, "Driver, that's our place. I think we will be an hour or so. See you then, or I'll call you if we need more time."

Forty-five minutes later, the group walked out of the store with bags filled with shoes, pants, shirts, and jackets. There were no fancy purchases, just dark, colored outfits.

The group arrived back at the airport and exited the SUV. As they began their journey, Franco said, "I noticed you did not tip the driver."

"Why would I tip him when he works for the group?"

Franco and his comrades boarded the group's jet. Franco exclaimed, "Wow, look at how this thing is appointed!"

The pilot said, "You should see the other two."

Franco said, "I was wondering how all of those people crowded into one plane. Is it a large plane?"

The pilot said, "Oh, yeah. It's a large new jet that can house all their family members. It's incredible. Okay, I need you guys to pick a seat and buckle up. We're out of here in a matter of minutes."

# # #

The plane taxied to the runway. It was number eight in line for take-off. As the captain and copilot looked out the window, four police vehicles raced towards the runway. The captain came on the intercom and said, "We have police vehicles racing our way. Is there something we should know before they board us if they board us?"

Franco yelled, "We are as sterile as virgins. We have not committed any offenses and we don't have any contraband on us."

The captain watched as the caravan of police vehicles zoomed pass them and stopped at the fifth plane in the que for take-off. He announced that the drama was for another plane. As soon as we are airborne, one of us will come back and provide you with drinks and snacks. Sit back and enjoy your flight, gentlemen."

As they pulled around the plane in question, the captain gave the other captain a salute. Five minutes later, the plane's engines roared and rumbled down the runway. Mario asked, inappropriately of Franco, "Did you have your way with that redhead?"

Franco replied, "Mario, have you ever known me to discuss my relationships with you? What makes you think you can breach that veil at this point?"

Mario responded, "*Senor*, you are the reason my family has a home and I have employment. Please forgive my moment of indiscretion, and I assure you it will never happen again."

The copilot came out and told the guys what was on the menu. They all wanted the rack of lamb, but there was only enough for two, and the other options was chicken. Franco said, "I really want the rack of lamb, but I'm willing to settle for chicken, so that one of you guys can enjoy it."

The men drank and enjoyed their meals and their access to as many drinks as they could consume. One-third of the way to their destination, the group was sound asleep. Their next sounds would be long yawns when the captain indicated that they were starting their descent into Maryland.

#

Without incident, the plane landed, and the Spanish contingency disembarked from their plane.

In the hangar, they could not avoid noticing the huge jet parked beside their plane. Franco said to Mario, "That's a helluva plane there. Look at the size of that thing."

The pilot overhearing the discussion said, "Oh, it's nice alright. That's the plane they fly together on."

Franco asked, "Who flies on that plane?"

The captain said, "The same people that you're going to meet with—Mr. Beckmire and associates."

Mario looked at Franco and said of the plane, "Much bigger plane, much bigger than I thought. They seem so humble and unassuming."

#

On the way to Virginia, Franco acknowledged, "This country is nothing, but highways and byways." As they headed down 495 South, they could see the piercing top of the Mormon Tabernacle pointing towards the heavens, as was explained by the driver.

Franco asked, "Aren't there airports in Virginia? Why would they land in Maryland and drive to Virginia?"

The driver said, "You should ask your host that question. I'm like an Uber or Lyft driver. We pick-up and deliver, that's all we do."

When the driver reached the road that led to the farm, he said, "This road is a little bumpy, so hold on tight." As the car rounded a bend, he said, "If you look to your left, you will see the farmhouse." A few minutes later, the driver pulled up into the circle and the group got out of the van.

Mallory saw them coming and decided to greet them since the Sarge was taking a nap. He welcomed them to the farm and told them to join him for a ride in the mule to where they were staying. He drove them to where the ex-senator once lived, told them to make themselves at home, and informed them that the Sarge and Jilkes would be there soon to officially welcome them.

#

An hour later, a mule pulled up to the house and the Sarge, Jilkes, John Lee, and Jong got out of it. The Sarge knocked on the door and Franco yelled, "The door is open."

The Sarge said, "Welcome to Virginia. I hope you had smooth flights. Jilkes and John Lee will walk you through the scenery and discuss options as well as elicit your suggestions for a smooth operation. I can only assume that Mr. Carter gave you the 411 on us. Let me say, and make one thing perfectly clear, we are not crooks, we don't sell drugs, we don't defraud banks and other financial institutions. We are law-abiding citizens, and not on anyone's watch list except those who do bad things. Also, I'm sure Mr. Carter told you not to think of our kindness as weakness. We are as passive and as gentle as humans can be. It's only when you mess with one of us that you will receive the wrath of all of us and we're good at what we do."

Franco replied, "Nice to see you too, *mi amigo*. Our flight was perfect! The food was excellent! Did you have any medical issues?"

"Franco, I'm just saying. We're the killing machine that people discuss. We are it, and now that you have decided, for the influx of money, you to want to be a part of our team, you should at least know how we play. Welcome brothers, are you hungry?"

Franco said, "We are definitely hungry. Do you have any Coors beer? I love that beer."

"Come on down to the main house and help yourself. I'm surprised there is none here, but I'm sure there is some at the other place."

Franco said, "Whose property is this?"

"It once belonged to a United States Senator who was too greedy for his own good. He died in New York, or somewhere, and we purchased the place dirt cheap. This is my first time here, and if you don't mind, I think I'll look around."

The Sarge and his crew began to walk around the well-appointed place and immediately realized that the place was bugged and had active cameras. He said, "Mr. Amazing, we're going to need your cousin out here in a hurry." He then tapped Franco on the arm and pointed to the security system. He whispered that they should not discuss any business in the house until he could discern where the feed led to.

At the farmhouse, Franco saw Courtney, and said to the Sarge, "Oh, I see your beautiful wife. Will it be okay if I pay my respects?"

The Sarge said, "As long as that's all you pay. Go ahead, Man. It's all good." He looked at Jong and told him to take Jilkes, John Lee, and find Mallory so they could give a thorough walk-through of the senator's ex-residence.

The Sarge saw Zanthius and called him over. He asked, "Did anyone walk through the ex-senator's property? There are active cameras there and I'm concerned about the feed."

Zanthius said, "Pops, I can't honestly say one way or the other. I think this all occurred while we were on our way out of town. I really don't remember. Why don't you ask Jong to get his cousin out here?"

"Already in the works, Son. My concern is I want our guests to be ghosts without a direct link to us. If that feed goes to an agency or even to my cousin, then our plan is dead in the water and we might be surprised."

The Sarge said to Jong, "Call your cousin and tell him we need him out here now. And delay that walk-through until we have had the placed swept. Also, give Franco and his crew some throw away phones, so they can call home if they must."

At 1600 hours, everyone began to talk about dinner arrangements. Jong made the announcement that Mary Alice had contacted her company and dinner would promptly be served at 1700 hours. He told the group the cocktail hour would start at 1630 hours.

The Sarge pulled Franco and his group aside and asked, "Did you guys speak about the operation we're planning in that house?"

Everyone looked around and shrugged their shoulders. Franco said, "We were glad to get here and were trying to figure out if we had time for a siesta? Why do you inquire?"

"That house was a recent acquisition, and I noticed the cameras in the place. I don't know where those cameras feed to, therefore, I'm concerned. We have our man coming to look at and disable the cameras."

"My friend, if I could be so forward and suggest that you let Mario peek and save you some money. He is the best AV guy in our part of the world."

"Okay, let me fetch a few of my guys and have them accompany Mario so that we have a record of exactly what was done."

# # #

While everyone else was enjoying cocktails, Mario, Jong, Gladstone, and McArthur walked through the ex-senator's house examining the camera system. Mario descended into the basement with Gladstone and they both were surprised that the senator was obviously, into S&M. Whips lined the walls, as did chains, restraints, mirrors, and multiple slab like beds. Dog collars, beads, feathers, and other strange objects were strewn around the room. Gladstone began to look at the different mirrors and noticed that the panes were symmetrical, save one. This panel was the size of a door jam. He gently pressed the pane, and it gave but did not open. He firmly pressed where a doorknob would normally be, and the heavy panel opened. He yelled for McArthur who came running and asked, "What the hell is this place?"

Gladstone said, "I need backup in this area. I have no idea what this sicko has in this place."

Meanwhile, Mario was following the RJ45 cables and bingo. It led to the same place where Gladstone and McArthur had disappeared. He banged on the panel, but it was the wrong one. McArthur saw him through the two-way mirrors and opened the invisible door. He told the men that the cable led to this room. As they walked deeper into the separate area, a light came on in a room that was filled with VHS tapes. Each tape was named. Mario suggested they look and see what was being filmed. Mario placed a random tape in the machine, and it showed several men in masks performing vile tasks on what appeared to be a despondent young female. Mario stopped the tape and said, "I assume these are all conquests."

Gladstone picked a tape that had 'MA' on it. He said, "Put this one in."

Mario said, "I want to disable the cameras. You guys can watch."

McArthur slid the tape in. It showed three men engaging in sex, in different positions with a woman. It was Mary Alice. Both men were shocked and damn near broke the machine when Jong banged on the panel. He walked in and asked, "What spooked you guys?"

"You banging on the door like that."

Mario yelled, "I need someone to hold a light."

Jong said, "I'll be right there. I wish the Sarge would make up his mind first before asking me to do things. My useless cousin is on his way here. Another worthless expense. By the way, what are these tapes about?"

McArthur said, "Just some freaky stuff that bad guys are doing to unsuspecting women, that's all."

Gladstone placed the VHS in the back of his pants and held a finger over his lips to McArthur. He yelled to Jong, "Mac and I are going to check out the upstairs. If you need us, give a shout."

When the two men were upstairs, Gladstone said, "No way in hell we can let this thing out? We got to burn this one in a hurry. Do you think we should tell the Sarge about it?"

"You know the Sarge is our leader, we can't let his man, our friend be blindsided by this heinous performance on a comatose individual. Why the hell did you pick that one?" McArthur asked.

"I just saw 'M A' and thought it was something new. I didn't know it was about our brother's wife and mother-to-be. Damn, damn, damn! We must decide this shit now. What's your take?" Gladstone asked.

"I say we burn and advise that we made the decision to do such a thing. However, we can't burn it now because it will cause undo suspicion. Damn, I feel like shit knowing that those old bastards drugged her and violated her beyond comprehension."

Jong shouted out their names and the two men hastily went back into the dungeon. They entered the recording room, saw Jong and Mario standing in front of two hidden closets filled with money to the ceiling. McArthur said, "Jesus, how do you steal this much money? How is it possible?"

Jong said, "I can't get reception down here, go upstairs, call the Sarge and tell him to bring a few other brothers and Franco."

#

When the Sarge arrived, his guys were outside of the house smoking Cuban cigars that were found in the house. The Sarge said, "Cigars, when did you people start smoking cigars?"

McArthur said, "Sarge, these are not just cigars, these are Cuban cigars, and we just discovered some real issues in this house. Jong, please show our leader, Mr. Brown, Mr. Bernstein, Mr. Whitmore, and our guest Mr. Franco, what his man found?"

The men entered the house, were appalled, and saddened by what they saw when entering the basement. McArthur explained to them that all the victims were drugged and filmed. He then led them into another room and opened the closet doors. Jong said, "Mario is the finder of this small fortune. He should be given a fortune cookie that says, 'you're rich'." The Sarge looked at McArthur and Gladstone and was not concerned about the cash in the closet, but something more important.

He said, "Mario, since you are a guest in our place, we will give you 5% if it's under $20 million with another percentage for your boss and your comrades with a cap at $50 million. Does that sound fair?"

Franco yelled, "Hell, yeah. Oh, my God! I met you people and I wanted to kill you. You turn us into honest businessmen, and we have become rich on this trip to do a job for you. Oh, my goodness! I'm so glad we shared wine that night instead of trading bullets."

The Sarge looked at him and said, "*Mi amigo*, I too am happy about our resolve to find a way to coexist and not to hurt each other. To my men, I say, 'what say you about my resolve'?"

McArthur looked at Gladstone and Whitmore, they nodded affirmatively. McArthur said, "I think we have an accord."

Mario said, "Are you people for real, or are you trying to con me?"

Franco responded, "In our previous life I think that would be a fair statement. Not now, my friend. We have been blessed and we're on the right road."

The Sarge requested, "Jong, escort our guests to the house so they can enjoy some food. I would like to make an announcement when I get back, so please people, don't upstage me."

When the group was out of sight, the Sarge said, "You know that Mary Alice was a victim of their shenanigans, don't you?"

"Unfortunately, we started viewing the tape. We stopped once we realized it was her. That's the truth, brother. Here is the tape and I think we need to close this place down until we completely sweep it. Too much shit in this place to just ignore," McArthur stated.

The Sarge said, "Okay, get our guests double rooms in the extension. I want that tape destroyed. Is that a problem or a concern?"

McArthur said, "Sarge we did not go looking for the tape. We wanted to know exactly what was being filmed and out of two randomly selected tapes, we had to pick one with our brother's woman costarring. It is burned in my brain, but it will never be discussed by me or Gladstone. When we realized that it was her, we stopped the tape and withdrew it from the box. We did not go looking for this and, damn, we're sorry it was us that found the thing."

"Would you have preferred that someone else found it? What's wrong with you guys? I'm happy you found it and not one of our guests or someone else with a much more sinister profile. This place needs to be sterilized. What the hell are we going to do with all of this cash?"

"That's a problem that I'm glad we have," Gladstone announced.

# # #

When the Sarge and the group showed up for dinner, he said, "People, it's a good day in paradise. Our new friend and family member, Mario, stand up Mario, alongside Mr. Amazing, discovered a hiding place in the ex-senator's house. These two guys sniffed out two closets filled from the floor to the ceiling with hundred-dollar bills. Give these two, new age-guys a hand. Listen, I'm your unelected leader and I think that Mr. Jilkes is making a run for my office."

Jilkes rose and said, "Your office, my fearless leader is for life. No one and, I mean, no one can make a run for your office. It is sanctioned and protected. You merely asked me to take control of an action and that's what I intend on doing. You my friend will move to the great beyond with the title of our leader." He turned to the group and said, "What say you?" There was a thunderous response.

Asiram raised her hand and the Sarge asked, "Why are you raising your hand? This is your home and we're your guests."

"Daddy-in-Law don't make me come up there and show you a few things. People don't ask my permission to enjoy what is here. This is no longer my house or home, but our house and our home. After all that we have been through—I mean, suicide vests, bullets flying, the doctor shooting people, Marisa and Monica blowing people to hell, to protect us all—

are you serious? Don't ask me how to enjoy your home, this is our place, not my place. Just like the resort is ours, this is ours, middle America is ours, but Daddy-in-Law, my Philly property is still mine until you fix it by paying for the repairs."

The Sarge said, "You're my soulmate and daughter-in-law. Me and my wife love you for all that you do for us. I don't want to recall how many of your places sustained damages, but I do want to say that when you pushed my son to Spain, in search of another Beckmire/De Lombardo, your stock went through the roof with us. Let me be clear, I'm placing the other house, the ex-senator's place, off limits until Jong's cousin has washed it. Our guests will assume housing in the addition. They have work to do tomorrow if, in fact, we can certify that when in the ex-senator's house, they didn't divulge any information about our plans."

The Sarge continued, "You all know, we're a close-knit group. It started with my guys in the Nam, then expanded to our relationships, our friends, our lovers and, in many cases, our new wives. I love all of you and I carry the burden of having to be concerned about the past, the present and the future. I mentioned playfully that Jilkes was making a run for my job. He's not making a run, but I do want him and Mallory to assume a greater leadership role in our organization. Listen, I'm getting older, they're getting older, and I can hardly keep that pretty wife of mine happy, because at the end of the day, I'm damn tired."

Franco raised his hand and suggested, "Perhaps you should try the Mediterranean diet for a while. *Mi amigo*, it gives you strength, character, and stamina."

The Sarge looked at him and said, "I already have those characteristics. I'm looking for someone to help me with all the functions of this damn group, including a bunch of Spaniards we were once going to turn into angels, and they were going to attempt to terminate us as well. I need more time with my grandbabies. Look at Rashida, that damn Juan, not Don Juan, has impregnated my baby girl. Asiram had a baby and magically found out that there was another. Mary Alice is pregnant, Yeshida, Somara, Yvette, and Okema are as well. I want to play with babies, babysit and start a granddaddy-daycare center. Hey, this is my confession. If you don't like it, go to the bar, and I'll join you later. I need to tell you people this because it is causing me many sleepless nights.

"Me and Mallory sat on a hill one night, long, long ago, drinking Jack Daniels. We decided that we had trained a group of guys who were the ultimate in soldiering. We knew when training them, they could run farther than any group before, save one country ass guy, hit targets, and do hand-to-hand combat better than any other group we had trained. Some were blue bloods, some middle class, some college dropouts, one-100% taught racist, and others, plain old poor people. I need you people to hear me out. You're sitting amongst your country's finest and most proven elite fighting machine.

"These people, as well as Mallory and me, have a shit load of souls waiting for us in hell to avenge their deaths. We're not proud of what our country asked us to do for it, but we, and I do mean we, bled together, suffered together, prayed as one and wreaked havoc on an entire nation, day after day, night after night until they placed individual bounties on our heads in the millions of dollars.

"Some despondent ass general gave us a one-way assignment and promised that we would be free from war if we would do one more insane breach. We did it and it caused a mobility issue with one of our beloved. We came back, we were one man short. He sent us on another, and we had another significant injury and he felt he could continue to hold us hostage. He too is one of those souls waiting for our entry into hell.

"A couple of our ingenious members decided to do an illicit deal that would empower and relinquish that poverty rope from around several of our necks. That deal was purely illicit and costly. It almost cost the life of one of our brothers, by the hands of a stepfather and the local mob. You mess with one of us and you will incur the wrath of us all. The entire mob in that area was decimated by a few good men, a stepfather was relieved of his life, and the product they thought was the panacea to success, was destroyed, and none of it reached the sick victims waiting on it. In other words, we did not start out as church mice. We started out as street rats who were fortunate enough to get control over the assets of that misguided adventure without any penalty to normal civilians.

"We have many titles, but the one we most appreciate is that we 'help people help themselves'. I know I never talk this much, but it's important that you know where we started and where we currently are. I know you're hungry, but I want to conclude with this information. We lost this property once, but we will not forfeit it again. We lost mid-America, but we will not forfeit it again. We have become a bunch of road runners. We have places, but we don't have individual homes. This is one of our homes. St. Thomas is one of our homes. Middle-America is one of our homes. Somewhere near John Lee and Jilkes, will be home for many of us. Soon to be, a resort in Valencia, Spain will be our home. We have three jets, lots of property, accounts all over the world, and enough cash to start an inquiry. My sons and I will soon have to venture to the Outback. We thought we had cleared up an issue, but there will be brazen attacks on our people by non-other than my cousin. This world is full of evil people."

Asiram rose from her seat and said, "Daddy-in-Law, are the cells in your brain decreasing? If you think my husband is going back to Australia without me, the children, and the rest of us, then I know you are having some mental issues."

"Honey, I asked him to show some authority and he asked me if I was crazy?" Zanthius stated.

"Pardon me. I'm Mr. Amazing and this is my wife, Mary Alice. I spent a lot of time looking at that disk that Helga left and to me it's all gibberish. Using a simple chemistry set, you can construct the model and get a bang, according to the disk. However, the final piece of the puzzle is embedded in the mind of the 'idiot spy'. What that means is impossible for me to understand, especially since he is called the 'idiot spy'."

The Sarge said, "Mr. Amazing, you have been called many things as well. Figure out what it means soon. Mike is missing because he is in communication with people about the Carbon Factor formula and a certain property that will hopefully, draw my cousin out into the open. I want to end this charade, people, and soon. While we are about to partake in a wonderful meal, my cousin is trying to figure out how and when to conclude our existence. We're in Virginia—everyone here has a damn gun. Stay vigilant and stay connected, not to the internet, but to your weapon."

Franco walked over to the Sarge and asked, "Was all of that true? I mean the war and mob stuff, is it true?"

"Do you think I would stand before my family and blow smoke up their asses? Don't answer that one. Yes, it is absolutely true and thanks to you, I didn't kill you. Your words about conversing first prior to fighting stuck with me. This new me, is because of you, *mi amigo*. We were about to put a real ass-whuppin on you and your men. After dinner, we'll find a place to huddle and go over the plans for Wednesday.   Nothing too serious, but just the latest intelligence on the area, and exit strategies."

# # #

Jong's cousin entered the road and text messages went out to most of the group that a vehicle was heading their way. Rashida and Juan, who had surveillance duty, walked to the monitoring area, and sent an all-clear text. They watched him from the moment he entered the road until he pulled up in front of the small circle. Jong met him and began yelling at him. He summoned Mario and they began to explain the layout of the cameras. Mario suggested that he look for an external antenna that could provide a signal outside of the house. Jong indicated they were distracted by some cash they found in the house and that they did not complete the task.

The Sarge saw Jong's cousin and walked over to Jong and said, "Tell your cousin we want the house cleaned of all bugs, and we want to know if the system can broadcast a signal somewhere other than in the house. Also, tell him there is a shit load of money in two closets and we want him to check it and make sure there are no traps."

Jong replied, "Why do you insist on telling me to tell him something? He speaks your language."

The Sarge just looked at him, and finally said, "Tell your cousin not to take his cut off the top as he has previously done!"

Jong looked at the Sarge and said, "That is a serious offense. Did he do such a thing? If so, when and how much?"

"Jong, tell him that I don't care about history, besides, you barely paid him enough money to make the trip out here, worthwhile."

"I pay his children's expensive college education fees. You should ask before you make assumptions."

"Mr. Amazing, do we have a problem?"

The Sarge's voice resonated throughout the place and things became extremely quiet as he waited for a response from Jong. Jong said, "One thousand apologies if I spoke against your will. It is because of you that I stand here. I need rest and time with my woman. Please forgive me for my sudden outburst."

"Mr. Amazing, you've been out bursting for a while now. I think there's something you want to say to me and now would be the best time to get it off your chest."

Jong fell to his knees, in front of his cousin, and said to the Sarge, "I sometimes feel less than a man, and those are the times I wish you had left me in the field."

The Sarge snatched him off his knees and suspended him in mid-air and said, "Don't you ever say that to me again. I killed eight people without a gun that night to save your ass. I don't do nothing for nothing. I love you, asshole."

Jong's cousin grabbed the Sarge's arm and Jong yelled a warning to him in their language. He backed off, bowing, and saying something in a foreign language.

#

Mike and Courtney fetched Carla from the hospital with Gladstone, Chakes, and Montomie performing back-up. All the women were waiting on her arrival to lend their support and to comfort her. They had learned to depend on her skills, after all, she was a masterful pilot.

She was amazed and whispered to Courtney, "I hope my husband doesn't know why I was in the hospital."

Courtney said, "I didn't tell him. Rashida didn't tell him. Did you tell him by chance?"

Carla asked, "Does Rashida know?"

"Years ago, Rashida met the wrong person, for the wrong reasons and received the same outcome as you. She told me about your symptoms and asked if her assumptions were correct. I never said affirmatively one way or the other, but she is not a small brain person," Courtney stated.

"I owe you guys a lot. What a way to start a new marriage. I feel so ashamed."

"You know what? You need to put that shit to bed and work the magic you put on Mike to the maximum. He's whipped, Girl. I mean this dude is so in love with you, he hasn't slept since you've been in the hospital. You might want to bestow some alternative loving on him just to ease his burden," Courtney stated.

"What's alternative loving?"

"Carla, think about it and you'll figure it out," Rashida said.

#

Tuesday afternoon, Franco, his guys, along with Jilkes, John Lee, Brown, Bernstein, and Whitmore, were given a ride by Jong's cousins to the area of the potential activity. Those breaching from the rear were let off on 11th Street, and they walked around to Ben's Chili Bowl at 10th & H Street, N.E. The individuals who would breach the front were let off on Florida Avenue between 10th and 11th Streets.

After the walk through and reversal of front and back surveillances, Franco said, "I am very much against the rear breach. It is a place where the entire exit can be blocked easily. One way in, one way out. I never like operating with that option."

Jilkes said, "I agree with you 100%. Once you're up in that alley, you're locked in without an exit. I think the best move is from the front during shift changes. I don't want to hurt people working for a living. Franco, I'm thinking, two will breach and secure, and two will begin the transport of cases. Since we don't know if the stash is in cases, you will carry fortified trash bags with you that will not burst open if dragged on the ground. As I see it, we have perfect cover from the front of the house. I'll set a team up at 8th & K, and another at 10th & K, to protect your exit. As you can see, there are no electric wires in the front of the houses, they're all in the rear. I will have my guys cut the main line with a ball like object to decrease suspicion. If you guys go in and find more cases or stacks than you can carry, Franco, raise your hand in the air and two more of my people will assist with the extraction. This is not a risk-taking event. It means little to us, but it draws out our arch enemy into the open, if successful."

An astute Franco said, "That street is very busy with buses and lots of car traffic."

Jilkes said, "I have accessed the bus schedule. There are opportune times when we should engage in this event. Once again, you are not to take any unnecessary chances. If this operation does not appear to be seamless, then we abort and forget about it. This mission is about making someone mad that people violated his haven. I don't want any heroes from this event."

When the group met back at the farm, John Lee said, "I hope you guys be listening to my man. If it don't look natural, like sheep on sheep, then walk the heck away from it. If you see a sheep and pig together, that there ain't natural. Those people at the property will defend what they're paid to do. We can walk away from this one and regroup to assault the Sarge's cousin on another front. If we must kill people trying to earn a living, then we ain't so happy about that one."

Jilkes said, "Study your approach. We'll meet for breakfast, decide the final course of action, and how many of us need to be engaged. I'll have your backs covered, no matter the circumstances."

Mike walked into the room and introduced himself to the group once again. He said, "I thought that it was one house, but that guy has three houses in a row. He has 903, 905, and 907. They have adjoining basements. There are security details at 903 and 905, but none at 907. It is surmised that his stash is in 905 and 907. It is probably best that we breach those two properties first and cover from afar. I'm assuming you might want to have your own people on the ground on this one unless Jong's cousin is willing to use some of his. Oh, and remember, the alleyway is one way in and the same way out. If necessary, and there are no other options available to us, we can breach the property on the corner from the rear. That would be 901. I will have my guys place a pull up ladder on the porch and then we're out of there. However, prior to that happening, if we are cornered, we will line the trucks up across the alleyway and blow them the hell up, giving us time to escape from 901."

Jilkes said, "I will lay out the plan in the morning after I have talked with the Sarge and Mallory. It appears to me we should have a lot of inside coverage as well as outside coverage. Mike, how reliable are your sources and can they be trusted?"

"I can only vouch for myself. Those guys live in the alleys of DC, and they were brothers of mine in the war who lost everything once they returned from the desert. I trust them, but I can't say if they got a better offer from someone else, what would be the outcome? I would bleed for them, and hopefully, they for me, but that thing called money speaks volumes."

Jilkes said, "I need to see Jong's cousin. I need him or his people to sweep that area and make sure there are no cameras on the other side of the street or in the alleyway. I also need them to provide alternative vehicles for us. In addition, if we come under siege, I would like to detonate a few vehicles in the area and create a distraction. Moreover, I would like to drop our vans somewhere not too distant from the target site and have some hot vehicles take us to the property. I assume that if those places have connecting basements, if we breach one, we shouldn't have an issue breaching the others."

John Lee said, "This here thing seems to be getting complicated. I be thinking you need to simplify the breach."

"How would you simplify it, Big Country?"

"I don't have no specific way, but it seems to me we might need more presence than just these here guys from Spain. We have a few people covering the places from their side, a one way in and out alley, a busy looking street, and we don't be knowing if it be a set-up or not," John Lee said.

"Those are all valid points, that's what I want to talk to the Sarge and Mallory about. I don't want to separate our people and leave the farm unprotected." Jilkes looked at John Lee, then at Mike and exclaimed, "Damn, I'm good! How about this, let's have everyone leave the farm, be near the target area, out of sight, but in range to help our people. Even have them provide distractions at every turn. We have plenty of vans, we get Franco and his group some hot wheels that are, hopefully, driven by Jong's people. We get our women involved, I mean they're all pregnant, but they're still mobile and hostile when need be. But more important, we make sure we can account for all our people. It might make sense for us to drive to Maryland after the job and fly to Virginia. I'm just thinking out loud, but I know if we are to do this job, we need everyone possible in an active role."

Mike's phone buzzed, and he answered it. One of his people living in the streets indicated that three guys walked into the front of the house at 905 and came out of the back of 907 with two exceptionally large suitcases. He yelled, "Guys, my people on the ground said that three suits went in through the front of 905 and came out of the back of 907 with two large suitcases. If I were a betting man, I would bet the action is in those two houses and not 903. I believe that was the subject's main residence when he was with his wife."

Jilkes said, "That limits our attack, but doesn't change my issue about splitting our resources. Did I hear someone say that, if necessary, we could breach the back of 901, the house on the corner?"

"You did hear that. That gives you three potential exits, the front of the properties, the one-way-in and one-way-out alley and breaching the property on the corner—901. Now, that clears the path for multiple breaches as well. We can breach the corner property, commandeer the alley, and storm the front. No matter how you look at it, we're going to need more people than the Spaniards. No offense intended, just saying the odds are against us with just you guys. Jilkes, you have those four, plus me. If you add in Larry, that's seven. We need six to breach and six to cover the retreat," Mike said.

"Listen, we don't need the money, but you guys do. I want you to think carefully about what you're about to do and be damn sure you will see this thing through, one way or the other. We can't start this thing and retreat at the first sign of trouble. Franco, did you say, one of your people is rather good at doing make-up?"

"He would be Mario. He's an excellent make-up artist."

John Lee asked, "Who are you thinking about being made up, you and me?"

Jilkes laughed and replied, I was considering making you look like Obama. I was not thinking of you, but I was going to take command of the event in person."

"Well, hell, Stupido, that ain't going to work. You can't go and do this without me protecting your dumb black ass. If you be wanting to debate this issue, then we be wasting a lot of time. We be needing two more, Gladstone and Whitmore. I think we'll also be needing Brown and Bernstein to prepare for the breach on the corner property, if all else fails. I think Walter must know by now that we be knowing about his stash and that we're coming for it. I don't be thinking he didn't get smart from them there other breaches of his stash houses."

Mike said, "I think everyone should be disguised. Can you do teeth, eyes and noses with your disguises and what do you need to make this happen?"

Mario began to speak in broken English. Franco told him to be precise and he would translate from Spanish to English. It appeared that his props were simple, untraceable, and readily available.

# # #

Later that evening, Jilkes and John Lee met with the Sarge and Mallory and presented their plan. The two men listened, took notes, and did not interrupt Jilkes and John Lee. At the end of the presentation, Mallory said, "You guys know we really don't need this heat, but some of our associates could use a score like this to get some of our people out of the sewers and into training programs. Who else are you going to use from our main group?"

John Lee stumbled in and said, "We be needing Brown, Bernstein, Gladstone, and Whitmore, along with the two of us."

The Sarge grunted, "That ain't going to happen."

Jilkes looked at him straight on and said, "I need you to sanction this mission, Sarge. John Lee needs you to sanction this mission. You are our leader for life, but you gave us this assignment. We don't want to be some backroom generals—we want immediate on the ground command of those who are committing to this event."

The Sarge looked at him and quickly realized that he should not inject any kind of vituperative responses to his two main men. He said, "I responded without thinking. Of course, you will want to be there, but I have just one question for you. What is the impact of you dividing our forces?"

"Sarge, we neglected to state that the farmhouse would be closed down because everyone would be near the target area, and that way we all have eyes on each other at all times." The Sarge looked at both men, then at Mallory, walked square to Jilkes, and gave him a man-size hug.

The Sarge then said, "This mission belongs to you two, my friends. Do your best knowing we'll have your backs at all times. Just tell us where you want us to be and it's operational. I'm once again, forever, and always, proud of you two dysfunctional individuals. We love you so much!"

As Mallory and the Sarge walked away, Mallory said, "Their proposal is full of holes. Why didn't you address your concerns?"

"Dude, that's called initiative. They're trying to help us not be so consumed with the very existence of our group. Listen, you and Monica want to adopt a child. Courtney wants me home more often and to take a nap every damn day. These are things we both can live with. We will be near, and we will have enough people there to stop a small army. We have got to start letting these guys command individual functions or we're going to lose them. I'm particularly worried about

Brown and Bernstein. You may not have noticed, but they're missing from a lot of our functions."

"I've noticed, and I even spoke to Monica about it. People might be getting homesick. I don't have a clue, but it's time we had a meeting with just our people."

"Now, that's easier said than done. We have been completely democratic and transparent in our approach with this group. I don't know if we call a meeting amongst ourselves, it will look suspicious."

"Sarge, call the meeting. No excuses take command of the outfit, or for an eternity, be saddened by the fact you made no attempt to sustain it. This is important. Plus, you're correct. Monica and I want to adopt some children, go to the damn zoo, watch baseball games. Dude, if ever you had one of those way-out speeches to give, the time is now."

The Sarge looked at Mallory and said, "This can't wait until tomorrow. This should happen, tonight. I'll leave you with the logistics, time, and the where."

# # #

That evening, a weary Sarge stood before his original group of men and said, "I must thank you from the bottom of my heart. You people are the best in the world when it comes to friendship, love, loyalty, and respect. You people came to my aide a while back and have been by my side ever since. We fought together in Viet Nam, a few of us fought together in Philadelphia, and now all of us have been fighting around the world for ourselves and what we believe in.

"My son, a person that I did not know existed, became the 'idiot spy'. I had not met him or heard about him in this world, until his mother invited me to one of my favorite restaurants and told me about the legend of Zanthius De Lombardo. People tried to kill her, me, and my wife, in that place. I stopped along the road, near Temple University where I saw a relic, a pay phone, and I called our 1-800 number. You came to my aide, we kicked some serious ass, and added another three to four hundred souls that are awaiting our arrival in hell. I love you and I owe you.

"Now, since that event the attempts to assassinate me and mine have increased exponentially. In the interim, we have made a shit load of money from there being a lack of people to receive payment. We have cash everywhere. We have funded youth programs, re-entry programs, purchased resorts, restaurants, and other things with some of that money. We have always done good and have attempted to help people help themselves. My wife, a doctor, who is sworn to save lives, has ended lives. Along the way, some of you have met your soulmates. I know you don't believe in that hocus pocus shit that I do, but each time it was right, it was sanctioned by one of my elders. I know you don't believe this, but in Australia, when Yvette was being accosted, I demanded that everyone hold tight and let her soulmate free her from her curse. Who stepped out of the vehicle and rescued her and has cared for her without requesting any carnal favors? It was Mr. Bernstein.

"In a bar in Hong Kong, three of you were manipulated by three beauties of Asian descent, who just happened to be spies. I knew they would all marry you people and have babies. Mr. Amazing looked at someone who was providing us with meals and fell in love. I knew he would marry her and that she too would be pregnant within a few months. I know, once again, me and my hocus pocus.

"I'll say this, when you people were in Australia, you know damn well the things you saw and felt were not your normal sights, thoughts, and/or feelings. I am Ben Beckmire, and my family is from Australia. I was appointed the unofficial leader of this group. However, I'm concluding my leadership because I believe you people need to find your own havens and love your families. I want to complete the mission on K Street tomorrow and then disband the group."

Mallory stood up and said, "Wait a minute. If your cousin is out there, we're all vulnerable to his vengeance. You might have forgotten, he's the same son-of-a-bitch that strapped suicide vests on your grandbabies. I don't think we're at a point where we can independently go our merry ways as if we have had no part in the conclusion of over 500 of his men and women."

Brown stood up and said, "What the hell is going on? Last, I heard, we were about to do a deal in the city and that we are all looking at land near John Lee's. Did I sleep through a coup or something?"

"Yeah, was I on the same drug?" Bernstein yelled.

Whitmore said, "Hold up, everyone. What the hell is going on? Are you saying, my leader, that you don't need us anymore and we don't need you either? That seems to be a pipe dream. I must ask a question. How many of you have pressing demands on your time back home, wherever, the hell, that may be? Don't be shy. Do you have something else to do with your life and your time? Do you have children back home asking, 'Where's my daddy'? Damn, not a single hand in the air. If we separate, we're as good as dead. If your cousin will place suicide vests on his own nephews and nieces, what the hell, do you think he will do with all the pregnant women and babies, including your grandchildren? Are you smoking some new shit or something? What is the deal with you? And Mallory, are you smoking the same shit?"

The Sarge started to reply when Chakes aggressively said, "Hold up. Am I being told we're no longer essential? Did we resolve the Carbon Factor problem and kill your fricken cousin? Did I sleep through this entire episode? If not, then I think the threat is real, still looking for us to disband, and go our merry way. It won't be merry because your cousin is a sick human being. He will isolate us and torture each one of us until he has the chance to skin you alive, Sarge. You need to rethink this proposition. If we separate, we will be annihilated. This is not the time for some bad dreams. This is the time to rethink and regroup our resources to prepare for the final confrontation."

Jilkes stood up and everyone knew not to make light or disrupt him. He asked, "What is happening in your life, Sarge, that you have decided on this course? I surely hope it's not the fact that John Lee and I were assigned this breaching function. Is it? You know I respect you and would stand in front of you in a firing squad. What on earth just happened?"

"Damn it, I just realized I have had you people captive for over two years, and I have not once asked about what you had going on before you abandoned it and came to my rescue. Not once have I asked."

Chakes yelled, "That's because we all know that you're a selfish bastard, plus that previous statement is not at all true."

The Sarge looked at him and broke into tears. Chakes said, "Oh my God! Sarge, you can't take a joke? What's going on guys? Now I'm serious. What the hell is happening Sarge? I apologize for being disrespectful, but it felt good. In all the years we have been associated, I have never said a word against you, your decisions, the battle plans, or the missions. You say jump and I ask to what planet. However, it did feel cathartic to yell at you instead of you yelling at me. I love you man and I too would stand before you in a firing squad."

The Sarge regained his composure and said, "What would I do without you, assholes? You continue to be the best there is at what we do no matter the curse of aging. What would I do without you? I'll tell you what I would do, I would go out there in the real world and get my feelings hurt without you guys. My sinister cousin would eat me alive without you. He would find me, cause injury to everything that matters to me, and that includes this band of misfits.

"I asked a question, and it was a hypothetical. It wasn't rooted in fact, just a scenario. I may have carried the ball beyond the end zone, but my intent was to get your real feelings about me and Mallory. I guess we both know them now. And Mr. Jilkes, I'm not concerned about you trying to steal my job. It would take a constitutional amendment for that to happen, buddy, so forget that idea. Also, I haven't been smoking anything, but I noticed that some of you are missing at events that we all should be attending."

Brown raised his hand and was recognized. He said, "Sarge, my wife is having a helluva time with this thing called pregnancy. She literally wants to hang me for impregnating her."

Bernstein said, "And, those sentiments go for your niece, as well. She's having a hard time with this waking up here and the next day you're on a different continent. I'm just trying to keep the peace in my dominion and be available for all missions you assign me. I'm sure Brown is feeling the same way. Perhaps, if you ask your overburdened bride to assist us in socializing our pregnant wives, it will allow us to be more visible, if you know what I mean. My lady looks in the mirror and cries her heart out. I need help and I'm officially asking for it."

The Sarge asked, "Jilkes, are you and John Lee experiencing these kinds of issues?"

Jilkes said, "Well, in my case, I have learned two new words—they are 'yes dear' to everything. I don't disagree, I just say, 'yes dear'. It certainly has helped me to socialize my bride. She loves me to rub her stomach and be near. Are you guys just hanging around like useless stuffed toys, or are you massaging their toes, rubbing their fat ass bellies, and telling them you want more children? It is time to step up your game. Ask big country what he's doing these days."

John Lee responded, "I be a little embarrassed to admit this, but I comb and brush my lady's hair each morning, and she just loves it. And I told her that we can't eat in the room, that we should share her beauty with the world and, therefore, I expect her to be out and about. Jilkes told me to say dumb shit like that, but it works. Maybe we should have a pregnant ladies brunch or something not too bright like that?"

The Sarge asked, "John Lee, how much land do you and Jilkes have down there in your neighborhood?"

"Last I checked, we have thousands of acres, plus I think we put in a bid on the land across the road which was another ten or so thousand acres of land."

"Oh my, I didn't know you had that much land. You have enough to see that each member of our group could have five hundred acres of land, if they wanted."

"That's exactly why we purchased the other parcels because we know that you people don't know how to plan ahead. Ain't that right my African American friend?"

"Why do you insist on calling him other than by his name?" the Sarge asked.

"Is it offensive or something? He don't seem to mind, and we been doing this thing for a long time. That don't mean I don't love him and him don't love me," John Lee retorted.

The Sarge said, "Since there have not been any constitutional amendments to replace me, then I assume I have control of this group of assholes for the next 100 years. Anyway, I need you guys to do whatever it takes to have your women be more visible and willing to pull the trigger.

"Chakes, you're absolutely, correct. If we separate, he'll track us down individually and do the nasty to each one of us including any children present. I say, we vacate the farmhouse tomorrow, be near where he may have some cash stashed, and wipe him out. This will bring him out, make him desperately determined to find, and destroy us. On another note, I don't trust anyone in the current government to turn over the final aspect of the Carbon Factor formula to. We need to have a conversation with Mike."

Whitmore asked, "Where is Mike? I thought we were going to include everyone in all future meetings."

"This meeting was for the ten plus two, exclusively. This was our bonding and purgation meeting. Whitmore, can you fetch him?"

John Lee asked Jilkes, "What that word mean, purgation?"

"It means to get shit off your chest or to vent," Jilkes stated.

#

Ten minutes later, Mike walked into the room and asked, "What's up guys? Did I do something inappropriate?"

The Sarge bellowed, "We don't know. Did you? Anyway, what's the latest on the Carbon Factor formula? We certainly don't want to turn it over to that senator, she has become tainted goods because of some of her associations. What I'm thinking is that we try to find a way, or a person in the former administration to present our information and documents to. I want to bleed my cousin dry tomorrow and rid ourselves of the Carbon Factor issue. Mr. Amazing, you've been extremely quiet during these discussions. Is there something troubling you?"

"I no have any problems other than the fact that my bride is being difficult as well. I no like rubbing bellies and combing hair. That is what girls do with dolls."

"I'm sorry, I was referring to the Carbon Factor formula. You have the final piece from Helga. Have you been able to discern anything from the disk?"

"I no scientist and I no understand any of this mess. I do understand the final piece rests with your son, the 'idiot spy', and he's yet to have any epiphanies concerning it. He's burdened with the same issue that many of us face except he has the by-product of intercourse. He no has time to figure out the hidden meaning of his mistress's formula. I don't know where to start suggesting."

The Sarge said, "I will have a conversation with him later tonight. Mike, what's your assessment of the project for tomorrow?"

"Sarge, I am breaching the places with Franco's group, and I hope the information is solid. Otherwise, I hope I have an old insurance policy that's still active."

The Sarge looked at him and said, "Now, that's an interesting thought. Mallory, have we taken policies out on our group, and if not, who can we call to make this happen in the next few days? I know it's not like we need the funds, but it would be great to take advantage of a system that usually takes advantage of us."

"I will consult with Monica tonight and figure out a process that will make this happen ASAP."

Mike said, "I hate to state this, but it has been rumored that the Russians are looking for the 'idiot spy' because they know he's the key to the Carbon Factor formula. Sarge, they have a $10 million bounty on his capture. Upon delivery of a full and proven package, another $10 million will be presented."

"The Russians don't have $20 million in cash in their entire country. Their president certainly has, but not the Russian people. This is a ruse to enlist other hungry and greedy people to join the task force and root out our 'idiot spy'. I ain't going to let this happen. And Jilkes, I'm glad you're running the show tomorrow, and you were smart enough to insist we all leave the farm rather than be half secured. I know Rashida, and Juan, and their toys are like having twenty additional personnel, but those are systems, we need humans to cover our backs. Any other information for the good of the order?"

Brown said, "Sarge, it doesn't matter if the Russians have the money or not. They're not going to honor their commitment, but it certainly puts more eyes on the ground looking for us as well as the 'idiot spy'."

"I don't disagree. I'm just saying they have bigger problems over there than the Carbon Factor."

Mike said, "If I can add one more comment that is floating around the streets and in the sewer systems, and that is the discounted senator has engaged a group of mercs through her liaison/lover to complete the mission on us. She believes you people gave false information about her connection to a departed senator whose land is now under title to one of your foundations. I don't know where this came from, but it's rumored she wants our heads, and I do mean 'our'."

# # #

After the meeting, Jilkes, John Lee, and Mike met with Franco and his group and gave them some of the pitfalls to the operation. He indicated that being caught with a loaded weapon in Washington, DC, was a major crime. He asked if they preferred tasers. Franco indicated to him that shooting bolts at a person firing a real gun ain't what they're used to. Franco told the group that they preferred two live weapons and two tasers. Jilkes asked Mike if his people in the street would be able to bury and destroy the weapons if things got crazy. Mike indicated that his people were trustworthy and were former soldiers, who even though they were down on their luck, would provide cover for the group.

John Lee reflected on that notion and inquired about the funds that had been set aside to begin the training programs. It was relayed to him that Allen oversaw that scenario and never got the opportunity to develop it since people were hunting the two of them. Mike indicated the funds were tucked away in one of Allen's accounts and allegedly was opened in his name as well, but he didn't know what institution he had used.

Jilkes indicated they were drifting away from the purpose of the meeting. He asserted that the time of the breach would be midday and the entire group would be in the neighborhood to lend support along with Jong's cousin and his people. He asked John Lee to remind him to make sure the plane in Miami was ready to leave once they dropped their passengers off. He then concluded the meeting, stressed that the group should get some rest after dinner, and he would see them at breakfast at 0800 hours.

Okema and Yvette along with Brown and Bernstein strolled in the kitchen and asked if they could lend assistance. Asiram said, "Where the heck have you two been hiding? Have you been playing that 'Mirror, Mirror on the Wall', shit? I know you have because I did, and I literally wanted to kill Zanthius after seeing my figure go from a size three to a size twelve. Until this mess is over, all we have is each other."

Okema said, "Asiram, I know we have never really talked, but I am so happy that it's you welcoming us back. For a while, we felt like outsiders and I guess it is because we wanted to keep what was happening to us, to ourselves. You just break things down to the penny. Thanks, and where are the babies?"

"They're in the basement with their dad. I was just warming up some milk."

Yvette asked, "You don't breast feed the boys?"

"Oh, honey, I do, but I naturally only had one. They both, in one sitting, could suck you dry. I try to make their diets one-third synthetic formula and two-thirds breast milk. I have been pumping a lot, but I can't keep up with those two beasts. They're as voracious as their dad is in some things. Listen, everyone knew you guys were missing a lot of activities and decided to let you have your space. It was only a matter of days before we intruded. As a matter of fact, Courtney and Ava were going to come knocking tomorrow, just so you know. Don't think for a minute, you ladies were not missed."

Okema asked, "Would it be alright if we came downstairs with you and watch what goes on?"

"Oh, absolutely, and by the way, Courtney and Ava are going to give parenting classes later during the week, depending on how well tomorrow goes."

Yvette said, "Oh, my God! I was going to ask her for help. I still consider myself a baby, and here I am having one. I'm scared to death. I mean sometimes it moves and I don't have a clue as to what's going on. I need to ask someone some questions, so I can do this thing right."

"Girl, once they pop out, everything becomes easy. You'll know exactly what to do and when to do it. It's the greatest thing that has ever happened to me."

The women headed to the basement where they found a basketball game on the television, Zanthius had a child in each arm, and they were all sound asleep. Asiram adamantly whispered.

"In a case like this, I don't dare wake them. I let them sleep, and when they go down, I try to get a nap as well. Now, that's an important lesson, otherwise you'll be up 24/7 and then you become the wicked witch from the East."

# # #

Franco pulled Mario aside and asked, "What are your thoughts about tomorrow? We've never done anything like this before."

"Boss, I'm concerned, but I also have faith in the Yanks that they'll have our backs. I think we'll be okay as long as we don't get creative and do something stupid."

"Those are my sentiments as well. I hope this goes smoothly so we can get back home and begin a legitimate enterprise and be partners. I mean if this thing pays off, why go it alone, blow our money on cars and women? Why not pool our money and make more money by doing what the Yanks are going to do with the resort and restaurant? We need to think ahead of the game and keep this thing quiet. I don't want any sudden fortunes raising eyebrows and inviting others into our new world. Make sure you speak to Giuseppe and Michele and tell them to not give any word back home about what we're doing and where we are."

Sometimes important things are considered after the fact and that is exactly what happened with Michele and his rabid tongue. He promised his girlfriend, who is also his cousin's lover, a massive wedding, and a huge diamond ring.

## CHAPTER TEN

At 0600 hours, 12 men who were so in tune with each other met on the porch without anyone planning it. At 0605 hours, Larry walked out of the main farmhouse door, trailed by a yawning Zanthius, and an obviously sleepy Mike. Larry asked, "Did you guys plan this gathering, and if so, why didn't you include us?"

The Sarge said, "On my honor, we did not. We've been together so long—we clairvoyantly communicate with each other."

Zanthius said, "Yeah, yeah, sounds like a bunch of crap to me."

The Sarge said, "The real crap is, how on earth did you heavy sleepers rise this early?"

"Don't know where you've been Pops, but we do this all the time. Let's go guys, so that we don't get in the way of their walk."

Mallory asked, "You remember when we could do that with no problem?"

"Yes sir, I do and that was a long time ago. Did you happen to see the bulges in their jackets?"

"I did, and I hope some of us are that smart. How about you, my leader? Do you have a weapon?"

The Sarge turned to his people and said, "If you don't have a weapon, go and secure one with an extra clip."

# # #

At 0930 hours, the farmhouse was placed on maximum lockdown and the security was high. Weapons were armed and ready for remote firing and all cameras were in play. Juan said to Rashida, "Honey, we should consider starting a security company once this adventure ends. We could earn some serious money developing security functions based upon the notions of gaming. We could expand our potential for income, diversify, and add other venues to the portfolio, thus ensuring our continued contribution to the group."

Rashida looked at Juan and said, "Really? Dude, he's my dad and she's, my mom. Really?"

Juan's head dropped as if he were rejected but Rashida was quick to notice that she had deflated her man's ego. She grabbed his hand and said, "Baby, if that's what you want to pursue, then LaGina and I are with you, and will support you with our own funds, if the group doesn't like the idea. However, as I said, he's my dad and I know how to get him to help me. That's a great idea and we have all the components. You know who would be key to your concept, if we can get him, is Jong's cousin. He knows this shit inside and out."

"You know what? You're right, he placed those machine pistols all over the place, the cameras, the detection systems, and the long guns. He would be an asset if we could get him," Juan reiterated.

"Honey, you need to put a paper together so that I, sorry, so that we can discuss this concept with my dad and Jong's cousin. It's not like we don't have the experience. This group has fought battles all over the world and will probably have a few more to deal with.   This is a great idea and let's plan a presentation to my dad," Rashida suggested.

# # #

At 1030 hours, Franco, Michele, and Giuseppe had completed their make-up session with Mario. Mario decided to wear an Obama mask in tribute to who he considered was one of the greatest presidents and humanitarians of all times. At 1100 hours, a disguised Mike, walked from Sherwood Playground at 9th & G Street, to 9th and I Street and entered the alleyway between 9th and 10th on I street. There he stumbled in the alley singing, *What the World Needs Now*.   He was carrying a bottle of wine. He saw two cameras facing the entry to the alley and two facing the exit. He spoke through his wrist piece to Jilkes and said, "Cameras are in play." As he started to retreat, a voice from the side of a garage asked, "Do you like my handy work? We took them from the block behind here and installed them for this ploy. Do you feel like sharing your bottle with a few men who are down on their luck?"

Mike asked, "Which house has the play?"

The person sitting in the alley said, "All three have cases. You might need to back three vans up in here to capture the goods. In exactly one hour, they're going to trade people. Don't kill them, they're with us and will need an immediate extraction once this deal is done. Can you do that?"

"What do you mean by extraction? Why the hell didn't you broach this before I got my ass up in this alley?"

"Because I knew you wouldn't be able to say no. These guys need to disappear for a different reason. Do I have your word?"

Mike said, "Let me check with the architect."

Jilkes listening to the chatter asked, "Do they have any forms of ID including a passport?"

Mike asked, "Do those people have passports?"

The guy laying between the garages said, "In their back pockets, and they each have $45 dollars to help pay for transit." Mike snickered and said, "Let me check with my man."

The Sarge was listening to the transmissions and said to Jilkes, "You're the architect. Your call, but it's time to do the work."

"Are Jong's cousin's people in place?" Jilkes inquired.

"They're sitting on the corner with the engines running. Call the play architect."

Jilkes hesitated and whispered to John Lee, "What do you think Big Country?"

"I live and will die with you. Call the play."

Jilkes said to Mike, "If we extract them from this place, there will be a world-wide search for them."

The guy in the alley said, "In the sewers, we have some sophisticated listening devices. We had to 'clean people' who murdered for property in one of our sewers. They match the color and the size of the people who will be transitioning in ten minutes. You grab the cases, we'll transfer the dead, and one of you will shoot the dead people in the face."

The Sarge broke protocol and said, "Mike, this guy seems as if he's been playing you all along. Ask him exactly what the hell he wants, and I know that he can hear me."

After a brief pause, a voice stated, "I want you to get those two men out of this corrupt situation, and I want you to finalize the program that Allen had promised us. I'm lost in hell, but I have a lot of good soldiers down here who could benefit from some of this money. Start the programs, build shelters, restore our dignity and belief in this country, and get us out of these sewers and alleys."

There was a silence on the line and the Sarge said, "You seem to have your hands in a lot of things. Do you know who we are?"

"Allen once told me about a group of dudes who took on a mob up north, fought a war that wasn't called a war but was nicked-named a 'Police Action'. I hear them people who they were fighting against over there put huge bounties on their heads. I also hear you people have done a lot for people like me and Mike. I hear a lot and I see a lot. I also know about that burden you're carrying on your back called the Carbon Factor. The sewers are a plethora of modern-day news. You should come down here and live awhile."

"Architect, this man knows who we are and knows what we are capable of doing. I, for one, trust him. I do want to start the process of getting our people out of the sewers, into homes, programs, and schools. As such, I will dedicate a portion of what is extracted from these premises to the notion of supporting our people as well as finding the funds entrusted with Allen. By the way, to the person listening in on our secure channel, you wouldn't happen to know what bank Allen deposited our initial investment towards that goal, would you?"

"As a matter of fact, I have a suspicion about what institution he visited and endowed with a deposit. If I'm not mistaken, it's on Florida Avenue and the architect should know where it is and the 'idiot spy' should know the account number access code. Just saying."

"We have got to meet one day soon. You seem to have a wealth of information and knowledge. Why not consider working for us?"

"Thank you for the offer, I think. It's a thing I will consider for the future but, for now, I must start getting my people out of the sewers. If we have an agreement, then I will signal the two people you're going to extract to play the part. Hit them hard, but don't hurt them. You have approximately twenty-six minutes to extract and clear the area without incident. The clock starts as soon as all three rear doors open."

Jilkes asked, "How about if we extract them through a single door?"

"That's brilliant, architect. In that case, you have thirty-seven minutes before the alarm sounds from an open door and I mean, precisely, thirty-seven minutes before a small army will arrive."

Mike said, "People, we have ten minutes to decide this mission."

John Lee looked at Jilkes and said, "You be the smartest person I know. I trust you and no matter what happens, I be behind you, and I got your back."

Jilkes smiled at him and said, "Mike, it's a go. I will call the mark in eight minutes."

There was a lull on the line then Jilkes came back on and said, "On my mark." At the 1:55 minute mark, he said, "We will execute in 5—4—3—2—1—mark."

Like clockwork, a security guard entered the house from the rear, and one came in from the front of the house at the same time. Jilkes said to Franco, "It's time to show your faces." Mario and Franco surprised the man in the rear, and Giuseppe and Michele attacked the guard in the front. The hidden figure positioned between the garages had his people bring the bodies of their two dead comrades out of a garage. Hoods were placed over their heads.

In less than a minute, eight people entered the buildings and began to remove, and stack black cases and fortified trash bags under the rear porch of 907. Two vans pulled into the alleyway and backed up towards the little breeze way. The vans were filled to the brim.

Jilkes told the Sarge that he needed more vans and the Sarge told him he would get back to him. The Sarge turned to Jong and said, "I need your cousin to take the truck up the alley and finish the loading."

Jong called his cousin and told him to head into the alley once both vans had cleared out and be ready to bail if necessary. Jilkes told the Sarge that so far everything was going okay but he wanted to leave with what they had and not take a chance of hidden or unknown alarm systems. Mike appeared from under the porch at 907 and said to Jilkes, "The clock is ticking. What's your call?"

"A truck should be entering the alleyway in less than a minute. There must be 12 additional cases in the front part of 903."

Mike said, "Let's get them all."

Jilkes responded, "Let's get what we can safely get away with and forget the rest. My concern is for our safety and those two guards who are trying to break free. Your man said we had 37 minutes. I want to be out of here in 27 minutes. Remember, you have to shoot those two corpses in the face with shotgun blasts."

"I'm on it, and I have a muzzle and blanket to place over their faces to stifle the sound and minimize the blood splatter.

I will gather the blankets and place them in a bag to be burned."

Jilkes yelled, "In 3 minutes people, we're going to breach that wall on 901 and that truck is going to be heading out of the alleyway with or without you. Don't be late."

Jilkes heard the double muffled sounds of the shotgun and said, "That's it people, we're out of here. Mike made his way down the alley and asked his informant do you want me to drop a case off or set up an account?"

"I can't handle a case. Do what you said you were going to do, and I'll be grateful. I'll need that MAC card soon because I'm running out of grease money. Catch you later."

Mike walked out of the alley and entered a van that was being driven by Carla who said, "Wow, my heart is beating like a drum. I was so worried about you."

Mike said, "Please drive slowly. You can tell me how much you love me once we get past North Capitol Street."

On K Street, SUVs began to appear and guys in suits and dark glasses exited them and approached each site with weapons in hand. The people entering the first site, 903, gave a thumb's up indicating that cases were still intact. The report for 905 and 907 lacked enthusiasm because the houses were fleeced of all contents. Unfortunately, for the person hiding the small fortune and tracking devices, the cases in 903 were touched but not extracted. The cases from 905 and 907 were clear and untraceable. Fortuitous for the group, since time and cargo space were their issues, the contents of 903 were left behind.

The van carrying Franco and his group, along with the two new passengers, arrived at the underpass at 2nd and K Streets Northeast. Franco and his crew were transferred to a clean vehicle and watched as the one they rode in was engulfed in flames. Jong's cousin's son took the six passengers directly to the airport in Maryland for their journey to Miami and eventually, across the waters to Spain.

The Sarge called Franco, told him to introduce himself to his new passengers, and to get acquainted with them because he was going to hire those guys for their projects in Spain.

Franco said to the Sarge, "I will not talk to anyone until I'm on your plane heading to Miami and have transferred on a plane for Valencia. I have to say, the execution of this job was absolutely, incredible! Your men, Jilkes and John Lee, without hesitation, indicated that enough of the stash had been secured and that it was time to go. They didn't blink an eye at the six or eight cases in the first house. I learned a lot today about execution and commitment. I, as well as my people, are thankful that you considered us professional enough to assist in pulling this caper off, even though we had never attempted anything on this level."

The Sarge said, "*Mi amigo*, I'm so happy I didn't kill you. You never had a chance to kill me, but I'm glad I didn't do you and your men. Franco, I would like you to operate with one philosophy or mission—that is 'to help people help themselves'. If you follow that principle, you will be a part of this group for as long as you live. Never take from the poor, never hurt the innocent, and always give away all the money in your pocket at Christmas time to a homeless person, no matter how much. I learned that from my friends Bongiavanni and Wallace. Call me when you get to the airport, and you're on the runway. My pilots have some cards for you guys, and I hope no one took any cash from the cases. We will have an approximate count by the time you land in Spain, will convert it, and send you the percentages as agreed. That's not to be confused with the funds for the resort and the restaurant constructions. Those funds should already be there. The new money, my friend, will be yours, your crews, and your two new employees. Set them up in a local hotel. Take care of their needs, give them cash, but not thousands of dollars to walk around with. I need you to put the fear of God in them to make sure they don't do stupid, like one of your guy's did. Mike will get me details on their skill sets, but I always want them looked after. I don't know those guys. Therefore, I need you and yours to provide them with phones that are tapped, and I need you to tap their rooms until I can get clearance on them. Is that a problem, *mi amigo*?"

"*Mi amigo*, I can dispense with my guy who broke protocol. I can leave him in a locker in Miami if you think he has compromised the operation. You have invested a lot in us, and I don't want to screw up this relationship. I will box his ass if you feel he is a weak link."

"When you put the fear of God in the two new guys, pull your man in and draw blood from him. Nothing serious, but a scar that will forever remind him of his treacherous deed and his compromising a multi-million-dollar chance in a lifetime event, for all of us. Need I be specific in the type of injury I want you to inflict? Do you think that you can handle this issue for me?"

"*Mi amigo*, I can leave a life-long visible indication of how he endangered this operation. I don't want to, but I will because he has made us vulnerable. I shall mark his left cheek and take away that arrogant look of his being such a machismo. I will let the world know there are others who possess what he lacks by the cut across his cheek."

"I don't want hideous. I want a reminder and a message for the new people until I find out who they are and their worth. You tell them if we have to come there as a result of them doing stupid—then they're already dead. Your man, until further notice, is not to be privy to our future conversations, and his cut in this caper is reduced to 50% and it will be handled by Sister Mary Marisa. He starts this new relationship, from ground zero! If he has a problem with this edict, then I will request that you handle this matter. If this is too personal for you, I will have my associates from Northern Africa, do the work."

# # #

The vans with the cases, stopped in the tunnel south of 4th and New York Avenue. Jong's cousin got out of the lead vehicle, raised the hood, and examined each case in all three vehicles with a scanner. None of the cases in the vehicles seemed to be bugged. Jong's cousin wasn't 100% sure if the technology he was using, was current in detecting any new devices that were being used by Walter. He placed a three-way routing signal in each van which assured him that tracking would be virtually impossible. He got back into the lead vehicle and headed to the farm.

Approximately thirty-five minutes later, he pulled into the parking lot of a strip mall in Virginia. Jong's cousin once again got out of vehicle and proceeded to each vehicle with strange looking apparatuses. He spent a total of 3 to 7 minutes in each van and then okayed them to proceed to the farm. Prior to his workers heading to the farm, he placed three additional devices in each vehicle that would distort any GPS devices hidden in the cases.

The vehicles were then driven to the ex-senator's house. The money in the cases were systematically substituted with the money in the closet. This was due to the idea that cleansing all the money on the premises was not a good idea. Jong weighed each case and told his cousin if there was the slightest change in variances, he would unleash his group on him and his family.

#

Hours later, at his cousin's place, the money was literally washed, dried, and packaged by his family members. In a single day, an additional $135 million was being added to the asset column of the group's books. That did not include the floor to ceiling amounts that were in the ex-senator's property. If all things were equal, in terms of height, width, and girth, there was at least another $135 million in cash, or $270 million sitting in two hidden closets and in three vans. When Jong's cousin reported the gross weights of the cases before and after cleaning, he said to his cousin, "You have another $135 million in those closets. I can't move this with the same group. I can use crooks to launder it, but I know you people don't do crooks."

Jong said, "We'll place real security around it. I need you to go the ex-senator's property tonight with explosives and rig the place to blow to bits if compromised."

His cousin responded, "I cannot go to the farm tonight."

Jong said, "Unless you've stolen a shit load of our money, then you will be there in precisely two hours. If not, I will ring the alarm that my family has betrayed me. You know how we roll."

"I will be there in the next hour or so with account numbers and temporary passwords that you must change within the next 48 hours. I am your family, but you are not mine. Your cost is too high for me."

"Cousin, I know that you have stolen $1.9 million from us on top of what we've paid you. Don't screw with me. I will be called to task if someone else does the bookkeeping. You understand, you are technologically smart, but a stupid ass thief?"

Jong's cousin lowered his head and murmured, "It was $1.4 million that I placed in a trust with your name and Mr. Beckmire's. Check your Industrial Bank account, cousin. I thought I could steal it, but I couldn't sleep at night, after realizing all that you have done for our families. It's in your name and Beckmire's. You have made me and my people rich. You also send my children to school and pay for protection for those back-home who want my head in a dirty bag. I am your servant, and I am loyal to you, my senior cousin. I will not defile our relationship. I make this vow on my children's lives."

"This I accept and agree to—on your children's lives. If you need anything and any amount, please confront me so that I can argue your case. We do not like treacherous people. We destroy them!" Jong exclaimed.

# # #

On one of the group's planes, Franco, his group, and two strangers, were being blasted into the air. Once the seat belt sign was turned off, Franco called Jilkes to report they were off to Miami.

In the meantime, Jilkes and Mike had spoken about the two new people who were looking for a new life. Mike told him that Lester and Leek had worked for him and Allen and were trying to find a way out of the watchmen's role. They had been loyal to Walter and had committed other crimes for him. He used the details of their crimes to keep them locked in his cellar. It had also been rumored they had entered a case or two and helped themselves to a substantial amount of money. The two men knew that you didn't steal from Walter because he would kill all who knew you and those, he thought, knew you. The timing was perfect for them to do the dash. Both men had served in the desert, and when they returned, their families had been destroyed. Their wives, played outside the rules of their vows.

Jilkes reiterated to Franco what the Sarge had said, "Put the fear of death in them. Also make certain to mark the one who had to have phone sex and gave away their plans to his girlfriend, who has many other boyfriends."

Jilkes told Franco to enjoy the plane ride and to not roll into Miami intoxicated. He suggested they relish the ride and the drinks, but to stay sharp until they were on that plane back to Valencia. He thanked them and told him that it looked as if each man on the plane, except the garrulous one, would earn $2 million, including the two new guys. Jilkes also told him that the money that was in the other property would net his guys another $1.5 to $2 million as well. Franco said, "Mr. Jilkes, I hope this is not some cruel joke you're playing on me."

"Franco, in the next few days, once we have account numbers and passwords developed, you will receive a call from your bank indicating your wire transfers are completed and what amounts are available. Also, an account will be established for you guys at the Monastery that will be managed by the real Sister Mary Marisa. We're doing this for your own sake and safety. We know what we're doing, and our commitment is as solid as our word; $2 million now and up to another $2 million in a few days. By the way, those debit/credit cards are worth a quarter of a million dollars as well. Follow the rules, my friend, and you'll be greatly rewarded. We look forward to hearing about the resort and restaurant in the next few days. That should be your focus. I know you guys are smarter than most, but it's necessary for me to advise you to not draw attention to yourselves by going ballistic and buying expensive toys. Take my word, you'll draw international attention that you don't want in your back yard. Nice and easy does it every time. Have a safe flight and break the news to your guys over a bottle of that special champagne in the refrigerator. Later!"

# # #

Hours later, Franco introduced himself to the two new guys and welcomed them on the journey. He, in turn, asked his people to introduce themselves as well. He said, "Michele, there is a price to pay for talking out of turn and potentially exposing the entire operation. The Yanks wanted me to assure them I would put a bullet in the back of your head."

Michele attempted to say something but was immediately cut off by Franco. Franco then said, "I pleaded with them because we had already lost a member of our group, and Mr. X stated, 'loyalty is not up for negotiation, will you take care of the problem'. I told him you are a good man but loved a woman who is not faithful. He indicated to me that you were to be marked so that you will remember you do not talk about business with people who are not involved in the business. In other words, I will give you a scar on your cheek or you can simply disappear and forfeit your earnings. I will give you until the plane lands to decide what you want to do."

Franco reached into the refrigerator, pulled out an expensive bottle of champagne, and said, "On another note, Mr. X indicated to me that every man, except one, on this plane, including you two new guys, would receive $2 million for the work in DC. My guys will receive another $1 million or so, for another job that was done for the group, except for the talkative one."

Mario interrupted him and said, "Franco, this kind of thing should not be played with. Is this fact or fiction and do you make a joke?"

"On all that is dear to me, I swear. Mr. X indicated those are the temporary numbers because a full count had not been completed."

Giuseppe asked, "Franco, please don't play. Is that what the Yank said?"

"Giuseppe, Mario, and Michele, I swear that is what the Yank promised each one of us, in addition to the cards that you got."

Mario asked, "What cards? You didn't give us any cards."

Franco hesitated and looked inside of his pouch and saw the cards and said, "*Dios mio*." Each man's name was crudely written on the envelope with the debit/credit cards inside with a temporary password. Franco said, "This was an oversight on my part. I did not open the package when the little Asian fellow gave it to me. I set it aside and attempted to blend in."

Giuseppe said, "Where is your card?"

Franco reached into the bag and said, "It's here. I know this does not look good, but I must admit to you, I was preoccupied by the scope of business that the Yanks do. It slipped my mind."

Mario said, "From what I know of the Yanks, there is no way Franco could have planned this one. It's a mistake because they gave him a deal he couldn't refuse. I'm going to discount this matter and forget about it because we have made more money in the past two weeks than we have made in our lifetime. I'm glad we didn't try to take those fellows on at the restaurant. It would have been disastrous for us."

Franco retrieved six champagne glasses and poured a generous amount into each glass. He said "Before we salute, I must give you the words of the Yanks as well. Mr. X said to me, "do not go ballistic and buy unaffordable toys. In essence he was saying, once the construction on the two places begin, we should be able to ease into some purchases that will have a legitimate backing with an aggressive earning potential. By the way, Sister Mary Marisa will have a portion of our funds in the auxiliary bank of the church. In other words, what we do has to benefit the monasteries and support those children.

The Yanks didn't say that, but I'll bet you $10 dollars that's going to be the impact.

"Now, the Yanks also had words for our two newest employees. Until they have a complete profile on you, you will go and do as we say. You, will not wander, elicit women, or buy foolish toys. Your money will be controlled by me, everything that you think you need, you will fill out a paper listing those items, and we will make sure you are accommodated. When it comes to companionship, we will take you into areas where there are wholesome Catholic women who are not like the person our comrade, Michele, has lost his mind over. He may have to annihilate her in the long run." He looked at Michele and asked, "Is that a problem?"

Leek looked at Lowery and Lowery said, "Listen, Walter accused us of stealing his money. We don't have a hundred bucks between us. You don't live when he has suspicions. We don't speak the language and, therefore, we'll be wherever you want us to be. Just remember, we don't do laundry."

Franco didn't get the joke, but Michele announced, "They're not our flunkies."

Franco frowned, approached the guy who made the comment, and announced, "You will do whatever I ask, including my fucking laundry, or you will not live to see the money you have earned."

There was a stillness in the plane when Franco said, "It is not I who will provide you with your last meal, but those who planned that last job. The Yanks will bury us all if one of us fucks this up. They are not the kind of people I would try to second guess."

"Franco proceeded to shake each man's hand and said, "Enough of talking about doing stupid. Agreed?

"On our plane ride to Spain, we should talk about pooling at least half of our funds, starting a construction company, and even a pay day loan program. We lend people money on their paychecks and they pay us a small fee. We then, as a function of them borrowing against their paychecks, require them to attend a 'money sense' program where we teach them the pitfalls of borrowing against paychecks and show them the value of smart money transactions and budgeting. If we can convince the Yanks what value this holds for them, then I'm sure they will invest in it as well, but it will be through the monasteries, I assure you. Now, if I'm not mistaken, you two must do good here because they bailed you out of a deadly situation. How about we ask the pilot to patch us through to them once we're on our way to Spain and hear it from their mouths?"

Michele said, "I feel that I betrayed you. You have been the only person trying to help us and keep us fed. What did you mean that the woman I love is not faithful?"

Franco shook his head, looked at Michele, and then stared aimlessly out of the window. He softly reentered the conversation by saying, "Your woman, is the woman to many others, my friend. Your woman once asked me to be her lover because you didn't have the resources to keep her and support her. I treasured our friendship, and prized your loyalty, more than her sex and beauty. I could not tell you because at times, the signs were right in your face," Franco stated.

Michele said, "I want to develop a partnership with you guys, and I will have my left cheek marked, which will tell people a lot about who I am. I'm willing to assume that, only hoping you will have me as a member of the group."

Franco looked at Giueseppe and Mario and said, "I'm no longer the boss and we each have a vote in everything we do going forward. I might have the largest brain, but all matters require a consensus. First, is that agreed upon?"

Mario and Giuseppe looked at each other and agreed. Mario said, "I think we need a director or president, and we need vice-presidents. Now, I will agree on that when we speak to our partners, we will show them we have developed a structure and an organization. Franco, I believe they will only listen to you, no matter the structure we put in place."

Franco said, "The question remains on the floor, do we terminate Michele or scar him with the tell-tell sign of the rat?" Each man voted to scar him for life.

## CHAPTER ELEVEN

Walter walked into the Senate Office Building at 1100 hours and went directly to the lady senator's office. Her aide told him she was in chambers, but he walked passed her and told her to sit down or suffer a stroke. He buzzed his way into her office and began to take pictures of the Colonel giving pleasure to her. She yelled, "What part of privacy don't you understand?"

"Don't trifle with me. And you, wipe your mouth and get the hell out of here."

Once Walter was alone in the senator's office, he said, "Somebody stole close to $150 million dollars from me and killed two of my men."

The senator looked at him and asked, "Who the hell did you steal it from and how much more do you have hidden away?"

"That's not the issue. The question is, who would have the audacity to break into my home, kill my people, and take away $150 million in broad day light?"

"Ah, Duh! How about your cousin, who so desperately wants your head on a pogo stick, you, crazy son-of-a-bitch?" Walter sprung at her, grabbed her by the throat and said, "Your next outbreak will be your last one. I will float a disk showing payoffs, your ménage trois, agreements for the termination of individuals, your shooting up and smoking crack cocaine, you fucking junkie. One more contrary word and I'll place the Colonel's head coming up from under your stinky derriere in that collection. Try me Senator. Now, why, and how would he know about those locations? Did you receive the final pieces to the Carbon Factor formula from him?"

"Absolutely not, but there are Russian agents all over the country looking for the 'idiot spy'. They want him bad. It appears your girl, or someone's girl, who was supposed to be dead, came back to life, is alive, and just had a baby," the Senator announced.

"What the hell are you talking about?"

"Helga Spengatsenburg is alive, allegedly had a baby by the 'idiot spy', or someone, and is now on the run again with the only copy of the final phase of the Carbon Factor formula. Oh, and you want to kill all of them before we can obtain the product? How smart is that Mein Fuhrer?"

The next sound to be heard was Walter's hand slapping the face of the senator. He said, "Your next disrespectful remark will leave you battered and dead bitch. Don't fuck with me. I own and control you, slut."

Outside of the office, everyone was in a panic because they knew not to interfere when Walter was in her office. The Colonel said, "I need to check on the senator."

One of Walter's men said, "That would be a mistake to enter a secure conversation. I'm sure she's okay, after all, she is a senator, right?"

Meanwhile in the senator's office, Walter asked, "Where is the bitch, and do you want me to secure her so I can finish that business with my cousin?"

"Unless you want to join the ranks of the CIA, FBI, NSA, HLS, and the military, then I suggest you do your own thing and remember that there are eyes and ears everywhere. You think you own me, but I'm about to gain my freedom from you because you've made a bad mistake."

"What mistake might that be, Senator?"

"You messed with the wrong old-head, and he happens to be related to you. Did you know he has contracts out on you to find out where you are? Not to engage you, but to know where you are? Oh, and he's financing it with your money, by the way."

Walter walked over to the senator and asked, "You want your daddy to beat you?"

"My daddy hasn't punished me in almost a year. I have to settle for colonels. I need to be spanked, Daddy. I need to be bruised. I need you to abuse me to show me who I belong to, Daddy."

"Do you go down on that fat fucking guy?"

"Don't be retarded. I only go down on you and the rest go down on me. I love you Daddy, and I've been bad. I need a spanking. Please Daddy, tell me when and where and I'll be there." Walter kissed her tenderly and walked towards the door. He turned and said, "If not tonight, then tomorrow. Will you be available?"

"I'll be there at a moment's notice. Love you, Daddy."

## CHAPTER TWELVE

The Sarge said to Jilkes and John Lee, "That was a pretty smooth operation, young boys. Smooth as silk, and you knew when to get the hell out of there and you didn't let that greed factor jump your bones. I'm proud of you, we're all proud of you. That means a lot to me and to Mallory because we're getting old, and the group is getting younger with our new additions. We need to develop some committees for each aspect of our operation. I know we have had that discussion before, but I really would like for us to pursue a division of responsibilities with the entire group. What say you?"

"We like things the way they are and will not concur with your committee notion," Jilkes stated.

"I need your help. We need assistance to relate to all the damn issues. In case you've forgotten, we have money everywhere and it needs to be accounted for. I need help, guys. The group needs help," the Sarge amplified.

"Sarge, this is a perfect time to engage our original smugglers," Jilkes said.

John Lee asked, "What you be talking about?"

"I'm talking about Bernstein and Brown. Who knows the ins and outs of money better than those two?"

"Oh, wow, you're right. Plus, they're having relationship problems with their pregnant wives. How is it that you two aren't having any issues?" the Sarge inquired.

John Lee said, "We be rubbing bellies, massaging toes, fixing snacks, and saying only two words, 'Yes, dear'."

"Damn smart men, I must admit. Say the right thing and everything goes your way. Did you tell your brothers to try that?"

"We did, but it takes time, or people will think it's contrived," Jilkes stated.

"Okay, I'm going to approach Brown, Jong, and Bernstein to be on the financial committee, but you two are still up for a committee. I hope you like it."

John Lee looked at Jilkes and said, "I leave you in charge one time and you make it difficult for us. Why do I trust your judgement?"

"Because you love me. Just admit it, and you'll be okay," Jilkes said.

# # #

As the plane began its descent into Miami, the two new guys had shared a lot of information about themselves. Leek and Lowery pretty much told the crew who they were and why they had to disappear once again, but this time without fear of being kidnapped or hijacked. Everyone agreed to consider pooling a portion of their funds and magnifying their impact on whatever business they decided to indulge in. Franco said, "We need to rest and get ready for customs. Does anyone have any contraband?"

# # #

As the men deplaned, they each thanked the pilots and wished them well. They entered customs to begin the next leg of their journey and were questioned because of their lack of bags and boxes. Franco answered his inquisitor by saying, "We did work in the states for a monastery in Valencia and we're going home to complete the destruction and re-construction of a huge resort and a perfect restaurant. As you can see, we entered your country on this date and we're leaving today, if you don't have a problem with us."

The customs official said, "Just so that I'll know if I ever decide to visit your country, what is the name of the monastery?"

Franco said, "While in Valencia, you must visit the Route of the Five Monasteries, and if you ask for Sister Mary Marisa you will be given a special tour, plus you will learn of the many things of goodness that me and my friends do around the world."

The customs official looked at him and thought, 'they have nothing, they got off a private plane and they're getting on another. Where is the crime? He looked at the men who didn't appear to have anything to declare other than themselves and raised his hands in the air. The passports were stamped, and they were allowed to enter their private jet for their ride to Valencia, Spain.

Once on the plane, several agents entered the plane with dogs, and the group remained calm and respectful. The custom officials casually looked around and knew that the plane had been sitting in the hangar with the engines plugged and was safety checked by technicians earlier in the day.

Franco asked, "Might I ask what you're looking for, perhaps if it's here, I can direct you to it. I assure you; we came with little and we're leaving with little."

The customs official walked into the cockpit and said, "If you people are ready to leave, then I'm clearing the plane for take-off. Have a safe flight and hopefully, we'll see each other again."

As the plane was towed from the hangar, the captain said, "I think we're on our way. Please stow all luggage and fasten your seatbelts. We're number four for takeoff."

#

The Sarge said to Jong, "I assume your cousin has washed most of that money. Why not have him bring the empty cases to the farm. That way, we can put that money in the safe in the basement in them. What are your thoughts?"

"I think that's a good idea. I will call him now and tell him to bring those empty cases. We have so much, cash. We need to involve Brown and Bernstein and get their thoughts," Jong suggested.

"I know. I'm trying to relax for the remainder of the day and find some time to spend with my bride," the Sarge stated.

"Why do you call her your bride? She's your wife," Jong reminded the Sarge.

"I guess because I love her as much today as I did when I first met and married her. She is more of a bride to me. A wife, after time, gets a little lazy and comfortable. A bride, is always trying to please her man."

"Now, I understand. I shall strive to make Mary Alice my bride as opposed to her being my wife."

"Jong don't go and do anything stupid.   This is a developing process, not one that happens overnight."

# # #

Later, Jong's cousin showed up with his guys and the cases and had them unload the money. The Sarge told Jong to wire the place, but to not attach any explosives. Jong was about to ask the Sarge why when the light bulb went on in his head. He told his cousin to lead the wires to a field down near the barn and they would attach a new kind of explosive that they had discovered. His cousin said to him, "I cannot handle this much money so soon. Word will spread, and people will begin to suspect me."

"How secure is your place?"

"Only a fool would attempt to break into it. I have the same auto-weapons system that you have, except I have refined mine."

"Why haven't you upgraded the system here?"

"I'm working on that and the fifty-five other projects you have asked me to do plus wash money, launder it, invest it, and collect checks and money orders. Am I on your payroll and, if so, dear cousin, where are you sending my paycheck? I no receive one yet."

"I'm still trying to figure out a way to tell my boss that you stole $1.9 million from us."

"It was $1.4 million, and it is in the Industrial Bank of Washington with you and Mr. Beckmire, as co-signers."

"Oh, that's great. You set up an account in my name and the Sarge's name and make us look like we're stealing the fucking money? Is that what you want the rest of the group to think, you tree swinging piece of dung?"

His cousin fell to his knees and said, "I have made two mistakes, my lord. I tried to steal from you and my conscience would not let me sleep. I tried to give it back and I made it look as if you and Mr. Sarge were stealing from the group. I swear to you once again, there will not be a third mistake. I will extract the $1.4 million and send it to your group."

"No, you will do nothing unless you are directed by me or the Sarge. You have such a thriving business and I want you to develop strategies where we can legitimately get rid of some of the cash we have on hand."

"I can do that easily if you give me five to ten days to arrange some things. I will develop a plan and present it to you."

"No, you will not present it to me because I don't want to know what you're doing with our money. Be something different for a change. Try to be smart."

#

Later that night, the group could hear the loud sounds of dogs barking and weapons being fired. Juan and Rashida entered the control room and saw that on the adjacent property, two young drunk men were playing a boom box and shooting possums. Rashida captured them with a high intensity beam and printed the words on the lenses—'Leave these woods now or remain in them forever'. The sounds decreased and the movement on the other property diminished until there were no foreign sounds.

# # #

In DC, during the middle of the night, Walter had his crew remove the remaining cases from 903, along with the two bodies. He told his people to take the bodies to a poor neighborhood and drop them on the side of the road and to wear gloves and torch the damn vehicle.

Unbeknownst to anyone other than John Lee and Jilkes, the two randomly placed tracking devices in three of the cases left in 903. When the two men saw Jong and the Sarge, Jilkes said, "We tried to narrow the playing field. We placed three tracking devices in the cases. We thought you should know that. We're not sure how this stuff works, so we thought we would ask Jong's cousin to figure it out for us."

The Sarge replied, "He has to do penance. I prefer you give it to Juan and Rashida, if they have questions, they can speak to his cousin while he is here. Are you good with that, Mr. Amazing?"

Jong gave the Sarge a thumbs up. The Sarge then paused for a moment and adamantly stated, "And, by the way, you two shouldn't mess with things that you don't know nothing about. Those cases could have exploded upon being opened. I need you guys to stick with the approved plans, and not modify them without pure knowledge of what it is you're doing or may be encountering."

Jilkes looked at John Lee and then at the Sarge and said, "You're absolutely correct boss and that is why you're the boss—you think beyond a simple task."

Jong after witnessing the Sarge kick his favorite people's ass, said, "I like the fact that we keep all our business within our immediate group. My cousin is faced with massive temptations. He made a mistake, stole money, tried to give it back, but it makes me and the Sarge look like cheap thieves. Him dumb ass makes it look like the Sarge and me stole $1.4 million. A measly $1.4 million in total. How many places do we have with that amount in cash? Him dumb ass is in atonement for an exceptionally long while."

The Sarge said, "I haven't spent any time with my daughter lately and this might be the perfect time to interface with her and Juan. I'm not completely sure about him yet."

John Lee said, "Oh, he be solid. He be in love with that daughter of yours. I almost want him to give me lessons. He's smooth like my African American friend."

As the guys entered the command center, Juan was gently rubbing Rashida's ever-expanding breasts, while he kissed the back of her neck. Unaware they had company, Rashida said, "I love it and it gives me pleasure when you suck my toes."

The Sarge banged on the door and said, "Are we interrupting anything?" The embarrassment was all over their faces, Juan said, "Sarge, I was attempting to alleviate some of the stress my wife is having being pregnant. Was there a particular matter on your mind?"

The Sarge said, "Well, first I want to see my daughter, and now that I've seen what good *hands*, she's in, I'll see her another day, and perhaps she and I can take a walk or a ride in the mule and visit with each other. Secondly, my two un-astute friends placed tracking devices in some of the cases they left behind on K Street. We were wondering between the foot kissing, neck rubbing, and stress reduction functions, if you two can figure out how to work these things and track them?"

Juan said, "Your daughter is the best and, between us, I'm sure we can deduce how these ancient tracking devices work. Perhaps you want to see it on the big screen?"

"Hey Juan, do I read a sense of sarcasm in your response?" the Sarge asked.

"Actually, I was attempting to confirm my love for your daughter, my wife, while you were here to let her know that I'm her husband, you approve of me, and sanction this marriage."

John Lee said, "Damn, he be done nailed that. Okay, you be letting us know how to work this soon?"

Rashida said, "I'll show you how to track them right now." The Sarge looked at Juan and stated, "Confirm your love. I like that. Good man."

After showing them the rudiments of how the tracking devices operated, Rashida took Jilkes, Jong, and John Lee's phones and placed an alert on them that would give a signal if the cases in question were moved.

Juan asked the Sarge if he could just have a single minute of his time and the Sarge agreed. As they walked away from Rashida's hearing range, Juan said, "I intended no disrespect to you, Sir. Your daughter, my wife, thinks we should hide our emotions from you. I have attempted to tell her we should celebrate our love. It's not poison, it's righteous."

The Sarge grabbed him and gave him a man-size hug and whispered, "If that was your purpose, you certainly accomplished it and with flying colors."

## CHAPTER THIRTEEN

Mallory was drinking in the family room alone and appeared to be well lit. As the Sarge walked through the main house with Jong trailing, he saw Mallory and said to Jong, "I need to address this one by myself. See you in the morning." He walked over to Mallory and asked, "You think you can afford to buy me a drink?"

Mallory stumbled through his stimulant depreciating vocabulary and found the words, "I ain't got no money."

The Sarge gleefully responded, "That's okay. Most of the booze here is free, anyway, to veterans. I bet you $20 dollars I know why you're here drinking yourself into stupid."

"Sarge, you don't know shit."

"Okay, Corporal. I will have people ready to perform back-up in the morning when Monica convinces you to follow up on the number the fake Sister Mary Marisa gave you. I will call Jilkes, John Lee, Whitmore, Chakes, and Larry to escort and keep an eye open on the horizon. Is that sufficient, or do you need more?"

"I need a wife that understands that I'm too old to be a father."

The Sarge jumped up from his sitting position, grabbed Mallory and hoisted him into the air. He said, "That adage will kill us all. You need to talk to your wife without whiskey in your system. I'll see you first thing in the morning."

The Sarge started to walk away when Mallory said, "I think I want out of my marriage. She is pushing me beyond my limits. I don't really want a baby. I just want tranquility and my wife."

The Sarge said, "Then why the hell did you put her through all of those fertility stints and shots? Why didn't you stop it then? You're a coward. You deceived her, and me, asshole. Go to sleep. The Mallory I'm looking at, disgusts me. Good night, asshole."

Jilkes and John Lee saw the interaction and decided to step in once the Sarge was out of sight. John Lee said, "Well, he can't go home like this. She be done cut his thing off and he won't even know it. Call Whitmore and Gladstone, maybe they can stow his ass away until he sobers up."

# # #

Mallory spent the night on the floor between Whitmore and Gladstone's beds. He snored the entire night. At 0730 hours, he woke up and yelled, "Honey, hurry up in the shower so I can get dressed." Whitmore and Gladstone sat up in their beds and looked at a bewildered and hungover Mallory.

Gladstone said, "Mallory, use our bathroom and take your time. We don't know what your issue is, but it seems like you have an appointment somewhere this morning. Is that right?"

Mallory stumbled through his words and finally said, "My wife wants to adopt a child. I personally don't want to, but I did make her a promise."

Whitmore said, "Congratulations, you lucky bastard. I wish I had a little Whitmore running behind me all day and calling me daddy. You're one lucky SOB. Congrats to you and the misses for taking the initiative. That's some heavy shit."

Gladstone said, "Yeah, right dude. That's where I would like to be one day instead of waking up to his ugly mug each morning."

At 0830 hours, Mallory, Jilkes, John Lee, Larry, and Chakes waited patiently for Monica to come downstairs and enter the van. When she stepped on the last rung, she spoke to the guys and told Mallory she would deal with him later. Larry was familiar with the weapons system in the vehicle and sat in the seat that controlled the guns. Monica asked him what he was doing, and he told her about the special aspects of the van they were in. She indicated to Larry that she would like to see a demonstration and had the perfect person to be the target. The look she gave Mallory was devastating.

When they reached the Catholic Charities offices, Monica got out of the car and waited for Mallory. He asked Jilkes if he was coming in and Jilkes told him he had to handle this on his own.

Inside the office, they met with a nun who was polite and straightforward. She asked them probing questions about their relationship, religion, age, mental and emotional health, as well as their finances. The nun was brutally honest about all aspects of the adoption process and that this would be the most challenging adventure they would ever embark on. She explained that many homes had been destroyed and relationships ended because both parties weren't really thrilled about the decision. She went on to tell Mallory and Monica that their age was a strong concern for her, but if they proved to her, that they were deserving and good people, she would overlook that. She asked them if they were interested in a male or female child, and Monica told her they were interested in one of each. Mallory looked at her but dared not open his mouth because he knew his mind was in turmoil. The nun asked, "Mr. Mallory, are you always this quiet and obedient?"

Mallory knew he had better say the most flattering words he had ever uttered out of his mouth. He chose to say, "We're so interested in this process and wanted to consummate it in Valencia, but we were encouraged by Sister Mary Marisa to visit your place in America, and perhaps escape some of the international issues incurred when adopting children from another country. My wife and I, and I do mean me when I say I, are so desperate to offer our homes to children. We would like to start the process as soon as possible. How do we go about meeting the children, spending time with them beforehand and ultimately, making our homes available to them?"

"Mr. Mallory, you keep speaking of homes. How many do you and Mrs. Mallory have?"

"We are currently breaking ground in a small community in the South, we are part owners of a resort in St. Thomas, a farm in Virginia, and a few other places. We have a lot to offer children, emotionally and financially, and my wife would be the best parent any child could ever wish for. She is a wonderful human being and I love her more than life. We have an extended family comprised of some of the greatest human beings on earth. I mean people who fought with me in the war, people who helped rid an entire city of drug dealers. My wife, as you know, is a lawyer, and a successful one at that. She manages our foundations and other interests and is perhaps the smartest woman I know and have ever met. Let me be very honest about this proposition, at first, and until recently, I was totally against this idea. My wife is a stubborn woman, and I respect her and love her. I'm only going to say this one time; we are extremely rich, smart, and centered with a group of wonderful friends and have a total support system including airplanes, farms, ranches, resorts, and international associations."

The nun said, "I know you have lots of money based upon my call from Valencia. My question is, do you have the commitment to provide parenting to a child that I release in your custody? In other words, forgive me for using language from the basement, what you say is the same bullshit I hear often. I need commitment and love. Our kids don't need connections and fancy things."

Mallory looked at the nun and said, "Touché! I have told my wife that I'm too old to be a father. She told me that if that's the case, then I'm too old to be married and have sex. I'm desperate for the touch of my wife who is the love of my life. I need your help in securing a relationship and I assure you that my wife and I have the ability to raise children as our own. We are not trying to buy our way into this process and will not do so. What we will do is make sure if there is ever a problem in your homes, you will be able to call on us."

Monica with tears streaming down her face, jumped up and said, "In front of God, I promise you the best relationship if you allow us to have a child."

Mallory looked at his wife and kissed her lips and said, "Forgive me and my stupor of last night. I'm on board. I am dedicated to making you and me parents." He kissed her lips and shouted, "This is the greatest moment of our lives."

The nun looked at the couple and surprisingly asked, "What is the status of the baby that was picked up and brought to the United States from Valencia?"

Mallory, suddenly began to put the pieces together and thought to himself, 'This is Helga. This is the 'idiot spy's' woman. He knew he had been compromised and that he had placed Monica in harm's way.

The nun said, "There are eyes from heaven all around us. I need you to walk with me, my son, for a moment."

Mallory started to say something, and the nun stated, "This is my show. You will be silent until I have exhausted my questions. I will be direct, and your input secures your Monica's life.

Later and away from where Monica was sitting, the nun said, "Is my son being cared for with the utmost of love? Is Asiram being a mother, or trying to figure out ways to discard my child?"

"Okay, stop the charade. How did you know we would be here?"

"Your wife is interested in being a mother, and you my friend, are secretly interested in being a father. The problem you have is that you just ripped off a stash from Beckmire's cousin that I was going to seize. We have a real fricken problem."

"No, we don't. Listen, we collected a significant amount of money on another junket. Tell me what you need and promise not to hurt my wife and perhaps we can make a deal."

"I had plans to hit 903 at 7 pm," Helga announced.

"If that was your plan, then you would have been caught and killed. The contents of 903 are still there and were wired to the maximum. They had tracking devices in the cases which were imbedded in the money. You just would have blown your ability to disappear and do whatever it is you do."

Mallory continued, "You're either dead or alive. You can't be both. My people will kill you if you say you're alive and so will Walter's. We'll drop the dime that it was you who hit his stash houses and then you will have double the trouble facing you. Also, you have another problem in that you have deceived my wife about adopting children, and for that, I will gut you like my man did Scottie. Leave us alone and find your own capers. Come near us again and you will officially be dead. Look at the dots on you, we never travel alone. You either disappear or we'll also let the Russians know that eyes were placed on you and that you were trying to sell the final piece of the Carbon Factor formula to us. Listen, you stole a million dollars from us in Spain. It's time that you found a new hustle because this one is closing in on you. As I mentioned, the Russians and various US agencies are looking for you. In addition, a certain senator that has her own hit team is looking for you and for us. I can mark you so they can easily find you."

"How much will you pay for the final piece of the Carbon Factor formula?"

"You have it all wrong. We don't want the pieces that we have. That mess is toxic and deadly. The 'idiot spy' just happened onto you, literally and figuratively, you helped him, and he helped you. You need to treat that one as a wash. Insofar as Walter is concerned, he will skin you alive because he has lost a lot of money, and he can sell it to one of those secret agencies. The senator already knows you're alive and a viper running for your life. She and her people will definitely increase the search now that you have the audacity to skip to the lou, like a nun."

"I have a proposition for you," Helga stated.

"I don't want to hear it. I'm here with my wife to begin an adoption process and you scandalously have tricked us again and threatened to hurt my woman."

"Wait, I have that under control. You will be granted permission to adopt as many as two children initially. If you enjoy parenting, then you will be able to adopt more. I can snap my fingers and make that happen, but I need you and your people to broker the sale of the final piece of the Carbon Factor formula. I will give you 20% of the sale, but it must be done mostly in cash and the rest in wire transfers."

Mallory paused for a moment and thought about the complexity of the situation they were in with all the funds found in the ex-senator's place. His wheels began to spin. He said to Helga, "Let me bring two of my people into the conversation. I know our leader, just yesterday, had a conversation with the sitting senator, but let me bring them over."

Mallory raised his left hand and rubbed his ear twice and Jilkes turned the perimeter over to Chakes and Larry. Jilkes and John Lee approached Mallory and the nun, with their hands on their weapons and their eyes scanning every possible weak point. Mallory said, "I thought you weren't coming in."

"We decided to sit in the lobby and watch you sweat."

Mallory said, "Gentlemen, I would like to introduce you to Helga, the 'idiot spy's lover and the mother of baby Zanthius." Helga looked at Mallory and asked, "Did they name my baby, Zanthius?"

Mallory responded, "That's his name and he's not your baby." Helga's eyes began to tear up. She wiped her tears away, and then said, "I need to be on the move. Ask your two comrades about my proposition."

Mallory took a few minutes to summarize privately with Jilkes and John Lee what he had discussed with Helga. He told them this could be a business arrangement, especially since they had a mountain of cash that was troubling management. Jilkes said, "So, in essence, we negotiate a price and pay her from the stash we have. We then collect ours from the senator through wire-transfers, thus officially laundering our funds."

"That is as simple as it can be. Do you think we should have the Sarge, and the others buy in, or just make a tentative deal subject to the approval of our board of directors?"

Both men agreed that the Sarge should be involved, and while they were walking back where Helga was standing, John Lee asked, "So, there ain't going to be no baby?"

Mallory exclaimed, "Oh, hell yeah, there's going to be a child or I'm going to kill a nun!"

Once back in the main office, Helga signed two forms, gave a copy of them to Monica and said, "These forms indicate you're suitable candidates as potential parents. It also gives you access to information about each child and any details that we might have even though the records are sealed. I'm doing this because of the ruse I used to track and follow you guys while eyeing my final exit strategy."

Monica asked, "What does that mean? The notion of ruse and final exit? Who are you?"

Mallory looked at Monica and said, "This is baby Zanthius's biological mother, Helga." Monica looked at her as if she were the devil's daughter.

Mallory asked, "How can you sign these forms? You're no nun."

Helga stated emphatically, "Mr. Mallory, I am a nun and I'm head of the east coast order of the Catholic Charities. This is no stunt and the signature I used is the one that is recognized by this church. I need to speak to you and your people while my people talk things over with your wife about when she would like to start the process. Through you, I want to present a number to the senator. I want $65 million for the final piece of the Carbon Factor formula. I want half in cash and half sent to accounts around the world. That's my proposition and a one-time offer. My next offer will be to the Chinese or the Russians."

# # #

Back at the farm, hours later, Mallory and the group went over the chance, but perhaps rewarding meeting with Helga. The Sarge was ecstatic over what he was hearing because it meant he was finally able to see the light at the end of the tunnel in relationship to the Carbon Factor formula. He immediately placed a call to the senator's cell phone. When she answered, she said, "Sergeant Beckmire, so nice to hear from you. I hope you have something special for me."

The Sarge replied, "A rogue agent contacted us and is offering the final piece, plus the entire original documents for the Carbon Factor formula. We indicated to the agent we did not want to be involved in any aspect of this cursed issue. She countered by signifying that she did not trust our government, so if we didn't broker the deal then the Chinese or the Russians would have the plans by this time tomorrow."

"Why are people always in a hurry to do business with foreign entities, and not trust their own government? Did this rogue agent have a number in mind for the final piece of the puzzle?" the Senator asked.

"Indeed, she does. She wants the small sum of $100 million."

The senator sighed and said, "Prior to paying sums that large, we need a full evaluation of the contents of the final piece."

The Sarge said, "I wouldn't expect anything less. However, you should have all the money in place prior to the evaluation. The agent is interested in a 50/50 payout between cash and wire-transfers. Those funds are to be placed in accounts associated with our businesses. The 50% in cash will be delivered to a to-be- arranged place in Virginia. These, according to the note that I have in my hand, are the conditions. Any failure to deliver nullifies the terms and the full item goes on sale on the international market at the minimum bid of $500 million. The agent is attempting to be patriotic. And, on a personal note, you could have saved yourselves a shit load of money had you been up front with us. I told you what we gave you was all we had. You insisted we had the total puzzle. Anyway, Senator, you have until midnight to agree to the terms because at 0100 hours, you'll be able to watch the bidding war begin on YouTube or whatever venue people hold open auctions on."

"Sergeant Beckmire, what's your take on this deal?"

"Senator, there are two monkeys on our backs. The first one is the Carbon Factor formula. The second one is my cousin. We want to live freely. Until those two things are put to bed, we keep plenty of guns, bombs, and contracts on people in high places, including where they live and work. I will await, or not await, your call before midnight. Goodbye."

When Beckmire hung up the phone, Mallory said, "You are one slick son-of-a-bitch. You damn near doubled our take for just facilitating a meeting and the delivery. You are a snake, Mr. Ben Beckmire."

John Lee said, "I don't have a clue about what just happened. Did you sell the Carbon Factor formula that you don't have, and did you just raise the price by some huge amount from what that woman be asking for? If you done did all that, then you know this here be why you be the leader of this raggedy army."

Jilkes chimed in and said, "That was a smooth hustle. And then you end it with, 'according to the note' you have in your hand. Where the hell did that come from? I was about to scream when you went in that direction."

The Sarge said, "Guys, they have been screwing us ever since this mess began. They sent people to kill us, placed suicide vests on our babies, burnt down our homes, and kept hiring people to kill us. Don't you think we need to charge them an excise fee or something?"

John Lee said, "What that be? Excise fee."

Jilkes said, "That be the tax or fee associated with specific goods or services that only privileged people can indulge in, I think."

Mallory said, "Sarge, we need to have a conversation with Asiram and Zanthius."

The Sarge said, "I'm not going to go further into this conversation without their knowledge. So, whatever you have to say to them, it will be the first time I will be hearing it as well."

#

Fifteen minutes later, Zanthius and Asiram walked down from their suite in the sky, smiling. She saw her father-in-law and said, "Your wife and Zanthius's mother are helpful with the kids. The babies are a handful, but I think me, and your son are doing a good job. Why are we here? What's going on?"

Mallory said, "You know that Monica and I went to an adoption agency today. Anyway, the woman that interviewed us turned out to be Helga. She knew everything about us, including you, Zanthius, and the baby. She asked about the baby's name and I told her. She thought she was going to blackmail us because she had planned to breach 903 K Street, as well. I indicated to her that she would have been caught and killed. I informed her the money in those cases was bugged with location devices and explosives. I also indicated to her that we did not breach 903 but the adjoining properties. I guess she was thankful she didn't. I say all of that to say, that she's still alive and wants us to do a massive deal with the senator for the final piece of the Carbon Factor formula. She threatened Monica, and that's when I told her she cannot be both dead and alive. I pointed to her outfit and that's when my friends showed their worth by marking her body with laser dots. In my estimation, she is desperate and has settled on an asking price of $65 million for the final formula. Your dad didn't know any of this, and that's why he's not, as usual, breaching the conversation. This part is new to him. Now, you're probably wondering why this is still relevant to you. You're a part of this ever-expanding family. We have tentatively agreed to broach the deal for her and send her on her merry way. It would have been bad karma to continue with these discussions without you guys knowing who the players involved were. I just thought that the conversation was needed because we're family."

Asiram walked over to Mallory, kissed him tenderly on his cheek, and hugged him passionately. She said, "The fact that you're concerned about us, even though we're not a part of every conversation states volumes to me about the core values of this group. There are no secrets, only transparency. You know I still might want to kill my husband for putting us in this situation. But I love my man, and when that baby was conceived, Zanthius was not my man at the time. Still, I'm proud of him for stepping up to the plate and saying, 'No Beckmire/De Lombardo stays in a monastery'. Thanks for the heads up. Do you expect any craziness from my sister?"

"I do not, but just in case, I'm going to ask the Sarge to make sure the security room is manned 24/7. I think she wants to get paid and then disappear. However, as usual, we watch the backs of each other."

# # #

The senator called the Sarge and asked, "Is gold bullion an acceptable source of payment?"

The Sarge answered, "According to my note, payment is to be made in cash and wire-transfers. If you would like me to reach out and ask that question, I will. However, as I read it, the directive was precise." The senator told him she would get back to him.

Mallory told the Sarge he had to check on Monica. The Sarge asked, "You're going to go and get between all those women talking about children? Are you stupid?"

"Where is she?"

"They're all in the barn, grooming the horses," the Sarge stated.

"I guess I should reconsider, and leave that one alone," Mallory announced.

"Also, I need you near because the senator is trying to bargain between cash and gold bullion. If it, were you, which would you prefer?" Beckmire inquired.

"Hell, who wants to deal with the weight of bullion? Cash is, ah, angelic," Mallory stated.

As the men sat around discussing the various ways to manage the cash, Brown and Bernstein walked in and fixed themselves a drink. Brown asked, "What are you people discussing?"

The Sarge said, "We're trying to figure out how to handle a lot of cash?"

Mallory said, "In four hours, we might solve some of the logistics, but we have to keep thinking about how to handle the rest of it."

Mallory's phone rang, from an unknown number. He looked at it and decided to answer it. It was Helga who said, "The Chinese just heard about the offer and indicated they are interested in purchasing the materials for $200 million. Tell your senator that the price just jumped to $200 million and another 10% for her office leaking the fact that it was presented to her."

Mallory stated exactly what had been told to him. The Sarge replied, "Hell, we might be able to wash all of that mess in the house behind the barn. Seems to me the senator has a significant leak in her place. It's only been three or four hours since this whole thing went down. How can the Chinese be on to it?"

Mallory said, "It doesn't matter if there is a leak because in the next four hours according to Helga, this thing will be decided. Sarge, I have never had direct contact with the senator and don't want to start now. You should make the call and tell her she has a leak in her office. Notify her that the price has jumped too, let's see, if we want to capitalize on this deal, say the price is $250 million. It's not like they don't have it at their disposal, we collected shy of $135 million from K Street. These numbers are staggering and unbelievable."

The Sarge called the senator's cell phone. When she answered it, he said, "You have a leak in your office, and the Chinese have offered $250 million for the product. The agent is asking for that amount since someone in your office has upped the price on her head. A full Russian contingent is now in the states looking for the agent and they want to have the head of the person with the formula on a platter."

There was a deep sigh on the other end of the phone. The senator pronounced, "Tell you what—tell that traitor to kiss my ass." She hung up the phone. The Sarge looked at the phone and said, "She wants me to forward a 'kiss her ass' message to the traitor."

Mallory asked, "Did you get disconnected?"

"No, I told you what happened. I guess we could lower the price but that would illustrate weakness. It would also show we're vacillating, and that the entire notion is a scam. Let's give her five minutes and see if she calls back."

The Sarge went to the cooler, grabbed a Coors's Light, and returned to the room. People stared at him in disbelief. Jilkes finally said, "Hey guys, I'm going to have a beer. Would anyone like one?" They all shouted, "Yes."

The Sarge said, "I'm sorry, guys, but I am trying to figure out what to say when she calls back."

John Lee asked, "How you be knowing she be calling you back?"

"John Lee, my brother, as much chaos and loss of life this thing has caused, would you let the fact of a $100 or more million deter you from what is, alleged, to be a weapon far superior then the nuclear bomb and exponentially less expensive? Oh, hell no, that wench will call me back and propose a deal."

Jilkes walked in and passed out beers and everyone yelled, "Thanks Sarge." He yelled, "Salute, assholes."

The Sarge's phone rang, and he announced, "It's the senator." He answered the phone by saying, "Ma'am this thing is no longer in our hands. I gave your message to the individual and I was told to tell you those are the exact sentiments of the Chinese towards you. I'm no longer in this relationship Senator, and the only person I want to find is my cousin."

"How can you be out of the discussion? It was less than seven minutes ago when we spoke?"

"Senator, when you call people traitors and tell them to kiss your ass, well, it doesn't take a mindless person to realize you're done with the talks."

"Listen, Sergeant Beckmire, I lost my cool and had to make sure we had that kind of money lying around."

"Senator, I don't believe you heard me. I'm no longer in contact with the agent."

"What if I told you that I could gift wrap your cousin and deliver him to you? Would that make you attempt to reach the seller?"

There was a long pause before the Sarge said, "Senator, I'm going to reach out to my contact and see if they've consummated the deal with the Chinese. As I stated, the price is $250 million plus the 10% for the leak in your office."

"Sergeant try to reach your contact and offer them the deal. I'll be waiting to hear from you." She abruptly hung up the phone without saying goodbye, a sign of continued defiance.

The Sarge looked at John Lee and said, "Everyone wants this damn formula. To me it spells the beginning of a new era of weapons development, and I'm not sure I want to be a part of that plan. I wish I knew a chemist or someone who knew what this mess is. How can you take coal, burn it, and capture enough materials to mix with other chemicals and create a milk carton size weapon with powers more destructive than nuclear based weapons? This is crazy, and I wish we could end this chapter of our lives by doing something that limits man's ability to destroy man. And besides, how can senators have private stashes like the one up the road, and this lady's ability to make a $250 million-dollar deal, without blinking an eye? The real question is, what are we leaving to our children and grandchildren by being a part of this mess?"

Jilkes said, "So, Sarge, how do we cancel this deal, make a deal with Helga, indict the senator, catch your cousin, and live happily ever after?"

"That's the $135 million-dollar question. We're acting as Helga's agent. You know what, I need Asiram and Zanthius in on this conversation. John Lee, can you fetch them for me?"

#

In the reconstruction of the house, two rooms were added at the east and west sides of the main house. The Sarge and Courtney occupied one, and Ava and Carlos occupied the other.

After knocking on Asiram and Zanthius's door. Zanthius replied, "It's open." John Lee walked in and said, "The Sarge be needing to see you and the misses. We be in a conversation that requires your input."

"John Lee, can you knock on those other two doors and ask Ava and Courtney if they have a moment to watch the boys?"

Later after acquiring temporary babysitters, Zanthius, Asiram, and John Lee entered the family room. The Sarge began, "We started a conversation and stopped in the middle because it involves an old friend and lover, Helga. She wants to give us the final piece of the Carbon Factor and from what I can tell, she is interested in us being her agent. The numbers being tossed around are staggering; $250 million. Since she is woven into your fabric, we thought you should be a part of this initial conversation regarding the Carbon Factor formula.

"As I see it, it's a poor man's way of participating in mass destruction and murder. China is importing more coal from that clown in the North and he doesn't have a clue. Can you imagine if the nut in the North got his hands on the formula, the destruction that it could cause. Me, well, I'd rather see my grandbabies grow up with the one threat that has been in front of man since it's invention, the nuclear threat. I think we have enough to buy the final piece from Helga with the cash that's in the house up the road. Now, this is just me talking, we buy it and publicly destroy it on camera."

Brown asked, "But Sarge, won't that senator think we had a hand in this matter? If this deal doesn't go through, they will want to talk with you because, after all, you were the one who developed the notion of a rogue agent with the final piece to the puzzle."

"Either way, we're in it. Again, I'm just talking and trying to figure out what's going to happen when Helga and the senator call and ask for details about delivery of the money and the formula. We're in this mess regardless," the Sarge announced.

Asiram said, "Boy, that Helga knows how to leave a footprint. She has already died several times and miraculously, has come back to life. We should try to make it happen one more time and give her remains to the Russians and the world. They might exonerate us on this one, but I highly doubt it. We're in this mess and she keeps us in it because she needs us to get her money and get her out of dodge, thus complicating our notion of denying any involvement. She's cunning, treacherous, and I like her unselfish manner of sharing the culpability. Brilliant, if I must say so. She knows unless they send the US military for us, everyone else becomes subject to annihilation, as proven in the past. We have no way out of this mess. However, I'll tell you one thing—I would rather turn it over to the senator than have her sell it to anyone else."

"Baby Girl, I feel you, but I think the senator is in cahoots with my cousin and together, they might sell it to a third world country. I don't trust her. Where and how can she come up with $250 million dollars? She's a senator, not the Bureau of Engraving. Last I heard, the bureau is the only one that prints money."

"Daddy-in-Law, we are in this mess until the end," Asiram stated.

Zanthius looked at her and said, "Honey, why must the end be on their terms and not ours? I mean, if we're in this thing until the end, then we should dictate when the end is. Listen, we secure the money she needs from the senator and we turn the product over to the Black Caucus or a committee of the Joint Chiefs of Staff, NSA, CIA, FBI, and every other clandestine agency in the country. We hold an outside news conference in the Capitol Rotunda, if necessary, and provide them with the materials. We can't let Helga keep pulling our strings like the master puppeteer she is, and we can't let that crooked senator get control of this kind of heat. We need to think of a way to draw them to a mutual outcome and have the entire government interface at one event—that would be the illusion. The misdirect would be to show the destruction of the product on camera. This is how I think this thing should go down."

The Sarge looked at his watch and said, "I'm expecting a call from Helga within the hour. I think the senator has made up her mind, is on board, and this whole thing will be concluded by 2400 hours."

"Hell, Dad, that's too soon. Any chance of delaying it until tomorrow or the next day? We should try to find righteous individuals within our government in the different agencies. I have an idea. I doubt if the senator can put $250 million dollars in a van and deliver it to us. Is any of the money to be wired?" Zanthius inquired.

"Why, yes, Helga is expecting a payout of 50% cash and 50% wire transfers."

"Excellent, Dad, excellent. Banks are closed on all sides of the water. This is going to take at least another 48 hours to consummate."

Asiram interrupted him and said, "Honey, I have to feed your children. Keep me informed, and I guess we all should begin to carry weapons again. Is that right, Daddy-in-Law?"

"Always stay safe, Baby Girl."

Zanthius said, "What I was about to say is we need to find honest politicians and try to convince them about our position on this issue. We can let the senator wire the money, and once that hits, we begin the misdirection. Guys, that bitch tried to have us killed, and she shouldn't be representing anyone. Furthermore, how can she control $250 million dollars? Is she a rogue agent for another government? I mean, come on now, we have been through a lot of shit, and if it weren't for each other, those guys would have had us coming and going. I don't trust her, never have, and never will. She is a viper."

"Why don't you really express how you feel about her, Son? Anyway, how can we get in front of a camera and have them believe us when the man in the big house calls all news, except his own, 'fake news'?"

"Pops, you're a brilliant man. We will create the illusion by stating that we have the most damning news on the new president, including a data disk, that represents his illegal holdings and proof of his continued manipulation of markets that he's deeply invested in, or something like that. On the other side of the street, we say that the senator and Walter have had an illicit liaison for years, have reaped billions in payoffs, received bribes from pay-to-play, contract surcharges, and providing arms to third world countries who murder for hire. We present the Joint Chiefs, Black Caucus, NSA, FBI, CIA, Senate Arms Committee members, and everyone else we can think of with the Carbon Factor formula and state that a certain senator was in negotiations with a foreign power to buy that very weapon capable of annihilating millions of Americans. We take her out, clean her clock, and hope she commits suicide at the same time. This is a crucifixion—not a court of peers review, or a slap on the wrist. We send her to hell in a dastardly fashion."

John Lee said, "It be apparent you hate that there woman. I hope you love all of us because you, my friend, didn't mix any notions of amnesty in your words."

"Did you with Scottie?" Zanthius retorted. There was a long pause and a, 'oh shit did he say that', kind of a moment'. Zanthius knew that his intent was distorted by his disdain for the senator. He walked over to John Lee and said, "I hope you didn't take that the wrong way. I mean these people will kill us including the children. I just hate the fact they're in control, and we have to resort to violence to make a point and to stay alive."

John Lee reached out and grabbed Zanthius's hand. He pulled Zanthius close and whispered, "I know your spirit and it comes from that man over there. You are family, and you don't have to dress up your words when addressing family."

The Sarge said, "If you two are through trying to mate each other, I would like to return to the notions on the floor. Now, my son, who is full of venom, and rightfully so, after all, if he hadn't kissed a woman and swallowed a capsule, we'd all be back at our respective homes enjoying Facetime with each other. Let's thank my son for kissing and swallowing." The group clapped, roared, and yelled, "King Zanthius—the greatest kisser on earth."

Mallory interrupted the festivities and said, "I like the general direction of his statement. We need to come clean with this thing and bury every living soul who comes at us. My question is simple—what do we do with Helga?"

Everyone looked at Zanthius. He paused before reminding people in a calm voice, "My wife's name is Asiram. I recuse myself from any vote on a one-night stand!"

Bernstein asked, "Did she come at us? Did she hire people to kill us? What did she do other than use your son to round us up and join us in the greatest adventure in my life, since Vietnam?" The group all toasted and screamed.

Bernstein stated, "In my view, she's off limits unless she tries to personally do stupid against us." Mallory concurred as did John Lee, Jilkes, and Brown.

The Sarge said, "I don't trust nobody that ain't on this farm. Mallory, I want our people on alert. From this moment forward, all gun cabinets are open, and all weapons are loaded with clips in view. By the way, where is Mr. Amazing?"

Mallory said, "Sarge, he is loading all of that cash from the dead senator's house to our vault in this basement."

"Hell, I don't want those cases in a place that is designed for humans if this thing goes south."

"No, Sarge, there is a below ground storage space in the tunnel as well."

"Damn, they thought of everything, didn't they?"

# # #

An hour or so later after the meeting, Jilkes saw Juan, told him that they were on full alert. He also told Juan that he was needed in the box. The Sarge was about to say something when his phone rang. It was Helga. She asked him about the status of his negotiations. The Sarge adamantly stated, "Let's get one thing straight, young lady. We're not negotiating for you or for the other side. We want out of this, and you have used your last string as our puppeteer. You will, from this point forward, follow instructions or learn to live a very destitute life. I can give you the direct number to the buyer, and you can fend for yourself. Your choice. You can't demand or expect anything from us that does not benefit us or enhances our security. In other words, if it's us or you, then you need to run because I will give them your last coordinates. Are we clear?"

"I am perfectly clear, Mr. Beckmire. How would you like to proceed from this point?"

"First, nothing is going to happen tonight. Banks are closed, and we don't feel like exposing ourselves to people with guns. Second, by the time the banks open on Monday, it will still take a moment to wire millions to various accounts. This amount and any cash payments will only happen once the formula is verified by the other side. If there is any chicanery, we will not wire you a single penny. Therefore, whatever you give me, or my people, had better be the real deal. Any deception and the deal is dead. We'll be off the radar; your picture will be transmitted to every news agency and airport in the world. Am I still clear?"

"Perfectly clear, Mr. Beckmire."

"Now, I haven't heard back from the senator, and I suspect she's trying to gather her resources to make the payments. We can offer you a better deal that gives you time to stall the process, get some money, allow you to disappear while we handle the bulk of the negotiations, and the transfer of the formula."

"I do respect you, and I understand what you're about to offer, but I want to make a statement," Helga announced.

"Your so-called proposed declaration is clouded by a payment request. Therefore, it has no meaning other than the fact that you stole or inherited a formula, and you are now trying to sell it on the black market to the highest bidder."

Silence prevailed on the phone before the Sarge said, "Nothing is going to happen tonight. Think about what I've said and early tomorrow I will reach out to you." He didn't wait for a response but hung up the phone.

Ten minutes later, his phone rang. An excited senator asked, "What happened?"

"Well, if you hadn't hung up, you might have been able to hear the details on a party line, firsthand. My question is more fundamental, Senator. Are you prepared to make wire-transfers and assemble the 50% cash requirement?"

"Everything is in play."

"Let's start all over again. Listen, I don't trust you and have truly little faith in what you say. I don't give a shit about the Carbon Factor formula, but you do. I'm being used by a grand puppeteer who is pulling our strings. Now, I'm going to try this again. Are you prepared to hand over 50% of the money in cash and conduct secure wire-transfers for the remaining 50% of the price? Yes or no, Senator? There's no need for fancy words?"

"Everything is ready except banks aren't open, and, therefore, no wire transfers can happen. Insofar as the cash requirements are concerned, my team and I figured you and your people have stolen a lot of money from the government."

Beckmire yelled, "Catch you much later, Senator, and good luck with that accusation. You must be on drugs. Goodnight."

Two minutes later, the Sarge's phone rang. The senator rushed her response, "Mr. Beckmire, please don't hang up on me. I have the money the thieves missed in one of our stash houses. It's enough to meet the cash requirements. I would like to make that payment first as a good faith demonstration. When the banks open, I'll begin the transfer process from other accounts."

"Senator, as I hear it, those stash houses belong to my cousin. Did you rip him off? Also, you mentioned the word, 'our'. Who are the others in that word? Do you have your own stash house?"

"Mr. Beckmire, I say this, and I mean no disrespect, but how and who I conduct my business with is certainly not essential to this agreement. Let us both stay on course and make this transaction as seamless as possible."

The Sarge had an idea as to who the other people were that made up the "our" word. He said, "You're correct; let's make this deal clean and without fracture. I need to find out where the agent wants the funds delivered."

The senator asked, "You didn't consider that in your equation from the beginning?"

"No, Senator, I didn't! We have no interest in this matter other than we prefer the formula land on American soil, and not in the hands of a rival or a fanatic." The senator mumbled something under her breath that sounded like, "good luck with that".

The Sarge asked her, "What did you say?"

The senator replied, "It was a cough. I had a tickle in my throat, that's all. Nothing more than a tickle."

The Sarge replied, "Oh, I see." He knew the conversation was being recorded. He said, "Listen, I will present your issues to the agent and you and she can have a face-to-face. I'll let you know where she wants the cash portion of this deal delivered. It will not happen tonight. Goodnight, Senator."

The Sarge hung up the phone and said to his team, "Deal with that bitch." He then punched the play button and listened to the last few minutes of the conversation with the group. Everyone heard her distinctly say, "good luck with that."

The Sarge called Helga and said, "Nothing is going to happen tonight. You must decide where you want the cash delivered and be very mindful of the fact that you're dealing with a conniving, treacherous, and despicable person. She'd back over your body and never stop. Make sure you know where you want the funds delivered and that you can escape once that aspect of the deal is done. Also remember part of the deal is being done on a good faith basis. Prior to the wire transfers, you must give up the formula. You might want to do that in stages. For this amount, you get this much of the formula and so on. You're on your own. And, by the way, the cases that they will provide you with will probably be loaded with explosives and tracking devices. We will rethink this in the morning prior to you giving a location. I'm not sure we can help you or want to help you. We'll sleep on it and make our decision in the morning. Goodnight."

The Sarge turned to his guys and said, "That *bruja*, the senator, has made a deal with a foreign government! I'll bet you $10. When I said, 'I prefer the formula landed in America and not with a rival', she distinctly mumbled under her breath, 'good luck with that'. After mumbling that phrase, I'm sure of it, she began to cough, and said she had a tickle in her throat. I started to say, 'Well, get that little thing out of your mouth. That wouldn't have been appropriate."

Jong slipped into the room and sat in a corner with his computer.

John Lee said, "Sarge, this here situation is only going to get complicated. If it goes bad, it's our fault, and if it goes without a hitch, then they'll say we be done sold that formula to China or Iran. I don't see how we can come out of this here thing without being hunted by the entire world."

"John Lee, I feel the same way, and that is why I think we should consider paying Helga off and taking control of the damn thing."

Jilkes stated, "Our dilemma is greater than paying her off. I'm more concerned about her screwing us, and still leaving the entire world looking to kick our butts. I mean, none of us are scientists and wouldn't know the Carbon Factor formula from that of baking soda. We have been pulled into this thing by both sides and we risk the most downside to this equation. One gets the money, the other gets the formula, and we get the traitor stamp when the Iranians or Chinese begin testing the product, with all indications that huge sums of money were transferred to our offshore accounts. We're in a bad place on this one, a real bad place."

The Sarge asked, "Zanthius, do you have any other ideas?"

"Dad, I'm sticking with my initial one that includes illusions and misdirection. Helga is bad news, and you can believe me when I say that she knows we should play a part. The question that's probably running around in her brain, is whether we will give her up, or side with the senator. The senator is looking at us as if the notion of a rogue agent is a ruse. They both have us compromised. We need the help of a scoundrel, or at least someone capable of playing that role. We need someone like that Clinton fellow or that preacher Jackson. I think that fellow Clinton is beyond our pay grade, that Jackson man is smart enough, loud enough to gain an audience, and participate in the illusion, but not the misdirection."

Bernstein said, "I have an idea about where you're going with this, but I think you need a little more yeast in the pan to make this thing rise. We need some white folks, black folks, Asians, Hispanics, Jews, Muslims, and everybody else to create the illusion. We only need a couple of people to make the misdirection possible. Also, since the volume or the percentage of the wired and cash payments are 50/50%, Helga might have to forfeit half and the senator will only have half a formula, initially."

"Yeah, but we don't know what half to give her because we don't know shit about this mess. I like the idea of getting everyone involved, but too many hands in this pot could be disastrous. Plus, if the formula is a blank, then we have an additional group of people on our ass for exploiting their beliefs and values," Brown stated.

The Sarge said, "Good point, Brown, you as well, Bernstein. There are parts of what you say that we can use once we figure out this misdirection and illusion mess that my son keeps speaking of. Guys, the immediate problem that we have is we don't have time to do a lot of trial runs, the clock is ticking. We purchased some time because the banks are closed, and transfers can't happen until Monday morning. We need to give that *bruja* account numbers. Mr. Amazing, you have any ideas on how to fix our problem?"

"Mr. Sarge, I don't know all the parts of the problem but here's what we do know. That woman who is momma to baby Zanthius has placed us in a bind. That other woman, the senator, thinks we hold the formula. One wants money to disappear, the other wants the formula to sell for twice, if not more the asking price, on the open market. I like the open market because we can get a billion for it. But we have nowhere to live if we do that. If we help the momma, we act like it is us all the time. We no be in a good place. This thing full of bad karma," Jong stated.

"Recognizing that this thing is full of bad karma, how do we turn it into good karma?" The Sarge asked.

"This never good karma. This is a bomb that kills good and innocent people. It will not, and can never, be good karma," Jong replied.

"If you had a choice, whose hands would you want to see this bad karma end up in?" the Sarge asked.

"Why you ask low question like that? No place like America, but I don't know about these new people who want to build a wall and run people out. They are not coming from a good place."

"Thank you for all your thoughts, Mr. Amazing. Guys, we're running out of time. I think we've had a long day, we all probably need to sleep, and come at it again in the morning, refreshed. I could use some rest. Some of you have wife and baby duties. Let's meet at 0700 hours and do a fast walk. Do we have security covered tonight?"

Mallory said, "Why don't we peek in and see what's happening?" They walked around the corner and looked in the expanded closet. They saw Rashida in a deep sleep, and Juan listening to the sounds of the woods and watching the animal movements. Juan turned to look at the Sarge and said, "We're taking turns, but you can see whose turn it is and will be for the balance of the night. Everything is good. I'm not only looking for movement when targeted by the radar, but I'm also listening to the various sounds of the night, especially since we haven't completely outfitted that property we annexed. By the way, isn't there a lot of cash in that place?"

The Sarge responded, "There is. Are you telling me we don't have cameras on that property?"

"Sarge, from the command center, I don't have any indication of movement at that perimeter. I think we should at least have a couple of guys sleep over in the place. If we found the stash, you can be sure others know about it as well."

"Mr. Amazing, can you have your thieving ass cousin come and set us up with cameras and weapons?"

"I will make the call. I'm sure he will come, and I know he has that place on a list of things to do," Jong stated.

The Sarge looked at Juan and said, "I'm happy you married my daughter. Let me see if I can get a couple of guys to sleep over in that place."

He turned to Mallory and said, "Can you handle this one for me? I need to get some sleep. Ask Whitmore, Gladstone, McArthur, and Chakes if they can manage that situation and you and I will relieve them in three hours. Tell them the place is wired, but I don't think its connected to any ordinances."

"What the hell does that mean? Either the place is wired or not."

"You know what—send out a group text indicating we need volunteers to watch the annexed property in a couple shifts and see who volunteers."

Mallory sent out the text and received 10 messages from people stating they were in. He relayed the information to the Sarge. The Sarge suggested he use the two lovers, John Lee and Jilkes, McArthur, and Gladstone for the first watch and then let the sun rise with Chakes, Montomie, Brown, and Bernstein.

Mallory sent out the selection, the assigned people assembled in the family room with full gear and weapons. The Sarge said, "I know you guys don't want to hear this, but I'm going to say it anyway. You're the best damn team that man has ever assembled. I love you and will see you later."

Juan peeked his head out of the command center and said, "Hey, guys, once you're in, hit me up with a text so I can focus the sound waves mainly on that area. Also, I need you guys to put your devices on channel 14. Is that a roger?"

John Lee responded, "Roger that."

#

McArthur didn't waste any time digging into the two married men's asses. He said, "So, tell me how it feels to come from being top dog in everything you do, to responding to requests and demands with words like, 'yes dear'? Do you feel emasculated? I mean, you two knuckleheads were, and remain, our bread and butter, and I just want to know how this shit works."

John Lee said, "Mac, you be trying to pick a fight?"

"No, my brother, I'm trying to figure out if I want to consummate a relationship."

Gladstone said, "If he wanted to fight you, you know I would have to help him whup your ass, right? However, he and I are under extreme pressure to make a commitment or forget about the women we like."

John Lee asked, "How long you be liking these women? And what makes me love and respect you guys, is that you, don't ever chase the married women when we're out. My African American friend over there thought you two had a special relationship going on."

Jilkes said, "John 'Crazy-Ass' Lee, don't spread bullshit on me like that. If I thought that and wanted to ask them, I would have come straight to the point and said my piece. You, you, country dung, throw me under the bus stating I had a question about their sexuality."

"Brother Jilkes, you're too sensitive. I don't give a hoot if they be banging each other or anybody else for that matter. I have one law—you screw with them; you screw with me. I know you got my back, just like they do. On another front, the Sarge asked us to watch the cash here—he didn't say we couldn't drink while on duty. It ain't like we're driving to town to chase prostitution," John Lee confirmed.

"John Lee, you chase prostitutes, not prostitution," McArthur said.

"Don't matter what you want to chase, but you got my meaning, right? And that is what I've been saying to my African American friend all these years. He pretends to not understand me, but he knows what I mean, each time."

"John Lee, you do know that McArthur and I are African Americans, don't you?"

"Oh yes, but my African American friend over there, is mine. I mean you two be mine too, but that one be mine for life. I love him as much as I love my woman, and if you tell anyone that, I'll slip a damn grenade under your bed."

Gladstone said, "Whatever—you're one crazy redneck, but I love you as well."

John Lee said, "Let's go and see if we can find where this ex-freak keeps his booze. I feel like it's a bourbon kind of night. How about you city boys?"

The group separated and started opening cabinets, and Jilkes yelled, "Eureka! Look at the top end booze in this closet." It was filled with high-end brands. He said, "Pick your poison and that way you don't have to worry about what I'm drinking."

The four men sat in the dark drinking with Sirius radio playing at a low volume. They soon were hammered and completely unfit for duty. They crossed the irresponsible point. They couldn't have helped anyone if their lives depended on it, but they weren't your ordinary ex-soldiers, either.

At 0330 hours, Juan started to doze off to sleep, but was alerted by the rustling of grass. He didn't have the system to view the annexed property as was installed at Asiram's, but he had some cameras and listening devices planted on the property borders. He shook his head and realized the noise patterns were too long to be animals. He deduced that the ex-senator's place was about to be breached. He frantically yelled into his mike, "Guys, I think someone is trying to violate your position." He got no answer because members of the group had removed their earpieces and were intoxicated. He hit the silent alarm and the pathway to the tunnel for civilians lit up as he shot a loud boom through each earpiece. Jilkes said, "What the shit was that?" Each man placed their earpiece in and heard Juan say, "Breach in less than five minutes."

Everyone in the main house and the auxiliary who had strategic assignments were up, vested, armed, and out of the door. Some ran away from the action, others ran to the action, and still others flanked their position. Brown and Bernstein ran east, away from the action, and pulled the magical rope on their outfield storage place and secured their long guns. The women raced to the tunnels in their robes and lingerie and grabbed machine pistols and clips on the way. It was clockwork. Everyone was accounted for and secured in a matter of three minutes. Larry, Carlos, Juan, and Mike had the farmhouse, and they were heavily armed at their four secured vantage points.

Rashida began to monitor the sound and determined that it was a false alarm. She was able to syncopate the foot traffic and realized that humans don't run on fours.

A few minutes later, she gave the all-clear signal and showed her husband a small detail he missed.

When the Sarge and Mallory entered the annexed property, they found their men wasted and barely able to stand straight. He called Brown, Bernstein, Chakes, and Montomie and asked them to relieve their brothers because it was apparent to him, they were intoxicated and unable to provide the kind of security necessary to protect the group from any real or artificial impending breach of the farm.

# # #

The balance of the night provided those who were awake with magnificent views of a full moon and sounds of a few lone wolves in the area. Juan asked his wife, "How did I miss that one?"

Rashida said, "Baby, it's okay. We need a false alarm once in a while to make sure people carry out their group and individual assignments. Did you happen to see my mom and Ava escorting Asiram and the babies down to the tunnel with two machine pistols each?"

"I didn't see that, but I would have loved to have taken a picture of it. You have a wonderful family and a group of friends that I don't think exist anywhere else in the world. I'm a little upset that I blew this and caused this craziness. I will apologize to the group tomorrow."

Rashida said, "Honey, tell them we decided we needed to have a drill and the only way to have a real drill is to sound the alarm in real time. That will get us off the hook, and we can point out areas that are lacking. Jilkes and his group were apparently drunk and unable to fulfill their duties. We can slightly attribute our decision to them, but don't let them know we screwed up, and, therefore, we're blaming them for the hit that they need to take from my dad."

"You are the most cunning woman I have ever met. Always thinking, always calculating, and looking to save your man from his stupid mistakes. I love you so much."

The Sarge walked back into the house and asked, "Who authorized this test?"

Juan looked at his wife, then at the Sarge, and said, "If a test is authorized and known to happen, then it is truly not a test. The people who have attempted to hurt us don't operate 'tests'. However, we must be organized if such a thing happens. We have taken notes and will address our concerns as heads of the security department later in the morning." Rashida slowly eased up to her man and placed her hand in his. The Sarge looked at them and said, "Damn, I love you guys. Keeping us on our toes and safe. Damn good show."

Thirty minutes later, when the houses had settled down and the occupants had fallen to sleep, Rashida slid next to her husband and placed her tongue in his ear. Juan turned around and inquired, "Are you trying to start trouble?" When he clearly focused on that wonderful jewel that was awaiting his touch and kiss, he proclaimed, "Now, that's what I'm talking about. I need to communicate with my baby and his momma." He began to kiss Rashida's earlobes and neck. He worked his way to her ever-swelling breasts and began to suckle them. He said, "Oh, my God! I just sucked a substance out of your breast."

Rashida said, "You need to continue on your mission and not stop and tell me about each new development. I need to be complete, only you know where to touch, and what to kiss to make me whole. Please, address the task that I have opened before you." Juan looked at the parted legs and knew it was time to do his job. The two found a way to be one and to enjoy the ecstasies of lovemaking, while being ever mindful of the fact there was no call for a beast to show up to make love to his woman. Her only needs were for her husband and lover to honor his commitment.

#

Miraculously, McArthur, Jilkes, John Lee, and Gladstone were in front of the farmhouse doing calisthenics and trying to ward off the hangover that was upon them. When the Sarge walked through the screen door, he said, "What on earth happened last night or this morning? You know you were our first line of defense from the northern front."

John Lee was about to say something, but was interrupted by McArthur who said, "Sarge, I will not disagree with the assessment of our conditions, but I will take exception to the fact that we weren't functional. We had ammo, weapons, and explosives."

Jilkes said, "Sarge, it was that redneck from the South who started this mess. Yes, we were intoxicated, but when the alarm went off, we took up our positions and were ready to die for the cause."

"See, that's the problem. I don't want anyone dying for any damn artificial cause. I want people fighting for the right to survive. I'm not interested in any casualties, especially amongst you people. My whole life has been with and about you assholes. You pull another stunt like that without me and Mallory, and we'll shoot you. We're pissed because you went on a binge and didn't include us. And, by the way, when you get a moment, thank Juan and Rashida for concocting an incredible fable to protect you guys. I mean you assholes go on assignment, find high-end booze, and don't share it? You're the most selfish assholes I have ever worked with. Don't let that shit happen again, or you will be shipped home."

The Sarge barely got the word home, out of his mouth when the door opened and there stood, Mike, Larry and Zanthius—the new guard. Larry said, "Dad, do you want us to walk alongside you, or do you want us to secure you a path?"

The Sarge said, "It's a sad day when my son says that I'm too old to travel with him. I'm crushed. I think I'm going to go back to my room and cry."

"Come on, Dad, you know I'm only kidding. Listen, Zanthius and I, along with Mike, will walk with you guys. However, when you're pausing to think about what it is you want to say, we'll takeoff and run a mile, coming, and going, and then by that time, you might remember what you people were talking about."

The Sarge said, "I just want my sons to be close to me at all times. Can you people make that situation happen?"

Zanthius looked at his father and realized that the joke had gone too far. He whispered to Larry, "They're too proud to let us kick their asses. In the process, they might try to prove us wrong, and someone might have a fricken heart attack. I'm not willing to accept that as a poorly stated joke. Are you?"

Larry responded by saying, "I'm going to apologize." He looked at the group of guys, some still intoxicated, others old and out of shape before saying, "Hey guys, I want to walk, jog, trek, or crawl alongside you. We collectively, couldn't hold a candle next to you people. I know what you've done and can do. So, I just want to thank you for taking the time and placing trust in me and my brother, from another mother, as well as Mike, who I don't have a clue about as to who he's from. It would be our privilege to run, walk, skip, or jog with the greatest group of warriors that has ever lived. I don't say that lightly or with jest. I'm giving you the essence of our true feelings."

The Sarge said, "Thanks, Son. That makes us feel a little better as we strive to stay abreast of you 21st century types. Way to go, Larry. I might have to make you the spokesman for our group in the future."

As the group prepared to make their run, a sleepy Juan walked out of the front door and pronounced, "When the farm is on full alert, you can't go running into the woods without getting your heads blown off. It would be nice if you told the security types that you're going for a long run, that way, we won't arm and engage machine pistols all over this place."

The Sarge said, "Hold up. You mean to tell me when friendlies are out and about, we need to disarm the system?"

Juan replied, "Duh! Sarge, that is correct. If we have friendlies and not so friendlies, in the woods, then it creates a problem for us to discern who is who, because you carry weapons, and so do those who want to conclude our existence. You see what I mean? Now, we do have those medallions in play, but how many of you have yours on you? You can't have it both ways. If you put the place on lockdown, then that is exactly what we do. Every movement in the woods becomes a target. We can't adjust for good versus bad until those medallions are in play. We gave badges to discriminate against good guys and bad guys, but if a good guy has a bad day like John Lee and McArthur, then they are in the firing line."

"Why did you pick those two individuals?"

"They don't have their IDs on them, so that puts them in the bad guys category."

Mallory walked over to the Sarge and whispered, "We need to disengage the system every night because our people aren't used to following rules, thanks to a certain leader."

The Sarge said, "Those days were different. We didn't have iPhones, Dick Tracey watches, and gadgets that do everything except stimulate you sexually. This is a new world, it's hard for old people like us to keep up with this technology."

He turned to Juan and said, "We're all armed, so shut down the system for now, but keep an eye out for unusual activity."

## CHAPTER FOURTEEN

In Valencia, Franco and his crew didn't waste any time preparing the two properties to be razed. The architect that they contracted with had prepared a simple, yet elegant, rendition of the new restaurant, and a highly visible and eye-catching structure for the resort. The architect knew he would have to explain each aspect of the drawings. He told Franco and Mario that the prints represent sketches or concepts of what he envisioned as the final facades. Franco liked what he saw and wanted a copy to send to his partners in America. He asked the architect what the impressions of the people who owned the properties, were. He was told they loved the sketches but were wondering if this was real or some caper. Franco told the architect that they used to have a different kind of relationship, but now he and his guys were the project managers, and the families had the right of first refusal. He asked the architect if he could travel to both places with him to make sure that this is what they wanted their respective businesses to look like.

#

An hour later, Franco, Mario, and the architect arrived at the resort and met with the owner, Don Carlo. Franco said, "This is a business deal, and it cannot happen until you provide your buy-off on the sketches. These pictures are concepts. Once, if they are approved, the dimensions and structural aspects will be added by engineers." Franco noticed the hesitancy on the owner's part and said, "Listen, I know we had a different kind of relationship in the past, I apologize for any and everything that was done to you in a bad way. You were going to forfeit the place one way or the other. The Yanks came along and saved us both—you from forfeiture and me from hell. This is your place. I'm only the project manager who must follow your lead in terms of approval or disapproval of the design."

Don Carlo looked at him and said, "I no trust you then. I no trust you now." He looked at the pictures, and it was as if a light went on in his head. His eyes opened wide, and his hands began to shake. He nervously looked at the architect and with a quivering voice asked, "You can make my place look like this picture?"

The architect exclaimed, "Absolutely! If you like this sketch, then I will put all the pieces together to make it work. Look carefully at the design and make sure this is what you want. Are the windows facing in the right direction? Are the doors the kind of doors you want, do you want the exterior made of brick or stucco?"

The architect said to Franco, "I have an idea. Let's leave the sketches with him, so that he can look carefully at them, make sure he absolutely loves the design, and that this is what he wants."

Franco said, "Great idea. How about if we meet for lunch and discuss your concerns, if any, tomorrow?"

Don Carlo said, "I will make notes, and bring them to the McDonald's at 1 pm." They bid each other farewell and left the resort. On the outside of the building, Franco noticed a seam extending from the base of the building to the roof. He walked to it and called the architect over, and asked, "What on earth could cause such a thing?"

The architect looked closer at the seam and said, "Let's look around the back to see if there is any similar damage."

The two men walked around to the back of the building and the architect exclaimed, "We need to shut this place down! It is crumbling from the inside out and could collapse at any moment. We must have a word with Don Carlo."

They walked back into the lobby, and the architect pointed at a seam running across the full length of the ceiling. Don Carlo asked, "Did you forget something?"

The architect pointed to the seam in the ceiling and told him that he also found two other such anomalies on the outside. He stridently suggested, "Don Carlo, I recommend you get your possessions and leave the building now. I must exercise my sworn duty to disclose fractures in public and private structures. Your resort could fall down at any minute," the architect urgently announced.

Don Carlo said, "That seam has been there for years."

The architect said, "And that's what scares me. Get whatever papers you need, vacate this place, and shut it down. If anyone is injured in this place, you will have hefty fines and the possibility of a jail term to face. I'm officially telling you to vacate and shutter these premises."

Don Carlo looked at Franco and said, "So, is this how you plan on swindling me?"

Franco said, "On my mother and every person I love. I swear to you I don't understand what he's talking about. I have no hand in what he has just said to you."

The architect said, "I must call the authorities and report what I see, Don Carlo. You have no guests, it's time to raze this structure before it collapses, and hurts someone. You should get out of here; those cracks are symptomatic of a bigger problem. Get your stuff and vacate this place." He turned to Franco and said, "When was the demolition phase of this project supposed to occur?"

Franco replied, "It was scheduled for this coming Monday. Some of the equipment should begin to arrive in a day or so, and then the crews will begin their tasks on Monday."

The architect called the Mayor's Office and stated, that he was recommending that Don Carlo's resort be cordoned off because he saw compromises in the structural integrity of the building. He advised that signs be placed around it, indicating that the building was a hazard and subject to collapse at any time.

Meanwhile, Don Carlo got his cellphone and called a sleeping Ben Beckmire. After waking Beckmire up, he said, "Mr. Beckmire, I think that scoundrel is up to his old tricks. He somehow convinced the architect to call the city and have them condemn my property."

A sleepy Ben Beckmire asked, "Why are they doing that?"

"They say that cracks in the ceiling and in the exterior structure indicate that the place isn't safe."

"Don Carlo, when we were there, I noticed that crack and thought to myself that the ceiling was going to fall on us. That is the reason we left Spain in a hurry—we didn't have alternative lodging that could accommodate us all—we don't like separation. The architect is a reliable man and Franco is a convert. The building is scheduled to be demolished next week anyway. I don't see any gain for them acting early unless the structure is vulnerable. Tell the architect to take pictures and send them to me at this number. I want to see what's going on. Have them do it now."

Don Carlo relayed Beckmire's request. The architect began to take photos of the ceiling and the exterior cracks. He took fifteen pictures and sent them to Ben Beckmire.

Ten minutes or so later, Beckmire called the architect back and told him to get everyone out of there. He asked him if he could speak to Don Carlo, and the architect gave the man his phone.

Ben Beckmire said, "That crack in the ceiling is wider than I remember. I'm in agreement with those guys. Shut the electric, gas, water, off. Please vacate the premises. There is nothing for them to gain by this action. Everything is on schedule and you're in control of this entire process. Look at the agreement you signed. You control this, but I can't let you do stupid and let the ceiling as well as the building collapse on you, my friend. Get what you can and shut the place down. No one can swindle you out of anything. We've got your back!"

Don Carlo felt good about hearing those words and said to Franco, "Don't you try any *stupido* shit or your *culo* will be handed to you in a net." Franco looked at him and bowed.

Don Carlo said, "I need you to go into the dungeon and shut off the gas and electric."

Franco said, "Don Carlo, I don't have a clue as to what and where those things are. I'll go with you, but I don't know what to do."

The architect said, "We'll all go and try to figure out where it is."

The three men struggled to open the door to the dungeon and when they opened it, the steps were lined with trash, chairs, tables, and rats running everywhere. Don Carlo said, "I hope we can kill these things before we rebuild."

Franco said, "You should have been shut down years, ago. Look at all of the rat droppings on the floor."

The architect said, "I just want to find those switches and get the hell out of here."

Mario came to the door and said, "The back of the building is peeling. You people need to get the hell out of there."

Don Carlo said, "Those are the switches over there on that back wall." Franco dashed across the floor and pulled the lever for the gas and electric to the off position. Surprisingly, the standby lighting system kicked on and he was able to find his way back to the stairs. The three men scaled the steps amongst the trash and furniture as Don Carlo began to have a panic attack.

Franco said, "You're making this too easy for me. Take deep breaths and let's get the hell out of here. I'm not leaving you behind, so let's move it."

At the top of the stairwell, Mario said, "This place really is compromised. Look at that crack in the ceiling."

On the outside of the resort's main building, Don Carlo said, "I wasn't feeling well back there."

"I know. And I was not going to leave you in there either," Franco replied.

"I know," Don Carlo responded.

CHAPTER FIFTEEN

At 0600 hours, the entire farm seemed to be up and busy. The Sarge asked his bride if she wanted to go on a run with him and she surprised him by saying she would be ready in ten minutes. Rashida and Juan had shut the weapons system down and were out in the middle of the field with LaGina watching the horses. The Sarge walked out of the farmhouse and saw his people were ready for a hike. He said good morning to them and proceeded to where his security experts were. LaGina ran to him, and he hoisted her into the air. She said, "PopPop, maybe one day I can have my own horse to take care of?"

Beckmire looked at the majestic beast and said, "Why not? If it's okay with your mom and dad."

LaGina turned to her parents and began to beg, "Can I Mom, can I Mom? Dad, can I, can I?"

Juan said, "A horse is a huge responsibility. You must feed it, love it, wash it, and take care of it. Are you ready to assume that responsibility?"

"I am, Dad."

"Okay, I will make a commitment to you to investigate the possibility of letting PopPop buy you a horse. It's a big job, and it takes a lot of research, but once we have ended our work, and when those bad guys aren't trying to hurt us, then I'll make sure you get a horse, my love." She thanked him.

The Sarge asked, "Are you people, okay? I mean it's six in the morning, and you're out here with the baby watching horses."

Rashida said, "Dad, we're doing more than watching horses. We're planning where we want to live. As a matter of fact, we are considering where John Lee and Jilkes are building. I hear you and mom have looked at designs as well."

"Honey, there's plenty of land available and I like the idea of you being close to me. Love you guys. We're going for a little walk and run."

"What's mom doing out there?"

"She's going for a run with her man. Catch you later."

The group started out with a slow walk that turned into a fast walk that turned into a slow run and then ended as a fast quarter mile. During the fast walk, footsteps could be heard from the rear. It was Zanthius, Mike, and Larry running at them at full speed.

The Sarge asked Mallory, "Do we have eyes on those hills over there?"

Mallory looked in the direction and saw a light flash. Mallory said, "I see what you mean." As the fast runners got closer, the Sarge stepped in the middle of the road and waved the youngsters down. He said, "Don't look now, but I think someone has eyes on us from those hills directly behind me. Are you people armed?"

Larry said, "We're armed. Do you want us to check it out?"

"That's the general idea my Son, but not at a risk of confrontation."

Larry said, "Mom, are you feeling, okay?" Courtney gave him the thumbs up sign.

Larry said, "I think we should flank them and hit that area hard. We will act like we tire at different points, and then run the rapids, zig, and zag until we reach the top. I'll give the signal for when we start the siege by raising my hand in a slow defeated manner and then we hit the area hard."

Meanwhile, LaGina was ecstatic about the idea of owning her own horse and said, "Dad, why is that light flashing on the hill? You told me never to point, but do you want me to show you?"

"No, baby, I see it. Rashida let's hold hands and hug our way back to the farmhouse."

They got up and Juan started tossing LaGina in the air and running with her around Rashida. Once in the house, he engaged the camera system and zeroed in on the approximate area. He engaged the long guns from the top of the roof and scoped the potential threat. He prepared the weapons to fire, but the alarm sounded when the system tracked friendlies heading in the same direction—Larry, Mike, and Zanthius. Rashida yelled, "Hit override."

The system focused three large caliber weapons on the targets. Juan said, "I'll be damn, it's a cow stuck in the bushes and that shining device is its cowbell." He broadcasted on the audio, "It's a cow. Stand-down from intrusion stance and proceed to assistance mode. I think it's a cow stuck in the bush."

As the three men got closer to where the cow was stuck, Larry said, "That damn cow smokes Marlboro." The three men pulled their weapons out and began to back away from the area, all in the same direction.

Juan witnessing this said, "Alert, apparent intrusion on the western front." Nothing else needed to be said, as the internal house alarm sounded, the occupants from both spaces made their dash to the tunnel while gathering their assigned weapons and survival kits. The Sarge hearing this knew they had to retreat to the farmhouse. He sent his fastest guys to provide security. Jilkes, John Lee, Chakes, and McArthur provided fifty-yard observation and security. Once at the farmhouse, each man rearmed themselves. Ava had Zanthius Jr, and Asiram had Ben, and all the kids had their headsets on and were listening or looking at their favorite show. Each adult in the tunnel had their favorite, or the weapon they were most proficient with. Carla, not knowing the drill, other than what happened when Juan and Rashida engaged the alarm system, said, "I need a rock or something. I don't have a weapon."

Asiram said, "I know you can fly a plane, but can you accurately fire a weapon?"

"How about adding expert marksperson to that pilot title? I am proficient in small arms, .50 caliber machine guns, sniper rifles and knives."

Ava asked, "Do you ever make love to your husband?"

Carla's head dropped before she said, "I just got married and I haven't had sex with my husband because I've been ill."

Ava grabbed her and said, "That was the most insensitive comment I have ever made. I promise, you will never hear anything that retarded from me again. I'm sorry, and I sincerely mean it. Listen, take my shotgun, I have my pistol."

Carla said, "I prefer a large caliber pistol and one of those assault weapons. I know how they work. That thing you have is too loud for me."

Once in the house, the Sarge asked, "Are all my people accounted for?"

Juan said, "I've been a little too busy to initiate a roll call. I'm watching the area where our people are backing away from. It appears to be staged and the cow was led to the area. I have three long guns trained on the area as they work this one out. We know what we're doing."

The Sarge threw his hands in the air as if he were surrendering and backed slowly and respectfully out of the command center. He yelled, "Brown and Bernstein, I need you to provide a retreat for my people out there in the field. Jilkes, John Lee, follow close and tell me what or who was on that hill. Chakes, Montomie, Gladstone, and McArthur, fix flanking positions and secure and discover who was there. Juan has his finger on the trigger. Make sure you have your medallions on so that the weapons system doesn't accidently target you assholes."

Jilkes yelled, "Oh, Sarge, we're feeling important again because you're calling us assholes and other nasty mantras."

People began to make their way to their assigned positions as others began to advance to check out the threat. Once back at the farmhouse, Larry and Zanthius went to their respective areas and outfitted themselves. Mike said, "I don't have none of that."

Larry said, "You have to earn this shit, mister."

Zanthius and Larry high-fived each other, but immediately realized they had emasculated an ally and friend. Larry said, "Once this threat is evaluated and over, I will personally outfit you. Sorry about the insensitivity we showed a few minutes ago. You are an important part of our team."

The Sarge looked at Larry and Zanthius and said, "I need you people to get in one of our vans and make your way to the road. Where is Mike?"

"Dad, he doesn't have a tailored made vest."

"Son, none of us do. Get Mike a vest. Zanthius, you cover the passenger side and Larry, you man the weapons in the van. Get to the top of the road and drive down to the next property's entrance and take pictures, capture me, if possible, a person to interrogate. He looked around the room and said, "Jong, you're up and senior in the group with my sons. Go, man, go!"

Mike drove up the road at lightning speed as Larry and Zanthius kept yelling, "Slow down before you run into a ditch."

Jong said, "We need to get to the road fast before those in question get away. I need you to drive faster, Mike."

When Jilkes and John Lee arrived at the scene, the cow was still stuck in the original position. John Lee began to look around and discerned what had happened and who had been there. He realized that Larry, Mike, and Zanthius did not take time to fully investigate. John Lee noticed that there were a variety of cigarette brands, marijuana butts, beer cans, glue and prescription pill bottles strewn about. John Lee looked further and saw a lot of condoms. He deduced the stage was too disorganized to be orchestrated, and that from the smell of the trees in the area, the girls wore a lot of cheap and smelly perfume. He ruled the site a "screw platform" for locals. He asked Brown and Bernstein to assume their positions because they were moving further into the neighbor's property.

In code and in country talk, John Lee gave the Sarge a summary of his findings by speaking to him about his favorite pig. The Sarge stated, "I guess I can't barbeque your pig tonight?"

"That would be a terrible sin and the pig savior would be placing a ring on our heads."

After the "all clear sign" was given and the cow was released from the fox trap, the group reassembled. The Sarge said, "In less than twenty-four hours, we've had two intrusion alerts."

He looked around the porch at all of the armed women and men and said, "I love this farm, but I think we need separation from when something can happen and when we can prepare for it. Here we are limited in response because this is a farm surrounded by trees, bushes, and neighbors. I think we need space, time, and the ability to mobilize. That can only happen at the ranch in middle America. What also troubles me is that, happily, a lot of our women are pregnant."

As he looked around the room, he saw Monica's head drop. He said, "In some cases, things are already in place for some of us to adopt children. I say, some things can be done virtually, if we need to make a road trip, then, so be it. I'm not leaving any conditions hanging without a possible resolution. Therefore, if we need to make frequent trips back here, then that is what we'll do. Does anyone have a problem with anything I've said?"

Seeing no objections, he continued, "Great. I need you people to complete all things that you were doing and make ready to leave the farm for a few days or until there is a decision about an adoption process that's in place."

# # #

Jilkes asked, "Boss, how can we orchestrate the symphony from afar?"

"Good question. We are bedamned if we do and bedamned if we don't. I like Zanthius's approach to the situation. I want to create the notion of things happening in one place and misdirect. Insofar as Helga is concerned, I'm not sure we owe her anything other than a portion of the funds she is requesting."

He looked at Mr. Amazing and asked, "Have you unloaded the cash from the other place and when will your cousin install the cameras and weapons system there?"

"Sarge, he's on his way. Unfortunately, we have another problem with that site."

The Sarge looked at him and asked, "Is this a guessing game, or are you going to tell me what's going on?"

Jong said, "I prefer to show you what is going on. That way, you might reconsider some of our plans."

# # #

Eighteen minutes later, after entering the house, Jong said, "Please, follow me. I would have told you earlier, but it appeared we were under siege."

Jong escorted the Sarge into the master bedroom, flicked the light switch on the wall twice, without thinking sat on the bed, and attempted to turn the lamp on. Without knowing it, he inadvertently unlocked the code which revealed a secret panel. The panel behind the king size headboard opened and featured 100 gold bars.

The Sarge said, "I'll be damned! No wonder our taxes are through the roof. These fricken guys and gals are thieves. What did they hope to do with all this mess?"

The Sarge radioed for his people to take a walk up to the house. He told them to leave Rashida and Juan in the box and in control.

When most of the group arrived, Jong yelled, "Up here, guys." The men piled into the room, Jong flicked the light switch, sat on the bed, and tried to turn the lamp on. The panel opened, and the guys stood in awe. McArthur said, "Now, that's beautiful, but tainted. Are there any rules governing these people?"

The Sarge responded, "Apparently not! Look, cash in his sordid dungeon, gold behind his head, and he is dead as a rock. Politicians are the biggest crooks on earth. Just look at that clown from Texas—his constituents were suffering from power outages and he takes his family to Mexico for a vacation."

"What are we going to do with this stuff? More importantly, what is this mess worth?" Mallory asked.

Jilkes stated, "Those 100 gold bars are probably worth shy of $10 million. Actually, looking at the closing price of gold today on the exchange, they are worth $9,942,000.00."

John Lee chimed in and asked, "How come you know so much about gold? You been holding out on me."

The Sarge stated, "People, let's stay focused."

Bernstein said, "We should put it in the bank. We should open a couple of security boxes and put this stuff in them. Our only problem is that those bullions are heavy. Perhaps we should get ten boxes and place ten bars in each."

The Sarge said, "How about for now, we get one of the mules, load this stuff in it, and put it in the tunnel with the cash. We need to switch gears and focus on the calls I'm going to receive around 9 am. Okay, let's load this stuff up. Jong, can you walk down and get another mule?"

"Why must I walk? Why can't someone drive me, to get a mule?" Jong inquired.

"Chakes, give the princess a ride, please," the Sarge chided.

Later, when the group got back to the house, everyone asked about the tainted gold. Bernstein said, "When we elect politicians, it appears we give them the keys to Fort Knox and the password to the Bureau of Engraving."

# # #

At 1600 hours, the team met in the barn and began to, once again, figure out what to do with the Carbon Factor issue, as well as Helga. Zanthius said, "Unless you guys forgot, we have a disk with the senator on it that has some extremely compromising positions, including with the dead senator. I don't mean when he was dead, but when he was alive. We have illicit sex, drugs, orgies, and she is the star in all those scenes. We have footage of her in cahoots with your cousin, Dad, and the insane conversations about payment for the Carbon Factor formula. I'm wondering if it makes more sense to try to get her to transfer the money first, or, how about this, make the 50% in cash payment as a sign of good faith. I'm sure she'll ask why the change in format and the answer is simple, the agent does not trust you or us and that is her demand. So, we have additional incriminating material from the wire transfer and the cash payment. Think about it. She's scandalous, nefarious, and a viper."

Brown said, "That all sounds good and I think it's as good a plan as we have, but why would she go for this change at the last minute?"

"Now, that's a good question and hopefully, the answer is because she doesn't control the flow of this activity. She is dictated to and, therefore, if there's any hesitation on her part, we make a deal with Helga. We then implement my illusion and misdirection plan, or some semblance of it," Zanthius said.

Brown asked, "Do you think Helga is that desperate that she's willing to give up a sizeable payday and settle for perhaps, half?"

"Helga is one manipulative '*Chika*' and has played us at every juncture. Remember, she stole, in the name of a nun, $1 million from us in Spain. She's desperate in my opinion. Look, she has the entire planet earth looking for her ass. It's a matter of time before someone gets a hand on her. I mean, I don't know for a fact that she's desperate, but according to the way she is playing this hand, I think she is cautious, scared, destitute, and broke. Her stint at the Catholic Charities is over, and she cannot go back there. The good news is, she did hook brother Mallory and his bride up before shunning her cloths for the final time. I don't have any evidence of what I'm saying, but I feel it in my bones," Zanthius stated.

The Sarge said, "Does anyone else have a plan or a scheme we can throw around?"

Larry said, "I think there are a few fundamental questions that need to be asked and answered before you entertain the calls, Pop. The first issue I have, is what are we going to do with the formula? The second concern of mine is, what is our purpose for being in the middle of this, albeit we were dragged into it. And, finally, do we want a connection between the senator, us, and cash money? Each concern is linked to the other and is essential to answer to make sure we know what we're doing. I've heard all kinds of commentary on this issue and it's never the same."

The Sarge inquired, "Son, what does your first item mean?"

"It's simple—are we going to turn the Carbon Factor formula over to some legitimate agency, so they have an additional capability to kill people? Or are we going to destroy it and hope there are no copies of it? I mean, what are we doing? Are we trying to save the planet, protect our children, make a statement, show corruption in the government, and get put on more hit lists? I think that should be our first discussion. Until that is decided, we will keep trying to figure out ways to increase our treasury. We can tell Helga that we'll give her $X and she can turn the formula over to us. We can then use my brother's illusions and misdirection game and destroy it in the name of mankind. Or we can attempt to extort, bring down the senator, plus capitalize on wire transfers, cash payments which makes us bandits, like she is, or recapture what we pay Helga, and then call it a day. There are so many avenues this thing can take, and until we answer that first question, we will remain caught up with the notion of increasing our fortune."

"Wow, Larry, that was some analysis and a great one at that," Mallory said. He paused for a moment and stated, "As I think about what you just said, it gives me reason to pause and think about our mission of helping people help themselves. Have we gotten that far from it that money colors our vision? I mean, we're rich as shit, and it just keeps rolling in. We have solid investments, we each have portfolios to die for, and not a single person in this room is worth less than $90 to $100 million."

Larry raised his hand and respectfully admitted, "I live in the hood. If I had that kind of money, I would be on a farm like this one." Everyone laughed.

Mike raised his hand and Gladstone said, "You just joined the tribe, and you did it by the back door—messing with our pilot. Put your hand down."

"Guys let's stay focused. The clock is ticking," the Sarge said.

Zanthius said, "Each word was meticulously selected and articulated. On my brother's first issue, I'm 100% committed to answering the question that controls our actions. He is correct, guys. What on earth are we doing this for? It sure ain't for money. We got more money than we can justify or individually count. Tomorrow is not that far away, meaning that my two boys and everyone else's child will be teenagers running down fields, or on courts, and enjoying life. Someone, somewhere, develops a bomb you can put in a milk carton. Can you imagine the impact of that product if it reaches the open market? This equation becomes catastrophic and our enemies, who, for whatever reason, don't like America, now can disrupt our system by these mini and ruinous devices. I'm with my brother, we buy it with our funds, and we destroy it in public."

Whitmore said, "I want to play the devil's advocate on the side of the devil. This new technology or formula will be recreated by someone, somewhere, and at some time. I say we bilk and expose the senator, pay the baby momma, and move silently to the islands with a shit load of secured money."

The Sarge looked at him. Whitmore added, "Okay, how about this one? We all consider what Larry said for the first premise and vote on it in secret, on pieces of paper. Perhaps there are some like-minded thinkers, who agree with me."

Mallory immediately said, "The clock is ticking. Let's take a vote on the most critical question surrounding the Carbon Factor formula, realizing that with any decision we make, we're going to have terminal enemies at the gate. Are there any objections to the notion of a vote?"

No one raised their hand. Mike blurted out, "Perhaps people are afraid of the oligarchs?"

Jilkes jumped up and said, "Have you lost your damn mind? The Sarge is not an oligarch."

Mike replied, "I was referring to Larry and Zanthius who seemingly have all the damn answers."

Zanthius said, "You're here by accident, but your input is critical. You just made a statement that got our attention. Please explain what you were referring to."

Mike hesitantly began to elaborate. "When I was in business school, some students could express themselves better than others. I was simply saying that Larry and you, Zanthius, are smart cookies and the rest of you are either tired, uninterested, or unaware of what is being proposed, or said. My contribution to this equation was to state my premise that woke everyone up."

The Sarge said, "Guys, in other words, Mike does not understand how we roll. He thinks I make all the decisions. He used Zanthius and Larry in sort of a third-party comparison. He was focusing his question on me. Is that correct, Mike?"

The room became deathly silent, and Mike dropped his head before replying, "You are one astute leader."

The Sarge said, "You don't know our history, and you would really have to have been there to understand where we come from and our commitment to each other. I don't have the time to address your issue, but I will say this—until you bleed together, watch others die amongst you, go into a situation without a working gun and kill six to eight people to rescue one of your own, you'll never understand that commitment. Zanthius doesn't understand that commitment, but Larry does. Mike, we will die for each other. Larry will kill for me. Those eleven guys will kill for me, and me for them. Until you've been to hell with us, then give us information that solves our problems and not questions about our leadership. We're good at that place because no one person makes the decision. I control combat. We have others who control different aspects of this raggedy army."

Mike dropped his head lower and said, "My mouth is forever shut."

Jilkes asked, "When are you packing your bags and leaving? Every voice has a platform here. You crossed the line before you were sanctioned, but you crossed at a critical juncture, and you asked an important question. Keep your head high and remember, we just didn't meet yesterday. We're family and we're trying to embrace you and Carla. John Lee and I will take you on and tell you how we came to be. We are the 'Killing Machine from Vietnam'. Our history is all over the world, but he and I will give you a modified version of what makes us family and how we got there."

CHAPTER SIXTEEN

At 0845 hours, a consensus had been reached on the Carbon Factor. It was also agreed that an offer would be made to Helga that she couldn't refuse, and that the entire deal would be financed by the senator. The only task that remained, in regard to the Carbon Factor formula, was how to stage the illusion and misdirection.

The group also reached an agreement on how much they would offer Helga, stipulating it was a "take it or leave it" deal. The idea was simple—everyone was tired of being on the run, living out of bags, boxes, and waking up in various parts of the world. Their goal was to incriminate the senator, get her and her cronies out of the facility that was supposed to protect the citizens and not rip them off.

The Sarge said, "I think we should reach out to the senator first and change the payment configuration. Since cash is angelic, we should ask for as much cash as possible and only minimally expose ourselves to the wire transfer stuff. Monica would know about the rules and penalties of wire transfers. I don't want to have us hanging out there with all kinds of criminal complaints if this thing goes terribly wrong. Mallory, would you ask your bride to join us for a minute?"

"Sarge, I think we should invite everyone to discuss our decisions regarding the product, Helga, and the senator," Mallory countered.

The Sarge looked at his people and said, "Show of hands who thinks we should invite them to discuss this issue in the next fifteen minutes?" The hands were slow to go up but Larry and Zanthius did not waste time raising theirs.

Zanthius said, "When the outcome of this vote is told to our brides and they spread it amongst each other, you people are going to have pay a high price for this one." Suddenly all the hands were raised.

The Sarge said, "Should we ask them if they want to be a part of how we decide to end this adventure, or would they like us to continue to operate in the best interest of the group?"

Mallory looked at Mike and said, "You see how he spends tales? That's why he's, our oligarch."

#

Later, as Monica and Mallory were on their way to the barn, Monica said, "Before you know it, tomorrow is going to be upon us and we're going to be looking at kids like some people look at cars. I hope they don't try to just push a child on us. I hope they let us observe, feel, smell, and cuddle with them. I want us to be happy and never look back on our decision. We never discussed this, but are you considering an older child or children, or little people? She looked at Mallory before continuing, "I'm wide open and scared at the same time."

"We'll do this thing together and, therefore, it's going to be okay. We're a good team, and we will be good parents," Mallory confirmed.

"Yes, I know that, but we're on the move, and it doesn't seem like it's going to end anytime soon," Monica replied.

"Look at LaGina and Larry's twins, they seem to be adjusting to this. We're at the point of trying to end this thing. We're almost there, honey. However, I don't want this to impact our decision making. We're going to do this thing and not look back," Mallory stated in an attempt to comfort his love.

In the barn, Monica was given the respect of a queen. The Sarge said, "Okay brigands, no foul words or you'll walk the plank."

The Sarge smiled at Monica, and asked, "In summary, if we accept funds from a crook by wire-transfer for the purpose of exposing them, what are our liabilities and how culpable are we?"

"Sarge, I would really have to examine the conditions, intent, the source of the funds, their purpose, any international treaties violated, sanctions circumvented, and a whole bunch of other legal applications. There are no simple rules, but I will tell you that international transfers are much harder to regulate because of the privacy rubrics and banking regulations. If someone transfers money to a foreign country, it becomes hard to detect. If possible, I would avoid such deals unless they are fully above board. However, with all the shadow associations, corporations, and LLCs you guys have based around the world, it will create a challenge to figure out the where and whom, almost like the new president's taxes. You guys have that Swiss relationship, the Cayman deals, as well as those banking relationships in the Islands, Spain, London, Paris, Germany, and South Africa, of all places. My suggestion is to be creative, but do not let me know what you're doing," Monica stated.

Jilkes asked, "What does that mean?"

"Ask my husband once I'm out of here so I won't know what you did in case I have to defend you. Anything else, gentlemen?" The Sarge thanked her and told her to take one of the mules back to the farmhouse.

At the door, Monica turned and said, "Each of you should have your affairs paid up, a couple of million in dumbass CDs, and a few million buried in your backyards in cash. I just heard that on CNBC—not my suggestion, but theirs. Good day, gentlemen."

At 0930 hours, the Sarge said, "Are there any other issues relative to how we relate to the senator? I sure would love to buy some more time to hash this thing out a little more. There are too many avenues to approach, and we're not seasoned in the clandestine art of lying and cheating. We're honest people who have been thrown into a volcano."

Larry said, "We need to change the configuration of the funds. How about 65% cash up front and the balance wired?"

Zanthius said, "This is not our deal. We were dragged into this mess by the agent. The agent does not trust the senator and that is the only deal that she will tender. Not to mention the fact that the agent has received some incredible offers from the East, the West, and from unstable parts of the world. We make all of this known and walk away from it. If Helga doesn't like what we have to offer, then so be it. We sell her latest picture to the press."

Larry said, "Dad, it's 0950 hours. You want to make that call?"

The Sarge looked at each person in the barn and tried to remember their input. He took a deep breath and said, "I just want out of this mess." He put his glasses on and found the senator's cell number. The phone rang eight times and then went to a voicemail that was full. The Sarge said, "I think she's been cooking the books as well and is playing us."

John Lee said, "Redial the number."

"Oh no, John Lee. If I did that, she would think we're anxious to get on with this event. Let the call resonate in her brain for a while, I'm sure she's going to call back."

Asiram drove up to the barn and asked her husband if they could have a conversation. She said to him, "I need to go to Philly and collect my mail. That place is where I had official and unofficial information sent to me in code."

He loudly exclaimed, "Damn! I need to do the same thing, but I feel the timing is not good. We're trying to conclude this thing with Helga, the Carbon Factor formula, and the senator. Do you think we can wait until tonight and the two of us slip away?"

"I'm not slipping away unless we have some bad ass dudes to protect our backs."

"I was just joking. I'm not leaving here without a full contingency of bad ass dudes and you're not leaving here without the eyes of your man on you at all times."

Somewhere during that statement, a light went on in Zanthius's head. He screamed to the top of his lungs, "Oh shit! I know exactly where the crucial piece of the Carbon Factor formula is and what the mathematical equation is to assemble it."

Zanthius paused and ran back into the barn and yelled, "Guys, Helga thinks we have all of the pieces to the Carbon Factor formula. But there is another part that I didn't secure because I never understood her cryptic message that baby Zanthius would have the final piece. We had Larry send a package to an unknown address we completely forgot about. I assumed she had the total formula. What we have is the conclusive piece of the formula that makes our part final. I mean, come now, we have been on the move, have been chased, and confronted with mayhem at every single turn. Getting rid of the formula was tantamount to our success, but we forgot about Larry sending a package to his nefarious post office box. I think somewhere in the middle, both formulas are needed to construct this reprehensible weapon. We need to postpone all interactions with the senator and Helga and proceed to DC. We need to visit Asiram's place in the Northeast, and Larry must remove the information from a box at the main GPO, if that's where he sent it."

Larry smiled and said, "Touché, my brother."

Zanthius loudly announced, "This is crazy, but please trust me. I think the formula is written like a symphony. Okay, stay with me. The formula code lines are written in two parts. Part one, Helga has, and part two, we have. That is where the numbers 234 come into play. Okay, what is 234's relevance, you ask? Well, the numbers 234 represent the room number in a hotel, in the Dominican Republic, that I used to frequent. My venue, of choice, was the resort, La Romana, in La Romana, Dominican Republic. It was a fabulous place next to the sugar processing plant that was operated by Gulf and Western. I was a little anal about my accommodations. Once I stayed in Room 234, it was my room of choice for the many future visits. I loved the land and was enthralled by it and its people. When I briefly disclosed this to Helga, she attached those numbers to my very existence, especially since that was my room number in St. Moritiz as well.

"Anyway, listen, the first two lines of the formula are in her possession. The next three parts of the formula are in ours. The next four lines of the formula are in hers and then it repeats itself. No wonder the Russians keep blowing themselves up. They never had the complete formula or anything close to it. That women is brilliant!" Zanthius exclaimed.

He turned to look at his wife and realized that he had just created a Saint Helga. He stated, "She may be a manipulative brilliant strategist, but it's my wife who saved my life and got me out of that country."

He then looked at his father, and said, "Pops, call Helga and attempt to make the deal with her. Tell her we need random sections of the formula to make sure this is not a ruse."

The Sarge called her number and received a message that the number had been disconnected." He shared this with his son, and Zanthius responded, "Give it a few minutes and answer a scrambled number. Ask her to send you five random lines of the formula so that you can make sure she is not sending you the recipe for baking soda."

Jong began to frantically play with his computer and realized the pieces of the formula he had did not transcend to the next stage. He immediately gave this information to the Sarge and Zanthius. Larry looked over his shoulder and suggested additional moves because it appeared to him the formula that Jong had was disjointed and out of sequence.

Zanthius turned to his father and said, "Pops, Asiram and I need to go to DC. Larry sent a package to somewhere that we must retrieve, and my wife has to visit her home in the Northeast to secure papers and other possessions.

The Sarge said, "I don't like splitting my security, but I'll have Rashida and Juan engage the security systems. Make sure the caretaker's light goes on, so he knows not to venture on to the farm. Okay, here's the deal. I'm requesting Larry, Brown, Bernstein, Jilkes, John Lee, and Mallory to provide security in two different vans for Asiram and Zanthius. I need, Jong, Gladstone, Carlos, Mike, Whitmore, Montomie, Chakes, and McArthur to take-up strategic positions along with me to defend the farm. I also need Okema, Yeshida and Somara on long guns as well. Mallory, make sure everyone has their earpieces in, with working and clean cell phones. Let's make this thing happen in the next thirty-minutes, people. Oh, you people heading to Philly and DC, remember, guns are prohibited. Don't carry but know that the vans are fully loaded. Asiram, how much time will you need at your place?"

"I should be in and out of there in thirty minutes unless someone found out where I keep my papers. The house has been rebuilt and secured, but the interior was not to be touched."

"Larry, are you comfortable with the idea of going back into the GPO?"

"Sarge, I may give the box stuff to one of the guys and direct him from the van. I'm not sure if my picture is floating around that place."

"Okay, work it out, but don't compromise yourself or your comrades."

# # #

A few hours later, the group stopped about one mile from Asiram's place. Mallory called for an Uber because he didn't want to have pictures of the vans and plates captured. He also had a fake account under the name of Luther Rackley.

The Uber arrived and took the group to their destination, Jilkes and John Lee accompanied Asiram into her house and told the Uber driver to wait. She entered her place and tears came to her eyes.

Jilkes said, "Don't become emotional—let's obtain what you need and get out of here." Asiram entered her bedroom and pushed a few buttons. Two panels moved, and two collapsible bags were displayed. She said, "Okay boys, that's what I need. Grab them and let's get out of here."

In the Uber after a few minutes of driving, Jilkes said to the driver, "I need you to drop us on the corner on your right, coming up." He threw three one-hundred-dollar bills at the driver and said, "Have a nice day."

Mallory and the crew drove up shortly, and the men threw the duffle bags into the back of the vans. On the ride to GPO in DC, Larry said, "I need you guys to go in and secure the package I sent there a year or so ago. I'm afraid to go in there because of obvious reasons. My box number is 1668. Secure the contents and don't dally around."

Jilkes looked at John Lee and said, "It means don't waste time or play around."

"Thanks, Mr. Webster."

#

An hour or so later, the two men entered the Grand Post Office without a hitch, found the box, retrieved the package, locked the box, and exited the premises.

Once in the van, John Lee said, "It's a good thing you didn't go waltzing your fancy ass up in that big place with all that wasted ceiling space."

"And why is that?" Larry inquired.

"There be wanted posters of your ass all over the place, and especially, in the bathrooms. They have a $25.00 reward for information leading to your arrest. Jilkes told them you were outside, and they told him that they were focusing on a $100 reward."

"Thanks, John Lee. Did you guys have any issues?"

"Naw, we walked in, followed your directions and picked up the package."

Zanthius said, "We need to leave and head back to the farm just in case this is not a soundproof operation. This city has cameras on every corner, and I want to get back to a place where I can, without challenge, have a weapon attached to my hip."

# # #

One hour later, Mallory called the Sarge and said, "We're two minutes away from the turn-off. Have them shut down the system but monitor us all the way to the farmhouse and keep an eye out for any attempt to breach the property."

The Sarge said, "As soon as you park, I need to know what your expectations regarding traveling to middle-America and the Catholic Charities, are. Monica thinks we're going to leave without you having the opportunity to visit the children there."

"Sarge, I will talk to her and we will let you know what our intent is once I get back. Thanks for thinking about us and our desired adventure."

# # #

When the people who were in Philly and DC got out of the van, Mallory asked Asiram, "Do you think you were able to access your place without detection? I'm only asking because the Sarge is going to ask me the same question."

Asiram looked at him and said, "I think we were in and out so fast, no one noticed. It's not a secret, but I had a significant amount of money hanging around in that place and, as a matter of fact, I have two more bags hidden deep down in the soil."

"If our foundation purchased that property from you to turn it into a shelter for homeless vets, would you be willing to part with it? I also saw a motel that looked like a dump that we could investigate, perhaps buy and turn into temporary housing for vets, as well," Mallory said.

"Mallory, I'm with my family and whatever my family wants to do, then I'm in on it. I also want to consider providing shelter for homeless and pregnant mothers who don't have any options available to them."

"Okay, I'm going to talk to the Sarge about both ideas. I'm guessing those two bags are filled with cash. Is that correct?"

"Your assumptions are accurate. However, I think you need to focus on a more personal issue, Mallory. You need to set the parameters for how long we stay and make it known to your wife this family is not leaving until you guys have decided or not decided on your quest. She's not in a good place because she thinks the majority rules. Ben Beckmire is the majority, and he rules when he's well informed," Asiram stated.

"I know. I don't think she believes I'm on board with her desire to adopt. I must admit, I tried to stall the process, but our fearless leader called me a chump and a coward, or something like that. Okay, have the guys help you with the bags. Also make sure Larry and Jong try to figure out Zanthius's symphonic notion while I attend to my bride."

Asiram walked over to Mallory and said, "She's deserving of an opportunity to be a mother. Every woman is!"

"I guess I'm selfish. It'll work out. Wait and see. This place and all of our places are going to become baby farms," Mallory stated.

# # #

At 2050 hours, an irate senator called Beckmire. She did not hide her annoyance as she said, "I hear the product is being sold to someone in the Middle East."

The Sarge said, "Good evening. I told you regardless of what you thought, we did not control this process. However, I can tell you that we secured our piece of the puzzle and unless it's a ruse, no one is selling anyone anything of value. We have the part of the symphony that makes it sound like music. The other noises are sounds of an orchestra rehearsing."

The Sarge didn't hear any background noise and asked, "Senator, are you there?" There was no indication that the line was still active. He thought to himself, "Why would she hang up on me after hearing that I had the confirming pieces in hand and was looking at them as we spoke."

The Sarge saw Mallory approaching and screamed, "Oh shit, I screwed up." He ran towards the farmhouse and yelled at Rashida, "Put the farm on full alert, immediately." Rashida didn't ask why but hit the activate button and the weapons system and cameras came online in a matter of minutes. He told her to hit the internal alarm and to state that this was not a drill.

In ten minutes, the entire farm was covered with long-guns and expert markspersons. Their weak link was the ex-senator's property. Jong's cousin had wired into the existing network and had forwarded a signal to the box. Juan said, "Honey, what is this signal that's beeping?" Rashida looked at the source, triangulated it and said, "We have 66% coverage at the other place that we haven't been to yet."

McArthur said, "It took us too long to react to that alarm. We've got to practice a quicker implementation if we live through this alert. Most people on the farm thought it was another drill to reduce the reaction time to the alarm."

At 2115 hours, Rashida yelled for her dad to enter the box. When he, Jilkes, John Lee, and Mallory entered, Rashida said, "Dad, this is for real. Those red dots are heat signatures and those green dots are weapons. We have an incursion about to happen." The Sarge looked at her screen and said, "There seems to be more dots west than east and significantly more north than south."

Rashida said, "Those east and west will be culled out quickly. Those approaching from the south will be terminated as well. My concern is we have not checked the system reporting from the north—the ex-senator's property."

Jilkes asked, "Who's on the roof and who is assigned to the barn?"

Rashida said, "You, John Lee, Mike and the Sarge are assigned to the barn." The Sarge asked, "When were we going to be notified?"

"Assignments are handed out each day, for the following day, Dad. When we had those two false alarms, you were texted your position as well as the rest of you guys."

"Is there anyone in the barn now?" the Sarge asked.

Rashida responded stridently, "Mike and Larry, and they're going to need back up ASAP."

The Sarge said, "What channel are we operating on tonight?"

Rashida rolled her eyes, shifted her head and replied, "Dad if we get through this incursion, I'm going to give you a spanking. You have got to pay attention to the information I feed you. If you designate others to handle specific aspects of our safety, then please announce it."

"That's it, I need to delegate or relegate assignments to others, rather than trying to assess or prescribe a solution and fulfill a scenario for every mission," the Sarge admitted.

Jilkes and John Lee had left 20 seconds prior to the Sarge who told his daughter, "There will be no quarter given tonight. I need you to be strong on this one and hit the buttons. Can I depend on you to do that?"

"Don't insult me, Dad. I'm pregnant and LaGina is here with all my family. I will shoot the Pope if he violates our boundaries."

Asiram got a call on her cell phone and it was her caretaker who stated, "There are a lot of people loading weapons at the top of the hill. Do you want me to summon the police?"

Asiram screamed, "No, no! Please don't do that. What I need you to do is call me if more show up. We'll handle the rest, and thanks for your awareness and discretion."

The largest intruding force came from the north. The living senator knew where the ex-senator kept his stash and was counting on his bank to support her bank. She also thought that the northern part of the property was unprotected.

# # #

In a matter of 1,380,000 milliseconds, or 1,380 seconds, or only 23 minutes, 131 individuals, got their tickets stamped to enter the last concert they would ever attend—'welcome to hell', enjoy your stay, were the final notes of the last song they would hear because Rashida pressed a button that read, 'engage'! The insatiable appetite of the ODS presented itself once again versus a foe who would never see it, know where it came from, but would realize that it's dedication to a conclusive response, was also preeminent, unseen, unknown, and unadulterated. As if it happened in slow motion, or as if time had stood still, the ODS searched methodically for intruders and calculated firing scenarios that would find the targets no matter where they took cover.

The notion of mechanized mayhem had been accepted as an alternative to field engagement. The older guys, initially against wholesale slaughter, realized that the ODS was a life saving tool that they should embrace, appreciate, and make as a permanent part of their survival tool kit.

#

Those approaching from the north had to contend with old fashion live shooters. At the top of the southern part of the road, the caretaker of the farm placed a shotgun to the head of an individual in a large van and said, "I don't know who you are, but you're trespassing, and I can blow your damn head off. If you move a single muscle, I will leave any heirs you have with a horrible picture of what a double blast to the head from a shotgun can do to a human."

Emerging from the van was the senator, who wanted to personally end the siege, kill the members on the farm, and collect the final part of the Carbon Factor formula. She announced, "I am a sitting United States Senator."

The caretaker replied, "And here I thought you were the Queen of the fucking Netherlands. Keep your hands where I can see them, or you will be shot for trespassing on my property. Any unwarranted movement will be met with a double barrel blast from this shotgun."

The caretaker called Asiram and said, "The whole damn state can hear all of that gunfire. I have some woman here claiming to be a senator, what should I do with her?"

"Hold her until we're given the all clear signal. Tie that broad up if you like. However, keep an eye on her. She's a trickster."

The senator literally sent men the colonel had wrestled up, to their immediate graves, from automatic gunfire that was hidden and controlled by a computer.

#

The Sarge and his group were under constant fire. Gladstone, Chakes, and Jong after focusing their attention on the east and west, began annihilating the advancing force from the north. The Sarge said, "If we live through this one, we had better place an order for more computer-operated-weapons. I'm getting too old for this mess—people shooting at me."

After two or three minutes, the shooting stopped. The Sarge stated, "That was too abrupt to be real. I know we didn't surrender, but I sure as hell hope they did. I've killed enough people for one night." He called the box and asked Juan, "What's the status of the incursion?"

"Sarge, we have lots of dormant bodies. As I scan the property, it seems as though someone has called a halt to the siege."

Asiram heard the discussion and said, "I think the caretaker took things into his own hands and forced the senator to order her people to surrender."

The Sarge asked, "What on earth are you talking about?"

"Our caretaker found a woman lurking in a vehicle at the top of the road and captured her. She announced that she was a sitting United States Senator. He may have forced her to conclude this event. Give me a moment and let me call him."

Asiram called the caretaker and asked, "Are you still in possession of your captive?"

"I have her tied from her head to her toe. Some colonel called her, and I made her tell him to retreat and that's when the gunfire stopped. I guess she's the woman in charge. Should I put her in my mule and bring her down to you?"

"I don't recommend that action since there still may be hostiles hiding in the woods. I will send two of ours in our van to fetch her. Please stay put and keep out of this mess. These people are dangerous, and I wouldn't want anything to happen to you or any of yours."

Asiram told the Sarge, "The person, who may be the senator, gave the retreat signal. I told the caretaker that we would send people to get her in one of our vans."

The Sarge said to Jong, "I need you to go up the road and pick up a human package from the caretaker. Pick up Chakes. I'll give him a heads up. Be careful because there still may be hostiles out there."

The Sarge then asked Asiram to make a call to the cleaners and to tell them that we have a lot of dry-cleaning needs.

On the way up the road, two bullets hit the side of van. Jong sped up and called Rashida and reported, "We just took enemy fire."

Rashida began to search out the assailants through the heat signature of the rounds that were fired. Deep in the woods in the east, the scanner picked up two moving targets with weapons. The machine pistols were out of ammunition and Rashida called upon the long guns. Two rounds were fired, and two intruders were hit. She called Jong, and said, "The road back should be clear. We'll do another scan, but you guys should be good in the van."

The Sarge asked for volunteers to sweep the ex-senator's property and to set up a perimeter. Carlos volunteered his guys to do the work, stating they were getting fat and lazy, and that this would be a good learning experience for them. He told the Sarge he was going with them, but they needed cover until they were certain the area was clear. The Sarge authorized Mike, Larry, John Lee, and Jilkes to advance and provide protection.

At the top of the road, the caretaker provided the group with a woman who was bound with her mouth taped shut. He said to Jong, "This woman keeps talking about she's a senator for the United States. I taped her mouth shut because I thought she was the Queen of the Netherlands or some other country."

# # #

Jong drove past the farmhouse and towards the barn. They drove the van into the barn and pulled the bound and gagged person out of the vehicle.

The Sarge exclaimed, "Well, I'll be damned! Senator, you back again? I thought the last time we made it perfectly clear that this not a public park and you can't just ride up in here with an army. You seem to like getting innocent people killed. Someone take that tape off her mouth."

The Sarge continued, "What would make a sitting United States senator, from another state, leave her golden perch and come down to the country to check on poor folks like us—not once, but twice? Oh, don't tell me, I think I have an idea. When I told you that I had the final piece in my hands, you decided to try to take it rather than pay for it, didn't you?"

"Mr. Beckmire, do you know the penalty for kidnapping a sitting United States senator?"

"Ma'am, which part of captive don't you get? You're not here." The Sarge looked around the room and asked, "Hey guys, has anyone seen a sitting United States senator here on the farm? And by the way, why would a sitting United States

Senator visit a farm in Virginia, especially when she wasn't invited? Okay, let's stop the horseshit. Is that television working?"

John Lee said, "It used to work, and we have film of people in this very same room that got their inners cut out. Do you want to show her the video of that Scottie woman?"

The Sarge looked at the senator and said, "This might entertain you a little. We shall see."

The Senator said, "How can you few conquer that many without a single casualty?"

The Sarge said, "Oh, we have casualties, but they're insignificant compared to what your people experienced. You know our history. You knew we were sent on one-way-missions and returned each time. If you really wanted to attack us, you should have dropped a damn bomb on us much like that stupid ass mayor in Philadelphia did to that group of protesters."

"If I survive this ordeal, I will consider it. That's if I ever come up against you people in the future. My question is simple—what are you going to do with all of those bodies around the property?"

Jong asked, "What bodies? I looked in the fields. There are no bodies there. Maybe they all went to hell in a hurry?"

"Your problem is that a sitting United States Senator will be missing tomorrow at roll call for some very important legislation."

Jong asked, "Are you referring to this person on the screen? That one in the center, is that you? How about the woman on the left, snorting white powder, is that you? Maybe the woman in bed with the recently deceased senator and his boyfriend, is that you? How about the woman who is in bed with two men and who is kissing a third person's private part, is that you? We be sure that none of those are you, but we be sure this one is you." Jong showed the senator being violated in a place that is usually reserved for alleviating waste with a Russian flag hanging out of her mouth.

John Lee said, "Now, here is my favorite part of the movie. That there woman named Scottie thought I didn't have the pig-power in me to do what I did to her. You might be knowing this, but I be stating it again. That woman cut my woman's inners out and hung my lady over my banister. I thought it was only fitting I return the favor. Now, that be the next scene that you will be seeing."

The television showed John Lee cutting away Scotties pants and inserting his huge blade into her private zone. He then without emotion, violently yanked it all the way to her brain. The senator passed out.

Jilkes woke her up and asked, "Can I get you anything, Senator?" A despondent Senator said, "I'm a sitting United States Senator, and I will report this activity."

Jilkes said, "You won't have the opportunity to report anything Senator because officially, no one knows you're here and we're going to gut you from your sex zone to your brain, wrap your remains up and take them out to the edge of the farm where the bears, wolves, foxes, rats, roaches, snakes, wild dogs, and a shit load of other little things, love fresh flesh. You were a sitting United States Senator. From this point forward, you are food for the indigenous animals."

She screamed, "What do you want?"

The Sarge yelled, "You have the audacity to ask that question of us. You sent hundreds of men to their graves, including perhaps, your part-time lover, the colonel. Perhaps the question is better asked from us to you, what is it you came here to take from us while killing all of us in the process, including our babies? Did you come to relieve our property of the gold bullion or the millions in cold hard cash? Oh, perhaps you came to obtain the Carbon Factor formula since I told you I had it in my hand? I know Senator, you came for all three—the money, the gold, and the formula. Let me tell you how this is going to proceed."

The Sarge was interrupted by Jong who whispered that the caretaker had called Asiram after he looked in the back of the senator's van. The caretaker told Asiram that he found three exceptionally large trunks. The Sarge told him to tell people to stand-down until someone checked for explosives.

The Sarge said to the senator, "We're going to give you the opportunity to resign your office, speak of all the collaborations you have had with people here and abroad to swindle the government of the United States out of what I estimate, is in the billions of dollars. Oh, it was mentioned to me there are three trunks in the vehicle you were riding in. Would you mind telling me what's in them?"

"Nothing that would interest you. More importantly, if you turn the Carbon Factor formula over to me, I can guarantee you people a half of a billion dollars," the Senator announced.

Jilkes said, "Sounds like you already have someone in mind who is willing to pay a lot of money for the formula." Jilkes then winked at the Sarge and said, "Senator, we have a country that will pay us a full billion for the formula, and we don't have to share it with you."

The Senator said, "You people don't have the international connections to pull off that kind of a deal. You're going to sell your country out and probably never get a single penny of the money."

The Sarge interjected, "We have a pre-payment of $500 million in our various accounts around the world. Our new scientist has encrypted the formula and removed key aspects of it until the other $500 million is deposited, otherwise the transfer is not completed. If you survive the night, perhaps we will show you what we're capable of doing."

The senator looked at the monitor and camera before asking, "Is that thing recording?"

The Sarge said, "No, it's not recording. Is there something you want to say?"

The Senator said, "Listen, can we please go outside where I don't have to worry about devices recording me and things coming back to haunt me after people doctor them?"

Jilkes asked, "Did anyone search her?" There was no reply. "In that case, I suggest that we keep her hands bound."

As the Sarge, Jilkes, Zanthius, and John Lee escorted the senator outside, Jong texted Rashida to record all movements and sounds from the barn area.

Once in the front of the barn, the senator said, "I can double or even triple the amount of money you're talking about. I have contacts in the 'Kingdom' who will, for this kind of technology, pay any price I ask. I mean, I must admit, my thought was to eliminate you people and make this a sole source deal. I'm not opposed to a partner and, I must say, a very astute one, at that, who is willing to earn two billion."

The Sarge said, "What would you earn on the deal, Senator?"

"I would earn the same amount as you—two billion. If you want to earn even more, I have contacts in some unstable places who will pay probably six for the product."

Zanthius said, "Are you serious? Someone will pay six billion for the Carbon Factor formula. Sarge, that's a lot of money and you know you always say, 'go with the highest bidder'."

The Sarge said, "The higher the price someone is willing to pay for the formula also equates to people with radical ideologies who may direct it against our country."

"Six billion is a lot of money and it gets us out of this mess with cash to burn," Jilkes said.

The senator incorrectly surmised that the group's decision was greed based and said, "Sergeant Beckmire, even your people realize how large this thing is. The money you've captured through unenlightened raids and other efforts, trifles compared to what I'm talking about. I'm speaking about a deal worth upwards of six to ten billion depending on how low in the 'hate America file', we want to dig. Listen, if I offered this thing to that disgusting person in North, he would be all over this deal. The problem there is that he doesn't have any real money and he would want to pay us on layaway, or with drugs and/or counterfeit money. Now, on the other hand, if we mentioned the possibility to the Iranians, hell, we're at the top or above the ten billion range. Russia has lost three billion and lots of lives trying to replicate a bad formula. I think the Kingdom would pay a premium for it, but there are others in the region that will try to outbid them."

The Sarge said, "Obviously, the leadership is interested in maximizing its profits and minimizing its costs, but we don't want the product to wind up in the hands of one of those regimes that absolutely hates America. We are interested, but we need to know who the final bidders are. We can conclude our current relationship by refunding the money and indicating to them the price has skyrocketed."

Zanthius said, "Sarge, we got to make this deal."

"Yeah man! That is a lot of money," Jilkes said.

"Why you be hesitating, Sarge? This here is more money than we can count. We got to get this money and sell the formula," John Lee announced.

The Senator once again thought avarice was the motivating factor and said, "Let me go and make a few calls and get this ball rolling. By this time tomorrow, we can all be billionaires at the click of the enter button on the keyboard."

Larry showed up at the front of the barn with one of the senator's men. The man had a bullet wound to the leg. Larry grabbed the duct tape and secured the man's wound.

The Sarge became vexed and said to the Senator, "I don't trust you and I never will."

"You don't have to trust me. Just count your money after I make the deal, and we part and never look back."

"Why would you consider doing this to the country that you were elected to one of the most prestigious positions to serve in?"

"Come now, Sergeant Beckmire. Money is the motivating factor for everything men, or women, do. That altruistic bull shit ain't American. What I'm proposing is the real America—make money on the backs of those who are poor and dumb."

Jong walked outside and said, "How they say that thing in Hollywood? That be a wrap."

Zanthius said, "No, Jong. The saying is, 'That's a wrap'."

Rashida and Juan tapped into Facebook while broadcasting the senator's live comments. Although the picture was blurry at points, it still gave a clear shot of her offering to sell her office and the American people for billions of dollars. There was also a blood sample taken from a too tight plastic restrainer that was acquired, 'by the book'.

This information went viral as soon as they left the barn. Rashida drove up to the barn and said, "Dad, everything said by the sitting senator is on FB. There are 550 hits already. It's only been three minutes, and it's beginning to spread like wildfire.

"I assume you're the not so smart Senator, who offered to talk to some extremely dangerous people about a product that will ultimately hurt Americans. I'm Rashida, the Sarge's daughter, and I want to thank you for the material. I know you'll deny it, but your credibility is shot to pieces. Nice to meet you."

As the senator's head slumped towards the ground, she said, "I guess I can't ask for an accommodation and expect one. Is such a thing possible?"

The Sarge asked, "What might you have in mind, a pirate's way out?"

"I'm no pirate, but I do recall their one-shot rule. Do you suppose you could afford me an honorable out?"

"Senator, you must be delirious. That is not an honorable way out. For you, it's quick, but for your remaining family, it's an embarrassment at every level and on every fricking day. You screwed with the wrong honest people. We had faith and trust in you, but you were owned by my cousin, a man who placed suicide vests on my grandbabies, and I will never forget that sight, or forgive those who had a hand in it. You're my cousin's lover, freak, puppet, and you marched to his beat. Now, you've exposed yourself by being involved in a direct assault on our farm."

The Sarge paused and looked as if he was having a stroke and yelled, "Full alert, engage the systems." Jong repeated the call to Juan, who was in the box. Some of the weapons in the system, were empty from the prior engagement. The only aspects of the system still in operation were the cameras and long guns.

The Senator said, "It appears to me you've found yourself in a place where you could term it, *détente*. I didn't know it would work out this way, but your daughter is probably in the hands of my people."

The sound of the long guns cranking and sorting out new targets could be heard. The new intruders eluded the detection system by donning special suits made of an unknown material.

The Sarge said, "Your people cannot get off this property alive. Those guns are precise, and if my daughter has as much as a broken fingernail, I will gut you here and now."

He looked at the merc with the leg wound, then at John Lee, and said, "I need to borrow your favorite knife." John Lee unsheathed it and handed it to the Sarge. He walked over to the injured man, got on his knees, plunged the knife into the man's scrotum and ran it up to his jaw. The senator fainted and hit her head on the floor.

John Lee exclaimed, "Damn, Sarge, you got to leave that kind of work to me and my friend!"

A few minutes later, Zanthius woke the senator up and said, "Fainting only delays the inevitable." In the background, three small caliber rounds were fired. The people apprehending Rashida saw she was pregnant and never bothered to search her. She was able to secure her .380 weapon and made three quick head shots. She started running, ran into Juan who was stalking the group who had lost their bearings, and unbeknownst to them, were heading deeper into the interior of the farm as opposed to leaving it.

Juan said, "Rashida, you knew I would find you and execute those bastards. I guess I didn't have to, did I?" He called Jong and told him that the package was secure and the people wearing funny suits were terminated by Rashida. Jong whispered to the Sarge what had been relayed to him by Juan. In essence, that all was okay. The Sarge commanded, "Make a call to the house and have someone report on the status of the people there."

The Sarge said to the senator, "Your plan was a good one, but your people didn't count on the resourcefulness of our group. What kind of material were they wearing to avoid detection?"

"I was not made aware of the operational details and/or materials of their uniforms," the Senator replied.

The Sarge said, "I guess it doesn't really matter."

# # #

Juan called Jong and told him the cleaning company was at the top of the hill. He also asked Jong if it was clear to engage them. The Sarge interrupted and instructed Jong to tell the cleaners there were possible active laundry in the fields and warned that they would have to wait until they conducted their own due diligence.

Juan called Jong back and said, "Tell the Sarge that there are 55,000 hits on FB about the senator."

Jong pulled the Sarge aside and told him that the FB count was up to 55,000. He smiled and said to the senator, "I'll escort you to your vehicle now."

Twenty minutes later and at the top of the road that accessed the farm, the Sarge said, "Senator, I'll not preach to you nor will I condemn your actions. I am neither priest nor angel. Goodbye!" The senator entered the van, hesitated, and gingerly turned the key. The vehicle started and she breathed a sigh of relief. She abruptly got out of the vehicle, walked to the back of the it, and opened the door. There was nothing to gaze upon because the good brigands had relieved her of any useable booty.

## CHAPTER SEVENTEEN

The senator went to her apartment, turned on her computer, and logged onto Facebook. It had taken her an hour to get home, and by the time she logged into her account, the hits had exceeded the 200,000 mark. Her cellphone was ringing off the hook, yet the only call she accepted was from Walter.

Walter asked, "Why on earth did you take on those people by yourself? You've exposed our entire network, and you know that ain't good. You need to get out of there, head to your safe house, and sort out your affairs. I suggest poison instead of a bullet, but if our associates get to you first, it's going to be a bullet, unless you can get out of DC and into Baltimore or Pennsylvania. I might be able to buy you some time. You have the entire world looking for you. I could have told you not to go down there and try to get them. That place is fortified. It produces mechanized mayhem. It's all controlled by computers with their own network and backup protocols."

The senator started to cry and said, "I thought I could do this one thing, and gain favor from you again. I miss being with you. I was forced to liaison with a bird colonel, and he was terrible. He told me his people could capture that place and be out of there with the formula within an hour. All those men were killed for nothing and my entire career and reputation destroyed." Walter thought to himself, "And you forfeited your life."

Walter said, "I can have a car come for you in the next ten to fifteen minutes. Pack only your passport, money, and credit cards. Don't pack any bags just in case you're being watched. Do you want me to implement this plan or what?"

"Please, honey. Rescue me from this mess."

"Okay, my people are going to bring you a wig, a hat, a walking cane, and sunglasses. Follow their instructions and don't try to be creative. I love you and I'll see you within the hour."

Twenty minutes after the call from Walter was concluded, a call from the concierge was placed to the senator's flat indicating that two gentlemen were there to see her. When they arrived to her flat, she opened the door and let them in. Three minutes later, the senator was dead from what would appear to be a self-induced toxin.

## CHAPTER EIGHTEEN

In less than twenty-four hours, 2.2 million people had viewed the senators comments on Facebook. When asked about the Facebook posts, the sitting president indicated that he believed it was more "fake news" from those unreliable stations.

After repeated calls to her cellphone from the concierge, the condo's maintenance man and a janitor, after knocking and banging on the door to the senator's flat, and in accordance with the policies of the condo, entered the premises to investigate. Upon entering the flat, they noticed the back of the head of the senator sitting in a chair. They called her name and there was no response. The janitor walked around to the front of the chair and noticed there was a foreign substance around her mouth and on her clothes. The staff immediately radioed the concierge and told him what they found. The concierge left his station and went to the senator's flat where he looked around. He saw that her purse was open and looked at his people. He knew they had removed any cash and would split it later with him. He picked up the senator's phone, dialed the police, and reported that the senator was dead.

The news of her death hit the news wires and went viral. The apparent cause of death was unknown, but it was reported that a strange substance was found on her clothes. The conspiracy theorists began to work different hypotheses and wondered if this was part of a larger plot, and if there were other co-conspirators. Questions about her relationships began to surface, but no one could identify any partner. Cameras from the condo's lobby showed pictures of the two men who visited the senator. Both men wore long coats, had gloves on their hands, and what appeared to be fake mustaches and beards. The concierge indicated the senator would often receive company, and people constantly delivered documents and gifts to her flat. He also said he wasn't suspicious about the appearances of the men because the two men had visited with the senator in the past with varying disguises. He indicated his role was to screen strangers, not draw attention to guests of the residents.

#

The people at the farm woke up to the news that a sitting senator was found dead in her flat with a yet to be analyzed substance in her mouth and on her clothes. The news also spoke of the Facebook posting that had surpassed 3.5 million hits. Images of the on-camera propositions showed the senator presenting to a group of unidentified individuals, who were later revealed to be billionaires, how to make billions of dollars on the sale of an unproven destructive formula. It was also reported that her constant companion, a colonel in the military, was missing.

#

At 0600 hours, the Sarge said he wanted to have a full group meeting at 0700 hours to discuss the events of the previous night and how one of their own was captured by the intruders. He spoke with Jong, asked him to have his cousin come to the farm and re-arm their weapons system, as well as explain how as many as three intruders could move around the farm without detection. He told Jong he feared and would not be surprised if there was more cash or items of interest stored in the ex-senator's house. Jong told the Sarge he had called his cousin last night and that he should arrive at the farm by 0800 hours.

The Sarge suspended the morning run/walk because the cleaning people were still at work in the woods. Asiram was in the kitchen with other people, and when she saw the Sarge, she said, "Don't forget to send people up the road to my caretaker's property to pick up those three cases. I would hate for him to get curious and detonate an ordinance."

The Sarge said, "I need two volunteers to run up the road and pick up some cases and leave them in the barn so that Jong's cousin can inspect and defuse them."

John Lee, Jilkes, Somara, and Yeshida were the selected volunteers. Somara asked John Lee, "When will we go south and check on our home?"

Yeshida chimed in and said, "Yes, when are we going home to see what has been done?"

John Lee looked at Jilkes who said, "Why don't we figure that out after the meeting. Listen, I know you guys are feeling closed in and need to have your own stuff, place, and privacy, but until we complete this mess, it's best we stay together to protect each other. What I will put on the table at the meeting is that we would like to divert our group to the south, and, perhaps to St. Thomas for a few days of sun and fun. Is that acceptable to you guys? I mean, John Lee, I'm not speaking for you, but I'm feeling the same way as the ladies. If we could make a stop prior to heading to the islands, that would also be fun. However, when we leave is dependent upon when Mallory and Monica go back to the adoption place."

Yeshida looked at her man and said, "I'm not putting pressure on you, because I do love this group and all of its members, but I do want to have a home to chase my child around in."

Jilkes dropped his head and replied, "Having two families can be traumatic. I will work this thing out my love."

John Lee looked at his bride and exclaimed, "I be feeling you! I just want to make you happy. I just need you to realize when we be alone, we be vulnerable. These people don't care about you or our baby, they be putting suicide vests on children." He kissed his wife before the two men went in the caretaker's barn and placed the three trunks in their vans.

At exactly 0700 hours, the Sarge said, "I want to delay this meeting until Jong's cousin has reinforced our machinery in the field. I'm not completely sure all the hostiles have been cleaned. Please forgive me for any inconvenience, but I want to make sure we have everyone's attention, and everybody is here and not in or on a lookout position. I will call a meeting once the weapons are restocked. Thanks, and by the way, the pancakes microwave at 3.5 seconds and are an amazing meal."

Jong's cousin, his favorite son and other members of his group appeared at the top of the road at 0725 hours and made the call. He drove his people onto the property, and they immediately began to reload, collect spent casings, and check the machine pistols. He decided to bring new pistols and larger magazines and installed them in the relevant places. At one of the locations, his son called to him to look at the corrosion on one of the weapons. Jong's cousin determined that the load of the ammunition was too high for constant firing. He placed a call to another son and told him to bring two cases of the 110 grain special loads for the .9 millimeter. He instructed his crew to replace the weapons, secure the connections and collect all shell casings. He indicated that he would be back to check each unit.

Jong's cousin entered one of his vehicles and advanced towards the farmhouse. Jong saw him coming and went outside to give him full instructions. When the van came to a complete stop, his cousin said, "I have taken it upon myself to replace some of the weapons in the field and to lower the grain load of the bullets. The weapons show signs of corrosion because of weather type issues. One day it be hot, next day it be cold, the next day it rains and the next day it snows. Not good for weapons."

Jong dismissed his cousin's concerns as if they were contrived. He directed his cousin to check out the cases in the barn before proceeding to the other property. He also told his cousin that he suspected they were booby trapped. His cousin thanked him for the opportunity to have his hands and head blown off in the name of something he didn't understand. Jong told him he was welcome and good luck with this one.

In the barn, an hour later, Jong's cousin very astutely recognized that the hinges on the cases faced outwards. For some odd reason, he focused on the hinges. He didn't touch the cases because he felt something was wrong. He summoned his cousin to the barn, along with his favorite son. He said, "I'm afraid to touch these cases because there is something unusual about them. There is something most different than the ones before. It is the outside that concerns me." He added, "I need to have time alone with these cases, and I must have good tea to drink to calm my nerves."

Jong said, "Would your low-life-ass require a bed while you fornicate the three cases?"

"I will not need a bed, but perhaps if you have a 25-year-old woman that no one wants, that might make me attend to the problem with the cases in an effective way. Sex makes me remember things."

Jong said, "You'll have to use your imagination. Everyone here is spoken for and stop your bullshit. You're not getting paid by the hour—I pay you by the task."

"I must speak to my lawyer. He told me my services were by the hour when I worked for you. Please cousin, and with respect, I ask you to remove your negative aura from barn, so that I may figure out what is different with these cases."

Jong turned and walked away, and his cousin told his favorite son to leave as well. He looked at him and said, "I don't know what is different, but this may be my ticket from my cousin. They all know you're my favorite and a transition will not be a problem."

Jong's cousin got his tea and looked at each case from all four angles. He studied the cases for over an hour. Jong knew there was a problem when he didn't have the solution in ten minutes. During the Sarge's meeting, Jong rose and said, "I feel I must be with my cousin at this moment. He has been studying those cases for close to an hour and has not breached one. There is something haunting him, and I must help ease his focus." The Sarge nodded, and off Jong went.

A few minutes later, Jong walked into the barn and said, "You have lost your touch. You're no longer capable of discerning issues and noticing differences."

His cousin slapped his hands together and said, "I am going to be disrespectful and acknowledge you at the same time. You be a masterful asshole of a family member. You're good because you keep our family safe and fed in our country and you send my children to the best schools. You're not good because you answer my riddle to myself about what is different about these cases. I now know what is different and unsuspecting."

Jong said, "Are you going to share it?"

His cousin said, "The person who planned this thing is a smart person because you would have to know about the other cases to recognize the slight difference in them."

Jong said, "You tell me now, or I'll have you sent home to a certain death."

His cousin smiled and replied, "Who would protect your pompous ass if I'm not here?" Both men smiled, as his cousin said, "Look at hinges on cases. You see difference?"

Jong said, "There is no difference. They all look alike."

His cousin said, "They do all look alike, but the other cases had the hinge pins pointing outwards. These pins are pointing inwards."

"What the hell does that have to do with anything? Pins pointing in or out, what's the issue?"

"These cases are armed, and I will stake my favorite son's life on it."

Jong asked, "Cousin, what do you need to confirm theory?"

"I need the high priestess to leave me alone, let me analyze, and convince myself of my own theory."

His cousin visualized the last cases he had breached and knew the difference was the placement of the hinges. He carefully slid the left pin out and saw it had a sensor like device embedded in it. He reversed its position. He did the same thing to the other side but left the one in the center undisturbed. He rationalized that if you took all three pins out, the case would come apart and the idea was to stop a thief, not waste time assembling a case. He hoped he was correct in his assumptions. He clicked the latches on the front of the case and gently opened it. After raising the top of the case, he looked inside and exclaimed, "Oh shit! I hope I'm correct." He was staring at a large stick of C-4 attached to a trigger but controlled by the polarity of the pins. He called Jong into the room, along with his favorite son, and said, "You pay me double or triple. You people would be dead without my brilliance. The hinge pins are the polarity factor that controls the trigger or detonator on the C-4."

He moved to the next case and said, "This one seems normal." He then removed a pin, and it had no sensors embedded in the device. He opened the case, and it was filled with cash. The same kind of thing was found in case number three. He removed the C-4 and asked his cousin if he could keep it. Jong asked him for what purpose and was told he could make miniature bombs from the stick.

#

The Sarge saw Mallory and Monica, walked over to them, and said, "Monica, I need to know what your plans are. We're going to try to stay here as long as possible with the single purpose of making sure you guys get to the adoption place and have time to do what people do when they go to one."

Monica said, "We have a meeting this afternoon, but I'm a little hesitant after the infraction last night. I thought you would want to leave here immediately?"

"My dear friends, we're not going anywhere until you tell me there is a window for us to head down south and then fly to St. Thomas for a few days. Once there, we can plan how to destroy a little disk that could bring us billions of dollars. It would also make us nomads because a lot of people would want us dead. No, my friends, you let me know what time you want to head to the agency, and I'll assign some people to make sure that everything turns out to be copacetic."

"Well, I would like to leave by noon for our appointment. Is that's okay?" Monica asked.

"Monica, you people are running this OP. You tell me, and I'll make it work," the Sarge replied.

# # #

Jong called the Sarge and asked him and Mallory to join him in the barn.

When the two men arrived, and looked at the display of cash, Mallory asked, "What the hell are we going to do with more cash?"

Jong's cousin raised his hand and asked for permission to speak. He said, "You give me $20 million, and I send you $19 million or so back. You give me $40 million, and I send you $38 million or so back to those accounts out in the world." The Sarge looked at him, then at Jong, and asked his cousin, "Could you give us a few minutes alone, please?" His cousin left the barn, and the Sarge asked, "I know he's a little crazy because he's related to you, but how can he do that? Isn't that called money laundering?"

Jong responded, "It's called anything you want it to be. I have heard of it but had forgotten about it because of the risks that are involved. He makes a few calls and people buy into the profit. The transactions are done in the bank, in the vault, in the safety deposit area. The problem sometimes is getting the money into the banks in Chinatown. There have been deadly incursions."

"Why couldn't it be done at a bank of our choosing, and they wire the money to our various accounts around the world?" the Sarge asked.

Jong replied, "Your banks have too many regulations and eyes. Our banks are banks within banks, within banks."

Mallory looked at the three cases and said, "Let's give him a shot. We have to go to DC this afternoon, so let's investigate this. How much security will we need?"

Jong's cousin who had been invited back in the room said, "You have armored cars and lots of people with guns. I leave when you leave, we open an account, get safety deposit boxes at my bank. I let banker within the other banks, know what is available and they will start the bidding war. They ask for more commission, but I tell them it is what it is. I say $20 million for $19.5 million. They say, something like real or play. I say real, and game is on."

Mallory said, "Sounds a little fishy."

Jong's cousin curiously looked at Mallory and replied, "Fishy no sound, fishy smell."

The Sarge looked at Jong and said, "Call Jilkes, John Lee, Gladstone, and Whitmore. I'll put the farm on alert when Mallory and Monica leave, and I'll stay here on guard."

# # #

When the guys arrived, John Lee asked, "What be happening?"

Mallory explained that he and Monica were going to the adoption center for the second and final part of the interview process. He then said, "Jong's cousin has a bank that will take $20 million and send $19 million or more, to our accounts. We have a shit load of cash and we need to begin moving it."

John Lee looked at Jong's cousin and said to him, "If this be a scam, I'll gut you like a fish."

Jong adamantly stated, "John Lee, this is my family. Would you like to apologize now, or after I kick the shit out of you?"

John Lee fell to his knees, held his arms out, and said, "I was only testing him."

Jong replied, "I was only testing you."

The Sarge said, "Testosterone—you guys need to chill out. I need you four to provide security for Monica and Mallory, and then follow Jong and his cousin to a bank to make a transaction."

John Lee said, "I think we be having to take our women with us because we promised them a trip."

The Sarge looked at him and said, "I'm sending you guys on a mission. Are you sure you want your pregnant wives tagging along?"

Jilkes said, "They can drive, they damn sure can shoot, and they speak the language. That gives us four to a car. The only problem I really see is getting out of a van with three huge cases."

Jong's cousin said, "You get smaller bags, we drop rolls of quarters and dimes on ground as we enter bank. You can open an account online and request safety deposit boxes that will hold an old magical urn or something. Cases much too big make people think things."

Mallory touched Jong on his shoulder and said, "I think this one's yours to call, my brother. Call your Op!"

Jong looked at his cousin and began to talk to him in a strident manner, while his cousin mumbled something and continued kowtowing. Jong said, "My low-life cousin is going to make calls to do an online account prior to us arriving. We can do this now, we can leave now, and head to the bank first, and then to Monica's place."

Mallory said, "Guys, we can't be late arriving at the adoption center."

Jong said, "It's 0915 hundred hours. If we leave in 30 minutes, we be in DC at 1030 hundred hours. We're out of the bank by 12 noon on the dot. No ifs, ands, or buts about it."

Jong turned to his cousin, continued ragging him in their language, and finally said, "My cousin is sure this will work because he has a son by another woman who is the head of an alternative bank and eager to show his worth. This would be huge for him."

The Sarge said, "Well, hell, man. Can he do $40 for $38.5?"

Jong looked at his cousin and began to badger him again. His cousin pulled out his cell phone and spoke rapidly to his son, who inquired, "When can you come in?" Jong's cousin told him that he would call him back.

Jong said to the Sarge, "Let's try to do this one successfully and then see if they want to do more. Too many things can go wrong, and we cannot be late getting Ms. Monica and Mallory to their meeting."

Mallory said, "I agree. Let's see if this can be done smoothly and then we'll keep his son as busy as he wants to be. I'm going to check on Monica and if she's ready, then we do this." He started to walk away, turned to Jong, and said, "Is the weapons system up and running yet?"

Jong said, "It is almost complete. They are switching out some of the machine pistols because of weather and the heavy grain-loads of the ammunition. They're also lowering the grain-loads of the bullets."

#

The group arrived at the bank at 1015 hundred hours. Jong, Jilkes, John Lee, and Jong's cousin walked into the bank leaving Mallory, Monica, Yeshida, and Somara in the vans in the no parking zone.

After a few minutes of introductions and procedural agreements, the men returned to the vans and extracted numerous bags loaded with cash. They reentered the bank and went to the basement where the vault was, leaving Jong with his cousin's son. The other three men extracted other bags from the vans and went back into the bank.

Jong's cousin said to his son, in perfect English, "You will count every damn bill and make sure it is the right amount. A single dollar difference will lead to a huge catastrophe in your life. Do not, and I repeat, do not screw this up. I, or rather they, can make you as rich as you want to be. And it is not illegal or stolen money. Do this right and you will be greatly rewarded."

Jong handed him a piece of paper with three account numbers on it, told him that they were foreign banks, and that they will confirm two hours after the transfer of the funds is made.

Jong's cousin said to his son, "Have this done in the next two hours. Get bankers from below to assist you, my son."

Jong's cousin's son asked, "Don't you want a receipt?"

His father said, "Your life is the receipt, my son."

The men turned, walked up the steps and exited the building. In front of his son was a total of $20 million dollars of which he and his institution would make a cool half a million or more for a "legal" transfer.

The men entered the vans, and Monica said to Mallory, "Honey, the guys left a bag in the car." He looked behind him and said, "Oh, shit." He called Jong and said, "There is a bag of money in my van."

Jong replied, "I know. His father is certifying his son's credibility, as well as, measuring his son's greed. There is a quarter of a million in the bag. I think my cousin needs it, but he told his son there was $20 million, will take him to task about it, and put the fear of the devil in his ass." Jong looked out of the window and asked, "Ms. Monica, would you like a Starbucks before we take you to your appointment?"

Monica smiled and said, "I think we all could use a good cup of coffee. We're so used to the stuff that's left in the morning that we might die from ingesting real coffee."

Everyone could hear the conversation between the two vehicles and yelled that they should stop for coffee.

The group filled up on lattes and other fancy named coffees. John Lee was looking out of the window and saw a sign that read, "How can I be a better husband?"

He turned to Somara and asked in front of Jilkes, "How can I be a better husband and love you to the best of my ability?" Somara unbuckled her seat belt and reached across the front seat where he was sitting. She kissed John Lee's neck and cheek until she found his lips.

John Lee exclaimed, "Jilkes, pull this thing over. I want to sit by my wife and the mother-to-be of my child!"

Jilkes pulled to the curb, and John Lee changed places with Yeshida. Jong, witnessing the activity, pulled over, inquired, "What they be doing back there? John Lee just got in the back seat." He eased his van to the curb and waited for some indication that all was okay. Jilkes kissed Yeshida when she sat in the front seat and said, "I'm asking you the same question. You are my world, my light, and I love you so much." Everyone in the van was crying, hugging, and kissing.

The group arrived at the adoption center forty-five minutes early. Jong and Mallory got out of their van and went back to the other one. Mallory asked, "What happened back there?"

Jilkes said, "Oh, we just felt love and wanted to express it to our women. When you get the feeling, you got to show it, and tell it, if you mean it."

Jong walked away and said, "Sounds like bullshit to me."

Mallory said, "At the rate you're going, Mary Alice is going to leave your ass."

Jong paused, and seriously inquired, "Why on earth would she do such a stupid thing when she loves me?"

"Dude, you had better learn to show it and mean it. Why do you think at my age, I'm here? Do you think I want to be like you old ass people, making babies and then kicking the bucket? I love my wife and have from the moment I first saw her. You have to do what makes them internally happy, not the glitz and bullshit, but real emotions that express who you are as a man and a husband."

"I would like for you to talk to me about this again when you're not busy. I'm not sure I'm being the best husband that I can be," Jong confessed.

The group lingered in the parking lot and caught the attention of the person in charge of the adoption process. She walked to the door and yelled, "Come on in. You're never too early or too late here."

Jilkes and John Lee gave Mallory the thumbs up sign.

# # #

It would be an hour and a half later before Monica and Mallory would exit the building. Monica said, "I am so sorry to keep you guys waiting. It's most appreciated." Everyone noticed the look on her face and knew the meeting had gone well. Mallory was aglow as well, and apparently satisfied with how things went. He walked up to his buddies and gave each one a hug.

Jong announced, "Everybody smile—no one say shit."

Mallory said, "We had a good meeting, met a couple kids, observed others, and are happy with the outcome. There's a five-and-a-half-year old and a four-and-a-half-year old, that we're focusing on. We want to look at our living arrangement options prior to making a final commitment, which brings me to you, John Lee. Everyone likes your farm and are considering moving into your neighborhood. Is there room for us?"

"Hell, man, we be brothers. If there ain't room for you then we'll make room for you. Jilkes and I purchased the land across the road from me and we have enough land for everyone to build a mansion and have 300 to 1,000 acres of land."

Monica said, "I would love to see it again, John Lee, but this time with an eye towards building and living there."

Jilkes said, "We're going to float that idea with the Sarge. Monica, you can help us move that proposition forward. We want to leave the farmhouse by tomorrow and head down south for a day or so, and then head to St. Thomas for a few days before heading to middle America."

John Lee said, "Our houses are being built. This way, those who are interested in the area can pick a plot and we can begin to have all the permits pulled. We can also have the architects talk to you through Facetime, Zoom, or some other medium."

Jong's cousin was about to say something when his cell phone rang. He answered it and looked at his cousin. Jong looked at the man whose head dropped and asked, "Do we have a problem?"

His cousin looked at him and asked, "Do you have any more money you need to forward to your other accounts? Check your email and see if that money has entered the circuit."

Jong pulled out his portable hotspot, turned it on, engaged his computer and logged into the organizations' general accounts. It showed that a transaction in the amount of $19,500,000 had been transferred into their account. Jong told his cousin to call his son and tell him they tested him. Let him know, we'll immediately reimburse him for the $250,000."

His cousin kowtowed and said, "You are the leader of our family." He called his son, gave him the news, and his son responded, "My partners in the bank helped me make up the $250,000." He asked his father if there was the ability to do business in the near future and his father said, "Since you made up the mistake I made, then I will beg, on your behalf."

Jong told the members of the group about the transaction and they began high fiving each other. Mallory said, "Call the Sarge and tell him that the banking is complete and in our accounts. Tell him I'm going to propose a number and see if our new banker is amenable."

After discussing the matter with the Sarge and members of the group, Jong said to his cousin, "Ask your boy if he wants to handle $60 for $59, non-negotiable?"

Jong's cousin made the call, and the immediate response was without any hesitation, "Absolutely."

Jong said to his cousin, "Tell your son we will call him at 0200 hours and set up a delivery time."

When the group arrived at the farm, the Sarge was standing in the circle waiting for them. He opened the door and helped Monica out. He hugged her and asked, "How did it go?" She unfolded the scenario and the anxiety attached to such an endeavor. She said, "We need to go to the lover's place, parcel out a piece of property, and have a stable address. We need to do that tomorrow and then I think we all should take a dive in the waters of St. Thomas, before heading west. Can you do that for me and the group?"

The Sarge looked her dead on, and said, "I'm here for you to command."

The Sarge then looked at Jong's cousin and said, "I need you to put cameras and everything else on that new property and keep it under surveillance until we raze it or reconstruct."

His cousin looked at Jong and asked in their native tongue, "What he mean by raze it? House high enough. How much higher he wants house?"

Jong said, "He means to demolish it and build a new one."

Jong's cousin said, "I can call other children to connect and install, while me and other children supply weapons in the field and collect expended shells."

The Sarge said, "I need you to count out $60 million for transfer tomorrow. Is that a problem?"

Jong's cousin looked at the Sarge and Jong. Jong said, "Don't look at me. Look at the Sarge—he asked the question."

His cousin slowly made eye contact with the massive human being in front of him and said, "I will count it to the penny, Mr. Sarge."

"Ah, we're not dealing with pennies. We are working with millions today and we surely don't want another Industrial Bank fiasco, now do we?"

# # #

That evening, the mood was festive, but cautious. The cleaners had people and dogs in the field bleaching and removing all evidence of a fatal occurrence. Mary Alice, from out of nowhere, asked Jong, "Do you love me?" He uncharacteristically froze in place and stared at her for a moment. Mary Alice stated, "I'm going to ask you again. Do you love me?"

Jong took a swig of his drink and recalled what he had heard from his brothers, and said, "Mary Alice, I've been meaning to talk to you about that. I do love you and the child that you soon will be birthing. In my culture, things are done differently, and I don't want to do things that way. I want to be your beast." He gently grabbed her, began to methodically kiss, and suckle her neck, and ears, while rubbing her thighs and gently massaging her belly. He said, "I want to rock your ship until it capsizes, and then you can rock mine until we right the ship."

She said, "You've been drinking a lot. Maybe we can have this conversation tomorrow when you're sober."

"I'm sober enough to know that I have loved you from the moment I first laid eyes on you. You're expecting my child, and that makes me happy."

"What if it isn't your child?"

Jong froze for a minute, but finally said, "If you will let me, I will be the best father to the child."

Mary Alice screamed and said, "Oh my God! You are the right man for me and my child. My husband, I need you to touch me, rub my belly, tell me you love me, and treat me like your woman. You practice too much machismo in my presence. I need a lover, not a warrior. I already know you're a warrior."

Jong slid close to her on the bench and whispered in her ear, "If the kids weren't still up, I would spray my juices in you right here. However, I will wait until you are ready to allow me in your chamber, so that I can wander around aimlessly searching for the most magnificent spot to harness your moon."

#

At 1900 hours, the Sarge tapped on his glass and asked, "People, can I have your attention for just a few moments? I know by now that all of you know that things are looking extremely positive for our brother and sister, Mallory, and Ms. Monica. I hope we all can say a prayer for them and support them in their quest. I'm going to need everyone to be ready to book from here at 1100 hours tomorrow. Any important possessions or information you want to secure in the vault, please have it in the hands of Rashida and Juan by 0900 hours. If it's alright with the group, I would like for us to head south to John Lee and Jilkes' land, where me and my bride are considering retiring and putting a bid on a lot. I also hear that others may be interested in that area as well. So, if it's for the good of the order, then I move we head that way in the morning. I hope that two days there will give those interested in living in the area, a chance to visit and look at available lots from our slum landlords, Jilkes, and his lover, John Lee.

"After those two days, I am proposing we spend a long weekend in St. Thomas. From St. Thomas, I would like to move the entire group to Middle America, where I feel the world will end or begin for us. As you all know, my cousin once placed suicide vests on the children in our group. Each night I wrestle with the fact that a human being could do such a dastardly thing and call himself a family member. I am thinking strategically, we stand a better chance of knowing something bad is on its way in middle America. That's where I want to draw my cousin out and conclude his life.

"Somehow, I am also getting visions of the outback when it comes to him. I want to play a game that was developed by my one son, and enhanced by the other, called 'illusions and misdirections'. This deadly game, so far, is the only way out of this quagmire we find ourselves in called, the Carbon Factor formula. Until those two items are completely dealt with, we should remain vagabonds. Individually, he will try to draw us out and draw us in. Collectively, he doesn't have a chance. I need you guys to think about what I've said and consider it tonight. I pray you make the right decision, and we all get on the same plane in the morning."

Bernstein rose from his seat while Yvette was trying to pull him down, and announced, "I'm confused, Sarge. This is perhaps the third time you've gone on this rampage. Unless I'm brainless, each of us realizes the importance of remaining as a unit. I mean, hell, we're all going south to see about buying homes. You should stop featuring Armageddon, describe nirvana, and how we all can achieve it together. Unless you have a description of a stoic person in our group who feels they can manifest a perfect existence without us, then I suggest you cancel that presentation in the future."

Quiet fell on the room, and the Sarge looked at him and said, "We have people with personal situations and requirements that may not fit neatly into our agenda. You all know that Mallory and Monica are in the adoption process and that takes time, involvement, and their presence. To that tune, it may not be conducive or safe for the group."

Brown stood up and said, "Sarge, perhaps it's time to consider splitting our forces?"

Mallory stood up and said, "That is neither plausible nor intelligent. Brown, you know we all have functions when it comes to our defenses, including the expecting mothers, as well as mothers. Even if we divided our forces equally, that would lead to our demise. However, I want to deal with the Sarge's issues. Monica and I can do what we must do without involving the entire group. Listen, if we have to ride this way, give me Jilkes, Brown, John Lee, and their women, and I assure you we can withstand an army."

The Sarge said, "But, you place them in danger because we will have appropriated insufficient resources for that operation. No, sir. I wasn't finished before Brown began to shoot off his mouth. What I was leading to is that we will fly in and out of this place, St. Thomas, and John Lee's place. I feel we're being tracked, but I want them to keep guessing where we are at any given point. Which leads me to the point, Jong. I need your favorite cousin to bug the offices of the adoption agency, and the key personnel's houses. Listen, people, they're looking for us at every corner. Our friends are in the midst of a major life adjusting experience. I need to fulfill this mission for them and keep us safe as well. Damn, I just thought of something else! Jong, I would like for your cousin to provide surveillance on the people who make the decisions at the adoption agency. I also want to invite Jong's cousin into our fold because he helps us in so many ways and is somewhat, trustworthy. These are the issues I bring to our group to respond to. What say you?" Everyone agreed.

The Sarge asked, "Where is your cousin, Jong?"

"He's delivering exactly $60 million to my nephew. He is also picking up more cameras to connect to the other property. I have a question. There was a quiet as Jong rose from his seat and stated, "We need to plan better food for the group, and we need to figure out what we are going to do with the gold bullion." Asiram rose from her chair and asked, "What gold bullion?"

The Sarge looked at her and said, "My bad, people. Behind the headboard at the ex-senator's house, was a panel that opened, and we discovered, I think, 100 gold bars."

"When were, you going to tell us about the gold?" Asiram with her hands on her expanded hips asked.

"Asiram, it slipped my mind and apparently, the mind of your husband."

"Daddy-in-Law, I'm just messing with you. You're the only man I know who don't give a shit about money or precious metals. If we all look at each other, we'll see what Ben Beckmire cares about, not riches, but us. I have one question before I sit down and that is, do we need a vetting program? I mean we keep adding people, but we never do background checks."

Zanthius said, "It's a damn good thing we didn't vet you."

The group laughed and Asiram asked, "Do you plan on sleeping with the horses tonight, dear?" There was no response.

The Sarge said, "I need ratification of my plan about our travel. Is everyone okay with here, John Lee's, and St. Thomas on a random basis?" The Sarge then asked Mallory and Monica to share their expectation of a time frame with the group.

Mallory stood and said, "I humbly thank you for supporting me and my wife in this adventure. It means the world to us. We count on a consistent environment of support from this group. Not judgement, but support. Anyhow, we want to spend at least tomorrow morning at the center and then we'll be ready to move on with the group. We're not sure who we're looking for, but we do know she wants a boy and I want a little girl. Go figure that one out. We have an appointment at 0800 hours, and I expect it to be over by 0900 hours, at which point we will head back to the farm and collect you people. The agency has agreed to provide us with a virtual tour of the individual or individuals we are interested in. Our problem is, we want to take them all home."

Asiram rose from her seat and said, "Why don't we take them all? I have enough of my own money to start a home that is a real home and not a shelter. You guys want to help vets. Well, I want to help children and families."

Courtney yelled, "Yes, Jesus! I'm with my daughter-in-law. I like the idea, so will my husband, or he'll be sleeping with Zanthius, and those damn horses as well tonight."

Rashida stood up and said, "Where my mom goes, I go." The women began to stand up one by one. Ava was the last to stand and said, "I go where my sisters need me to go."

CHAPTER NINETEEN

The Sarge received a cryptic text message from Franco. The message read, 'Forces are trying to separate the harmony that you created. Equipment is being destroyed, and the families of the resort and restaurant are in hiding. It is being made to look like I'm the perpetrator. My man Mario was shot, and his body placed in front of the resort with his tongue cut out'. We're being strong-armed. I want to draw arms, but I want to stay out of the old life."

The Sarge sent him an immediate response, 'Tell those who go against you, they go against the 'killing machine'. We will protect what's ours. If we come there, we will give no quarter to any man, woman, or child involved directly or indirectly. We will do this most dastardly thing in public, and it will be loud and disgusting. And, insofar as any equipment that was destroyed, it must be replaced. Tell those attempting to strong-arm our relationship, if we come there, the force we bring will be nuclear!"

As the group was enjoying the balance of the night, the Sarge yelled, "It appears that I might have to head to Spain. Our people on the ground are being threatened by hostiles, but I told our people to tell the hostiles they just engaged the 'killing machine'." There was a loud roar. He then said, "We need to diversify some of our projects. For instance, I need someone to step-up and take control of the Spanish projects. I need someone to work with Jong and his cousin to reduce our cash on hand and to reconcile them into various accounts around the world. We have Juan and Rashida in charge of our security system here, but what about in the islands or in middle America? We also need someone to work with Jong on where we go, when we go, and the rotation factor with our pilots, even though our number one pilot is connected to someone who wants to join our merry band. In other words, people I need you guys to help me make decisions that impact all of us. Are there any volunteers?" The hands flew in the air immediately. The Sarge looked at Mallory and said, "Make assignments, but take people out of their comfort zones and place them into new areas that will make them learn a new skill. Sort of like continuing education courses."

Mallory said, "Sarge, before we make assignments, we need to be clear about what it is we're doing here. We cannot have everyone making decisions about projects and then reporting on them. What we need is for people to know the intricate details of an assignment and then report back to leadership with a recommendation for a decision. Unless someone thinks differently, I believe our system has worked well so far. What we're trying to do is minimize your detailed knowledge of a task, or an action and have you listen to suggestions and/or directions. People, so far, am I correct? We don't want to remove him or me from the decision-making process, we just want to limit the amount of details we receive but burden the project teams with the minutia. Am I on track or off?"

John Lee said, "I be thinking that is exactly what we be saying. We shovel the shit and ask him where he be wanting it." Everyone laughed but agreed with the simple reasoning.

Mallory said, "Brown, Bernstein, McArthur, and Gladstone are assigned to Jong who is the leader of the group. Jilkes, John Lee, Chakes, and Montomie oversee the foreign projects and Jilkes is the lead on that one. Whitmore, you Zanthius, Larry, and Carlos are responsible for the most important aspect of our union—getting rid of the Carbon Factor formula and drawing the Sarge's cousin out into the open as well as other duties as assigned."

Bernstein said, "Unless you involve the women in these groups, then we're not going to get far. They are demanding inclusion, not exclusion, decision-making ability on travel, and where we stay. They want to decorate both the resort and restaurant in Spain and the two new properties in The Sanctuary."

"How do you know so much about what they want to do?" the Sarge asked.

"Because I have to listen to your niece tell me what tasks I need to champion for her. Any other questions on that subject?"

The Sarge said, "I need you guys to be completely honest with me. Do you think Rashida and Juan do a good job, or do we need one of our own in that box?"

Whitmore yelled, "Hell, yeah. That shit is all computerized. They know the difference between animals and people with guns. They triangulate approaches, and they don't hesitate to hit that engage button. Sarge, our hand and eye coordination are too slow to do what they do in split seconds. I say, if it works, don't mess with it." Everyone roared and agreed with Whitmore.

The Sarge said, "Bernstein, since you're the only one amongst us who listens to his wife, can you tell me if the wives are interested in being a vocal and an equal part of meetings like this one?"

"Hell no, Sarge. They say we meet and talk too much. On the contrary, I don't think we meet and talk enough. Of late, we have been reacting as opposed to planning what we're going to do. Crisis after crisis has been our game. We attract trouble like shit attracts flies. We took Allen to the islands, and he's killed by our landlord's family. I'm not picking on that particular instance, but we attract trouble! Case closed."

The Sarge asked, "Is there any way we should behave differently to not attract trouble?"

Bernstein replied, "Virtually impossible, Sarge. We're the fricken 'killing machine'. The very nature of our past is like an open invitation to a gunfight. We are who we are, like *Butch Cassidy and the Sundance Kid*, or that asshole Clint Eastwood, in those spaghetti westerns. Until we decriminalize ourselves by destroying that toxic Carbon Factor formula and finally drawing straws to see who gets to gut your cousin, then it is what it is. That is why we are at risk if we consider separation. When we're all in the same place, we are feared!"

The room got quiet until John Lee asked Zanthius, "Did you learn to kiss without swallowing?" The room erupted into loud laughter.

The Sarge said, "I would like to spend ten minutes with each group and discuss how you want to report your events or findings. Jong, I'm counting on you and your guys to figure out ways to move money to our banks in St. Thomas and in Spain. I wish there were a way we could ship funds to the convent without a lot of problems. Anyway, we'll work on that during our initial meeting. I want to get with Jilkes first because he has an immediate decision to make relative to Valencia."

# # #

The men talked, and after a while, agreed to send another text message to Franco requesting a phone number and time that a conversation could be held to discuss the issues and demands by those attempting to strong-arm the group.

Jilkes didn't want to vociferously threaten people from afar but wanted to listen to what it was they thought they could achieve from underestimating people that they didn't know. The Sarge smiled and said, "I sent the text and included your name and number. Let me know how you want to proceed."

The Sarge moved over to Jong's group and said, "People, your task will require you to think like a crook for the good of the order. As you know, we have gold bullion, $115 million from the ex-senator, probably another $150 million plus in the ground beneath us, and at least $100 million in middle America. Is that correct, Jong?"

"Almost correct. We also have $40 to $50 in the ground here, and another $60 million of Asiram's in three cases. In other words, we have probably over a half billion dollars in cash that we need to convert," Jong stated.

"I think we should always keep $50 million liquid," the Sarge said.

Jong said, "What would we do with $50 million? You want to buy the White House? No one lives there who runs the government. Him live in Florida."

"Okay, brother Jong. That's why we need your brain and the others to concoct a way to turn this cash cow into negotiable assets."

#

Two hours later, the groups were enjoying cocktails when Jilkes' phone rang. On the other end of the call Franco announced, "*Mi amigo*, this is Franco in Valencia. I have on the phone with me the person who feels you should pay him an entitlement fee. His name is Shamone. Shamone, you are now linked to my US backers and probably the people who will bury you."

Jilkes said, "Whoa! No need in starting a conversation talking about death when we're the death dealers. Can you guys hold the phone for just a moment?" Jilkes made a call to Northern Africa and connected a person who owed the group a lot of money. He told the guy to be silent until he was introduced.

Jilkes reconnected with Franco and Mr. Shamone, and said, "Guys, I've been drinking, and I don't really want to spend a lot of time discussing the notion of respect. We have a financial relationship with the resort, the restaurant, Franco, and his people. Franco told me that Mario was murdered, and his tongue cut out. Let me be perfectly clear to you, Sir. There are two ways this will end. You will further hurt our people over there which we don't want to happen. The other is we take a contract out on you, your family, and everyone with your last name with our friends in Northern Africa, who have a huge presence in your town and who owe us close to $20 million dollars. That's a single call, and as a matter of fact,

I'm sorry, I meant to tell you our contact is on the phone as well. Mukherjee, say hello to my man Franco and his adversary Shamone." Murkherjee uttered some strange sound and asked, "Jilkes, do all of these people know the entire government of Vietnam wanted you dead and had a standing offer of $10 million for each of your heads?"

Jilkes said, "I don't know what Mr. Shamone knows. I only know we'll reduce your $20 million debt to $18 if you kill his wife, kids, and anyone who knows his ass, for killing my friend Mario. If we come back to Spain, I will gut his mother from her midsection to her brain. I'm hanging up the phone. In ten minutes, someone had better call me and tell me this guy took up residency in South Africa, or somewhere, but before he left, he paid for all of the equipment that was destroyed. Also, before he goes, 'tell him the killing machine is coming'." Jilkes disconnected the phone and took a swig of his drink.

John Lee said, "Tell him the killing machine is coming. What the hell is that supposed to mean?"

"Big Country. Didn't you see the movie starring Burt Lancaster called, *Valdez is Coming*.

"I ain't seen no dumb shit like that. When did it come out?"

"I guess in the early seventies, maybe 1971 or 72. You should stop watching pigs screwing and look at the cowboy movies. There's a lot of sayings to be learned. Valdez was a Mexican Constable trying to collect $100 for an Indian woman whose man was murdered by a mob for a murder he didn't commit." Jilkes, as well as everyone else heard the sound of his phone ringing. He placed the phone in the amplifying cradle and said, "This is Jilkes."

Franco asked, "Do you have a minute?"

Jilkes said, "Franco, that's all I have! What's the deal?"

Franco said, "Shamone feels as though you should pay him $10,000 for backing down from what he considers a legitimate claim."

"See you in the next two days. He can ask me for it in person before I gut his ass. Don't call me back," Jilkes hung up the phone.

Chakes said, "Shit, you scared me on that one. Perfectly played, my brother."

Jilkes was about to say something when he received a text that said, 'Please answer the phone when I call in two minutes. Please, I beg you'. Jilkes showed the text to the group, and Chakes said, "Perhaps that guy didn't buy the threat."

Jilkes exclaimed, "Oh well, he'll regret that decision!"

Jilkes' phone rang and he once again placed it in the cradle. He said, "Franco, you and I already did this dance, and it costs lives. What part of do not call me, don't you understand?"

"Please, Mr. Jilkes, Shamone wants to offer you a deal."

"Offer me a damn deal? John Lee, call our pilot in command and have them make ready the plane."

"Mr. Jilkes, please, just listen."

Shamone said, "I'm well connected, and I can make sure your permits don't receive any bureaucratic reviews. I'm just trying to not create a problem with a potential partner."

Jilkes said, "I want to know who killed Mario and why."

Shamone said, "I did not kill him nor cut his tongue out. I simply knew that no one would assume responsibility, it would increase my notoriety, and access in the region if it was assumed that it was my work. In all honesty, he was caught with his tongue in the wrong place, on the wrong woman, by a husband who liberated the notorious legend."

Jilkes asked, "So, do we have an accord?"

"Mr. Jilkes, you have more than an accord. I will have my people watch over the works, without a single penny of cost to you and your group. I'm happy we discussed the issue like adults before we started shooting at each other."

Jilkes said, "Thank you, but you will pay for the damage to my equipment. Good night."

# # #

The Sarge went to Jong's group and asked, "Just how much money can your cousin's son handle?"

Jong said, "I'm not sure, I hope greed doesn't set in, compromise him, and us."

Bernstein said, "We only heard pieces of this caper, can you give us the full scope of the relationship, the venue, and how he's able to be a banker and not violate the banking laws and regulations?"

Jong articulated the details of the deals and the cost. It was a long conversation that ended with Brown asking, "How much more can he handle and are there competing forces we can involve in this process without starting a war?"

# # #

When the Sarge walked over to Whitmore's group, he said, "Forget about the bullshit. The money and gold are nothing compared to us ending our relationship with the Carbon Factor formula and providing justice to someone who considers himself a relative. I need your best thinking and scheming tactics on this one. You have the problems and now I need solutions."

The Sarge started walking up the stairs and said, "By the way, I want real solutions in the morning. I don't want, what 'if's'. I want direct answers to your assigned situations."

CHAPTER TWENTY

As the plane headed down the runway, the group watched as Carla almost did a vertical climb into the heavens. From the airport in Maryland, she blasted their plane into the air with runway to spare. Once she leveled off, she said, "Sorry if I worried anyone, but with this group, I have to be able to put this thing in the air in minutes and on short runways." Everyone clapped but secretly felt that the experience was a bit scary. The captain came back on the line and said, "According to our flight plan, our first stop will be in Birmingham, Alabama for a two day stay and then on to St. Thomas until Monday or so, with a continuing trip to middle America. That takeoff was an indication of how we're prepared to get our group up, up, and away, in record time. I don't like doing that, but it's important that me and my crew know how to 'Get the hell out of dodge' in a hurry'."

Courtney said, "Damn, I hope she isn't a mental case."

The Sarge looked at her and said, "How the hell would we know if she was or wasn't? For that matter, how can we know the sanity of any pilot?"

# # #

An hour or so later, the captain came on the intercom and said, "We're on our descent. Please prepare the plane for arrival."

As the plane began its descent, alarms began to sound. On the starboard side of the plane, another plane was detected on the same approach. Someone in the tower was responsible for an almost mid-air collision. Captain Carla backed down her engines and received an urgent message from the tower to abort the landing and was given a new heading and altitude. Everyone on the starboard side of the plane saw the other jet and knew it was too close for comfort. Captain Carla said, "Folks, on the right side of our plane you will notice another plane a bit too close. We have been given instructions to abort the landing, go around, and approach again. This hiccup was not our fault, but the fault of those in the tower."

On the second approach to the airport, everything appeared to be in order and the plane landed safely. Courtney said, "Sarge, I still think you should talk to her and have her give us a warning when she is about to takeoff, like a rocket instead of a plane." He looked at Courtney and said, "Honey, if you think she's a nut, then it appears to me no one is better prepared to assess that than you. We're all just soldiers, you're the doctor."

"Sarge, I don't think she's a nut. I just want to know when she's going to blast this thing into space, that's all."

"Honey, please talk to her and see if you detect depression, anxiety or some of those other things you studied that I wouldn't know or recognize."

Once the plane was safely at the gate, Courtney rose from her seat and headed towards the cockpit. Monica said to Mallory, "She's going to fire the captain. I know that look."

In the cockpit, Courtney said, "Captain Carla, really? Was that takeoff necessary?"

"Dr. Beckmire, in our manual for the operation of this plane, we are required to conduct two such maneuvers every 200 hours of operation. We're also supposed to conduct a stall, but we'll do that when you guys aren't onboard. That event may have seemed unnecessary to you, but to us it is as important as kicking the tires. My concern is for everyone on this plane, and, therefore, we don't do any stunts. We fly according to the manual. Perhaps the next time we're required to do that, we'll make sure that you guys are on the ground."

"This is a lot of responsibility, we put a lot of faith in you, and your crew. I don't like flying! Half of the people back there don't like planes. I'm sure you can understand how we feel when you go vertical. Let's coordinate your training thing in the future. You can land the plane, without the theatrics, we can watch you from the ground as you fulfill the requirements and test your skill set. Can we agree to that?"

An accord was reached as one would expect.

#

John Lee had texted his people and told them that he was coming in for a few days and needed people to pick them up at the airport. When the group exited the plane, a row of black SUVs were waiting. The Sarge asked, "Some rock star showing up down here?"

"Yeah, me and my peoples. Couldn't put you in the back of a pick-up truck with all these pregnant women. Now, could I?"

"Well, I guess not. Do you have space for all these people?"

"Sarge, there always be space in the country. There be some daylight left, maybe you and some of the others be wanting to look at our land and figure out where you be wanting to build that there retirement home. I'm sure Ms. Courtney is going to take you up on your offer. She and Ms. Monica are dying to settle down and stop this here gallivanting around the world," John Lee stated.

Jong, Brown, Bernstein, Gladstone, and McArthur were continuing their discussions about the group's money issues when Jong's phone rang. His cousin called and said, "There is a bid for $100 for $95. I don't make decisions, but I told them to stick pig's feet up their asses."

Jong said, "I'm going to put you on speaker phone. Repeat what you said to me."

His cousin said, "There is a bid for $100 for $95. I told them that is not possible. They tell me to ask?"

McArthur asked, "Can we call you back in five or ten minutes?" His cousin answered, "Yes."

McArthur said, "Why on earth would we give up $5 and take $95? It makes no sense to me. I am against that much discounting."

Brown said, "I'm with you. I think we should first state we don't negotiate. I would propose that for $100 we take $97. Jong, is that number coming from your cousin's son or from a competing source?"

Jong said, "Let's call my cousin and ask."

Jong called his cousin and asked him the question. His cousin said, "I would slap my son for being greedy. It was from a competing source."

Jong said, "Tell those who look at today and not to tomorrow, our numbers are non-negotiable, and for this relationship, $100 gets us $98.5."

Jong's cousin asked, "Why not $99 or $99.2?"

McArthur said, "I like his thinking. We don't know these people or what they do. We at least know Jong's cousin, and hopefully his son, represents their family in a good light."

Everyone agreed on the number. Ten minutes later, Jong's cousin called back and said, "They ask for more money, and I tell them what you say. They finally agreed. When would you like this to take place?"

Jong said, "I will get back to you and let you know."

Bernstein said, "Guys, I like that deal. I mean we give up $1 million, get our requested amount cleaned, and entered into our accounts. Our problem is, how much can these guys move? We're talking about a half-a-billion-dollars, not peanuts by any stretch of the imagination. Do you think we should divide the gold twelve ways and be done with it?"

Brown said, "And where would you keep yours? Dude, we're too mobile right now. Until we conclude the pressing business in front of us, we don't need to carry bullions around in our pockets, weighing us down when we're trying to escape people shooting at us."

Jong said, "I want to stop talking, get my bride, ride around the property, and pick a place for my home before all that's left is back road and no plumbing."

"Come on now, that's not what we're up against. There's plenty of land. The issue you might have is who your neighbor is. I don't want to be a mile or two away from you guys. Maybe a hundred yards or better, but if more than that, we might as well not follow through on this. We don't do well personally when we isolate and talk by Facetime," Brown stated.

Bernstein said, "You're absolutely correct. I should be able to walk to your place, and you to mine. Our kids should have a pathway through our properties so that they don't have to relate to the roads."

# # #

Those who were married took a tour of the property, everyone witnessed a majestic sunset, and learned where the sun rose and set.

John Lee's people rented out the dining room of a downtown hotel for dinner. When the group gathered and entered vehicles for the ride downtown, the Sarge said to Courtney, "At least we know which way the sun rises and sets. I want to have the sun wake me in the morning and make me sleepy in the evening. I also want to become a farmer, grow food for the poor, and let the poor grow food on my land to sell and to eat, as long as they pay a small amount to a fund that supports other struggling farms and families."

"You are one wonderful human being, Ben Beckmire. You're always looking out for the little guy, and you always help people help themselves. That's why I love you. You know, I think I'll be sad when this journey ends. I know it's full of drama and death, but normal life is as well. We've done some bad things to people who came to hurt us, but we never went looking for a fight. The fight was always brought to our doorstep and, therefore, I can justify shooting a human being. Not a perfect justification, but one that I can live with. How big do you think our place should be?"

"You move from one topic to another without taking a pause. I certainly don't want anything over 4,000 square feet. I mean that gives us five bedrooms, four baths, a family room, a living room, a dining room, and a kitchen that can accommodate at least twelve, with three fireplaces, and a sunroom. Not sure if I want a pool unless it has an electric metal covering to protect grandkids from falling into, if unattended," Beckmire stated.

"Honey, you sure you don't want a mansion with a spiral staircase and a grand foyer? I kind of think I would like something a little more upscale than what you're speaking about."

"Courtney, you asked me a question and that was my answer. Once we pick the property out and get financing through our slum landlords, then we'll see what we can afford. But let me be very clear—I want a home and not a place where in a few years we're going to need people to wait on us and help us up all those damn stairs."

"Yeah, I see what you mean. We'll negotiate this one later. I think we should have a property that is central to the entire group that's planning on the move. By the way, how many of your people are joining us?"

"Last I heard, they're all looking for property, but it's contingent upon the taxes the two slum landlords will charge."

"Stop calling them that. They're your best and most loyal."

"That, my dear, is where you're wrong. They're two of the best and as loyal as any other member of the group."

Courtney smiled and thought to herself, "What a catch. I love this guy so much."

# # #

In the dining room, John Lee stood up and said, "I want to be the first Alabamian to welcome you to Alabama. We done bought a lot of property down here on both sides of the road, and we be mighty happy if you people accept as much land as you think you can handle up to 1,000 acres. We ask that you let my kin down here take you through the land. Me and Jilkes, well, we don't want nothing in return other than your continued friendship."

Jong stood up and said, "You called him Jilkes. You two marry since we left?"

John Lee said, "You be having that rice stuff in your ears. I said my African American brother." Everyone roared! Jilkes stood up and said, "After all these years of dealing with this dude, do you think I care what he calls me? As long as it ain't 'honey', I can deal with the rest." The group roared with loud laughter. Somara walked up to her husband and kissed him on his cheek. Yeshida did the same thing to her husband.

The chef interrupted the group and said, "We have a wonderful menu for you guys to enjoy. We got fish, we got chicken, and we got steaks. We can't serve any pork products because a certain person here raises them as his pets. I ain't calling no names. We also have sushi, and an entire menu of Asian delights. The bar is open, and the food is ready for you to partake in this feast."

Captain Carla and the other pilots were in attendance. Carla said to Mike, "Dr. Beckmire came into the cockpit and basically chastised me for the way we put the bird in the air. I explained to her this was a common thing, and that it was important that our group understood how to do that in case of an emergency. Do you think I should have another conversation with her?"

"Sweetheart, I think you should do what you think is best for you and the group. I must admit, that was a pretty aggressive takeoff." That was not the information that Carla wanted to hear, but, nonetheless, it led her to decide to attempt to have a conversation with Dr. Beckmire.

Courtney and Monica made their way to the bar, and Carla saw an opportunity to engage them. As Courtney and Monica were in the process of ordering, Courtney saw Carla in the mirror. She said, "Carla, let me buy you a drink."

"I wish that were possible. I could use a stiff drink right about now, but I'm on duty."

"We're not flying again for two days. Have a drink," Courtney suggested.

"Thank you, but I have to refuse. If there is an emergency and we must leave in a hurry, you wouldn't want a person with alcohol in their system to fly the plane, would you?"

Monica said, "Now, I like that. How about a Coke or Seven-Up?"

"Naw, just a bottle of water."

"I neglected to ask you how you're feeling down there. Any recurrence of pain? Did you take the pain medicine?"

"No, Dr. Beckmire, no pain and definitely no need for those pills. That, too, would have been a breach of my responsibilities to fly the plane. About today, perhaps I need to apologize to you guys for that takeoff."

Courtney said, "I don't think you need to apologize to us for anything. After I thought about it, I remembered that runway in St. Thomas, not much room for error. Was that the same kind of takeoff?"

"Dr. Beckmire, today's takeoff simulated a small landing strip for single engine planes. St. Thomas has another 40 or more seconds of runway."

"Here's the deal—I want you to continue to fly the plane safely, and when you need to do something out of the ordinary, give us a heads-up. Okay? Now, give me a hug."

# # #

After fixing Mary Alice a plate, Jong saw the Sarge and said, "We can do $100 for $98.5, hopefully."

The Sarge shook his head and said, "That's a good deal. No one gets hurt in this mess, right?"

"I hope not. People must do what they say they can do and not cheat. Simply good business and no funny stuff, that's all," Jong concluded.

CHAPTER TWENTY-ONE

Two days later, after people had tentatively identified their plots of land, the plane was airborne, and on its way to The Sanctuary in St. Thomas. The flight was uneventful as most would desire.

After landing, and going through customs, the group headed to the welcoming station for some rum punch. When Chakes tasted the punch, he exclaimed, "This is much better than what they make at The Sanctuary! Perhaps we should have this person come out there and teach our people how to make punch like this?"

Mallory said, "You know you're right. Why don't you see if you can strike up a deal with her to come out and show us how to make it?"

#

Later, as the group was enjoying the rum punch, Chakes approached the woman pouring it, and said, "I would like you to come out to our place and show our people how to make rum punch as good as yours. Your rum punch always leaves a desire for more, and ours, well, after the first one, you're done."

"Man, I under contract with the Tourism Bureau. I can't freelance."

"I'm not interested in causing you any problems. I just want you to teach our people how to make a punch as good as yours."

"I no can do this thing you ask. They're strict about people doing parties and side jobs."

"How long have you worked here?" Chakes asked.

"Way before you be born, way before."

"How many hours do you work a day?"

"I work the welcome booth eight to ten hours a day during high season and just when planes arrive during off season."

"Is the pay good, and do they give you benefits?" Chakes queried.

"Man, why you ask so many questions?" the lady inquired.

"Because if you won't show us how to make it, we'll hire you to make it exclusively for us. How much do they pay you if you don't mind my asking?"

"They pay me enough to get by."

Chakes in a respectful manner, lowered his head and said, "Sister, you been getting by all your life. Why don't you come work for us, and we'll double what they pay you plus, you only have to work a few hours a week."

Montomie came up to Chakes and said, "Dude, you're holding up the caravan."

"Tell them I'll be right there. I'm trying to convince this sister to come and work for us and ease into retirement. Can I call you to discuss this further?"

"Man, I no rich. I don't have a telephone."

"Well, Sister, you do now. Take my phone and you name what it will take for you to come work for us at The Sanctuary." Chakes pulled out a $100 bill and said, "Take this money and buy the charger for the phone inside the airport. You can call wherever in the world you want. Even if you don't want to work for us, you can keep the phone."

"I can't afford no telephone bill."

Chakes exclaimed, "I can! Keep it Sister. I know the number, and I will call you later. You can tell me how much you want to earn. I hope this works for us when I call you later tonight."

He left her booth and headed towards the vans. Mallory yelled, "Did she give you the recipe?"

"No, but I offered her a job, gave her my phone, and told her I would call her later to figure out if she wants to come on board with us."

"Good job! I hope she seriously considers it," Mallory stated.

"Oh, I think she will. I could see her eyes glowing and almost in tears. I don't think she believes I'm serious," Chakes announced.

The Sarge yelled, "What's the hold up?" Mallory explained what was going on, and the Sarge said, "Tell him we'll give him another five minutes."

Chakes went back to her booth and said, "Sister, I ain't leaving here without an answer. I see you must be done for the day. What you do with that punch? You no give it away?"

"I have to pour it out. Can't be seen contributing to the drinking problems on the island."

"Okay, my people are giving me five minutes to convince you. Where you live, Sister?"

"I live where the problems are. My granddaughter should be here any minute to pick me up. Where is that Sanctuary place, you mentioned?"

"You know Mr. Christopher Carter? We are his partners. We demolished his place and rebuilt it."

"Oh, yeah, I hear about that. You the people who do that bend in the beach. You people rebuild those places and make it high end so poor people can't afford to come and stay there."

"Sister, we have to make a profit. Maybe you can come and tell us what we should be doing on the island to make it a better place for everyone. Sister, can we give you a ride?"

"I no get in a car with a strange man who gives me a phone and $100. You may be one of those freaky people from the mainland."

"Sister, I assure you, I'm no freak."

"Oh, here's my granddaughter." Chakes turned around and damn near fell to his knees. A woman appearing to be in her early to mid-thirties, bronze in color, with sandy long hair, and green eyes walked towards the booth. She asked, "Hey Grandma, are you ready to go?"

Chakes stared at the woman and froze. The woman said, "Hello, I'm Luana. Who are you?"

Her grandmother said, "This guy gave me a phone and $100 for me to buy a charger so I can call him later."

Her granddaughter said, "Mister, you had better put distance between this booth and my grandmother, or I'm going to scream that nasty word."

Chakes exclaimed, "Wait a minute, please, please!" He looked at her grandmother and said, "Please tell her why I gave you the phone."

"He wants me to come and work for him at Chris Carter's place. He's one of the new owners."

Chakes said, "We're not the owners—we are investors. Mr. Carter and his family will own that land and property no matter what."

Luana softened her demeanor and said, "I'm one of the lawyers who reviewed that one-sided document."

Chakes said, "I have a caravan of people waiting to go to The Sanctuary. I would like to send a van for you and your grandmother to come to the resort this evening and have dinner with me and my family."

Luana said, "I'm not sure I would be good company with your wife in attendance, or for that matter, any time."

Chakes said, "Oh, I see. Listen, my family is a group of people who I work with, live with, and travel the world with. If you'd come outside for a moment, you'll at least see what I mean. I'm not married, and I pray to God, you aren't either. Come outside, wave but keep the phone, and I will call you. If you know Mr. Carter, give him a call. Ask him to vouch for my character. Just give me a chance to get your grandmother out of this booth and working for us making that fabulous rum punch. Please, both of you come and hear me out before you scream that nasty word. We help people help themselves. We don't screw them over. Ask Mr. Bassman, or the owners of those properties that make up The Sanctuary."

Luana walked her grandmother outside and saw all the vans with people waving to them. Chakes said, "That multi-colored, multi-ethnic bunch of people is the family I was referring to. I'm not married, but I sure would like to have a serious conversation about the things you like to do and what kind of man could possibly win your heart. I just might be that guy. Please call."

He walked them to their car and said, "You need to get that muffler fixed. Please call."

Chakes entered the van Mallory, Monica, and others were in. Monica said, "Oh my, God! That woman is absolutely stunning. She's drop dead gorgeous and built like a brick 'S' house. Who the hell is she?"

Chakes still in shock and smitten, mumbled, "She's a lawyer like you. She's a lawyer like you."

"I hope you invited her to dinner."

"She's a lawyer like you. I invited her grandmother."

"You didn't invite the woman to The Sanctuary?"

"I gave them my phone. I don't know the number to my phone. Does anyone know the number to my phone?"

Montomie laughed at the way he was responding and said, "Brother, we know your number."

When the group arrived at the resort, the buzz was viral. "Who was that woman, was a constant question?" Chakes just kept walking without acknowledging anyone.

Once in his suite, Chakes picked up the house phone called Montomie and asked him for his phone number. After retrieving it, he made a call to his phone. When the voice on the other end answered the phone, he said, "This is Mr. Chakes calling. I met you at the booth dispensing rum punch at the airport. I would like to send a car for you and your granddaughter so that you can have dinner with me and my friends. If you feel you need to bring a male chaperone, that's fine as well. Please forgive me for not asking your name, Sister. I just like the way 'Sister', sounded, and decided to address you that way until you felt comfortable enough to tell me your name."

"Mr. Chakes, I'm an old woman and I don't have nothing for anyone to steal. Do you promise me that you're no thief or philandering cherry picker?"

"Sister, I am none of those things. I was once married, but my wife loved another. I wouldn't know how to philander, even if there was a road map. I'm a good Catholic boy who loved his mother and obeyed most of the commandments."

"Which ones didn't you obey, Mr. Chakes?"

"Sister give me the address, let me tell you about me and my friends over dinner. I assure you, it's not a boring story, and it has its roots, here on your island."

The woman gave Chakes the address and told him she would prefer dinner at five if it was okay with him. He told her they would be there waiting on her. She said, "I would like to bring my great-granddaughter as well."

"Sister, you can bring your entire family if you like, but please include your granddaughter."

Chakes went to the lobby where he saw Mr. Carter and asked him to provide transportation for his guests. He gave him the address. Mr. Carter gave the address to his son, asked him to pick them up, and deliver them to The Sanctuary by five pm. Mr. Carter said, "Might I suggest dinner on the beach in an enclosed net?"

Chakes said, "That would be perfect, and that way, no one is gawking at me and making me feel extremely nervous. I don't know what they eat, so we'll have to wait until they get here and show them the menu or have them tell us what they would like to eat. Is that okay with you, Mr. Carter?"

"Mr. Chakes, you people don't get it, do you? We're here to make your life perfect. You don't have to ask my permission to demand what you want."

"Mr. Carter, we're partners. We don't own you, and you don't own us. If any in our group appear to play Kunadakhain on you, let me know. Slavery ended, officially, oh, I don't know when, but that ain't how we roll. You're our partner and never hesitate to ask any of us for anything. We're who we are, and having people bow to us, ain't who we be." Mr. Carter grabbed him and said, "That is what all of us can't fathom. You people come here like you're guests."

Chakes sternly stated, "Mr. Carter, we are guests and don't forget it. Nothing special and nothing required. On another note, can I ask you, sort of a 'man to man' question?"

"How can I assist you?"

"Do you know anything about the grandmother, granddaughter and great-granddaughter that are coming for dinner?"

"I thought you would never ask. She's probably one of the most beautiful women on the island. She has been widowed for four years. Her husband died in Desert Storm. Her daughter is four years old. She's a lawyer, a wonderful granddaughter, mother, and hasn't bothered to look at another man for that many years. The fact that she's accompanying her grandmother here, speaks volumes, Mr. Chakes. She must have smiled at you at some point. I know she did."

"Mr. Carter, I have to reverse some of the bullshit I said earlier. Prior to meeting the granddaughter, I begged the grandmother for the formula to her rum punch. I gave the sister my phone and told her I would hire her to work for us. Do you have a problem with me obligating you and our business? I mean, if necessary, I will provide funds for her from my pocket, but she doesn't need to know that, right?"

"Mr. Chakes, if you can convince her to work for us and the four institutions in The Sanctuary, we would all be obliged and in debt to you. None of us can replicate her rum punch. If you drink her rum punch, you drink it until you pass out. You drink our rum punch, well, you have one, you're done, and then you move on to something else. That would be a major coup for this part of the island, if you can make that happen. I can have the other owners come down and tell them what a great human being you are and bullshit like that, if you like?"

"Mr. Carter, I don't want bullshit. I just want an honest opportunity to convince a woman I don't know that I'm not a brigand, but a guy who wants to learn about her, her granddaughter, and convince her to work for us in management. Just kidding."

Chakes looked out towards the beach and saw the assistants pitching a tent. He said, "I guess someone else has the same idea?"

"No, Mr. Chakes. That is an exclusive presentation for you, my friend."

# # #

At 1630 hours, Chakes had finished his shower, shaved his nappy face, and styled his hair. He knew when in the islands, do as the islanders do, dress lightly and whitely.

At 1645 hours, Montomie knocked on his door and said, "Your guests will be here at exactly 1700 hours. You should be down on the beach and make your way back to the lobby, all while they're watching you make your grand entrance, your majesty. Listen, this is important. Try to remain calm, greet the grandmother first, then the great-granddaughter and then her mom. Make her mom last. This way, you're gaining supporters for your efforts. Now, let me caution you on one thing, my Brother. If you're out to get laid, then attempt to hire the grandmother and be done. We don't hurt children and we don't hustle women for sex. Are we clear?"

Chakes looked at him and said, "Is my cologne too strong?"

"Barely noticeable. What is it?"

"Bulgari, I love that scent. Okay, I'm off to the beach."

# # #

At 1658 hours, the van pulled up to the resort and the staff graciously helped the occupants out of the van. They entered the lobby and were overwhelmed by the opulence and the aesthetics of the building. Mr. Carter was first to greet them and said, "Oh, there's Mr. Chakes, he was walking on the beach." They watched as Chakes majestically walked towards the entrance, while looking at his watch. He entered the lobby and said, "Sister, thank you for accepting my invitation." He reached for her hand and kissed it gently. He looked at the beautiful little girl and said, "My name is Maurice Chakes, and you are an exceptionally beautiful little girl. What is your name?"

The child responded, "My mother told me to never tell strangers my name."

Chakes said, "Your mother is a very smart woman." He moved in front of Luana and said, "Welcome to The Sanctuary." He reached for her hand and kissed it lightly, but passionately. He said, "What is your daughter's name, or do I call her 'Cutie' for the balance of the evening?"

Luana said, "Honey, this is a friend of grandmother's and Mommy's. It's okay to tell him your name."

The child looked at Chakes and said, "My name is Beatrice."

"Nice to meet you, Beatrice." He smiled at her, then returned his attention to sister and said, "Let me show you and your family around the property. You want to take the van, the mule, or walk?"

Beatrice said, "I want to ride on the mule."

"Beatrice, it's a mechanical mule with four wheels," Chakes advised.

During their ride, around the property, Beatrice saw Larry's kids playing on the beach and said, "I want to play in the sand with them."

Chakes said, "Why don't we all play with them? Let me introduce you to one of our leader's sons."

Chakes stopped the mule and approached Larry. He said, "This little beauty is Beatrice, her mother is Luana, and this lady, for now, goes by the name, Sister."

Larry introduced his family, and after some small talk, suggested that Luana leave Beatrice with him and Marisa while they went on the short sight-seeing trip.

Later, Chakes said, "When you turned off the main road, you entered what we call The Sanctuary. The two properties at the beginning of the cul-de-sac, as you could see, were demolished and new structures will be built with hotel accommodations and, of course food service. We rebuilt Mr. Carter's property in record time by running three shifts of different workers each day for six days. By doing it that way, we placed a small dent in the unemployment rate on the island."

Luana asked, "Why are you doing it and making the agreements so flexible? Don't you have an attorney to structure these relationships?"

"Aw, I see you saw that. Anyway, we do, and she's a brilliant one at that. This is how it works for us—we help people help themselves. We invest in individuals and not businesses. If Mr. Carter wants to take advantage of us, he could, as well as the rest of the owners. Mr. Carter and the others create jobs, which in turn creates demand for products, and people spend their money, however, some will invest it. We are altruistic in nature but are the residual product of a mean set of circumstances. There are twelve of us who fought in the jungle for an awfully long time. We have a lot of souls in hell, waiting on our arrival. We were all living our lives separately when the call came in that one of our members, was under siege. This has been a work in progress for the past few years. Our group has expanded, wives have been added, they have become pregnant, and we spend a lot of time in different places around the world."

Sister asked, "When will you settle down?"

"I have settled down. We were in Alabama yesterday selecting plots of land to build our houses on. Now, Sister, I want to know, will you come and work for us? We will pay you well, give you benefits, and secure you a position for life. All you have to do is make that fabulous rum punch for our guests. Mr. Carter is very accepting of you and has agreed to any arrangement I develop with you."

Luana said, "I have to feed Beatrice as well as myself. Can we continue the conversation over dinner?"

#

At dinner, Beatrice continued to play with the twins, as well as with LaGina. Courtney saw Luana, walked over to the table and announced, "Hi, I am Courtney Beckmire."

"Hi, I'm Luana and this is my grandmother, Ms. Viola. I'm hoping you know this scoundrel sitting across from me."

"Ah, a scoundrel he is, but a great one. We're so happy you could join us for dinner. Ms. Viola, we all love your rum punch, perhaps a little too much. Rather than have people keep coming over, once we're all here, I'll announce that we have guests, everyone should just say hi, and not intrude on the delicate negotiations that have to happen between Ms. Viola and Chakes."

Ms. Viola said, "Man, I asked you before, which commandments did you violate? Is this group like the mob, and are you people into bad things?"

Chakes paused and said, "We were soldiers in Vietnam, and we probably killed more enemy than the average group over there. We were called the 'killing machine' by the Viet Cong. That tall good-looking guy over there with the woman and two babies is the reason why we're in this mess. He's our leader's son. He kissed a spy, swallowed a capsule, and became the most hunted human being on the planet earth by every major power. He's known as the 'idiot spy'. This is a complicated story, and we're fighting a new war where the people we trust in our government are trying to get their hands on a non-nuclear, but deadly bomb, manufactured with carbon. It's called the Carbon Factor."

Sister said, "So, are all you people spies? And whose plane is that you flew in on?"

Chakes smiled and adamantly stated, "No, Sister! We are not spies. That's our plane and we have two others. We have foundations and charities all over the world, and we're all somewhat rich. We don't steal, sell drugs, manufacture drugs, or relate to drugs in any way shape or form. We're much like modern day Robin Hoods!"

"Grandma, I think he's probably told us all that he's going to about their business. I would like to order something to eat."

"Mr. Chakes, I'm going to give that phone to my granddaughter. Her life is miserable, perhaps you can help her get back on track."

"Grandma! You don't know this scoundrel."

"I knew that when he came back for the second time to talk to me that you would be there by then. I like him as a scoundrel."

"You're kinda embarrassing me. I don't need you to play matchmaker."

"You need someone to play it!"

Chakes said, "Let's order something to eat." He looked up and saw Jilkes, John Lee, and the Sarge heading his way. He said, "Okay, here comes the insults."

The Sarge stood over the group and Chakes said, "Sarge, John Lee, and Jilkes, meet Ms. Viola, her granddaughter Luana, and the little one with Larry's kids is Beatrice." Everyone cordially said hello and the Sarge said, "I want to welcome you to our little world and hope you can come to terms with his proposal, Ms. Viola and Ms. Luana, you would be a welcome breath of fresh air for our comrade."

Courtney returned with Monica and said, "Sarge, lead your squad away before you people scare his guests away."

Courtney then said, "This is Monica, our lawyer and friend. Okay, I promise, no more interruptions."

Ms. Viola asked, "Would it be rude to get something to go? I want to watch TV for a while before I go to sleep?"

"I guess that's the cue. You may order anything your heart desires and you can as well, Luana," Chakes announced.

Ms. Viola said, "I'm leaving them here in your care. I want to watch Scandal and the Blacklist. Those are my favorites. To tell the truth, I didn't think we would be here this long, but I learned to respect my gut feelings that told me you're a good person and you're surrounded by good people. Luana, you do want to enjoy a night out, don't you? Come on girl, don't be playing shy."

Luana said, "When I get home, young lady, I'm going to give you a spanking. Is this evening contrived in any way?"

Chakes said, "I wish. I tried to hire, Sister, you turned the corner and I've been in a stupor ever since."

"Okay, both of you, leave the game alone. Grandma, what would you like to eat?"

Chakes said, "I have an idea. Why don't we put you in one of the rooms to watch television, you can eat there and order whatever you like? Meanwhile, I can look after Beatrice and try to interest Luana in my less than polished game. And, if you decide to spend the night, it will give me additional time to talk to Luana. My people are watching me, and I'm not particularly good at this dating thing. In the past two years we've been all over the world and no one has caught my eye like you."

Luana said, "Mr. Chakes, this is all very flattering, but I would like to propose an alternate course. If you're free tomorrow, we can come for lunch, perhaps take a swim, and you can provide us with accommodations. We'll be your guests all day. What's your reaction to that?"

"I like that idea and it sounds like a plan. Okay, Sister, what would you like to eat?"

They ordered dinner, and it was obvious that Beatrice was extremely happy playing with the other children. She came over to the table and whispered to her mother, "They asked me to spend the night. Can I?"

"Oh, honey, not tonight. How about if we come tomorrow? Perhaps we can stay tomorrow night if you want to."

Beatrice ran across the dining room floor and said, "My mother said I can't stay tonight, but maybe tomorrow night if you invite me."

The meal was scrumptious, plentiful, and it was getting late. Sister asked, "How can you stay in business giving away this much food?"

"Sister, maybe they do a little extra for you since you be special and all."

"Man, you be so full of it, but I like you and I like the people in this community. Do you think I could see a room before I leave?"

"Sister, what you talking about? You should come tomorrow and soak those tired feet in your waters. This party started with you and you're the glue until I hit the right note."

"Man, from where I sit, I think you be done hit all the right notes."

Luana said, "That little taste of wine has impacted her brain. I think we should be getting home."

Chakes said, "Okay. Let me round up a driver and some support, and I'll be right with you."

He walked over to the Sarge and said, "I need an escort." The Sarge looked around the room and summoned, Whitmore, Gladstone, Montomie, and McArthur. He said, "Escort Romeo and his friends home, but have our people at the resort drive two vans. Be discrete and not let on that you're following him."

Marisa said to Luana, referring to Beatrice, "What a darling. So how early can you guys come tomorrow? Can you come for breakfast that way we can swim a little, go into town, and shop a little?" Luana began to feel almost obligated and said, "How about ten?"

Marisa said, "Great, I'll reserve one of the vans to pick you guys up at 0930 hours."

"We have a car, and I can drive," Luana said.

"Luana, let us be your hosts and pick you up. Oh wait, we should come to you since you're in town and pick you up. Do you have his phone number?"

"I do not." Chakes asked me if I had a cell phone. I really don't have a need for one," Luana confessed. Chakes handed Luana his phone and smiled.

"Okay, Mr. Nice Guy. You just gave me your phone, so you don't have one. How do I reach you?" Luana asked.

"Mallory, do you have an extra phone?" Chakes inquired.

"I do. Didn't you have two?" Mallory asked.

"They're in use. I need a new one," Chakes confessed.

Luana said, "Listen, you gave my grandmother a phone. I'll use hers if it's okay with her."

Chakes gave her the number and told her they would speak later or tomorrow to finalize the details.

# # #

The ride to her place was quick and fast. When they arrived, Luana said, "I would invite you up, but I'm sure your security team wants to get back."

"You spotted them, eh? Anyway, we don't travel alone and even when you don't see us, my friends are around and vice versa. We live a complicated, but an honest life, one that I hope to share more details about with you tomorrow. If you like, I'll be back at The Sanctuary in thirty minutes, I would love to talk to you on the phone."

"Mr. Chakes, I'm tired and overwhelmed. This has been a wonderful evening. I thank you for dinner, the ride, the escort, and the magnificent company. I will call you in the morning."

Chakes extended his hand and gently shook hers. He said to Beatrice, "It was so cool meeting you. I will see you tomorrow. Goodnight." He turned to Ms. Viola and said, "Sister, you be good vibes, Man. I be seeing you in the morning." He kissed her hand and watched them enter their apartment building. He turned to walk away and saw three guys near the property. One of them said, "Yankee man not safe when mess with island women."

Chakes responded, "Island man not safe when screw with Yankee man." The doors to the van opened on both sides, his security team got out of it, and advanced towards the men. McArthur walked up to them taking pictures. He said, "The next time you see my friend, you run away. If he suffers any insults from you, our team will come down here and clean this place up. Am I clear?"

The leader turned without saying anything. McArthur hoisted his ass off the ground and asked, "Am I clear?"

"Yes, Sir. Yes Sir."

Gladstone asked, "Do you two have a problem?"

"No, Sir."

The men turned to walk away and Chakes looked at the windows to see if anyone was watching. He knew that Sister was watching the interaction.

# # #

Back at the resort, Chakes thanked the guys and bid them goodnight. He entered his room and saw that the light on his phone was on. The message stated, "I saw what you did, I thank you for that. They're like flies. Sister!"

At 2315 hours, the phone in Chake's room rang. He grabbed it and said, "Hello."

"I'm sorry, did I awake you?" Luana asked.

"I'm okay, I mean I'm not asleep. Nice to hear from you."

"Listen, can I be brutally frank with you?" Luana inquired.

"Oh goodness, I guess I didn't make a good impression or I'm just not your type. Which one is it?"

Luana said, "Ye, of so little faith. The jury is still out on that. I called to thank you again for a wonderful evening that included my grandmother who absolutely adores you. By the way, your life is complicated, and you're apparently always on the move. Is that a fair assessment?"

"That would be a fair statement. I would love for you and Beatrice to join us sometime."

"Listen, please be mindful of the fact, we just met and there are some normal things that people go through prior to being asked to be whisked off to some unknown destination. I like you because you didn't have a con, other than the one you tried on my grandmother which makes me believe you and your people are legitimate. I mean, I like you, but I just met you.   You   understand   where   I'm   going   with   this conversation?"

"I'm going to let you in on a little secret. I have not been with another woman in years. When I found out about my wife, I checked women off the list. I saw you and had a natural reaction to your beauty and the sculpture of your body. I saw you and lusted for you because I had forgotten about that aspect of life. I listened to you address me, felt the warmth in your heart, and the discontent in your voice when sister told you that I gave her a phone and $100. She really set me up with that one. However, we're still talking and I'm running out of words because I have such a vision of you, Beatrice, Sister, and me. I like you and them so much, and I don't know a thing about you guys except sister makes the best rum punch. I wish you had stayed here tonight. We could have walked on the beach, talked, and found out what each other likes. I think I'm talking too much."

"How else will we learn about each other? I'm going to follow my grandmother's advice and tell you about me. My husband was killed during Desert Storm by an IED. Immediately after his funeral, his married friends started chasing me and insisting that I enjoy life with them, but on the side. I shut down completely and refused to answer calls or letters, hence, no cell phone. I loved my husband very much at one time, but he was a player. He was not happy with the attention of one woman but needed the rapture of many. He hurt me in many ways. He abused me verbally, he hit me frequently, he disrespected my body and gave me an STD. His death was a blessing to me, and I affirmed before God, that I would never allow a man to humiliate me or touch me in a violent manner. If a man could not give me the same depth of love that I gave to him then I didn't need a man. Therefore, Mr. Chakes, I love deeply and permanently. I suggest you don't start anything you can't finish."

"I would like the chance to start something that I will finish. I saw you and became comatose and speechless. I have never felt that way before. I have never felt embarrassed to open my mouth because I wasn't sure who was talking. Given the opportunity, and if you believe in, ah, let me not spoil this."

"What were you going to say Mr. Chakes?"

"Let's start by getting rid of that Mr. Chakes stuff. Why not call me Maurice?"

"I like being formal with you, Mr. Chakes, if that's okay with you?"

"Listen, Luana, I'm turned on to your spirit. You might not believe in signs and things, but when we were in Australia, I saw you in a dream, and I have seen you in other dreams of mine. The Sarge and Zanthius, his son, are Beckmire's, and they're Australian. We all traveled there, and we all had out of body experiences. I saw you, I saw me, I saw Sister, and I saw Beatrice. I also saw a new baby boy. Please don't think me crazy or on drugs. I saw these things and I'm not crazy. Now, perhaps they were dreams, but the person in them looked like you."

"Maurice, do you have a strange tattoo on your leg in the back around the knee area?"

"Why do you ask?"

"I dreamt two days ago of a relationship with a man who all I could see was the back of his leg. Now, how crazy is that?"

"That's not crazy at all. I have a tattoo that I do not remember receiving while we were in the outback. This is getting a little weird. I hope you don't think of me as a nut or a person with a mental issue."

"Hell, man I just told you about a dream I had about a man with a tattoo on the back of his leg and I don't know what he looks like," Luana said.

"Of course, you do. I'm volunteering for that job. How crazy do we sound at almost midnight?"

"Isn't that when the nuts come out to play? At midnight, and on the night of a full moon," Luana stated.

Chakes said, "We should be together." There was silence and then a sigh.

"Why is that Mr. Chakes?"

"The topics we're sharing are things that should be reserved for in-person discussions. I want you to see my expressions, look into my eyes, and realize that I'm not whistling Dixie here."

"Maurice, I want to digest this conversation and be prepared to continue it in the morning. I'll say one thing before I say goodnight. I feel a comfort level around you and your extended family. My question is simple, if we proceed down this road, can you give me the respect I demand, the appreciation I require, and pure love without compromise? Goodnight, Mr. Chakes. I will call you in the morning."

# # #

This was a night to receive messages from faraway places. Jilkes received a text message from Franco stating, "We poured concrete today my friend. It's happening." Jilkes smiled and broadcasted the message to the rest of the group.

The Sarge received a message from the outback. It said, "Under siege by European lawyers and hired bad guys. They are trying to steal the land legally through intimidation, threats and murder." He called Mallory and said, "We need to make a call to the outback. Tell Monica that a group of European lawyers are there trying to file an injunction staying the previous agreements. They are stating that there are no true owners in Australia, that they are entitled to the land and, therefore, they're filing a petition to seize the land by a series of legal maneuvers."

Monica said, "Tell the Sarge, if we're not there to file an opposing petition, they're likely to take the land free of charge. Tell him I said, we should head there in the morning!"

Mallory broadcasted the information to the group and told them to prepare to leave for the outback by 1100 hours. When Chakes woke up and saw the message, he yelled, "I can't believe this. I fall in love and then I must fly the hell away. Cruel is this world." He began pacing and yelled, "Shit, she's going to think I hustled her and them." McArthur walked by his room, heard the discourse, and banged on the door. Chakes answered it and asked, "Did you see the damn broadcast?"

McArthur said, "I saw it. What's the big deal?"

"The deal, knucklehead, is that I'm supposed to have guests later. I'm sorry, I didn't mean to call you a name. I like this woman and when we were last in the outback, I dreamt of her and now I must leave her. She's going to think I'm a bullshitter."

"Not if you ask them to come along," McArthur advocated.

"What?"

"Pick up the phone, inform the grandmother that there is an emergency in Australia that we have to deal with and that you're begging her, her granddaughter and great grandbaby to come along. All they need are passports. Dude beg the grandmother. She is the controlling factor."

Chakes said, "It's a legal issue. Perhaps Luana can assist Monica in the proceedings."

"Dude, now you're thinking and concocting."

Chakes paced around the room and finally made the call. He said, "Sister, I know it's late, but this is an emergency. I want you and your family to accompany us to Australia in the morning. We have a bunch of thieves trying to steal native lands through legal maneuvering. I need Luana, I need you, and I need Beatrice to be at the airport with passports or citizenship papers by ten. Sister, if you can't go, and they can't go, then I will not go and protect my brothers' backs. I will stay here and try to gain the favor of the woman I feel I could love."

"Man, you been drinking that rum punch?"

"Chakes in his accent and character that he used with Ms. Viola, said "Sister, I no drink at all tonight. I need you to have blind faith, trust in me, and be at the airport in the morning. Pack lightly or not at all. No one will need a thing. We will provide everything."

"Man, I know you been drinking that rum punch."

"Sister, I swear, I no drink anything tonight. The only punch I drink is the sweet nectar of Luana's voice over the phone for the last two hours. I'm sober as the Pope."

"Man, we don't just run off with the first Yankee we meet. You can't expect me to put my babies at risk with people I really don't know. Come on, Man, what you think we made of? There are no paper dolls here, we're real humans with brains. Man, you no call here with this kind of request again. Sleep well, Man."

# # #

At 0945 hours, people were preparing to make the trip to the airport. Captain Carla and crew were already at the airport, preparing the plane for departure. The plane had been stocked with provisions, fueled, safety checked three times by air and ground crews, and was ready for takeoff.

At 1030 hours, the weary group arrived at the airport and went through customs. The Sarge knew Chakes was not in a good place and decided to offer him an option. The Sarge walked up to him and said, "If I saw Courtney for the first time and felt the way I did then, as I do now, I would miss this flight."

Chakes bellowed, "Bullshit."

The Sarge said, "I know we're brothers and our bond has survived all kinds of exigencies from women—my son kissing a spy, people shooting at us, placing suicide vests on the children, blowing up where we live and a whole host of other crazy shit. She's a winner, and she will be here when you get back if you chose to leave. I need you. But you have got to have faith!"

The Sarge, with both hands on Chake's shoulders, hesitated for a moment, smiled, then laughed, before saying, "It appears that I'm running my mouth for nothing. Turn around, you, dazzling Romeo."

"Man, I've never been to Australia, and I want to make sure you're not trying to hoodwink my girls into some craziness," Sister stated. Chakes fell to his knees and began to cry and the Sarge told him to stand up and act excited.

Chakes said, "Sister, I am the happiest and luckiest man in the world. I was so despondent, and my leader, the Sarge, told me to have faith. Sister, I will take care of you and them. This here long plane ride gives us an opportunity to talk about what you want to do with that neighborhood of yours. I know you saw me and mine about to hurt a couple of young hustlers. It also gives you, Luana, and Beatrice an opportunity to interact with our group." In the middle of the customs area, he yelled, "Jong, I need three more first class seats."

Sister said, "I got this text message and didn't believe it at first, but I then realized that you and my granddaughter are in love but were afraid to make a commitment because you don't even know each other's last name. I need to help you two reach the next level, as they say, or is it to the next base?"

A customs agent asked for Beatrice's papers and her mother asked, "Grandma, did you take the papers off the table?"

"I thought you did," Ms. Viola responded.

The agent said, "I can't allow her on the plane without proper documentation. You people ought to know that by now."

Chakes turned to the Sarge and said, "Hell, this ain't United or Southwest Airlines. This is our plane."

Chakes paused and asked, "Mallory, can you call Mr. Carter and ask him to come back to the airport and give us a ride to Ms. Viola's place?"

The Sarge said, "Mr. Carter doesn't leave until our wheels are tucked under the belly of this beast. Whitmore, Gladstone, Montomie and McArthur, give my brother an escort."

McArthur said, "Sarge, we had a little difficulty there last night. Perhaps we can change the escort team to, Jilkes, John Lee, Bernstein, and Brown?"

"Done! Escort Chakes and Ms. Luana to her place."

# # #

Approximately thirty-five minutes later, the two vehicles arrived at the airport with proper documentation for Beatrice. Ms. Viola, during the wait period, had the opportunity to substantiate from the Sarge that he ran a true and Christian ship. He attempted to convince her, but only Chakes could work the magic needed on her.

At 1134 hours, Captain Carla came on the intercom and said, "I like to give myself as much separation from those hills in front of us as possible. I need you guys to hold tight and realize that we know what we're doing up here. I will lift off, our second officer will make most of the trip, a long one at that, with our two alternate pilots, and I will oversee the landing in Sydney, Australia. We are well-stocked with food and booze. You know the drill, have fun, watch your movies, but more importantly, talk to each other. To our new guests, welcome aboard and enjoy the ride. That little girl is such a cutie. I need to have one like her. Mike, are you listening?" The entire cabin laughed at the thought.

Ms. Viola said to her granddaughter, "I hope I haven't gotten us in over our heads. I thought we could expose him on the invitation to Australia and here we are about to go down under. Damn, this be some ride."

Chakes let Luana sit in the aisle seat so she could see her daughter and grandmother. Captain Carla came on the intercom and said, "Courtney, this is going to be fast." She throttled the engines to the point the plane was vibrating on the runway. She released the breaks and then bam! The plane roared down the runway and in record time, the wheels were lifting off the ground.

Minutes later, after the plane was airborne, Courtney walked to the cockpit, opened the door, and said to Captain Carla, "That one wasn't so bad. The other one felt like we went straight up." They laughed and she asked Carla to come and see her when she took a break.

Meanwhile, Monica went back to where Luana was sitting and said, "I hear you're a lawyer and that you questioned the contractual relationship between us, Mr. Carter, and the rest of the people in The Sanctuary." Luana looked over at Chakes, who felt her discomfort.

"Monica continued, "The banks were about to repossess all of their properties and build a high-end community, much like we did. The difference is, we're partners, and all the owners can screw us if they like, and we wouldn't have a leg to stand on. We help people help themselves. We don't want to own the properties. We want to make sure that decent human beings aren't screwed out of their assets. That agreement was drafted in their favor and they can buy us out at any time. They don't have to worry about foreclosure or any legal maneuvering. They and their families own those properties.

"Now, I'm going to need your help once we get to the outback. I would like you to be my assistant and co-counsel on this matter, caution me when necessary and correct me when needed. This relationship is critical because we're going to be up against some real sharks. Their goal is to steal land from the Aborigines. That's a no-no, Ben Beckmire, the Sarge, ain't going to let that happen, and neither are the rest of us. Is that something you think you can assist me with?"

Luana said, "Certainly, and that way, it allows me to earn credit towards this expensive trip we just barged in on."

"Honey, you didn't barge in because that's impossible. You were invited in by a certain gentleman whom I will vouch for."

Ms. Viola asked, "So, Ms. Monica, this here man is not a scoundrel?"

"No, Ms. Viola. This one is special. They're all incredibly special. A few years ago, I almost lost my husband because I gave him an ultimatum—them or me. Once I got off my high horse, I realized these guys are as much of a family to him as I am. They bled together. All I did was nag him. Now, these guys are well tempered until you go against one of them and then you suffer the wrath of all of them. They permanently remove obstacles."

"You mean they bury people?"

"Naw, they don't bury them; they kill them, others bury them.

"So, Ms. Monica, are my grandbabies safe and secure?"

Monica looked at Ms. Viola in a perplexing manner and flatly stated, "Ms. Viola, no one is safe and secure. We're in a damn plane that could fall out of the sky. You could choke on a bone, and the baby could slip and hit her head. If someone comes to hurt you or your babies, would you shoot them?"

"I would do what is necessary to protect them," Ms. Viola confessed.

"That is what we do—whatever is necessary to protect our community. Some of us women have had to exercise our rights and end the lives of intruders. I don't want to scare you, but we look after our own and anyone who needs our help. I'm sure Mr. Chakes is going to tell you more about what we do and I'm going to save it for him. I just wanted to solicit your help, Luana, on the problem that we're going to face. Nice to have you guys on board. This is a fabulous place, Ms. Viola, I hope you'll have fun. We're going to spend the day in Sydney and then head to the Northern Territory in the morning, I guess."

# # #

The kids were near the back of the plane watching movies. LaGina asked Beatrice if she would like to come back with them.

Sister started playing with the buttons and found that the seats turned into small beds. After twenty minutes of tossing and turning, she found her soft spot, and was out for the duration.

Chakes asked Luana, "Are you hungry?"

"I'm not hungry right now, but I need to check on Beatrice and see if she wants something to eat."

"Trust me, the kids will show her how the system works, and she'll order what she wants. It's basically healthy foods.

At this hour, it's programmed for lunch, and that includes, real turkey breast, with whatever you want, as well as pastrami, hamburgers, kosher hot dogs, real cod fillets, or a salad of your choice. Does Beatrice have any allergies?"

"No, thank goodness."

"I'm going to have me a Bloody Mary and then I'm going to talk your head off. Do you want a Coke or something?"

"Really? You're having a Bloody Mary and you offer me a Coke? Is this the considerate man I met a day or so ago, or is it a man who thinks he has convinced someone that he is the prize?"

"This is the guy who begged Sister to come along on this journey, and to bring you and Beatrice. I mean, you didn't have a glass of anything last night, so I figured, I wouldn't try to put peer pressure on you. Having said all of that, would you like a Bloody Mary?"

"Thank you, yes."

Later, the two toasted and Chakes said, "How did I get you guys on this airplane?"

Luana looked at her grandmother and said, "She woke me up in the middle of the night after she saw the text message." She said, "Mr. Chakes has a message about Australia. I think he and his people will be off to that island." She then said, "Honey, I don't want to talk about all the things I told you not to do, and you did. I mean you were just like your mother, God rest her soul, but she was foolish and wild. I didn't want you to marry that man because I knew he was rotten to the core!" She also said, "This Mr. Chakes is solid, ambitious, dedicated to a premise, loyal and in love with you. I paused for a moment and then asked, "Grandma, how do you know so much about a man you just met a few days ago?"

She told me, "You had her rum punch before and that you smiled at her and slipped her $100 dollars. What's with you giving older women $100?"

"Sister is special to me. She smiled, laughed, and cautioned me about the rum punch and the island women. You're not going to believe this, but she said, "I have someone you should meet if your soul is righteous.""

"You know I'm going to ask her to confirm that statement."

"Listen, I don't believe in that love at first sight mess. However, I do believe that you and I are destined to be. You saw the back of my leg; I saw you, Sister, Beatrice, and a baby boy in my dream. So, in other words, whether you stay in love with me or not, you're going to have a boy."

"Maurice, I may be beyond that baby making stage."

"Luana, I'm only interested in this woman sitting next to me on this plane heading to the land of spirits. I was once a skeptic about my experiences in the Nam until I realized we never faced an enemy who was willing to die, but one who wanted to kill us. I began to rely on those guys in every manner. I've had them pick slogs off my penis, burn wounds shut, and bite miniature ticks off my ass. We probably have several thousand souls roaming around in hell, waiting on our arrival.

"In the last two years and over that Carbon Factor formula mess, we've probably killed over 500 people. In the Nam, I'm thinking we did thousands or more. The Sarge and Dr. Courtney went to lunch to meet his ex-lover when she told him that he had a son who was under siege. The threesome were having drinks and waiting for lunch to be served when people began shooting at them. They did that to send a message to the 'idiot spy'.

"He called us when he realized this thing was bigger than him busting up a couple of people. It turned out that hundreds of people wanted his son, as well as, all of his family. We regrouped, they shot up Asiram's place in Philly, and placed suicide vests on those kids that are playing with your daughter, in middle America. They blew up her ranch with us in it. I'm telling you all of this because I believe in destiny and not sex. I was totally numb after seeing you. It was like Sister spiked my rum punch with your name in it."

Luana touched Chakes' hand before saying, "I trust her and her wisdom. I saw you talking to her and wondered, "Who is that guy? When you turned around and looked at me and was unable to make a complete sentence, I thought that was perfect, and deserved a smile. I know that people think, and have said, that I'm one of the most beautiful women on the island. I don't agree because my soul is conflicted, as a result of my past relationship. I smiled at you, a thing I haven't done when meeting a man in many years. My grandmother showed me the text about this place and said, "You got to go with him if he asks." I said to her, "Grandma, I don't know him."

She said, "I don't know him either, but he be the scoundrel to catch and to love." Two seconds later, you called, and she went through that charade with you and I heard every word. Once she hung up on you, we discussed it all night. Beatrice woke up and said, "Mom, I like him, and I want to go". Speaking of which, please excuse me, I need to check on my daughter."

After checking on Beatrice, when she returned to her seat, Chakes was fast asleep. Luana's grandmother said, "I told you he was the one." Luana was considering debating that notion when she realized her grandmother was sound asleep again. She looked in the overhead bin and saw there were pillows and blankets. She placed one on her grandmother and one on Chakes. She retrieved another one and placed it on herself, closed her eyes, and entered dreamland.

Carla left the cockpit and saw Mike staring at her in a very strange way. When she was close to him, she said, "The first thing I want to do when this plane lands, is make love to my husband for the first time."

He stood up and kissed her and said, "I need you to be honest with me. Have you concluded all of your relationships?"

"Mike is that all you want to ask me?"

"That is the only thing I want to know."

"Baby, I concluded everything the moment I first laid eyes on you. I got sick, but now I'm well. I need you to hold me, love me, and make sure I'm loved for the rest of my life. And Mike, I really want to have a baby. Will you make love to me until I'm pregnant and beyond?"

CHAPTER TWENTY-TWO

The plane began its descent into Sydney, where the group intended on spending the balance of the day and night, before leaving for the Northern Territory in the morning. The Sarge placed a few phone calls to relatives, but to no avail. He said to Zanthius, "I think we need to get to Northern Territory as soon as possible. I'm having bad feelings about being here." He saw Jong and said, "We have two additional pilots on board. Why can't we refuel, and they take us to the Territory, now?"

Jong said, "Sarge, people were counting on spending the night in this wonderful city."

"So was I, but I have a bad feeling about being here rather than there. Let's make this happen in the next two hours."

The Sarge called the constable and said, "Constable, this is Ben Beckmire. How the heck have you been?"

"I've seen better days for my people. Things are going bad in the Northern Territory. On Monday, those crooks are presenting a case for ownership and discovery in court. There have been several severe beatings of potential witnesses, and it seems like they're just going to take the land."

"I called my people and can't seem to get an answer. What's going on out there?"

"Mr. Beckmire, those people have cut all telephone service in the area. They communicate by using those satellite phones and their private email servers."

"Why are they so desperate to acquire that land?"

"I have no idea, but your ancestor has been summoned, and he's on the move. Are you people going out? If so, it might be for nothing."

"Actually, we're refueling our plane now and will be there later tonight. Is there any way you can get that magical school bus to meet us and deliver us to one of the tribes?"

There was a long pause and seemingly, the sigh of disappointment. The constable said, "Text me when your plane departs. I will have them pick you up and supply you with bows and arrows. I know you have other things, but we want it to look like the natives got tired of taking shit and revolted. By the way, how is Yvette doing?"

"She is married and near term to have her child. She married the man who intervened in that issue, and she's happy. She's scared because she's seen the kinds of things we have to do, but she is a member of this community and I do mean a full member."

"Nice to hear that fairy tales do come true," the Constable stated.

Beckmire responded, "Our plane is to be airborne within two hours and I will text you once we are in the air. Nice to hear your voice, my friend, and on the way back, we will set a foundation in place to protect that land and others around the country. The one thing you might have to consider is retiring from the force and becoming the president of the foundation, hire you some big butt kickers, both black and white, then a staff to investigate and secure the properties that are under siege. We have two lawyers with us, I might leave one behind because this is her first trip, and we might have to bleed some rocks."

"My friend, I need young, educated Aborigines to help with this process, and they have to be paid."

"My friend, I will leave you in charge of a million dollars initially, and once you have a structure in place, we will endow you at the $5 million level if the board agrees. Hiring good people and providing them with good benefits will not be the problem. Finding good people who are committed to their heritage might be an issue. Thank you, my brother, and please make the connection for us. We have an unusual number of pregnant, and want to be pregnant, women in this group."

"Understood, Mr. Beckmire. Not to worry, all things will be in place and I'm sure your ancestor knows you will be on their sacred ground soon and will handle the issue."

The Sarge saw Jilkes and John Lee. He signaled them over to him. He said, "I need Mallory in on this as well."

John Lee said, "In on what?"

"Man open your eyes. Look at Chakes and his new family, they're all like in a trance, except the grandmother. We need to secure them in a hotel here in Sydney because I'm sure there is going to be trouble where we're heading. That wouldn't be a good first impression. Now, would it?"

Jilkes said, "Sarge, I don't quite agree with you on this one. Instead of your option, let's present them with another. Let's just lay it out that we may encounter danger and we want them to be safe."

"Damn, that's why I like committees. You get a fresh opinion, rather than your same old stale one."

# # #

John Lee asked, "Can I make a suggestion to Beatrice?"

Her mother agreed, and he said, "We would like to talk to your mother and grandmother in adult talk. Do you mind sitting on that bench over there, where everyone can keep an eye on you?"

Chakes inquired, "What's up, guys?"

Jilkes said, "Listen, people, we're not going to spend the night in Sydney. Instead, we're heading directly to the Northern Territory. Apparently, the problem is worse than we thought. Luana and Ms. Viola, we want to put you guys up in a hotel here in Sydney, and you can play that tourist thing until we finish our work in the outback. Don't worry about anything. Each of you ladies will have $10,000 in pocket money and you each will have debit cards with $50,000 to use to get back home if we're unsuccessful in the Northern Territory. We think our mission might be a bit bloody, and we certainly don't want anything to happen to you guys."

Ms. Viola looked around and asked, "Is little LaGina and the other kids going?"

Jilkes said, "Yes Ma'am."

"Are all those pregnant women going?" Ms. Viola inquired.

"Yes, Ma'am."

"Then if you ain't trying to get rid of us, we be going too."

The Sarge interjected, "Ms. Viola and Ms. Luana, we might have to kill some people and they're certainly going to try to kill us."

Ms. Viola looked at the Sarge and said, "Are they going to try to kill your grandbabies?"

The Sarge said, "At our place in the Midwest, the intruders strapped suicide vests on the children. These people kill for money."

Ms. Viola turned to face Chakes before saying, "Man, you be done brought us into the rain. We been wet before and we ain't staying in no hotel. You show us how to work weapons, and we will violate the commandment."

Chakes looked at Luana and said, "It's dangerous and people might have to count on you to protect them. You don't have to be or show any machismo here. I want you guys safe. Those other women, have ended lives in order to protect us."

Ms. Viola said, "Man, when we got up in that plane, we knew life would never be the same. My granddaughter has found a potential mate. I like him and trust him. He calls me 'Sister'. If'n, he goes, we go with him. Thank you, gentlemen. We be done here."

John Lee said, "That there woman is the only person in this group I be fully understanding. She speaks the right language."

Luana looked at Chakes and said, "I'm trusting you to be my first line of defense. After that, me and Grandma will cover your back. Just show us how to use the tools you have."

#

Carla, out of uniform, walked out of the cockpit. Mallory asked, "Captain, do we have an issue?"

"No sir, Mr. Mallory. I will be in the cockpit, but I'm over my flight time hours. Our copilots will fly this beautiful beast into the Northern Territory. I want to sleep in my man's arms," Carla answered, smiling, as Courtney winked at her.

Beatrice asked her mom if she could sit with the other kids? Her mother told her she could after the plane takes off and the captain turns off the fasten seat belt sign. Luana turned to Chakes and said, "You know I'm scared, and we're putting a lot of blind faith in a man my grandmother met twice while giving him stimulants. Doesn't bode well with me. She's been acting like some spiritual being in the last few days talking about a new way of life. When Mr. Beckmire broadcasted that event about Australia, she woke me up and said, "We're not having breakfast on the island in the morning, but we will have breakfast on an island." She also told me to pack a light bag for Beatrice, one for myself, and I'll be damn, we're on a plane to some unknown place in Australia."

"Sister is a wise woman. She plotted me to you, and I'll forever be beholden to her. You will see, I won't lead the discussion or try to plant a thought in your head, but you will find this place to be magical. You will find work to do here and you will do it well. I'm telling you, when we were in the Nam, the Sarge used to tell us about his relatives and especially about the one called the 'Great Saltie'. Legend has it the Great Saltie could transmogrify into human form, or into the largest saltwater crocodile ever seen. I know you think these are old wives tales, but I know for a fact, there are forces that supersede the knowledge of science."

"Enough of that, my love."

"Oh, my! You called me 'your love'."

"I guess it was a Freudian Slip," Luana acknowledged.

"Regardless of whose slip it was, you called me 'my love'."

"Maurice, tell me things about you. Tell me what matters to you and how you feel about humanity."

"Wow!"

For the next two hours, they both shared their lists of likes and dislikes. They laughed loudly and boldly, as if they were the only people on the plane. She touched his arm lightly, and he touched her nose. She hit his knee, punched his shoulder and he melted from the impacts. He asked her why she didn't date in four years and she told him if she wanted to get laid, she would lay herself. She in turn asked him why he hadn't hooked up like his brothers and he told her they met their soul mates in strange and defining places. He indicated to her all he met were people who wanted to screw. She asked him "What's wrong with screwing?" He told her if screwing was all there was to a relationship, then he didn't need it. He indicated that a jar of Vaseline was much more satisfying in the morning next to him, rather than a person whose name he could not remember. He said to Luana, "I hope my selfish ambitions haven't placed your family in any danger."

"Maurice, I hope not as well. My grandmother is so into you that it scares me. Did you have an affair with her or something?"

"Luana, no! Why would you ask such a thing?"

"My grandmother told me my first husband was a piece of shit after shaking his hands and examining them. When he left our apartment, she said, "Him like dog; he sniff and sniff until he humps the camel. After he humps the camel, he no sniff, no more. He now sniffs new camel! With you, and we've known each other for only two damn days, she swears on the bible about you. She said, 'He no wants to sniff you. He wants to know your mind and your passions. He no wants to immediately hump the camel. He wants to drain the brain, know the camel before he humps the camel. He no wants to hump the camel and then know the brain, unlike that last piece of shit that sent his friends to corrupt you, so he could divorce you and marry that twenty-five-year old pole dancer'.

"She told me that you're clean, righteous and loyal. I asked her, "How you know so much about this man, you want him for your lover?' Anyway, my grandmother slapped me into a coma. She said to me before she closed her bedroom door, 'I speak the truth. He unlike any man you met, but him a man. He will provide for you, Beatrice, your new baby, be a loyal family man and role model for your children. Beatrice will love her daddy and her brother. She will forget the shit that you brought home'."

Chakes looked at her, studied her face, her eyes, and then asked, "She spoke of a little boy?"

"Maurice, I just read you, her book. She said, 'Beatrice will love her father and brother," Luana replied. A stillness came over the box they were in. Maurice looked out of the window and studied the landscape below the plane. He said to himself, "How could she know about a little boy?"

Luana noticed the lull in the conversation and felt uneasy since she had performed catharsis on herself. She thought perhaps she had given Maurice too much information but wasn't sure. She turned to him to say something and he raised two fingers in the air. The quiet continued for perhaps another two minutes before Maurice turned to her and asked, "Did you tell your grandmother about my dream about a son?"

"No, I absolutely did not."

"How did she know about my dream?"

"Maurice, I will direct you to her, for a one-on-one conversation. Don't include me in this situation. I haven't shared anything about you because I frankly don't know anything about you. I'm living vicariously through the eyes of my grandmother when it comes to you. This is all so weird, but strangely wonderful."

"I'm sorry to spazz out on you, but at this point in time, I want to get to know you and that might include not sharing information with your grandmother."

"Honey, I didn't tell her a thing about your dreams."

"Oh, my! You called me 'honey'."

"Yes, I did. Do you have a problem with that? Listen, you're either interested in me or you're not. I'm interested in you, but I'm not going to be your easy conquest. I don't know what making love is because I have never made love. My responsibility was to perform the acts that his majesty wanted. I've faked and attempted to reach that thing my girlfriends call 'the bomb'. I don't think I've ever been there or would know it if it happened."

"How many boyfriends have you had?"

"I've had three. Melvin in kindergarten, Paul in high school, and my husband. Why?"

"I'm intruding into your past with this question, but how many lovers have you had?" Chakes asked.

"I had my husband, and he was pretty much it. I unfolded my wings one night with him. I found myself intoxicated, in the back seat of a car. His head was in a precarious place until I threw up on him. That's the extent of my sexual knowledge."

Chakes looked at her and said, "I did something I'm not proud of. I asked you questions about your history that shouldn't matter, and it really doesn't. I still have a bad taste in my mouth from my ex-wife. I trusted her and relied on her to be my partner. She plied her trade with members of my family and my friends. I didn't know she was one of those

Spike Lee girls that had to have it. My house was like a community—'Come Screw Me' place. So many people screwed my wife. It wasn't about money; she just had to have it.

"Once, she asked me to go to the store and get olives for drinks. I returned early because I knew that there were olives in the house, I parked my car on the street and walked towards the closed garage. I heard this banging noise and looked into the laundry room. There she was, on top of the dryer with my cousin, screwing her brains out. They saw me, and she smiled. That lecherous woman smiled at me while she screwed my cousin.

"What I feel for you far surpasses any emotions I had for her, and I was married to her. When I see you, Beatrice, and Sister, I feel connected to the ground and space. My emotions are centered, solid and my desires are focused on spirit and not sex."

Luana said, "I'm going to take a nap. Go watch and talk to your daughter, Mr. Man." Chakes told her to take the window seat so he could watch out for her and the others.

When he went back to check on Beatrice, he found her crying. He got on his knees and asked, "Beatrice, why are you crying? What made you sad?" Chakes stroked her hair and pulled a tissue from the box in front of her. He asked, "Were the other kids not nice to you?"

Beatrice said, "I like them a lot. I don't think they like me."

"Why do you say that?"

"They all said they were tired and didn't want to play or watch a movie with me." Chakes told her he would be right back. He walked to where the kids sat, and they were out like a light. He walked back to Beatrice and said, "I need you to come with me, but I need you to be very quiet."

Beatrice unbuckled her seatbelt and grabbed Chake's hand. He looked at this little person accepting his friendship and walked her to the seats where the other kids were. He got on his knees and said, "Look they're all tired and sleepy. That's why they didn't want to play anymore."

"But they left me in my seat, and I need to use the bathroom." Chakes escorted her to the restroom and explained how things worked on a plane. He saw Courtney watching him, so he motioned for her to help. Courtney went into the oversized space with Beatrice, explained to her how the vacuum flush toilet worked, and how to use the soap dispenser. She showed her how to lock and unlock the door. When she came out, Chakes said, "She thought the other kids didn't like her. They left her in her seat, when really what happened was that they wanted to take a nap. No one showed her how to leave her seat or use the restroom."

Courtney said, "You should take the time and give her a set of rules. I guess no one expected a new child aboard the plane. I like that family, and Sister ain't to be played with."

When Beatrice came out of the restroom, she said, "I made a mistake. Can you get my mom?" He walked up the aisle and gently ran his hand along the side of Luana's face. He said, "Luana, Beatrice made a mistake and needs you in the restroom."

"Why can't you help her?"

"Luana, I haven't been sanctioned by you or Sister and, therefore, I'm not going to ask your daughter, what's the problem." Luana looked at him and said, "Some babysitter you are."

Beatrice's little problem was just that, a little mistake. Luana said to Chakes, "You're right. We haven't sanctioned you with my daughter, and it will take a while before that happens. There are a lot of nuts running around and I haven't decided if you're free from that title yet."

"Thank you for the vote of confidence. I completely understand how difficult that decision might be. Just for the record, I'm solid as a rock, her interest, your interest, and Sister's interest, are my fundamental reason for existing from this point forward. However, I also must state for the record, my reasons are subject to change, unless there is concrete evidence this infatuation is moving towards the heavens. One should always have an escape route. Listen, all jokes aside, why didn't you guys stay in Sydney, enjoy our hospitality for as long as you wanted to, and enjoy $10,000 dollars each, plus cards that you could fly you anywhere on us at no cost to you? What made you guys want to trek into a dangerous part of the country with complete strangers?"

Luana looked at him and said, "See that stubborn old lady sleeping in that chair next to my now sleeping daughter, that's the answer. She knew you wanted to stay but couldn't. She also knew this group is more than a bunch of friends on an outing. She told me this was a trip that we had to take for my sake. She told me if I didn't seize this opportunity, that another in a distant land would sweep you up, up, and away. She has always been mysterious, but accurate at forecasting events. Sometimes, I think she can conjure up stuff and make it happen. Before my husband was shipped to the desert, we got into an argument and he slapped me. We all lived with my grandmother. She told him that a real man didn't have to hit his woman. He jokingly came at her with his hand raised, and she told him to enjoy his war. He was on the ground for one day when the vehicle he was riding in ran over an IED. He was the only casualty. When I got home from work, a day or so later, she told me the man I was married to was no more. She went into her bedroom and stayed there for three days. Man, and I don't know why, that woman believes you're the second coming of Christ. She talks about your calmness, your relationships with the other people, your insistent drive to get your way, and your need for a good woman with a starter family."

"Why you be putting all those things on Sister?"

"Listen JC-Jr, I'm not making this up because this is not who I am. I am an introvert trying to find the right avenue that navigates me to my freedom. So far, and thanks to you, I believe I'm at the corner of infatuation and happy, and according to my GPS, I should arrive at decision and trust in the next few miles."

Ms. Viola woke up and said, "Those are sweet words to an old woman's ears who doesn't have a lot of time left on this earth. Praise be to God. Man, I no never hear her calculate her emotions before. Yeah, I tell her you be special and all, but I also tell her that you be forever a scoundrel, too."

"Grandma, can you go back to sleep and let me tell my story? He already knows you love him." She turned to Chakes and said, "How you gonna handle so much true love, Man?"

"The same way I get it, the same way I give it. I have never felt weak and dizzy from looking at a woman. When I turned around and saw you, you knew it was to be. I felt it, I saw you, and now you and your family are trusting me and my friends to keep you happy and safe. Let me say this, unless there is a dark side to you that is absolutely reprehensible, I would venture to marry you tomorrow and never look back. That's how confident I am in what I feel for you. I've never felt that strong for another woman, including the one I was married to."

"Maurice, those are some powerful and serious words. Let me say this, unless there is a dark side to you that is solely condemnable, then I would marry you next year or a few years later." They both laughed, and she broke protocol and kissed him on his cheek covering just the right amount of lip to indicate desire. Maurice slouched in his chair and said, "I would like to have another one of those in the same place and for the same amount of time." His wish was granted.

## CHAPTER TWENTY-THREE

Captain Carla woke up when she felt the engines decelerate and the plane began its descent into the Northern Territory. She kissed her sleepy husband and told him that she would see him later.

Once in the cockpit, she said nothing, but watched as the pilots completed their checklist. Satisfied, she said, "Gentlemen, continue your descent and your communication with the tower." She knew every conversation in the cockpit was recorded. She tapped her friend on the shoulder and through hand signals indicated the runway was extremely short. He raised his thumb in the air and made the notion clear to the copilot. The additional pilots were securing the cabin and making sure everyone was buckled in.

The landing became complicated because of a crosswind. Captain Carla kept a close eye on the instruments, the actions, and calmness of the pilot-in-command. She noticed the copilot was extremely loud, fidgety, and placed her hand on his shoulder and suggested he slow his breathing down. Everyone on the plane noticed the angle of the approach, saw the lights on the runway, and realized the plane was approaching sideways. Courtney said, "Sarge, we're landing sideways. Is there a problem?"

"Courtney, when you're in surgery, do you change your approach if conditions are not standard?"

"Is Captain Carla flying the plane?"

"She is not. We have excellent pilots, my love. Trust the system." Everyone at this time was holding on to each other as the plane was being whipped around. There was a sudden and definitive blast from the GE engines, and subsequently, the correction of the path of the plane, a bumpy landing, but a good one.

Captain Carla looked at her ex-lover and said, "I taught you everything you know. You're a better pilot than I am." He turned the docking process over to the copilot and turned around in his seat and said, "You're the best damn teacher in the world."

"How did you know exactly when to throttle and redirect? That was damn textbook and excellent." The three pilots began a dialogue and everyone on the plane realized the crew of pilots were the best.

Sister woke up and said, "Man, when you be marrying my granddaughter?"

"Sister, I be marrying her as soon as she proves to me that she is no longer married in mind and body."

"Yankee Man, what that mean?"

Chakes in his dialect for Ms. Viola, said, "That means, Sister, I no longer marry you, but I marry your granddaughter. We be good, Sister? We discuss a lot of things and we make a lot of decisions, but we no consummate a false existence in the name of sex. This relationship was designed by a more powerful existence than she and I, Sister. We be on a solid road. We be at the corner of Infatuation and Happy and real close to the streets, Decision and Trust."

She smiled and looked towards the heavens. She said to her granddaughter, "I need you to sit next to me. Beatrice, do you mind sitting next to Mr. Chakes while I talk to your mother?"

Ms. Viola then turned to her granddaughter, "I be an old lady and I done watched you and my daughter make dumb mistakes. This adventure you be on is going to be my last."

Luana's eyes began to water as Ms. Viola continued. "You think I live forever? I no want to live forever. I just want to see my granddaughter married and happy. I know you think I don't be knowing what I say when I talk about the Yankee. That Yankee is as pure as the blood that flows through your veins. You both be needing each other, and Beatrice be needing you both. Don't stay on that high horse that I know you can ride but introduce him to the wonderful and beautiful lady I raised. He be deserving of it."

"Grandma, are you sick? Why are you saying these things now?"

"Honey, I be tired. He knows what I want him to do. He will tell you one day, but he knows what I want him to do."

"You're not making any sense and you're upsetting me. Let's talk once we're off the plane. I just want you to be honest with me and tell me if you're sick."

# # #

The group disembarked from the plane and were happy to place their feet on the ground. Courtney said, "You know, Ben, I'm getting tired of all this travel. We seem to pick up, leave places, and every time we leave a place, we seem to pick up new and interesting people. I think Chakes has found his match and she seems well grounded."

"I agree, he's walking this one with patience. Sister loves him dearly, and they've only known each other a few days. I guess that's how it was after you met me and insisted, I take you to dinner," the Sarge reflected.

"Whatever! I'm glad I liked a cop instead of that young intern who was following me around every night. He was so young and cute, I must admit."

Ben said, "Whatever, I don't remember any intern following you around."

"Honey, that's the point. You were not there every night or day, but he was, with his fine self. But I guess I made the right decision by marrying a policeman. Love you, too."

# # #

As the group entered the lobby of the airport, a very stately gentleman who could transition between the physical and spiritual world (so it was rumored) walked towards the group and said, "Ben Beckmire, welcome home. I see you bring two lady lawyers with you and lots of associates. Associates, many of you I remember from your last trip here. My name is Wajickee and I will be your guide and your host. If you follow me, we will enter the bus and head to the village. No need in worrying about attire, our people will outfit you and you will feel comfortable sleeping under the stars."

Wajickee looked at Ms. Viola and said, "Sista, you gone be alright. We take care of what ails you here. You gone be alright."

Everyone was amazed at how much he knew. Most of the group got on the bus, but Wajickee told Ben that he and Zanthius would take another journey to see an ancestor. As the men prepared to kiss their wives and children, and bid them farewell, Wajickee said, "There is another person that must be welcomed on this journey. Larry, tell your family you will see them soon."

Larry was astonished and Ben Beckmire began to cry, for he loved Larry like none other.

Wajickee instructed his people to watch the plane from afar and to make sure the pilots were fed, had showers, and could walk freely from harm. Prior to the bus closing its doors, he stood at the front of the bus and everyone gave him their attention.

He said, "Many of you have been here before—since before, things have changed. This is our home and your home. Don't hurt the animals and they won't hurt you. Be kind to my kin, and they will be kind to you. The outback is unforgiving. Please do not wander off without my people in attendance and drink plenty of water. We will be back in the morning to fix this disease that has spread upon our land. I thank you all for coming, and do not fear your dreams for they truly are a representation of your life."

The four men piled into a jeep that had its own driver. They drove to the water's edge, and Wajickee said, "I'm going on Walkabout and will return before midnight. This young fellow will attend to your needs in my absence. Larry, in this land, many things are not what they seem. Trust your father and your brother for they have journeyed here before." The men were watching shooting stars, and when they turned to speak to Wajickee, he was no more. Larry asked, "Where did he go?"

The Sarge asked, "Do you remember when I used to tell you stories about Walkabout and Dreamtime? Well, that's where Wajickee is. It's a magical place as I told you, it's full of our history and stories. This is an enchanted place, Son, and it's a place of beauty, freedom, and spirits." The Sarge looked at their guide and stated, "I feel as if I know you."

"Uncle, I am Darryl Andre Beckmire, and I'm from a long line of honorable men and women. This mission secures my transition into manhood. It's an honor to meet you, Zanthius and Larry. I hope one day I will be able to travel and enjoy adventures like my cousin, Yvette. She is a generation above me."

Ben Beckmire said, "That fire is magnificent and bright. I would like you to tell me what has been going on since my last visit. How have things deteriorated so rapidly?"

Darryl said, "Uncle and cousins, I was assigned to look after you because my ancestors believe I craft such ridiculous stories. I have an opinion that is not shared by anyone."

Beckmire excused his rudeness for interrupting and asked, "Do you know the constable in Sydney that I want to place in charge of our efforts here?"

"The constable plays both sides of the road. He was the hidden character behind the enslavement of our cousin Yvette. He's remarkably familiar with the white devils who are trying to manipulate their crafts to become owners of our natural land. I have an opinion that is not shared by anyone else. I believe those devils have found some mineral, or something, on our land," Darryl proclaimed.

Zanthius said, "You keep saying our land. What are the boundaries of our land and are there treaties in writing to state that?"

"That's why the two lawyers are here to determine this information based upon documents from our historical vaults," Darryl confessed.

"Where are these historical vaults?" Zanthius asked.

"They're in the village. The lawyers are reviewing them as we speak."

Larry inquired, "How do you know what they're doing?"

"Oh, Cousin, I know what everyone is doing that has a critical role to our penetrating the evil forces. You will come to learn that good can always visit righteous, but evil must corrupt good in order to hold court. This thing called world order is bigger than you think. As a matter of fact, Uncle Beckmire, one of your group had a relative who was an adversary of your forefathers. Mr. Cheeks laid a seed, who laid a seed, who laid a seed, and who laid another seed. In the laying of those seeds, Mr. Cheeks became Mr. Chakes over time. Your Mr. Chakes is the seed of Mr. Cheeks who was the cause of the matriarch of this family's death. So, Larry, on Walkabout and during Dreamtime, many things are capable to see and understand. During Dreamtime, we see all and learn all. I'm just a vessel, a link between this world and the spirit world."

He looked at Zanthius and said, "You asked about territory, and I was about to explain. I portend some devil found something valuable on this land and only the Great Saltie can sort this thing out. He will make himself visible to you Uncle, and to cousins Zanthius and Larry, but he will only speak to Uncle Ben."

Ben Beckmire after feeling the passion and spirits of the land asked, "Darryl, how certain are you about the credentials of the constable?"

"As sure as the fact that if Larry doesn't knock that spider off his arm in the next ten seconds, he will be bit by the Sydney funnel-web spider. Somehow, you must have transported it from Sydney. I will have my family detox your plane before taking off." Larry saw the spider, plucked it off, and asked, "Was it poisonous?"

Darryl smiled and replied, "Perhaps the most poisonous spider in the Eastern part of Australia."

Wajickee strolled into camp with two gutted and skinned rabbits and said, "I guess you people are hungry. What tales has your cousin been telling you? Let me guess. He's been saying that the devils found some precious mineral on the land and, therefore, will eradicate our people to gain control over it."

Ben Beckmire asked, "More importantly, did you know the constable is a bad man and that he had helped put Yvette in slavery?"

"I can't see into towns and villages where the people are all devils. I'm blinded and tone deaf against their music, the isolation, and their smell. He probably knew this and recognized the fact that in the spirit world I can't visit chaos. Now, Darryl on the other hand, fits right into their genre. He can sense, decipher, decode the hidden messages of their music, and their thoughts. I on the other hand find the sounds frightening to my senses and those who power me."

Darryl said, "Dinner is ready."

Larry said, "No way. He just returned from catching those things."

Zanthius strolled up beside Larry, and said, "If you close your mind, your mind will be closed. Here, my brother, things, and spirits, can do what we in another place and time would consider impossible. Don't focus on norms—think about the fact that it is, what it is."

Wajickee said, "With Darryl, the spirits are confused about his assumptions, his thoughts, his beliefs, his interest, and his music. He doesn't like the didgeridoo but prefers that electronic combusted music. He enters the center of devil land, smells everything and senses all. He was there when you rescued Yvette. He's not your normal person or spirit. He just graduated from college and instead of wanting to enter the world of hustle, he wants to secure the properties of our people. His next journey is to secure a law degree. He's not your normal Aborigine—he's a Beckmire, and is sanctioned by the Great Saltie, and that's why you're here. Darryl will transition the Aborigine people into the 21st Century, for it is that age we must conquer or be conquered by."

At 2300 hours, Wajickee said, "That was a late meal, but a good meal. If you have thoughts that are not pure, I beg you to realize them, and stay away from the water's edge. At midnight, the Great Saltie will present himself to his kin and expose the object of the devil's quest." Wajickee further reiterated the fact about thoughts that were impure. He concocted a potion that would lessen the impact of the enormity of the event and presented it to the group as a body cleansing and mind purifying potion.

At 2330 hours, the group ventured to the water's edge where a massive fire burned. Zanthius and Larry were intoxicated from the potion that was provided by Wajickee who said to Ben Beckmire, "Trauma is the anticipated result of witnessing the Great Saltie. Your family will see him, will debate his size, structure, and what beast he was, but between themselves."

Beckmire thanked Wajickee and said, "To this day, I find his being an anomaly and a scary one."

Wajickee announced, "I want you to take Darryl back to the States when you leave and enroll him in the law school that the two lawyers agree upon. He will have fun, enjoy life, and will eventually, bring his American/Asian family back home to begin the work you're prepared to spot for him. The constable's journey ended tonight. He was bit by a dangerous spider."

"Must we worry about our families and children in the village? Seems like spiders are showing up and are prepared to do harm to all in this area," Beckmire said. After a pause, he asked, "And, what do you mean about Darryl's Asian family?"

"All in good time my friend. This thing you are hearing, you will forget in the next 2 minutes.

Wajickee smiled and stated, "Everyone is having a wonderful out of body experience. Your families former nemesis, Mr. Cheeks, now your lifelong friend and loyal protector Mr. Chakes, is being told the story of his ancestors. Just accommodate him when you're reunited. He's a great friend and good human being. We're going to help Ms. Viola see better days and learn to not hide what afflicts her," Wajickee stated.

At 2350 hours, Wajickee became quiet and proclaimed, "It is time. Please follow me."

At the edge of the billabong, Wajickee told Larry and Zanthius to have a seat. He told Darryl to watch over them and keep them calm. Larry whispered to Zanthius, "Is this real or are we in a hypnotic state?"

Zanthius said, "You should decide that on your own. Just be calm and remain still."

Darryl said, "No more talking or you'll distract the essence of what you will see."

At 2357 hours, Ben Beckmire and Wajickee sat at the water's edge and a stillness could be felt in the air. There were no natural sounds to be heard.

At 2400 hours, the area was still, and the night noises were absent. There was a large splash in the water, followed by two additional violent splashes. It was the Great Saltie. Larry and Zanthius's senses were impeded by the drink that they consumed. Ben Beckmire lowered his head and listened to a roar that would be heard throughout the outback.

In the village where the guests were, everyone huddled around the fire. The leader of the village began to tell them what the roar was and who it was that was making the scary noise. He spent time telling the group about man's propensity for greed and how, historically, it has led to man's downfall. He spoke of the Great Saltie in terms that were reverent and powerful. He told the story of Mr. Cheeks and other co-conspirators who plotted against the Aborigine people for their land and would commit unspeakable crimes against them. He told how a boy by the name of Andy Beckmire was selected by the spirits to protect the Aborigine people and their lands from evil people and schemes. He spoke of how this young boy could transmogrify into the largest saltwater crocodile ever seen by man. He said this beast or spirit is more than thirty-nine feet long. He also went on to tell the group there was one among them who was from the seed of one of the initial co-conspirators. Everyone wanted to know who it was, but he insisted Wajickee or Mr. Beckmire would reveal the identity of that person.

# # #

At the water's edge, the Great Saltie shook his head and flung a huge item onto the shore. He moved gently beside Ben Beckmire, looked into his eyes, and moved slowly back into the billabong. Ben Beckmire walked over to the item that was flung from the Great Saltie's mouth and exclaimed, "I'll be damned! Unless I'm mistaken or misinterpreting what just happened, there are diamonds on this land and that's what those people are trying to steal from us—diamonds."

He walked over to a semiconscious Larry and Zanthius and said, "This problem is about diamonds, and from the size of this one, there must be a fortune to be mined here." He looked at Darryl and said, "I will never doubt your word again. You were correct from the start." He looked at Wajickee and asked, "You clearly must have known this yourself?"

"Indeed, I did. It was not my place to inform you of your new mission in life, but to connect you to the one who would inform you. Your lawyers are very tenacious and are putting together a legal complaint that will temporarily keep the dingoes away from the doors. What's important, is that intimidation be taken away from the devils and true horror be implemented from our side. It will require you and your men to use strong-arm tactics while me and the spirits will, how do you say it, scare the shit out of them. I can make all kinds of things happen to slow the process, but eventually, we must win in the court system. They are not native friendly because some authorities agree with trying to build a new Australia—free of darkies," Wajickee noted.

# # #

That night, everyone would sleep well and long under the stars in the middle of the outback.

At 0700 hours, the group began to stir. Monica and Luana had worked throughout the night preparing their opening statement and looking over documents that were stored in the sacred vault. They felt confident they could legally get a continuance but did not know the politics of the system.

The women were led to a billabong first and they watched how the water gently flowed up-stream to where they were. It was a new experience for them, but one that turned into joyful play. The children absolutely loved the clear water. Beatrice asked Courtney, "What was that loud roar last night? Was it the devil?"

Courtney smiled and said, "When my husband shows up in a little while, I want you to ask him that question. You won't forget, will you?" Beatrice ran off.

Luana saw her grandmother and said, "You look rested and refreshed. What did you eat or drink last night?"

"I had the same thing you had, but when I drank that potion, my body just kicked into gear, I mean it's like one of those energy drinks. The nice lady said it would make me feel better. Did you tell them I wasn't feeling well?"

"Grandma, Monica and I were whisked away, and we worked all night long. We drank something to keep us awake as well. Some weird tasting plant juice, I didn't tell anyone anything about you. Perhaps they could tell that you weren't well."

"Well, I be feeling good and energetic today," Ms. Viola announced.

# # #

Beckmire's group got in their jeep and headed for the village. Wajickee told them he would meet them there. When they turned to acknowledge his comment, he was gone.

When they arrived at the village, Wajickee was there sending different people into a cave. Larry asked, "How did he beat us here?"

Zanthius said, "For you and me, it's complicated. Just let it go, man."

In the cave, Wajickee began to tell a story and explain what the drawings on the walls meant. For over fifteen minutes, he explained the nature of the beast they were about to deal with and their resolve to run the Aborigine off their land. He turned to Beckmire and said, "Ben Beckmire, relative of the Great Saltie, show them why they want this land so badly and will kill each of us, and each other to get it."

The Sarge dug his hand into his pocket and pulled out an item that was symmetrical and was the size of two square ice-cubes, stacked. He threw it on the ground, and everyone stared at it in awe. It was a diamond like no-others. It had been taken by an intruder who was devoured by the Great Saltie as he tried to make his escape along the billabong.

The Sarge said, "This is what this mess is about people. They will kill every living soul here to gain access to this land. Can you imagine what this could do for the Aborigine people and Australia as well? This stone alone must be worth $50 to $60 million, if not more. Look at the size of it and the clarity."

Jong asked, "How did you come upon such a prize, if you don't mind me asking?"

"My ancestor that I've talked about, spit it on the shore last night and gave me a clear message that I'm sharing with everyone for the first time. This atrocity stops today or all who participate in this evil event will be eviscerated."

Wajickee picked the stone off the ground, handed it to Jong and said, "It is your responsibility to figure out its value and open an account with names that Ben Beckmire will give you next week. Ben Beckmire loves you and all of the rest and would die horribly to make sure that you people are not injured."

Jong looked at Wajickee and attempted to say something, but the words would not come out. He bowed and ran to Mary Alice. Once he saw her, Jong cried out, "I want to go home. This place is full of things I don't understand and spirits that I now believe in. I'm scared."

# # #

At 0830 hours, the group arrived at the judicial center and were met by hundreds of Aborigine people. Some of them were in their bush clothes, and others in garments recommended by those in charge. It was a massive showing and one not to be trifled with. A limited number of local people were allowed in the hearings while others waited patiently outside to hear the outcome of the proceedings. At 0900 hours, the gavel hit the pad and the court was in session.

The people who were trying to steal the land portrayed the indigenous people as backwards, tribal, and against modernization. The lawyers stated that the land in question, would provide the area with a new university, hospitals, government offices, schools, commerce, and a tax base that would contribute as much as 20% of all revenue to the new Northern Territory. They showed the judge renderings of a renovated part of the country and kept emphasizing that it was the only way into a profitable future that all could share in, including the Abos.

The judge slammed his gavel down and said, "There will be no disrespecting any individual or culture in this courtroom."

The lead attorney said, "Your Honor, I can assure you that there was no disrespect intended in the use of that word."

The judge said, "Your plans are admirable, but this case is not predicated on history, development, or land reformations. This court is also the wrong body to petition for land. What are your legal rights, claims, easements, or other certified notifications for land in the outback that is culturally Aborigine, historically Aborigine, and functionally Aborigine, is what is at stake? Let me ask you a question that will lead to a series of other questions and perhaps an indication of why so many Aborigine people ave been missing and/or ave turned up dead in recent months.

"Did you or the people you work for discover anything, and I use the word exponentially, that could be turned into a benefit or a profit for those who seek this land? Let me be clear—you and your entire team, as well as everyone in this court, are under oath. Let me also announce, that any perjury in the legal system will be criminally charged to the maximum. In this jurisdiction, I am the supreme officer.

"Now, for the record, I will ask that question again, but in a different manner. Is there anyone that you know of, or ave contact with, who may be involved in any manner to deprive the Aborigine people of their land because of some resource that was discovered on it? This resource could be nuts, gold, emeralds, oil, rocks, spiders, snakes, or anything else of value."

"Your Honor, to the best of our knowledge, we are unaware of any attempt to swindle the Aborigine people out of their land. As a matter of fact, we are prepared to offer them a grand total of $5 million, and we will relocate them westward or to any place they desire."

"Is the relocation cost considered in the $5 million? And why did you use the word 'swindle'?"

"Yes, your Honor, it is. I used the word to alleviate the notion that your Honor assumed that these attorneys are involved in a scheme to de-land the Aborigine people in this region," the lead attorney stated.

Monica added, "Your Honor, that question is on the record. I would like to have a moment to consult with our clients, who are also family, to present information that can be substantiated that the individuals on the other side, along with a long list of investors, not only want to develop the land, but also this development will occur after they have raped it of its natural resources."

Monica approached Beckmire, who whispered, "I know exactly what you want to do and I'm with you." He looked at Wajickee and said, "Once we clear the path to ownership, we should expose these people by showing what they found on

Aborigine land. Once this has been settled legally, we can clearly show that they are crooks."

Monica said, "Your Honor, I want to take this matter in another direction. I want to first of all expose their investors and ask you to set a $100-million requirement for further discussion of the land, that must be in place by 12 noon tomorrow. This way, their investors must come from under the rocks they live and present themselves as honorable men and women with a desire to build this area into the future."

Luana touched her arm and whispered, "The only downside to that is they might require you to do the same thing."

Monica said, "Ben Beckmire is not going to let his people, or any people, be robbed of what is rightfully theirs. He and his team will put the money up."

"How can you be so sure? That's a lot of money. Do they have that to gamble with?"

"Welcome to the ride, Luana. These guys do not let people get swindled. They will double that number if necessary."

The judge cleared his throat to indicate that it was time to continue with the trial. Monica said, "Your Honor, I'm so sorry to take so long. My clients are under the impression there are some raw materials to be gained from access to this land. They reject the $5 million, totally, and laugh at the amount. They instead want to propose an initial offer of $100 million to begin the discussion and another $100 million to conclude the deal. Those are the tentative terms my clients will agree to. In addition, Your Honor, my clients' relatives are willing to put up another $200 million to secure land in the following coordinates according to tribal documents. May I approach the bench?"

The judge said, "I will recess the court for thirty minutes while I discuss the parameters of the land in question with both parties. Since there are so many people in attendance, I will allow four people from each side. However, I will only allow two to ave discussions with me."

In his chamber, the lead attorney for the other side said, "Your Honor, what hyperbole? Look at these people. They don't have that kind of money, but the people I represent certainly do." The judge considered the allegation and decided that nothing was going to be settled in chambers.

The judge reminded the attorneys, "You're under oath to notify the court if there is anything of significance within the coordinates that the Aborigine people ave held since the beginning of time. We will resume in 5 minutes."

The judge fixed his eyes on Ben Beckmire and asked, "Sir, I would like to ave a word with you." After the lawyers left his chambers, he asked, "What is your role in this matter?"

"Your Honor, my only role in this matter is to make sure my people are not swindled out of their land because it has significant value."

"And if they're swindled, what would be your resolve?" Who are you, anyway, and what again is your role in this matter?"

"Your Honor, my name is Ben Beckmire, and these people are my family."

The judge dropped his head and said, "That's funny, I thought the name Beckmire was a legend told to children."

Beckmire responded, "Your Honor, I'm not old enough to be a legend and besides, the real reason these guys and their backers want this land, is for profit. Under oath they lied to you, but I have something that will make them rethink their testimony."

The judge said, "I find it ineffective to try to resolve issues in chambers." Please return to the courtroom. I will be there shortly."

Ten minutes later, the judge entered the courtroom and said, "I thought this case was complicated, but as I listen to the exchanges, I find it's another case of people trying to steal land owned and occupied by Aborigine people. I also believe the $5 million is a miniscule sum for the land featured in the prescribed coordinates. In addition, I agree with the team representing the Aborigine people. If the other side wants to actively pursue this land, then at least $100 million must be placed into an account suitable to the lawyers of the people. There must be an express notification that if anything, including camel shit, is found on the land within the coordinates, then the Aborigine people can consult with their lawyers and petition the court for consideration. Also, the $100 million escrow is forfeited, if the facts from either side are not accurate, or ave intent of collusion attached to them."

The judge paused for a minute and looked over his notes before saying to Monica, "It was your suggestion and, therefore, I must ask—do you or your clients ave $100 million to place into escrow realizing that if you fail to prove any aspect of this case, you forfeit $100 million and the land annotated in the stated coordinates?" Monica turned around and looked Ben Beckmire squarely in the eyes. He looked at his crew, then back at her and gave her the thumbs up.

The judge looked at the other side and stated the same question. Without any assistance from anyone, the lead lawyer responded, "We will put $100 million in escrow, Your Honor."

The judge replied, "I am recessing court until tomorrow at noon, at which time, I expect each of you would ave directed assets to the bank and in the account being provided to you by the bailiff. There should be no uncertainty about my resolve in this matter. If you do not show up with the appropriate escrow amount, $100 million, you will be held in contempt and all known assets will be seized, placed in default, and awarded to the other side. I ave maintained the amount of $100 million because I believe any millions placed in an escrow account by both parties is enough to satisfy and determine the seriousness of the case. I will say again, young lady, this is your suggestion and I want you to make sure you can make this happen by tomorrow, no second chances. If you can't produce the escrow amount, the stated land will be turned over to the petitioning group. Are there any questions or concerns?" The judge paused for a moment and then said, "I ave stated the tenets of this action, and those are the only tenets I will accept in adjudicating this claim! Court dismissed."

The Sarge looked at Jong, who was staring at him in disbelief. The Sarge said, "Don't stare at me. Get on the phone and make it happen."

Wajickee said, "That lawyer was correct that hospitals, universities, and other institutions would be built to help empower the Aborigine people. I think this day we should all be happy to ave family, and we should ave a huge feast tonight."

Leaving the courthouse, Beckmire as well as Jilkes, Chakes, John Lee, and Brown, saw who they considered were the people most likely to be their adversaries. Wajickee said, "I see you ave visually met those who ave inflicted harm on our people."

Ben Beckmire said, "My people have them in their sights. Let's announce we're going to have a huge celebration in the 'Cave of Stories'. That will draw them out, and I'm sure they're going to attempt an assault on us. Can you get the tools we'll need from our plane to fend them off?"

Wajickee looked at Darryl. He nodded his head and disappeared into the crowd. Wajickee said, "Call your people and tell them to expect guests looking for gifts. I'm afraid this thing is large and they're going to ave a large contingency of people to try to annihilate us."

"If you get us bow and arrows, as well as pistols for our ladies, from the plane, we can handle these guys. You see, these guys advertised who they are. It also might be a great time to call in the dingoes, wombats, snakes, and spiders. You do know that if they put up $100 million and they fail, you get to keep their money. If we fail, then they get to keep our money," Ben Beckmire stated.

"Is that how that works? That is why we must get Darryl and others enrolled in law school to handle this newness or we'll be raped at every turn. This kind of thing is happening all over Australia. I'm going to need you people back here in a month or so once we handle these thieves and murderers," Wajickee requested.

#

The rest of the day included face painting, wall painting, the children learning what animals to approach, and which ones to stay away from. It was a learning experience as well as a back to nature trip where the means of natural purgation were completed after the construction of a personal loo.

Later that afternoon, Mike and Carla left the airport with Darryl carrying a case full of pistols, ammunition, and two cases loaded with high tension bows and arrows. There was no customs function at the airport because the trip started within the country.

At the village, Ben Beckmire called a meeting of his people and included Wajickee and Darryl. He indicated he suspected that there would be trouble in the village tonight. He said to Rashida, "Honey, I need you to construct a defense system in the cave. I have secured those weapons you ladies like and plenty of ammunition. Me and the boys will try to hedge our bets and meet them in the bush, but we will always have a direct line to you people.

"Once we lock down the cave, the only way anyone gets in is by saying, 'Baby and Zanthius'. If you don't hear those words, then shoot. The guys and I will go jungle on them and do our bow and arrow thing. They expect us to have a huge celebration tonight, and that's when I suspect they'll try to kill us. Now, listen, you all saw the size of that diamond, and there may be plenty more like that on this land. It would do wonders for the Aborigine countrywide to help build schools, roads, infrastructure, hospitals, and businesses. For riches, those other people will try to wipe us out, and I mean the babies as well. Keep a fire going and a metal rod hot. If you get shot, slap the iron on it and keep shooting.

"Ms. Viola, I must apologize to you and Ms. Luana, but we're not taking the fight to them. They're coming for us and that includes you guys. I want you two to stay in the deepest part of the cave with the children. These pregnant women know what they must do. For the balance of the day, don't act strange or fearful, act as if you're going to a party. Any questions?"

There were no questions. The Sarge said, "Mallory make assignments."

Chakes approached Sister and said, "Man, you no worry. We be knowing what we do, and we be good at it. You just find yourself a nice spot in that cave and it'll all be over by morning." He looked at Luana and said, "I was serious about what I said."

"Which thing are we talking about now?"

"I told you if there was nothing reprehensible about you, I would marry you today. I was serious about that."

She smiled and said, "I hope so. I was serious about what I said too." He approached her, kissed her lips lightly, and hugged her. Beatrice said, "Mom, he kissed you."

"Honey, that was like a friendship kiss. I'll let you know when and if he really kisses me."

# # #

Wajickee and Darryl mapped out the area for Beckmire and his group, and suggested they not venture beyond the Boab Trees. Wajickee said, "Many animals will feed on the dead and the living as well. The night noises will be filled with suffering, but the little ones won't hear it. They'll only hear the sweet sounds of the didgeridoo. If they approach from along the billabong, they will become dinner for the many large crocs that have gathered. If they approach from the west, they will encounter a huge pack of dingoes and in the east,

Darryl and I will attend to them. Your positions will be north, but again, do not go beyond the Boab trees."

John Lee asked, "Can you tell me what one of them there trees looks like?"

Wajickee said, "You'll know one when you see it." He looked at Beckmire and said, "I will return in time to alert you of their numbers and positions."

# # #

After dinner, the group meandered around in no particular fashion acting as if they were not being watched. There was no indication that a raid was on the horizon.

The night noises in the outback are usually a function of trees, or the lack thereof, and the weather. Where there are trees, there are birds. When there are no trees, there are other animals that make noises during the night. Around the campfire, there were sleeping bags filled with grass. All the villagers and their guests were tucked deep inside of a cave. The Sarge and his men made themselves scarce using their technology to communicate with each other. Each man had a pistol with a silencer and a belt full of ammunition clips. Larry said, "Hey, Dad, we're kind of laying around in the dirt. You know I had that spider on me."

Darryl said, "The dirt you lay in is snake-proof, bug-proof, spider-proof, and evil-proof." He then said, "Uncle Beckmire, now would be an excellent time to tell your people about Mr. Cheeks and his association with your group."

Ben Beckmire paused and said, "Okay, guys, I'm going to tell you a fantastic fable about my ancestor's existence on this land and the exigencies they faced from a person who wanted them dead, so that he and his group could take their land for the wealth that it contained." The chatter between the guys stopped, and he had everyone's attention. He confessed, "The matriarch of the Beckmire clan was a woman by the name of Marisa who married Andy Beckmire. It has been said that Andy Beckmire is the Great Saltie. I'm going to give you the abbreviated version of this story because it could fill a book and it did. The book is titled *BODYBAY*, by a little known author, I can't remember his name. I don't know how he came to write the story, but nevertheless, he did.

"Anyway, my great-great-great-grandfather could transmogrify into the largest croc ever seen, the Great Saltie. During that point in time, the crimes against the Aborigine people were unspeakable. Violence against the Aborigine was countrywide, and places like Massacre Bays, Deadman's Creeks and Murdering Gullies where Aborigine people were summarily murdered and herded like cattle and driven off cliffs. White settlers would drink too much piss, what we know as beer, and go into the outback and shoot Aborigine people like they do the kangaroo. Anyhow, it was told to me that the great spirits were appalled at the manner in which good Aborigine people entered the great beyond. My ancestor, it was alleged, was chosen by the great spirits of the country. Pigeon was one of them, and he led an armed and deadly revolt against the whites and went on a killing spree.

"Mr. Cheeks and a group of co-conspirators wanted the land that the Aborigine people lived on and hired some awfully bad men to eradicate them by conducting raids during the night. The plan was to expunge all the darkies from the continent because they didn't look like them, didn't eat like them, didn't speak like them, and they didn't worship their imported god. The real reason is the same as why we're here today, supporting and trying to legalize ownership of the land we're on and not let land grabbers take it from the indigenous people."

The Sarge began to cry, and everyone knew that this story was not going to end well. He apologized and said, "I'm sorry, but I find it hard to understand how people find valuable resources and decide to just kill people for it, rather than pay a fair price. Anyway, a man by the name of Mr. Cheeks was responsible for killing the matriarch of the Beckmire clan. It is also alleged that the Great Saltie destroyed all the co-conspirators, but spared Mr. Cheek's life. He wanted to send a message, and he did. He severed Mr. Cheek's arms at the shoulder, his legs at his thighs, and gauged out his eyes. The bottom line to this story is that after generations and generations and iterations of the spelling of his last name, it has been discerned by Wajickee and Darryl that our Mr. Chakes is a long-lost seed of the man who created so much mayhem in the outback. How ironic is it that my brother, who has bled with me, killed with me, has been an intricate part of our family, is here defending my family from the very thing his ancestor is probably turning over in hell about?"

#

Montomie and Chakes were staked out together when Chakes said, "The Sarge must be drinking some really bad shit. The story had meaning until he connected it to me." Suddenly, Wajickee appeared next to Chakes and scared the daylights out of him. Chakes said, "Whoa, where the hell did you come from?"

Wajickee said, "I'm from the spirit world, and I want to make sure you understand that even though it was your bloodline, it does not represent who you are. You're a member of this tribe and your unofficial leader is Ben Beckmire, a person who will take you to see the most incredible sight you will ever see in this lifetime. Your blood is that of Mr. Cheeks. I know because I was there, and I know his blood and those who are connected.   Although your great-great-great-grandmother was a wonderful woman, she was a woman that lived by her own rules. Her name was Paula. This is all coming to you fast and furious, but it is the truth. Before you board your plane and decide to marry Luana, you will see your ancestor's adversary and realize why he failed in terminating all Aborigines from this magnificent land."

Montomie asked, "Dude, are you okay?"

"Didn't you hear that Wajickee fellow talking to me?"

"Okay, Brother. I need you to slow your breathing and focus your attention." Montomie then called the Sarge on the open band and said, "I need you to make your way to our position. Chakes is freaking me out. He thinks he was in a conversation with that Wajickee fellow. Sarge, I've been here the entire time. No one has been in this area but Chakes and me."

The Sarge said, "Montomie, we're in Australia and in the outback. He'll be okay in a few minutes."

From out of space and time, Wajickee slithered close to the Sarge and Mallory and said, "Forces are amassing from all sides. Your challenge will be from the north. The other areas are well covered."

At 2300 hours, the sounds of dingoes could be heard. From the north, the sound of birds fleeing their nests could be heard. Ben Beckmire said, "I don't know how many are coming from the north, but I want head shots and tandem firing. Do not fire consistently because if you do, they can target you. Unless we are overrun, fire from left to right and work your way to the center and begin that firing process again. Keep your heads down and no hero crap. We want to be in that courtroom in the morning, and on our plane in the afternoon without a single casualty. So be damn careful people, less I be going on a one-man killing spree."

At 2345 hours, the loud sounds of wild dogs, gunfire, and horrific sounding human screams could be heard. From the north, the Sarge said, "Guys, I think I see movement, remember, fire left then far right and then work backwards in the firing pattern. Head shots, gentlemen, and give no quarters, for if they overrun us, they will show our women none."

Mallory said, "The first shot is mine and it is happening in 5-4-3-2-1-'puff'." As a muffled sound was made by his weapon, the impact and placement of his shot was conclusive. He hit the intruder in the head from 100 yards east of his position. 'Puff', and another head shot by the outlying team was made. Between those two shots, the rotation and the kill shots, their position had been exposed. The Sarge went viral and said, "Bow and arrows."

Into the night, the whistling sound of arrows could be heard. These guys were still good with the bow and arrow. From the east, west, and south, there was little chance anyone could possibly survive the defenses of the animals and nature. The crocs gouged themselves on those who attempted to travel along the billabong. The dingoes made a call to their brethren and indicated there was a feast in progress.

There was no indication of what Wajickee and Darryl did to uninvite those from their area. It was conclusive in the north from a series of head shots from guns and bow and arrows. It was obvious that the breaching force lacked planning. Wajickee and Darryl entered the camp with crude ropes around two dingoes. Wajickee rubbed their heads and released them. Into the night, they raced and found two wounded individuals attempting to escape. They signaled to their associates and surrounded the escaping men.

When Beckmire and his crew reached the area where the men were surrounded, the dingoes raced off to another feast that was in play. He looked at one of the men and said, "Today when I first laid eyes on you, your reaction was unsettling. Do you wish to give me that same look?"

"I ain't got nothing to say to you, bloke."

Wajickee magically appeared and said, "That statement might be a bit premature, mate." Darryl showed up with a burlap sack that had two poisonous snakes in them and a jar with two deadly spiders. He emptied the bag and placed the spiders on the individuals.

Wajickee asked, "Is there anything you would like to tell us?" The men began to beg him to remove the spiders and the snakes. Wajickee picked the snakes up and took them to the boundaries of the village and did the same thing with the spiders.

Ben Beckmire said, "In my estimation, I assume you guys are mercs. Am I correct in that assessment?"

"You be right about that, mister."

"Let me introduce myself to you. My name is Ben Beckmire and these guys are my family. We have left wives, girlfriends, and lovers to be with each other because if you screw with one of us, you take on our entire clan. This box I'm holding is a recording device. I want you to tell me your mission here tonight and give me the names of those who employed you. Now, let's make sure we understand the rules. I don't control the snakes, spiders, dingoes, or crocs. Only my friend and this handsome guy to my left, are capable of doing that. I need you to tell me everything about your mission and be willing to restate your mission in court tomorrow."

#

The group sat around the campfire, and the two men gave up everyone that they were connected to, including who paid them a few thousand dollars, in order that they could earn billions. Monica and Luana listened to them and took copious notes. Beckmire interrupted the catharsis and asked, "Are there more of you?" He was told they did not know of any others in the area. Beckmire asked Wajickee, "What shall we do with these two who came to the village to kill us, our women, and our children?"

Monica said, "We need them in the courtroom tomorrow and let the judge decide their fate, if it gets to that. I don't think we need to take the law into our own hands because the law of the outback seems conclusive to me. If they make a good showing tomorrow, we should let them go. If they show up in court with amnesia and decide to tell a different story, then we let the animals have a go at them." Mallory listened to his wife and was amazed at the words coming out of her mouth.

# # #

Most of the group was still on duty when Beckmire asked Wajickee, "Do you think we have to keep watch for the balance of the night?"

"No, Ben Beckmire. I believe we will be okay."

When Chakes saw Luana, he smiled at her. She winked at him and asked, "Are you okay? Are we safe?"

"I believe so. How's Sister?

"Oh, she's doing very well. They gave her some roots and told her how to prepare them. Everyone seems to like her. She's a good woman, but I worry about her."

"It's getting late, you should get some rest. We're going to hang around to make sure nothing else jumps off." Luana grabbed his hand and pulled him close to her and gave Chakes another peck on his lips.

For the balance of the night, the only sounds to be heard were from a didgeridoo playing somewhere in the outback. Everyone would sleep well knowing they were in the company of spirits and that the Great Saltie was near.

At 0200 hours, Beckmire, Wajickee, and Chakes made their way to the water's edge. What Chakes saw lounging near the water frightened him. It was the Great Saltie.

Chakes fell to his knees and began to pray for deliverance. He admitted his faults, his terminating actions, but most impressively, he confessed, he was committed to his new starter family. He prayed for deliverance.

# # #

After breakfast, people went to the billabong and bathed. The children played in the water until it was time for everyone to thank the villagers for their hospitality and head to the courthouse.

At 1130 hours, the group arrived at the courthouse. Jong had worked his magic. In a sanctioned bank account, with the dictated numbers given by the judge, Jong was prepared to hand over $100 million to a judge that no one knew. On the other side of the aisle, those who thought the land would be forfeited because the other side could not obtain the escrow amount of $100 million were in for a horrible shock on two fronts. First, Beckmire's group survived the night. Second, they provided the judge with the $100 million obligation.

At noon, the gavel hit the pad and the administrator called the court to order. Beckmire's people had a look of defeat on their faces as suggested by Jilkes. The judge looked at the plaintiff's statement and it reflected that, indeed, $100 million had been entered into an escrow account for the land within the prescribed coordinates.

The plaintiffs saw the discontent on the other side and began to celebrate prematurely. The judge looked at Monica and said, "Apparently, you heard me, and you made the decision to contest the other side. Let it be known that both parties to this event have placed in escrow, $100 million." The lawyer on the other side fell to his knees and yelled, "Who are these people? Are they drug dealers or robbers? Again, I ask, who are these people?"

The judge said, "Who they are or what they do was never a consideration or challenge in this matter; it was only if they could support the locals and put the $100 million in an escrow account. Based on everything that I'm looking at, they ave accomplished that task and you yourselves ave placed $100 million in the approved account as well." He looked at Monica and asked, "Do you have any additional information or items you would like to enter as support for your claim?"

Monica said, "I do, your Honor."

Luana whispered something in Monica's ear. Monica acknowledged her. Monica then said, "Your Honor, I would like to identify one item, and request that the cultivation, extraction, sale, trade, or use in any form whatsoever, of this indigenous product of the land articulated by the latitude and longitude coordinates, as stated in the filings be prohibited. Furthermore, the item that will be identified can only be used for the benefit of the Aborigine people who reside within the prescribed coordinates and those who live from East to West, and from North to South on the continent of Australia."

The judge said, "What is the natural resource, or resources that is indigenous to the longitude and latitude expressed in this legal matter that both groups have placed $100 million in escrow. What is so valuable? Can we have a picture of it and estimates of its inherent value? The other side states that it just wants to bring this part of the outback into the 21st Century."

Monica called Jong forward and said, "Give me that which is what this entire case is about." Jong turned his back to the judge and handed Monica the diamond.

Monica said, "Your Honor, this case is about another attempt to find, secure, and dispel the rightful owners of their property by a group of people who found the mother of all jewels, for non-Aborigine individuals' financial enhancement."

The judge said, "Please bring that item forward, and for the record, what is it?"

Monica said, "Your Honor, this large diamond was found within the coordinates of the land that is documented to be Aborigine land. Those who are pretending to want to modernize this area are only trying to build a cage around a product that will make them rich and powerful on the backs of the rightful owners."

The judge looked at the petitioning lawyers and asked, "Did I not ask you if you were aware of any natural resources that could provide profits within the designated coordinates? However, if you were not aware of the resources, you can still petition the court to let you work for the Aborigine people. Otherwise, I hold you in contempt of court, and I sentence you to 90 days in prison, starting now. I will also turn your $100 million in escrow funds over to the Aborigine people to be used as they see fit to empower their people."

The judge paused for a moment before commanding, "Constable, remove and process these thieves."

He then looked at Monica and Luana and said, "Good job and good presentation, ladies. I'm sure we'll be seeing more of you until this thing is completely adjudicated. I suggest you file all your papers before you leave the country. I will allow some forms to be handled from afar, but you need a local lawyer or someone who can be here to handle some of the paperwork. If you don't have anyone, I have a clerk who can probably help you. She is, of course, a lawyer, who just happens to be a conscientious and heritage-centered Aborigine woman. If you people want to independently hire her, I will allow that and will accept her resignation today. She is a smart woman and a good lawyer. She just happens to be my clerk and a damn good one."

Monica said, "We would like to, perhaps, interview her. She'd also need to meet our unelected leader, Ben Beckmire."

The judge said he would hold everything in place and make sure the stated coordinates had no liens on them and that the group could move forward with registering the claim, land, and authenticating the borders. He then looked to the back of the courtroom and asked Mr. Beckmire to meet him in his chambers.

Ben Beckmire entered the judge's chamber. The judge asked, "Are you a member of the famed Beckmire family that is responsible for the folklore called the Great Saltie?"

Beckmire smiled and said, "Your Honor, once again, I believe I am from that group of people who manufactured that fable."

"By chance, did you hear the roar of an animal last night around midnight?"

"I did hear that extremely frightening sound," Beckmire stated.

"When did you and your group arrive here in the outback and where did you get that diamond from, if it is a diamond?"

"I received it from the mouth of the Great Saltie, the same semiaquatic reptile that made the roar that could be heard all over the outback."

"Why are you here in the outback, Mr. Beckmire? How did you happen to show up in time for the proceedings and in time to hear the roar of a reptile? How did you people show up with the largest diamond I've ever seen? Tell me the facts,

Mr. Beckmire. Are you people good human beings, or are you people here for the bling?"

Ben Beckmire smiled at the judge and said, "We are all that is right. The bling means nothing to us. We cleaned up the local riff-raff on our last trip here. We were summoned back when our people did not have the proper legal team to advance their cause. We now have a team in place and sufficient funds to fight this thing for a lifetime. Let it be known everywhere in the outback—if there is treachery, we will be there in some form or fashion to right all wrongs against our people."

"That's what I was afraid of, and also, what I wanted to hear, Mr. Beckmire. I know I don't look like an Aborigine, but I'm half Aborigine and committed to ending the fraud against our people. I have your attorneys' numbers. If anything of a pressing nature appears, I will be in immediate contact."

Beckmire asked, "Where are your people from?"

"The West Coast," the judge indicated.

"Good to meet you, and if you need references, go on Walkabout and talk to my family and my protector, Wajickee. I'm sure we'll be seeing a lot of each other in the coming months. It would help if you kept a lid on the publicity about the find until we can install a leadership council and manage what's going to be a lot of people trying to slip into the territory and mine illegally."

The judge replied, "That's their problem. This territory is unforgiving and filled with spirits, snakes, and spiders that, seemingly, don't bother Aborigine people. Will see you soon, Mr. Beckmire. Will see you soon. When are you planning to leave the Northern Territory?"

"Your Honor, our plans were to leave after the hearing, but it has come to my attention that we need to send a clear message to those who would perpetrate this fraud against the Aborigine people.   Therefore, we won't leave until tomorrow."

#

At the village, Ben Beckmire said to Wajickee, "We have the legal aspects of the matter temporarily under control and now we need to kick some butt. Do you have a list of names of those who are involved in this conspiracy?"

"Ben Beckmire, I don't, but Darryl has a book with their names, addresses, and their businesses."

Ben Beckmire nodded and asked, "How far, and how much influence or intimidation can Darryl visit upon the key players? I need to get some reaction while we're here so that me and my guys can do what we do best, and that's kick butts."

Wajickee summoned Darryl. When he appeared, he had a crude list of names with the amounts of money they had pledged towards the project. Convenient was the fact that the four largest investors were in the same land and title development building. Beckmire asked Darryl, "Can you get me and a few of my people a meeting with the head man?"

Darryl said, "They're close by. They're playing golf on the course near the airport."

"Is there any water near the course?"

"It's right next to a billabong, why?"

"I'm going to see if we can get a few crocs to do some work."

#

An hour later, Beckmire, Zanthius, Larry, and Darryl waltzed into the exclusive members-only club and asked if a Mr. Sonay was there. The person behind the counter said, "No Abo's are allowed in this establishment, Mate."

Beckmire walked towards the desk and punched the man in the head, rendering him unconscious. Larry said, "Dad, you still have that right hand punch."

Another attendant hearing the noise came from behind closed doors and said, "What's going on here? I hope you guys realize this is a private club and that no Aborigines are allowed, other than those who provide a service."

Beckmire said, "I'm looking for Sonay. I have an urgent message for him about some land he's trying to steal from the Aborigine people."

The attendant said, "You know what, I don't like that racist son-of-a-bitch. Go through those doors and turn right. You'll find him and three others conspiring to get their hands on some land not too far from here. I'll give you ten minutes or until that bloke wakes up, and then I'll ave to call the constable."

The four men walked through the doors and turned right, where they saw four people huddled together speaking extremely softly. Beckmire said, "I'm looking for Mr. Sonay."

Mr. Sonay stood up and said, "No darkies are allowed in this club."

"Sir, are you Mr. Sonay?"

"I am, and I order you darkies to leave at once or I shall ave to call the constable." Beckmire walked over to the man and said, "It's going to be a while before you're able to eat again." He hit the man in the jaw and broke it on contact. He looked at Darryl and said, "What's the next name on that list?"

Darryl said, "Mr. John Weaver." Beckmire walked over to the table and said, "Any name calling will result in a broken jaw or a shattered brain. Here is the message. Any further attempts to infringe upon lands owned by the Aborigine people for profit will result in the complete annihilation of your entire family, including any babies or small children. This will be done by the spider, the snake, the dingoes, and wombats, as well as the Great Saltie. Consult your history and watch what will become of any person who speaks of conspiring against the Aborigine people. Your lawyers are in jail, and as an example of our wrath, one will die the day after he is released. You will write a letter to the newspaper apologizing for your scheme to defraud the Aborigine people out of their land, and you will work to improve their properties, without receiving pay. If an Aborigine goes missing or is found dead, we will kill twenty rich people and their families. Also, if you are still a member of this club in one month, and this place isn't available to all people in Australia, you will feel our vengeance. Take that 'white only' sign down immediately."

As the men were leaving the building, Darryl said, "Uncle, you don't take no shit, do you?"

"And neither should you, Darryl. They put their pants on the same way we do. They want exclusive, find another planet."

When the group returned to the village, Wajickee said, "You are a force to be reckoned with, Ben Beckmire. You ave the temperament of your ancestor as well as his might. That fellow you punched will not eat solids for many months."

"That fellow started the conversation off by calling names." Beckmire then announced he might have legal issues and wasn't quite sure if it was smart to pull up and leave but felt that they needed to remain in the outback for another day.

# # #

That evening, everyone enjoyed a wonderful meal, native drinks, and stories of Walkabout and Dreamtime. Wajickee was masterful in spinning his tales about the Beckmire clan, and said, that two of the women there were named in honor of their matriarch, Marisa and Asiram which is Marisa spelled backwards. Both women felt honored by the comment.

Beckmire sensed that Monica had a heavy load on her mind. He eased next to her and Mallory and said, "Listen, guys, if there is no storm or fall-out from my actions today, then we're out of here tomorrow for an arrival in the states in the morning so that you can do what you have to do. Don't feel abandoned. You know I got your backs. I'll either be arrested or thanked at the airport."

# # #

The next morning, at 0800 hours, Darryl showed up and said, "Uncle, I have my passport, driver's license, birth certificate, and $500. Where will I stay?"

When Wajickee appeared, Ben Beckmire responded to Darryl, by saying, "I'm going to place you with Jong's people until we have time to do this thing the right way. Eventually, we'll get you an apartment and lay out the law in terms of what you can do and what you can't do. By the way, how old are you?"

"I will be 21 on March 16th of next year." The Sarge saw Jong and Mary Alice and summoned them over. He said, "Good morning Mary Alice, you're looking lovely and pregnant."

Mary Alice smiled and the Sarge said, "Jong, I must take my nephew back with us and set him up. He starts school at Georgetown next week. I need your cousin to accommodate him and get him situated in school. I don't want him living alone. I want him living with your family until we can pay attention to this matter. Give your cousin $100 thousand for his tuition, books, and clothes. Tell your cousin, Beckmire men do not wear clothes that show their undergarments. I thought about taking him with us, but then he gets noticed and placed on the radar. Is this a thing your family can do for my humble family?"

Jong said, "In a hegemony, we do as we're instructed, oh mighty one."

Ben Beckmire said to Darryl, "You will be the respectful Beckmire that I know you are. His cousin is a little weird, but he's a good man, and we rely on him to do the impossible for us. I want you to load up on courses. No normal load, I want you finished in one year and a half, or sooner, if possible. Do we have an accord?"

"Indeed, we do, Uncle. I thank you now for the experience and the opportunity. I will not let you or my people down."

At 0900 hours, Beckmire told Jong, "Have our people saddle up. We're out of here by 1100 hours and in the air by noon. What an existence! This is the greatest show on earth, and we're the ring leaders."

He saw Wajickee and asked, "Are you expecting any human issues from anyone?"

"The air is cool and the wind is mild, my friend. All is well that has been attended to but must be placed on the docket for further oversight."

Beckmire said, "This will not be placed on the back burner. I will start the conversation on the plane with Monica and Luana to discern the boundaries of the properties based upon the documents we took from the vault. I will need you to get a group together to manage $100 million, and the billions that will follow. I just need good names on a document. Darryl is going to head this thing. I need time to cultivate him and show him how my boys and I work especially, when the good sometimes have to be the bad, in order to destroy the wicked."

He looked at Wajickee and said, "I'm sure you know that Mallory and his wife want to adopt a child or children, and that we must be back in the States by tomorrow."

"Yes, I'm aware. I have aligned them with two mixed race children that are one-third Aborigine, but who's counting parts?"

"Thank you, old friend. I will take care of Darryl, but you know there are two monkeys that we have to get off our backs—the Carbon Factor formula and my cousin."

"Your approach to the Carbon Factor formula is solid. Destroy it publicly, and let the world forget about another method of self-destruction. That formula appears to be volatile, explosive, and temperature based."

"How do you know so much about the formula, Wajickee?"

"Ben Beckmire, do you think Jong is really that lucky, or that smart to partition a device and hold back indispensable phases of a formula? I'm with you now as I was with your ancestors then. I assisted Jong in partitioning the formula. I need your people to be at the airport by 1030 hours. At 1115 hours, a massive force will be scouring the airport looking for tourists heading to Tahiti. That is the destination of the alleged group that assaulted those people at the golf place. I will send a messenger to each of those men to tell them their activities today will require punishment. Each wife will be hospitalized at 1145 hours, nothing serious, just a warning."

"Wajickee, my old friend, you have been, and will always be, my guide to understanding what must be done. I could never learn enough from you, and I wish that you continue to watch me from afar and make sure I do what is right by my people and all people. I will give you notice of when we'll return. Thank you, my friend."

Beckmire went to Jong and said, "We have to be on the plane and on the runway before 1030, hours or I will be arrested for assault."

Jong saw the urgency in the Sarge's eyes and announced, "People, we have to leave now!" He yelled, "We leave now, or we leave in thirty days after the Sarge gets out of jail."

There was a beehive of activity and when Jong took a head count, he realized he was short one person. He looked around the bus and said, "I'll be damned. Where is our pilot and her husband?"

Mary Alice said, "Baby, I last saw them on the beach."

He yelled, "There are no beaches in the outback. There are only billabongs and that's where big animals hang for their next meal."

He yelled, "Brown and Bernstein, come with me. We have to find them before they become food for a large predator."

#

When Jong and his group arrived at the billabong, Jong said, "They're having sex and the crocs are watching them. What a weird place and scene." He picked up a rock, threw it near them, and got their attention. As Carla turned to her rear, large carnivorous animals were eyeing their machinations. She said to Mike, "Whatever you do, do it slowly. There are five or six large crocs behind us. I'm going to ease off you, head towards Jong and the others without any clothes on but with one of those towels. I suggest that you roll over on your stomach slowly. Get up and slowly walk away from beach."

Mike watched his bride walk away and did exactly as she had suggested. Once he reached where she was standing, he turned around and saw the large crocs lounging at the water's edge. He felt weak in the knees and needed assistance in vacating the area. Jong slowly walked towards him and helped him out of what could have been a potential feeding frenzy.

#

On the bus, a few minutes later, Jong said, "Something still wrong. I now have one too many people."

The Sarge said, "Remember, Darryl is coming with us, and your family is going to keep him until we settle two issues." He looked at Jong and motioned him to where he was seated. The Sarge continued, "Get this thing moving or I'm going to be arrested and then there is going be a lot of trouble for all of us. Do it now, my brother!"

Jong said to the driver, "I need you to get us to the airport safely and quickly. We're in a hurry."

# # #

At 1005 hours, the group walked out of customs and entered the hangar and boarded their plane. The push back tug was attached and ready to extract the plane from the hangar.

Once everyone was aboard, Captain Carla said to the passengers, "This is a short runway and we're going to dispense with a lot of pre-flight information to our guests. You people know the drill and I'm signaling the tug driver to get us the hell out of his hangar before we are surrounded by hostiles."

The copilot had performed the pre-flight checks and the other two pilots gave Captain Carla, a thumb's up. They had gone through their checklist and the plane was prepared for departure.

Captain Carla said over the intercom, "We have clearance from the tower, and if you look out the port side of the plane, you will see a large contingency of emergency lights approaching the airport. I'm not second guessing anyone, but I assume we're the target of the lights, so hold on to your arm-rests. I'm going to blast this wonderful lady into the air in a hurry."

Captain Carla gunned the engines while holding the plane in place by engaging the brakes. She released the brakes and the roar of those GE engines could be heard in a distance as they screamed down the short runway and blasted the plane into the heavens, like a rocket in search of the planet Mars.

As the plane began to level off, it became obvious to everyone that the outback is a spectacular place, filled with wonderful out of body experiences, and a belief that there are higher powers in the universe. However, most of the group also realized that the Carbon Factor formula and Walter would provide the group with new challenges, filled with adventure, suspense, romance, birthing, and plenty of newfound money.

As the plane leveled off, Beatrice said to her great-grandmother, "I guess mommy must really like Mr. Chakes. They're really kissing a lot."

the end

also in the 'idiot spy' series

Available at Amazon and BarnesandNoble.com

www.ingramcontent.com/pod-product-compliance
Lightning Source LLC
Chambersburg PA
CBHW051509250626
47156CB00001B/22